work in PROGRESS

STACI HART

Cover by **Quirky Bird**

Photography by **Perrywinkle Photography**

Edited by **Jovana Shirley, Unforeseen Editing**

Book design by **Inkstain Design Studio**

Proofread by **Love N Books**

Playlist: https://spoti.fi/2TLCqqX

Pin Board: http://bit.ly/2zGGe5L

work in
PROGRESS

To the quiet girls,
The soft girls,
The girls with more thoughts
than words:
Love speaks loud and clear.

Unforgivable Sins

AMELIA

Three more people.

The girl in front of me shifted the weight of her bag on her shoulder, the bulk of which rested under her arm like a pack mule. I eyed the bag, wondering how many books were inside, like one of those *How Many Jelly Beans Are in the Jar?* games I was terrible at.

There were eleven, if I had to guess.

I might not have spatial awareness of jelly beans, but I could probably sniff that bag and determine how many books were inside.

Two more people.

Sweat bloomed in my palms as we all shuffled a few steps closer to the table where Thomas Bane sat.

All I could see between bodies was an unrecognizable sliver of face and a bit of his elbow, clad in a black leather jacket.

I took a breath—a deep, thick, anxious breath—and recited the

It's nice to meet you.
I'm Amelia Hall with the USA Times.
Please sign that generic.
I'm fine, thank you.
Yes, I've read every word you've ever written.
No, I actually didn't enjoy them at all.

Okay, that last one wasn't on the list. And the truth was, I'd devoured every book he'd written since he broke out six years ago. I might have hate-read them, but read them I had, every word.

Thomas Bane, the sensation. At twenty-four, he'd shown up first in pop culture, dating a Hollywood *It* girl—the one tapped to star in half a dozen romantic comedies in half as many years. The crowd went wild, the media clamoring to find out everything they could about the tall, dark, and cavalier Thomas Bane. And in the height of the media frenzy, he'd dropped his first fantasy novel.

He was a legend, the name on everyone's lips. There were entire websites devoted to speculating about his girlfriends—comprised of a long and famous list of models and pop singers and actresses—and his relationship status. He had somewhere in the neighborhood of fifty bazillion followers on Instagram, and there was a fan account devoted strictly to his hair.

His hair, guys. His hair had its own Instagram.

I'd say I didn't follow it, but I was a terrible liar.

And there he was, just a few feet away. And in two—*shit*—one person, it would be my turn to meet him.

The best I could hope for was that I could survive the meeting without fainting, running away, or squeaking like a farmhouse door.

If it wasn't for my brand new gig blogging for the *USA Times'* book division, I never would have found myself standing in the hip little bookstore in the East Village. But my boss, who happened to be a terrifying, brilliant shark, had assigned me my first real gig—come to the book signing, meet Thomas Bane, have a few books signed, and try not to have a stroke when I had to have an actual conversation with him.

My therapist had said the exposure would be good for me. If I was ever going to pursue my dream of editing for a publisher, I figured I'd have to learn to speak to strangers.

The girl in front of me unloaded her haul onto the table with shaking hands.

… nine, ten, eleven. Ha!

A rumbling laugh from the other side of the table. He said something I couldn't make out, something in a snarky, smoky baritone that did something inexplicable to my insides.

I chalked it up to nerves.

Remember the ABCs—acknowledge, breathe, connect, I recited to myself matter-of-factly, sucking in a noisy breath through my nose that garnered me a glance from the girl in front of me.

I hadn't purchased groceries at the actual market in well over a year. I hadn't answered the phone for anyone but my best friends or parents in at least five. And I didn't go *anywhere* without a buffer who, in case of emergency, could speak for me.

It was almost always a case of emergency.

My speechlessness wasn't an enigma, but it was most definitely inconvenient. God knew I had enough words in my head, words in my heart, chittering chattering words that never saw the light of day when the spotlight was on me.

It didn't even have to be a spotlight. A flashlight was plenty.

It was rare to hear me speak outside the company of people who I knew loved and accepted me. People I could trust.

Thomas Bane was most certainly *not* one of those people. And if he recognized my name, I was well and truly fucked.

I'd reviewed every book of his at three stars or less.

Three stars! you say. *But that's average!*

Not to authors, it wasn't. I'd been blogging books since college, but a couple of years ago, one of my reviews—on one of Thomas Bane's books—had gone viral, and my blog had exploded.

Let me tell you something—there were few perks to being someone's top-rated negative review on Amazon, at least for someone like me who hated confrontation almost as much as I hated keeping my opinion to myself. Online, it was easy to be myself. With a screen firmly between me and the masses, my personality was bold and outgoing. Real life was another story. Put me in front of a cashier and watch me lock up like rigor mortis.

I cursed Janessa again for sending me here, wondering if she'd been intentionally cruel. Maybe she was hoping for me to return with some famous Thomas Bane quip or one-liner. Maybe she was hoping he'd confront me about my reviews, be an asshole, and load us up with material to write an article on.

Notorious bad-boy Thomas Bane. Model-dating, ultra-rich, devil-may-care, super-famous, fist-wielding, public-drunken and indecent-exposure Thomas Bane, fantasy author with a rap sheet the length of my arm.

"Do you want a picture?" I heard him ask. I thought I could hear him smiling.

"N-n-n-no, thanks," the girl stuttered.

My guts turned to ice.

She'd been talking her brains out with her friend not ten minutes ago with sword-brandishing bravado about how she was going to French kiss him there in front of God and everybody. If *she* couldn't answer a simple question from him, I was never going to make it out of the building.

I took another breath and straightened my spine, stretching me to the extent that my five-foot-one frame would allow. But when she moved out of the way, I almost went out like a candle.

His eyes shifted from the parting girl to fix on me, and the air left my lungs in a vacuum that would have snuffed an entire *room* full of candles.

They were dark as midnight, the iris indistinguishable from his pupil, his lashes thick and long and absolutely ridiculous. Ridiculous, every inch of him. The cut of his jaw, covered in a shadow from his casually kept beard. His nose, strong and long and masculine. Those cursed eyes, which had to be brown, but I couldn't make out even a hint of anything but bottomless black. His hair, long enough to fall over his shoulders, wavy and so thick, I'd bet his ponytail was at least seven times the diameter of mine.

But the most ridiculous part of his absolutely ridiculous face was his lips, wide and full, the bottom in a constant pout, the top a little bit thicker, slanted at a *ridiculous* angle that had me wondering what it'd be like to suck on it.

Which was ridiculous in and of itself. I'd never even been kissed.

But whenever I was, God, grant me lips like those.

Hands planted themselves on my shoulder blades and shoved.

Thomas Bane laughed, and I was unsurprised to find that his smile was ridiculous, too. What utterly unfair bullshit that a man should be that gorgeous.

I wondered if anyone ever called him by anything other than his full name. He was like Celine Dion but with better hair. No one called Celine Dion just plain old *Celine.* I imagined even her kids called her Celine Dion, yelling through their multitrillion dollar home, *Celine Dion, wipe my butt!* I also imagined that on Sundays, she wore a ballroom gown and tiara to lie around on the couch and watch Netflix.

I cleared my throat and unloaded the books the paper had sent with me. I couldn't meet his eyes again.

"Hi"—he paused, probably looking for the name tag stuck to my tiny boob—"Amelia. It's good to see you," he said as if we'd met a hundred times.

My lips wouldn't move.

Say hi. Say hello. Say hi, Amelia, goddammit.

I made the mistake of looking up, and my tongue tripled in size.

Don't look at him, you idiot! ABCs—acknowledge, breathe, and CHRIST, he is hot.

My eyes darted back down to my hands. I swallowed.

"H-hi," I whispered.

God, I could feel him watching me. I could *feel* him smirking.

He took a book as I set it down, his hand entering my line of vision like a giant, manly, long-fingered version of my tiny pale one.

"Who should I personalize this to?" he asked.

"No personalization," I answered before I lost my nerve.

Another soft chuckle as I added to the stack. "No problem." The sound of a Sharpie scratching the page filled the silence.

Say something! You are a mess, Amelia Hall. You have to tell him who you are. Janessa will shit a brick if you don't.

I swallowed the sticky lump in my throat, arranging the book pile without purpose. "I ... I'm Amelia Hall. W-with the *U-USA Times*."

The book closed with a soft thump.

"Amelia Hall? As in the blogger for Halls of Books?" The question was thick with meaning.

The blood in my body rushed from every extremity, racing up my neck in a blush so hard, I could feel the tingling crawl of it on my skin.

Like a dummy, I looked up. An affirmative word was on my stupid, fat tongue, stuck there in my mouth like a gum ball in a water hose. I nodded.

He was smirking, lips together, a tilted smile that set a glimmer of amusement in his eyes. "You're the blogger who hates me so much."

I frowned and spoke without thinking. "I-I don't hate you. I just hold issue with your idea of romance."

The words left me without thought or attempt or desire to reel them back in.

I might not be able to order a pizza over the phone, but I could stand up for a little old lady who someone had cut in front of or the kid who was getting picked on. And my ideals. I could stand up for those too, especially when questioned.

The corner of his sardonic mouth climbed. "Well, lucky for me, I don't write romance."

A derisive sound left me. *Lucky for all of us.* "I don't hate your books," I insisted.

He shrugged and took the next book off the pile to sign. "Wouldn't guess so from your reviews. My least favorite phrase on the planet is *unforgivable sin*, thanks to you."

The heat in my cheeks flared again, this time in defense. "Your world- building is incredible. Your imagery is so brilliant, sometimes I have to set my book down and stare at a wall just to absorb it. But every hero you write is, frankly, an"—*an asshole*, was what I was going to say but instead landed on—" unkind man."

He nodded at the title page as he scrawled his name. "Viggo?"

"He left Djuna because she was pregnant with his half-breed baby. And she took him back even though he wouldn't even commit to her for good."

"Blaze?"

I rolled my eyes. "He didn't come for Luna because he was more worried about himself. He could have saved her from the Liath!" My hand rose in the universal sign for *what the hell* and lowered to slap my thigh with a snap.

"Even Zavon? He's everyone's favorite."

My face flattened. "He cheated on her out of spite. *That*, sir, is the ultimate unforgivable sin. And if that wasn't bad enough, she took him back for no reason. *He didn't even apologize.*" I said the words as if it were *me* he'd cheated on. Honestly, it felt that way.

He slid the book to me and picked up another. But he didn't sign it. Instead, he turned that godforsaken smirk on me, which subsequently turned my knees into jelly.

"But he loved her. Isn't love enough to forgive?"

It was that tingle again, climbing up my face like fire. "Of course it is, but your heroes never make heroic decisions about the women who love them. In fact, they don't seem to love their women at all, not enough to sacrifice their own comfort. They're irredeemable. Why isn't love enough to make them act less like assholes?" I clapped a hand over my mouth, my eyes widening so far, they stung from exposure to air.

Something in his eyes changed, sharpened with an idea. He was otherwise unaffected, chuckling as he opened the book and turned his attention to his Sharpie again. "I mean, you're not wrong, Amelia."

The way he'd said my name, the depth and timbre and rolling reverberation slipped over me.

I blinked. "I'm not?"

His eyes shifted to meet mine for only a heartbeat before dropping to the page again. "You're not. Every time I publish a book, I wait for your review to see if I've finally won you over." He closed the book, pushing it across the table to me before reaching for the last. "Would you consider helping me with my next novel?"

Somewhere, a needle scratched. Tires squealed from a pumping of brakes. Crickets chirped in a chorus in an empty room.

Help him?

"Yes, help me," he answered as he signed. I didn't realize I'd spoken the question. "I could use a critical voice on my team. I have a feeling they've been telling me yes for years when they should have been telling me no. I need a no." He looked up again and asked, "Are you interested?"

"Interested?" I echoed stupidly.

"Are you interested in being my no?"

I blinked at him. "What a strange question."

A chuckle rumbled through a closed, sideways smile. His eyes had to be black, black as sin. "I've got to admit, I'm usually asking for a yes, especially where women are concerned."

My face flattened, not only because he was a cocky bastard, but for the flash of rejection that I wasn't considered a woman worthy of a yes. "What would the job entail?"

He watched me with an intensity that made me want to crawl out of my skin, which all of a sudden felt too small for everything inside me. "Be available for meetings to plot and character develop. Read for me when I send the manuscript and provide critical feedback. Talk me off any ledges or push me off them, if that's what you think I need. Help me make my stories better."

I said nothing. Absently, I realized my mouth was open as if I were about to speak.

When I didn't, he smiled. "Why don't we meet up tomorrow? We can discuss the details. What do you say?"

What *could* I say? Thomas Bane was a sensation—famous not only in the literary world, but in the pop culture stream. *Page Six* followed him around like he was their only job. He was, at that very moment, on a forty-foot billboard for TAG Heuer in Times Square. On top of all that, he was a phenomenal writer even if his stories *did* need a fresh set of eyes.

And he was asking *me* for help.

"Say yes, you idiot!" the girl behind me hissed, presumably the one who'd shoved me toward his table when my feet failed me.

Thomas Bane's smile tilted higher. Otherwise, he didn't react.

Say something. You have to answer right now.

In the span of a handful of seconds, I weighed it out. He wanted my help, and I *loved* to help. I'd beta read for authors a hundred times and always found it fulfilling to offer my advice in order to make a story the best it could be. In fact, I loved it and took every opportunity to say yes, should it arise.

So why wasn't I jumping at the chance to help Thomas Oh-My-God-Quit-Smiling-At-Me-Like-That Bane?

On paper, there was no reason. Floating around in my head were a hundred, the topmost being that when he looked like that, I actually felt like my panties were on fire.

He expectantly watched me. But when that smile of his dropped incrementally in defeat, coupled with the almost infinitesimal draw of his brows, I caved.

Thomas Bane wanted my help, and I had the rare opportunity to give it.

"No."

His eyes narrowed in confusion. "Wait. No as in yes? Or no as in no?"

"I…I think I'd like to help. So if you need someone to tell you no, I'm your girl."

There it was again—that smile that probably cost more than most people's cars. "I like the sound of that. I'll message you through your blog, and we can set up a time to meet." He arranged the stack of books, straightening their corners before moving them a couple of inches closer to me.

The gesture was strangely nervous and utterly disarming.

I found myself smiling. I picked up the books and deposited them in my bag. "I'll look forward to it."

"Do you want a picture?" he asked.

I got the distinct impression he asked everyone that question simply because there was no way in hell anyone could have the constitution to request a picture on their own. Not with his energy sapping everyone in a twenty-foot radius of their wits.

"I...erm..."

He was out of his seat and stepping around the table before I could say no again, and this time, I'd have meant the word in full. But there he was, approaching like a thunderstorm. My chin lifted as he approached. He was at least a foot taller than me, the air around him charged, everything about him dark. His hair. His beard. His bottomless eyes. His jacket that smelled like Italian leather and combat boots to match, the laces half-untied and the top gaping open with irreverence.

My senses abandoned me completely. The effect of him amplified with proximity, and there was nothing to do but submit. So there I was, tucked into Thomas Bane's side with his arm wrapped around me like hot, heavy steel.

It took every ounce of willpower I possessed not to curl into him, fist the lapels of his jacket, and bury my face in his chest for a good, long whiff of him.

If my nose didn't come approximately to his nipples, I would have smelled his hair, too.

"Do you have your phone?" he asked, but the rumble of the words through his chest vibrated through me to the point of absolute distraction.

"Ah...um..."

"Here, we'll take one with mine." With a slight shift, he retrieved his phone, holding it out for a selfie. "Say *irredeemable asshole*!"

A laugh burst out of me. And then his hand lowered.

I stiffened. "Wait, did you take it?"

He nodded, smiling down at his phone. "I'll tag your blog on Instagram."

"But...I mean...is it okay? I'm not..."

He looked down at me, and for a second, I lost myself in the vision of him this close, from this angle. I could see the fine lines in his lips, the thick clusters of his lashes, the depth of his eyes. The brown was finally visible, so deep, there were almost hints of a deep, dark crimson.

"You're gorgeous. See?"

Gorgeous? Me? The words sounded like Greek, a mush of sound that made no sense.

I tore my eyes away from his to glance at his phone and almost didn't recognize myself. My eyes were closed, my nose scrunched, my smile big and wide and happy as I'd unwittingly leaned into him.

A hot flutter brushed my ribs. "Oh…that's…"

He laughed, a short sound through his nose as he pulled away. "I'm glad you came today. Tell Janessa to email my brother if she wants any more books signed, and we'll send them to the office."

"O-okay."

"Thanks, Amelia. For everything. I'm looking forward to seeing you soon."

Hysterical laughter crackled in my throat, but I swallowed it down in a feat of self-control.

The girl behind me cleared her throat, and I glanced back at her apologetically. She looked furious.

"Sorry," I said quietly.

"Ugh, life is just not fair." She brushed past me and plunked a stack of books on the table.

Thomas Bane's smiling eyes were on me as he took his seat, and I waved lamely before turning to walk away.

I swore, I felt those eyes singeing a hole in my back the whole way out the door.

Pocket-Sized

TOMMY

"**Y**ou did what?"

Theo's arms were folded, his frown the mirror of my smirk. It wasn't the only thing that was mirrored. My twin was an exact copy of me but with a practical haircut to match his practical suit. We were almost indistinguishable from each other beyond the hair, which had really put a damper on our ability to fuck with girls.

I pulled off my jacket. "I asked Amelia Hall to read for me. Be a critique partner."

"The girl who hates you?" he asked flatly.

"She doesn't hate me, and she's not wrong." I tossed my jacket on his couch.

"She *does* hate you, which is exactly why Blackbird Books keeps sending her your releases. Her bad reviews sell your books."

"She *doesn't* hate me, and she's gonna help. She's smart, Theo. And articulate. And if you hadn't told me not to, I would have asked her for help a long time ago."

He snorted a laugh. "God knows you fucking need it if you're ever gonna turn in a book again."

"I told my editor I'd have the book to him soon."

"Soon is not a measure of time, Tommy."

I smiled. "They've waited six months. What's a few more weeks?"

"A few more weeks would imply you were close to being finished."

"Who says I'm not?"

One of his dark brows rose.

I sighed. "All right, fine. I'm not, but I will be. Soon, which *is* a measure of time. I have a good feeling about this."

That climbing eyebrow jacked a few more millimeters. "Oh? And which one are you gonna send? The mpreg werewolf or the space opera that feels suspiciously like *Firefly*?"

I gave him a look. "I'll have you know, male-pregnancy fantasy makes a shitload of money. Throw in a werewolf, and we can probably afford a jet."

"You're playing with fire. She's working for the *Times*…for *Janessa*. What happens when she writes her tell-all?"

I rolled my eyes and walked past him toward the kitchen. "I don't have to tell her anything, *Teddy*."

He glared at me. "Nice try. You're not goading me into a fight just because you know I'm right. This is a bad idea, man."

"Or it's a *great* idea." I opened the fridge and reached for a beer. "She's smart. She knows the market. I'll have her sign an NDA. What's the problem?"

"First of all, NDAs only keep honest people honest." Theo strode toward me, stopping on the other side of the kitchen island. "And secondly, my *problem* is that you never think anything through. You never think *at all*. You just act."

I popped the cap with a hiss and tossed the tin in the sink with a clink. "I like to think of it as recognizing an opportunity when it lands in my lap. That's the difference between you and me. You're a thinker, and I'm a doer. It's why we're such a stellar team."

"You mean I'm the fixer."

Ma's voice came from behind him. "What are you fixing now, Teddy?"

Everything about him softened as he turned to face her, and I found myself relaxing, too.

"Oh, just Tommy's mess, as usual."

She chuckled, shuffling into the room, her arms oddly still. Theo grabbed her arm to stabilize her and helped her take a seat at the island bar. "Well, that's nothing new."

"It's not a mess, Ma. In fact, I think I've solved all my problems."

Her brow rose, just like Theo's had. "Oh? You found a cure for writer's block?"

I smiled. "Sure did—in the form of a tiny little blonde with too many opinions for her own good."

She laughed, the sound a tight, trembling echo of what it had been before Parkinson's. "A girl's gonna save you?"

I leaned on the island across from her, still smiling. "A smart girl, one who isn't afraid to tell me I'm being an idiot."

"Well, bless her for trying."

"Listen," I said, meeting Ma's eyes, then Theo's before I continued, "I'm not too proud to admit that I need help—"

Theo snorted a laugh, his gaze brushing the ceiling.

I ignored him. "I have a good feeling about this. There's something about her… I don't know how to explain it."

"Some writer you are," Theo shot without any bite.

"It's not that, dick. I haven't had time to process anything. I've been on for the last four hours. Cut me some slack."

He kept his mouth shut. I took a sip of my beer to keep my lips occupied and dug into my repository for a way to explain in words.

What had it been exactly? Something had stopped me on the sight of her, halted my thought. Something in the air between us, tight and humming, a spark of awareness, a zing of connection.

She had been stunned, the small, colorless girl with eyes so wide, the irises were ringed in white.

No, not colorless. She was composed of shades of porcelain and sunshine; the gleam of her platinum hair, unfussed, long and natural; her skin, creamy and smooth, tinged with the slightest pink at her cheeks, though the color rose to crimson in the span of a few heartbeats when faced with the likes of me. Her eyes were blue—so light, they were almost silver—wide and big, as if they wanted to drink in the whole world, as long as it was from a safe distance.

The size of her was enamoring, like a pocket-sized girl, a tiny thing to fit in the palm of your hand. Delicate. Breakable. Soft and gentle, like a snow-white sparrow. When I'd tucked her under my arm for the photo, I'd felt the urge to keep her there, where she'd be safe from clumsy hands.

Amelia Hall.

I'd read all her reviews—I couldn't help it—and she was always right. I'd meant what I said to her. Every time I published a book, I hoped I'd finally win her over.

I had been disappointed every time. I'd considered asking her to be on my team a dozen times, but Theo always said no—too dangerous to let anybody in. But our meeting today had sealed the deal. Not only had she disarmed me with her nerves and the delectable way she squirmed under my attention, but she'd fired back with unexpected heat and fervency, sparking something in me, plucking a creative string that reverberated ideas and inspiration.

While I was writing, Amelia Hall would whisper in the back of my mind, her presence pressing me to take a harder look at my stories. If that had happened strictly through her reviews, I couldn't fathom how she would affect me while working by my side.

It was like I had this big, fat blind spot that she'd point at after the car already crashed. But not this time. This time, she'd be right there to give me a solid slap if I was going the wrong way on a one-way street.

The first item of business would be to get some semblance of a story together. I was a perfectionist, which was part of the reason I had a stack of manuscripts that would never make it past twenty thousand words and should never see the light of day. Every day, I sat down to write. Every day, I walked away with jack shit.

I'd never had a muse, but I'd always wanted one. And today, with Amelia Hall shooting down my heroes like tin cans, I felt like she might become mine.

My thoughts finally landed on something I could give voice. "When we talked about my story, I felt inspired. It was a sense of possibility, a sense of understanding. When I think about my stories, it's like … it's like playing tag in the fog. The ideas are there, but the second I reach out to grab them, they're gone. But talking to her was like a break in the clouds. I thought for a second I could see." I took another swig. "How's that for writer-y, Teddy?"

"Passable," he offered.

My smile hitched up on one side. "Send her the NDA, would you?"

"Yeah, all right," he conceded. "I think she should come here. I wanna meet her, and I don't want any of your manuscripts emailed."

"Sure," I started, unsurprised by his suspicion. "Have her come to the house in the morning, if she's around."

Theo's phone appeared in his hand like magic, his gaze dropping to the screen along with his attention. "I'm on it."

My brother, jack of all trades. He was my manager, my publicist, my assistant, and a pain in my ass. He also happened to be my best friend, but I wouldn't admit it to him, even under duress.

He wandered back toward the living room, absorbed in the slab of titanium and silicone in his hand.

"How are you really, baby?" Ma asked gently, her accent—the one I tried so hard to hide—betraying our Bronx roots.

I met her soft, dark eyes and felt my resolve crack. "I'm okay. How are *you*?"

She chuckled. "Oh, no. Nice try. You're not turning it around on me." She watched me for a beat. "You really think she can help you?"

"I do," I answered honestly. "A new perspective will do me good. I'm one breakthrough away from everything being peachy keen."

"I just worry," she said, looking down at her hands where they rested on one another on the granite surface. The top hand trembled. We watched it without acknowledgment.

"I know, Ma. But I'm telling you not to. I'm gonna figure this book out and make Blackbird a dump truck full of hundred-dollar bills."

"And you're not gonna get in any trouble," she added.

My smile was back, irreverent and cocksure as always. "You say that like it's impossible to imagine."

That earned me a laugh. "And you say *that* like I didn't raise you. You and your brother were the angel and the devil, day and night. My straight arrow and my rule-breaker. I've never met a more stubborn kid. Or one so eager to find trouble."

"I'd argue that trouble found me."

"You'd argue the paint off a wall, Tommy," she said on a chuckle. "And you'd muscle your way into a fight in a heartbeat."

"Hey, it's not my fault I have a sour taste for assholes."

"Like Paulie Russo?"

My face pinched in distaste, a surge of anger rising at the mention of his name. "Paulie Russo was a stupid piece of shit who liked to make himself feel big by beating up on Jenny Costa. It's not my fault he ran into my fist at prom."

Her face flattened. "I'm sure Jenny appreciated that, but you almost got kicked out of school. It nearly cost you your diploma. And history repeats itself, honey. You almost lost your career because half of America thinks you're a Nazi."

That surge of anger roared to a tsunami in my chest at the mention of the coup de grâce of bullshit lies. "God, I will never hear the end of this, not in a hundred years. I broke a skinhead's nose. How am I not a goddamn national treasure?"

"I know you had nothin' to do with them. There was no way you coulda known when you drunk stumbled on them in Washington Square that they were white supremacists—"

"Half of them were in suits! It's not like they walk around wearing swastikas."

"I know," she soothed.

"And I stopped to listen, wondering what they were on about. I mean, there were cops everywhere, just waiting for them to step outta line. I shoulda known to keep walking."

"And not to run your mouth to a skinhead."

I frowned. "That son of a bitch deserved that broken nose and the two black eyes. He deserved worse than that."

"I mean, honey, you started a riot."

"He hit me," I argued.

"And you got arrested at a rally. Of course the papers ran with it." She shook her head, the furrows in her brow deep. "You can justify anything, and I'm not saying you were in the wrong."

"Well, good, because I wasn't," I shot without heat.

"I'm just saying, you don't know when to walk away from a fight."

"It pisses me off not to do the right thing. And if I get hit? I don't have it in me to just walk away from that, Ma. *Know thyself.*" I shook my head. "This is why nobody knows anything about me.

'hem to put their dirty hands on my life and my past
the truth doesn't matter. They'll make up whatever story
sells magazines, whether it's true or not. So instead, I give them all
the fake relationships they desire to vomit back up on TMZ."

She drew a breath and let it out in a sigh that weighed a thousand
pounds. "But that's my point. It didn't matter if you did the right thing
or not, and you were dropped by your publisher and all your sponsors.
TAG is the first company willing to touch you in two years." She
reached for my hand. "Your life is public, and you chose that path—"

"Because I can control the narrative this way—"

"*But* that means that what you do matters. What you say matters
even if it's phony. I know this was how you boys decided to kick-start
your career. A boy like you with a face like that dates a famous actress,
and people want to know you. Smoke screen your life so you can hide
your truth. I get it—but you put yourself out there."

"I wish I hadn't," I admitted. Grumbled really. "It seemed like
such a genius move at twenty-four to start my career in the public
eye. But now, I'm theirs."

"I know. And I know you'd get out if you could. But everyone's
watching, which means you gotta keep your nose clean. That morality
clause was the only way Blackbird Books would take you after that
arrest, and they're your last shot at a Big Five publisher."

"And I did what they wanted. My nose has been squeaky clean
ever since."

A small smirk, a more feminine version of mine. "Thanks to your
brother keeping you."

I rolled my eyes.

"Don't act so put out. He does it because he loves you."

Theo snorted from the other room. Ma ignored him.

"I know you've got a streak in you, but you've gotta keep it put
away. Make a box for that, open the lid, and put that urge inside."

I sighed and reached for her hands, feeling her bones shake, her muscles firing against her will. "I've been good for almost two years, Ma. I'm not gonna break my streak now. Plus, if I can get Amelia to help me and we get an story moving, I'm gonna be locked up until it's done."

"If she even agrees," Theo said from the living room, his eyes on his phone.

She let out a sigh of her own, her smile cautious. "Am I gonna meet her? This girl who's gonna save you like Saint Michael?"

I chuffed at her comparison of Amelia to an archangel. She wasn't far off, if my intuition was right, which it almost always was. "Ma, you know you can't meet her," I said gently.

"She's a reporter," Theo added.

"She's a book blogger, dude," I volleyed. "She's not dangerous."

Theo made a derisive noise.

"My gut says she's good."

A snort. "Because *that's* never gotten you in trouble before."

"It's gotten me into fights maybe, but I have no trouble with girls."

Theo looked up with the sole purpose of laying a heavy look on me. "Vivienne Thorne."

Those guts I prided myself on clenched at the mention of the reporter's name. The reporter who I'd made the mistake of sleeping with without any kind of contract.

The reporter who I'd woken up to find trying to break into my computer.

"That was a mistake I won't make again. I was drunk, and drunk Tommy isn't always smart Tommy."

"Well, I hope this works, honey. I hope she can help." Her eyes softened even more, now with worry.

So I offered a smirk, squeezing her hand before pushing off the island. "Don't worry, Ma. I always land on my feet."

"Like a black cat with thirty-one lives."

I laughed, pressing a kiss into her hair as I passed. She leaned into me, patting my hand cupping her shoulder.

"I love you, Ma."

"You too, Tommy."

I strode into the living room, swiping my jacket off the back of the couch with a jerk of my chin at Theo. "Keep me posted about tomorrow, would ya?"

He jerked his chin back. "Yeah, you got it."

"I'll see you guys at dinner," I said over my shoulder, heading for the door.

And with their goodbyes at my back, I stepped outside.

I took a hard left and trotted up the cement steps of our brownstone in Greenwich Village. It had been my first big purchase with the obscene advance I'd gotten for my second series. The first thing we'd done was renovate, converting the ground floor to a walkout for Ma. She was already supposed to use a walker, though I didn't think I could pay her to actually get behind it. And eventually, she'd be bound to a wheelchair. Ground access was nonnegotiable.

I brushed away thoughts of the future, the plague of imaginings of how much worse it would get for her. And there was nothing I could do but take care of her as best as I was able.

She'd always taken care of us, even when things were tough. Especially after my dad left. The busybody bitches in the neighborhood were relentless. Rumors spread about her like wildfire. Her coffee friends quit inviting her over. I still remembered her loneliness in a time when she'd already been abandoned.

Fucking gossips. The truth didn't matter to gossips.

Better to control what they thought than leave them to their own devices.

I slipped my key in the lock. Theo had taken the second floor of

Ma's place, and the upper two floors were mine.

I barely made it through the door when Gus barreled into me, seventy pounds of slobbering, happy, hairy golden retriever.

"Heya, bud." I grabbed his face with both hands and gave it a good mussing.

He arfed his hello at an ear-splitting volume before getting back on all fours and taking off for the living room for a tennis ball.

Otherwise, the house was silent as a tomb.

I immediately turned on music. A gritty guitar riff slipped out of the speakers installed in every room of the house, even those empty ones I never used.

It was too much house for me. I used three rooms—the kitchen, my office, and my bedroom. The other rooms could have been part of a model home, and the only person who stepped foot in them was my housekeeper.

I wandered upstairs and into my office. Took a seat at my desk and opened my laptop, pulling up the shitty, half-baked stories to print them off one by one. If Amelia was willing, I'd have her critique them and help me figure out if any of them were viable. I needed a plan, which had never been my strong suit. Theo planned. I was much more comfortable winging it with blind optimism that everything would work out. It always had before.

This was bound to, too.

But a plan wouldn't hurt.

Amelia rose in my mind. She'd agreed to help me, which was saying something. I'd been a pariah ever since my contract with Simpson and Schubert was thrown in the dumpster fire that was my arrest and subsequent scandal. It had taken an inordinate amount of coercion to persuade another publisher to take me on, and Blackbird was the last of the Big Five to give me a chance. And that was only granted on a mountain of conditions.

First and foremost being a morality clause.

Keep your nose clean. That part had proven easier than dealing with my long-past deadline. If I stayed home, trouble couldn't find me, and I couldn't stumble into it. Because that was always when it happened—a drunken stumbling into a fight where my mouth would write checks that my ass absolutely could and would cash.

But if I had no book, it was all moot.

My printer spit out page after page of garbage in a lonely room in Greenwich Village. My mother sat with shaking hands on one of the floors below me, her well-being in my hands. And my brother fixed my life for me with cell phone in hand because that was what he did.

That was what we all did. We took care of each other.

And if I could get Amelia's help, I might be able to find a way to fulfill my obligations so I wouldn't let them down.

Insta-Famous

AMELIA

It took the entire train ride to Midtown for my skin to return to its natural shade of oatmeal.

But my mind couldn't process the afternoon as easily as my body could metabolize my adrenaline. As I wandered into the *USA Times* building, avoiding all possible eye contact, I replayed the exchange for the thirtieth time in as many minutes.

Thomas Bane wanted my help.

I would have laughed if I hadn't been so astonished. Stupefied really.

I was starting to wonder why I'd agreed now that I was out of his blast radius. Maybe he'd fritzed my brain. Scrambled my frequency. It almost felt like warfare. Chemical warfare, and his primary weapon was pheromones.

I didn't stand a chance.

The elevator was wall-to-wall people, from delivery guys to a pack of suits with briefcases, with me in the middle, tiny and pale and

I muttered, *"Excuse me,"* weaving around people to exit once the doors opened, only slightly relieved to have open air. Because that open air buzzed with frenetic energy.

People zipped around the office, which hummed with the sounds of clicking keys and chatter, rustling papers and commotion. I thanked my lucky stars I hadn't had to actually interview here. When my blog had gone viral, Janessa Hughes had reached out to invite me to blog for the paper as part of their Fiction Reviews column.

It was an opportunity I couldn't pass up. But Janessa had no idea I was a nervous mute in public.

It was a physiological response to a psychological hurdle I'd never overcome. Such was my curse as the colorlessly pale, eccentrically shy daughter of the Slap Chop fortune, who had grown up with a speech impediment. Not only was I an odd only child of inventors, and not only were we the wealthiest people in our provincial South Dakota town, but I couldn't pronounce Ls or Rs.

I realize it doesn't seem like that big of a deal. When I was five, it was adorable. When I was ten, I was a pariah. And thanks to the cruelness of children, I'd spent my formative years crying in excess and escaping into books. I had a million friends there.

Even when my impediment had been corrected with years of speech therapy, I barely spoke. Which somehow made the bullying worse. I knew every word that rhymed with Amelia, and none of them were pleasant—pedophilia, necrophilia, achylia—the absence of gastric juices—plus a dozen other "philias" that were equally disturbing. Although, Popillia wasn't the worst. But they were still a genus of beetle, and such was my lot in life.

Not exactly a happy place for a twelve-year-old girl. I was a ghost, pallid and silent, drifting through the halls in the hopes that no one would see me.

Sometimes, they didn't. Sometimes, they did.

But I'd become a ghost girl through and through. And now, I had years of conditioning to break if I ever wanted my dream job.

Bag in hand, I made my way down the wide aisle bracketed with cubicles, heading for my editor's office.

Janessa Hughes stood behind her desk, tall and beautiful. Her dark hair was loose and wavy, falling over the shoulders of her blazer. She looked comfortable there in her corner office, the floor-to-ceiling windows behind her looking out over the tip of Manhattan and the Atlantic beyond.

She was the epitome of power and control, everything about her lovely and severe. Her eyes sharpened when I passed through her open doorway, her lips lifting in a composed smile.

She waved me in, her gaze dropping to her phone. "Charles, don't bullshit me. Can you get the story or not?"

"That's what I'm trying to explain. There's a hang-up. If I can't get Senator Williams to meet, I can't—"

"Then I guess you'd better figure out how to secure a meeting whether he wants it or not. I want the story on my desk Monday, Chuck. Otherwise, don't bother coming in."

Before he had a chance to respond, she disconnected the line with a cold press of a button.

When she smiled, it was warm and friendly and the exact opposite of the woman who had just hung up on poor Chuck.

"Amelia Hall," she said amicably as she smoothed the rump of her pencil skirt and sat. "It's nice to finally meet you in person. Please, have a seat."

My heart galloped in my chest, and I was grateful she had given me an objective so I didn't have to respond. I had a whole separate list of lines for this meeting, but as I sat, I found I couldn't remember a single one. So I reached into my bag and started unloading books in lieu of trying to formulate sentences or—God forbid—instigate an entire conversation.

Maybe if I hadn't been in public all day.

Maybe if I weren't actually me.

"Ah, Thomas Bane." As she reached for the books, her smile curled into something more wicked. "He's a real looker, isn't he?" She took one of the books and opened it up to inspect his signature.

"Mmhmm," I hummed, completing the stack. I then focused all my attention on my hands as I folded my bag into equal parts with far more precision than was necessary.

Janessa didn't seem to notice. "I mean, seriously, he's gorgeous in print but in person? I'm salivating just thinking about it."

I imagined Janessa turning into a stammering, blushing fool around him, and the thought that she was actually flappable relaxed me infinitesimally.

"So," she started, turning her full attention on me, "how did it go?"

I fiddled with the bag in my lap. "It went—" I croaked and cleared my throat. "It went well, I think."

She chuckled. "I'd say it went better than that. I saw the picture of you two on his Instagram."

My gaze snapped up to meet hers. "He already posted that?"

"He did, Tagged you, and the *Times*, too." She picked up her phone, swiped at it a couple times, and turned it around in display.

There we were—me and Thomas Bane, laughing in the bookstore like old friends.

"That is so weird," I breathed.

She laughed aloud at that. "Glad to see you're enjoying the perks of blogging for a newspaper—getting to get a good whiff of Thomas Bane."

Had I been in different company, I would have groaned my agreement. "That leather jacket."

"And his soap maybe. His shampoo? With all that hair...I swear, it's like a diffuser. Something citrus and spicy and...mmm," she hummed, setting down her phone. She leaned toward me, her eyes sharp and smile wry. "So, did he hit on you? Come on to you? Start a fight with any readers? Tell me he at least squeezed your ass. Or that you at least squeezed his."

A painful flush climbed up my neck. "No! Of course not."

"Well, that's a shame. Would have made a good story." She sighed and sat back in her chair. "Did you get any dirt on his next novel? I've heard a thousand rumors, and I'm dying to know the real story."

"No, not exactly. But he asked for my help with it." The words felt like a betrayal the second they left my mouth.

She shifted, sparking with intrigue. The tension in the room thickened. "Oh, really?"

I tried to smile, my tongue sticky and thick. "I-I'm not even sure I'll do it," I hedged.

"Oh, you'll do it all right," she insisted.

Shit.

"Thomas Bane's story has been sought after by every major news syndicate ever since he broke out. His social life, the women he dates, his history. Who he *really* is, because the charm and swagger he wears like head-to-toe plate armor is nothing but a mask. We all know there's more to him. But no one's been able to get close enough to learn the truth. *This* sounds like a golden opportunity."

I blinked, trying to sort out how I'd gotten here, to the threshold of her suggestion. "I... I'm sorry. I'm not really a reporter, Ms. Hughes."

"Please, call me Janessa. And I realize this is out of your wheelhouse, but think about it," she said, her face softening, opening, brimming with charisma. "He read your reviews, I'm guessing?" When I nodded, she continued, "He respects your opinion. You'll be spending time with him, learning about him, working with him. You've already proven you're a fantastic writer by the scores of reviews you've written and the wide-scale popularity of your blog. What if I offered you a permanent position at the newspaper as a journalist in exchange for a piece about him?"

My brows drew together, the weight of her proposition tugging the corners of my lips. Before I found the wherewithal to speak, she beat me to the punch.

"I'm sure you've never considered it—at least, not like this. Don't answer me now."

"I…I don't want to be a journalist, Ms. Hughes. Janessa."

Something in her tightened, and the predatory feeling it gave me triggered an instinct to bolt.

"Well then, what *do* you want, Amelia?"

I swallowed hard enough that my throat clicked. "To be an editor for a publishing house."

Her smile curled at the edges. "Your reviews are stellar, critical and constructive without being overbearing. With the success of your blog, your master's degree in English, and credits reading for other authors, I can see you moving in that direction. Your résumé is impressive. And I can get you an internship."

A flash of hope ripped through me like lightning.

"All you have to do is consider writing a piece about what you learn working with Thomas Bane."

The crack of thunder in my chest that followed was deafening.

One doesn't sit in the office of one of the most influential editors in New York and say no, especially not when she was dangling the carrot of your dreams in front of you, and especially not someone like me who couldn't say no to her cat.

So I tried to smile and offered the only promise I could, "I'll consider it."

LESS THAN AN HOUR LATER, I dragged myself across the threshold of my brownstone in the Village, mentally exhausted and aching to be alone.

I was peopled the fuck out.

Between Thomas Bane's pheromone overload, Janessa's proposition, and the several thousand people I'd just shared air with, my energy was completely sapped along with my ability to brain. But a long, hot bath with a book was waiting for me, and I'd been obsessing about it since I burst out of the *Times'* building like someone was chasing me.

Which was why I found myself uncharacteristically disappointed to find all my roommates in the kitchen, laughing. Any other day, I would have been overjoyed for us all to be together, as rare as it was these days. Val and Rin were in serious relationships, and most of their time was spent with their boyfriends. Coming back to our place—to *my* place—was becoming more and more of a chore for them, though I knew they'd never admit it. They did it for Katherine's and my benefit.

God help us once they were all married. I'd end up alone in this big house. One cat wouldn't be enough. I'd need at least three more if I was really going to commit.

I sighed, hanging up my coat, scarf, and bag, grateful that there were no men in my kitchen. Thomas Bane had given me enough male presence for a month.

"Hey!" Val called from her spot in front of the stove, brushing her curly hair from her forehead with the back of her hand.

Rin and Katherine turned, smiling. Well, Rin was smiling. Katherine just wasn't frowning. Even sullen, Katherine was pretty, her dark hair straight and perfect, her face untouched by makeup, her shirtdress tailored to calculated precision. To be honest, she *looked* like a librarian—strict, smart, and stern. I'd bet she'd dole out a solid spanking, too.

"Hey," I echoed, trying to sound peppy as I hauled my jellybrained self to the kitchen island and plopped down on a stool.

"That good, huh?" Val asked with a teasing smile, turning for the pan of sizzling paella on the stove.

I groaned. "Too many people. The bookstore was crazy. Midtown was packed. The *USA Times'* office alone is enough to make me crawl into bed for a year."

Val's heart-shaped face pinched. "So I guess now's a bad time to tell you that Sam and Court are coming over for dinner?"

Another groan, this one drawn out and accompanied by a magnificent slump of my shoulders.

Rin's face fell. "We should cancel. The boys won't mind."

I sighed, straightening up. "No, no. Don't cancel it. Just don't be offended if I dip out early to lock myself in my room."

"You sure?" Val asked, her face mirroring Rin's.

"Positive. I'd feel a hundred times worse if they didn't come on account of me." I put on a smile, though I knew it was weary.

They relaxed, seeming relieved.

Val pushed the paella around the pan, her curvaceous hip leaning on the counter. "So how did it go meeting Thomas Bane?"

"Well, I didn't faint."

They chuckled, and I found myself smiling genuinely, my exhaustion and anxiety seeping out of me now that I was home and with my friends.

"He's…intense. Very intense, very smirky, and he smells *very* good."

Katherine gave me a look. "You got close enough to smell him?"

"We took a picture together."

Now all three of them were looking at me.

"At his insistence. Janessa said it was already on Instagram."

Simultaneously, the three of them reached for their phones. Belatedly, I reached for mine. I hadn't considered *really* looking. I'd been too focused on navigating all the *people*.

"Oh my God," Val breathed. "He *is* gorgeous."

"Look at you." Rin beamed. "What a great picture, Amelia."

"This already has twelve thousand likes," Katherine noted.

"Holy shit, it does." Val gaped at her phone. "How many new followers do you have?"

I swallowed hard and pulled up my account. My eyes nearly popped out of their sockets. "Two thousand. That can't be right." I checked my analytics. "Or it can." With a nervous laugh, I set my phone facedown on the counter, not ready to deal with whatever the hell *that* meant. "He asked me to help him with his next book."

Three faces swiveled in my direction.

"But you hate his books." Val's brows drew together.

"Why does everyone keep saying that?" My forehead furrowed. "Just because I don't leave him five-star reviews doesn't mean I hate his books. I love his books. I hate his heroes."

"Ugh, like that one you made me read. You know the one. With the guy who slept with that other girl just because his ego was bruised? God, he was the worst. Fuck that guy," Val said.

"That's close to what I told him."

Val laughed. "You didn't!"

I shrugged. "He asked."

Her smile fell. "I mean…you actually talked to him?"

"I did," I said, half in wonder. "He accused me of hating him too, so I explained myself. And then he asked me to be on his team. To tell him no."

Katherine frowned. "As in to refuse his request?"

"No, as in to help him by telling him to stop writing assholes."

"And you said no," Katherine added.

"I said yes."

They blinked.

"Don't look at me like that. If you were standing in front of him and he asked you for anything, you'd give it to him. I mean it. Anything."

"A blow job?" Katherine countered. "With your exceptionally small palate?"

"Your ass?" Val asked with a smirk.

"I was just gonna say a kiss," Rin said, "but I feel like I should up the ante."

I laughed. "Anything. I couldn't have been more surprised if he'd asked me to fly to Vegas to get married."

"You wouldn't have said yes to that," Val said on a laugh.

"I dunno. I don't think I could have said no to anything. Even the invasion of my tiny mouth or ass."

We looked at each other for a silent moment before bursting into laughter.

"But really, I'd love to help him. Plus, it's an opportunity to add another book to my résumé when I'm ready to start applying for internships—and a book by *Thomas Bane* to boot."

"I can't believe Thomas Bane asked you to help him with his book," Rin said, shaking her head. She still wore a pencil skirt and tailored shirt from her day at The Met, though she'd kicked off her heels, which took her back to a solid six feet from an almost astronomic height. Her hair was dark and shiny, her bee-sting lips full and crimson. Her skin was even fairer than mine, thanks to her Korean-Dutch roots.

Seriously, she should have been a model. But she was almost as shy as I was. Well, before she'd started working at the museum at least.

"Wasn't he just one of *People*'s Sexiest Men Alive?" Val asked.

"Yes," Katherine answered, slipping off her stool. "It's right here in my knitting basket." She shuffled around in the living room.

Val snorted a laugh. "Care to explain why you're trolling sexy men in *People*?"

"I read it for the ads," Katherine said flatly.

I was mostly sure she was kidding. A second later, the magazine hit the countertop with a smack, opened to his page.

We leaned over it in unison. The spread was a series of shots of him in Washington Square with a golden retriever, looking happy and carefree while also somehow managing to smolder. I attributed it to that ridiculously luscious mouth of his. The title of his segment was, "Bad Boy Bane: Love to Hate Him." Although I didn't know how anyone could hate him when he was scruffing his dog's face or whipping a tennis ball with that arm of his that looked Photoshopped. If I hadn't had that python wrapped around me earlier, I wouldn't have believed it myself.

"He came out of nowhere," Val said. "No one had ever heard of him, and then he started dating Olivia Nash and broke the internet with his hair."

I laughed. "Have you seen that video of him putting his hair into a bun in slow motion?"

"Pretty sure I got a hysterical pregnancy from that video," Val said. "Man, when he and Olivia Nash broke up, GIFs of their breakup was in my news feed for a week."

"When she took off her Manolos one by one and threw them at him? Oh my God, in that moment, she was every woman," Rin added.

"I use that GIF all the time," Val said on a laugh. "When it bounces off his face? I die." She wrenched her face up and pretended to get hit in slow motion.

"That was just before his first book came out," Katherine noted.

"He has gotten some of the best and worst publicity," Val said. "Though I'm not at all mad he dated Marley Monroe. That breakup album is one of my favorites of hers."

Rin bopped in her seat and sang, "*I don't care if you look like an angel.*"

"*All I want is for you to be faithful,*" Val chimed in.

And we all sang, "*But all you give is the hot, lovin' danger. And all you were was a beautiful stranger.*"

"God," I said on a giggle, "he's just too much. I can't believe I'm going to work with him. Like, all the time."

"When are you supposed to start?" Katherine asked.

"Tomorrow, I think," I answered. "He's supposed to get in touch."

"Well, has he?" she pressed.

I picked up my phone to prove her wrong. "He couldn't have. It's only been a few—" My email notification bubble said I had three emails, and when I opened the app, all three were from his office. I scanned the first email. "His assistant wants me to come over in the morning to discuss payment, timelines, and materials. There's…" I swallowed. "There's a nondisclosure for me to sign." I lowered my phone. "I already told my boss."

Katherine shrugged. "Let him know. You're not in breach. You haven't signed anything yet."

"God, remember when he got arrested at that rally?" Val asked. "The coverage of his arrest was awful."

Katherine snorted a laugh. "I don't care what *Us Weekly* says. With hair like his, there's no way he's a skinhead. Not that they're mutually exclusive. But I believe him when he said he was at the wrong place at the wrong time. Plus, why else would he be all beat up? I think he stumbled into that rally and picked a fight, just like he said. I think it's hot," she said with a shrug. "I'd do a guy who punched a Nazi in the face."

Val laughed. "Like Indiana Jones. *It belongs in a museum!*"

I couldn't help but giggle. "No, I think you're right. But man, the firestorm was horrible. He got dropped from his publisher and lost all his sponsorships. No one would touch him. It's a miracle he picked up a contract with Blackbird after such awful press. And who could blame them? When coupled with public indecency and a penchant for getting in fights at nightclubs all over the city, he's a publicist's nightmare."

"Or dream come true," Katherine countered. "Depends on their angle. Maybe the whole thing was a show for media attention. In which case, he's performing exceptionally well."

I chuckled. "Maybe. But everyone dropped him like a bad habit. That couldn't have been part of anyone's plan."

"Not everyone," Katherine amended. "You've seen the TAG billboards. He doesn't seem to be hurting."

"Well," I started, "it's been two years, and the public is split. People *love* to argue about the truth. Remember the *Team Tommy* T-shirts?"

"I have one," Katherine said.

We all turned to stare at her.

"What? All proceeds went to a fund for the New York Public Library."

I shook my head. "See? The controversy keeps him relevant."

"And now you're going to be associated with him." Rin frowned.

"But it's not like anyone will *know*. Trust me, I will still be as invisible as ever." I sighed. "I really do think I can help him with his story. Although I don't know why he'd want me after I doled out a boatload of criticism on books he couldn't change."

"Maybe he's sick in the head," Val offered. "Or a masochist. Maybe Marley Monroe and Thomas Bane broke up because he secretly loved being spanked with a riding crop, and that was just too much pressure for her."

"Maybe. Tomorrow will tell the tale," I said.

"What about the NDA?" Rin asked. "I guess we won't ever know how it goes if you're gagged."

"I mean, if she's lucky she'll get gagged," Val said with a waggle of her brows.

"I am one hundred percent sure there's no way I can survive this without you guys," I said. "Trust me, you will know even if I have to make you sign an NDA of my own."

The doorbell rang, and Rin and Val both lit up with smiles.

"I'll get it," Rin said, slipping off her stool and striding to the front door.

I heard Sam's voice first. Val's gaze shifted to a spot behind me, her eyes eager as a puppy at a barbecue. And then I heard Court, followed by a smooch.

"Hey," Sam said, pulling off his jacket and hanging it next to the door. He glided into the room, his eyes locked on Val's as he approached. The second he was in arm's length, he scooped her up for a kiss, her paella spoon in hand.

I sighed with a schmoopy smile on my face as he broke the kiss and set her to rights.

"Smells delicious," he said, grabbing a spoon to dip into the pan.

But she popped his hand, laughing. "Get outta there, you."

He smirked. "Can't. Won't." And he kissed her nose, distracting her so he could lift a spoonful when she wasn't looking.

She rolled her eyes. "I hope you burn your mouth."

The way he was chewing, I had a feeling her wish came true.

Rin took her seat next to me again, and Court stood behind her, smiling.

They were all too much. Especially seeing Court so gooey. The man was about as light and easy as a Brontë novel. Which was to say, not at all.

I looked over both couples, considering how they'd come about. And I daydreamed for a moment as they conversed around me that I'd find someone someday, too. That somehow I'd meet a man who would see all the things I thought were faults and love every one of them until I did, too. Just like Rin and Val had.

Of course, I'd have to leave the house for that to happen.

And with a small, resigned smile, I submitted to my fate as a spinster.

Absolutely Ridiculous

TOMMY

"**W**hat the fuck are you doing?"

Theo stood in the entrance of my living room, brows drawn and arms folded across his chest.

I fluffed the pillow in my hand and set it in the corner of the couch. "Making sausage. What the fuck does it look like I'm doing?" I spotted a rogue sock peeking out from under the coffee table and kicked it under the couch. "My housekeeper doesn't come until tomorrow. This place is a mess." I stopped, lifting my nose. I sniffed. "Does it smell weird in here to you?"

Theo rolled his eyes. "Seriously, what is wrong with you?"

"Nothing," I said, moving for the bookshelf where a candle sat. I stuck the tip of my nose in the opening and sniffed again with a shrug.

"You're lighting a candle."

"Well, it smells like a shoe in here." I opened a drawer in my desk, looking for a lighter.

"It smells like it always does." The flick of flint sounded before the lighter appeared in my periphery.

I tilted the candle, meeting the flame to the wick. "How come you never told me I lived in a pigsty?"

"You never asked." He returned the lighter to his slacks pocket, leaving his hand there. He eyed me with suspicion.

"What time is it?" I asked as I set the candle on the sideboard.

"She'll be here any second. What are you so nervous about?"

I laughed. "I'm not nervous."

"Right. I know how into candles you are. Maybe you should throw a Scentsy party."

My face quirked. "A what?"

He sighed. "Never mind."

I huffed, moving to the couch. "I don't know, man," I said as I sat, reaching for the manuscripts I'd printed up for her so I could organize them. Again. "She judges me for a living." I noticed a film of dust on the glass top of the coffee table and frowned, swiping at it. A streak the size of my hand graced the top, and I swore, storming into the kitchen to rummage around under the sink for something to clean it with.

Theo sighed when I came back with some wipe things I'd found. "That'll streak." He headed to the kitchen and came back with glass cleaner and a paper towel. "She might judge your writing, but she's not going to be judging your housekeeping. She probably won't even notice."

"Easy for you to say. Nobody trips on dildos or C-rings at your place."

He made a face at me, pausing mid-swipe. "Dude. I live with Ma."

The doorbell rang, and I perked up, smiling as I headed to the door. I paused in front of the hall mirror for a split second to smooth a hand over my hair and check my teeth before trotting the rest of the way.

I'd say I hadn't thought about her once, not at all, not even for a second, but that would be a lie. And I only lied about who I was dating.

Truth was, she'd been occupying my thoughts since she walked away from me yesterday, and the reason was simple: Amelia Hall was the embodiment of hope.

All I had to do was not fuck up.

With that positive reinforcement at my back, I took a deep breath and opened the door.

Amelia seemed smaller than I remembered, her hair long and mostly straight. The flaxen strands held rings of the slightest natural wave. She was bundled up from top to toe in ten shades of white— her snow-white felt coat, her cream knit scarf, an ivory skirt, tights the color of chalk. In fact, the most colorful thing about her was her eyes, as blue and bright as the silvery winter sky above us.

Scratch that. The most colorful thing about her was the flush of her cheeks that rose like a blooming flower, peach and soft and delicate.

"Hey," I said, stepping back and pulling the door open wider with me. "Come on in."

Her flush deepened, but she smiled, dipping her head as she passed.

I closed the door behind her without looking as my eyes followed her into my entryway.

She paused by the bench and coat hooks, setting down her bag.

"Thanks for coming so soon," I said, stepping toward her, reaching for her coat to help her out of it.

She stiffened in surprise, but she was still smiling. "M-my pleasure."

I hung her coat on the rack as she unwound her scarf. Her blouse was creamy white too, and sheer, dotted with a tiny pattern I couldn't make out.

"Are those..." I started, leaning in with my eyes squinted.

"Tabby cats," she said matter-of-factly as she picked up her bag from the bench.

I chuckled once through my nose. "Of course they are."

Her small face pinched in suspicion. "What's that supposed to mean?"

With a smile, I stepped into her space for the briefest moment. She took a breath, her face open and eyes blinking.

"You're unconventional, Amelia Hall." I angled closer. "And I like it."

I removed myself from the intimacy and walked away, heading for the living room with my blood thrumming and my smile immovable.

"Can I get you something to drink?" I asked over my shoulder, feeling her behind me.

"N-no, thanks," she answered, stopping in the living room and shuffling around.

I was about to speak—the words right there on the tip of my tongue—but when I turned around, they were instantly inconsequential and slipped from my mind, never to be recovered.

Amelia Hall was digging through her bag, hinged at the waist with her back straight, her ass out, and her hair falling over her shoulder, tucked behind her ear to frame her profile. Her ass was shaped just like a heart, stretching the construction of her skirt.

If I'd ever passed Amelia Hall on the street, she wouldn't have caught my attention. But that was the thing about girls like her. Once you saw them, there was no *un*seeing them.

Theo cleared his throat from somewhere behind me, and Amelia shot upright, her hands clutching a notebook and pen and her face open as a 7-Eleven.

Her eyes bounced from me, to Theo, then back at least a half-dozen times.

I sighed.

It was always like this. On our own, my brother and I tended to evoke a reaction from women. But when we were *together*? Women occasionally ceased motor function. I would have smiled if it wasn't for a pang of annoyance that she was looking at my brother that way.

I attributed my usual upper hand in such situations to a combination of my hair and leather jacket. The thought that she might prefer the clean-cut, responsible version of me was a little too much to stomach.

Theo stepped toward her, smiling amicably. "Hello, Amelia. I'm Theo. We emailed yesterday." He stuck out his hand.

Her cheeks were flushed as she blinked, looking at his hand, then up at him, then back at me. "There are two of you."

Theo's smirk rose. "Yeah, but too bad for Tommy that I got all the charm and good looks."

Amelia smiled in the most timid curve of her lips. She extended her hand with apprehension, and it disappeared into his. "Nice to meet you," she answered so softly, I barely heard her.

Theo didn't miss a beat. "It's a pleasure to meet you, too. Thanks for coming to bail him out," he said with a smile and a nod in my direction. He leaned in conspiratorially. "He's hopeless, you know."

She smiled at that, relaxing incrementally. "Nothing's hopeless. With a little hard work, anything can be saved."

"Coming from you, I believe it," he said, laying it on so thick, I fought a baffling impulse to physically remove his hand from hers.

Fortunately for all of us, he let her go on his own.

"Don't listen to Teddy," I said, smiling wider when he scowled at me. "He's the brains. I'm the face."

Amelia stifled a laugh. "You literally look exactly alike."

I moved to Theo's side. "You say that now," I said, pausing to wet my bottom lip, "but you'll figure out our differences soon enough."

Her eyes were on my lips. "I … ah …" Just as I began patting myself on the back, she finished her thought, "One of your teeth is crooked. Right here." She bared her teeth comically and pointed at an incisor.

Theo barked a laugh, and my face flattened.

And Amelia Hall smiled, her cheeks rosy and high, her pretty, smartass lips together.

I moved to the couch, turning my attention and wounded pride to the manuscripts waiting there. "Anyway, Teddy here was just leaving. Weren't you, Theo?"

He slipped his hands in his pockets and shrugged. "I dunno. Maybe I'll hang around for a while."

The look I shot him had him rolling his eyes. But he let out a resigned sigh.

"All right. Amelia, let me know if you need anything. And Tommy, don't forget to arrange Amelia's payment."

"Oh, no," she said as she sat on the couch opposite me. "I don't expect to be paid. I just do this for fun."

I frowned. "I'm sorry, I just don't feel right *not* paying you."

Theo nodded. "I don't think you realize what a pain in your ass he's gonna be."

She shrugged. "It's all right. Really. I insist."

My frown deepened. "No, *I* insist. Everyone can use extra cash. I mean, unless I'm mistaken as to how much bloggers make."

Now Amelia was frowning, too, her little mouth downturned in such a way that she almost looked like she was pouting. It was so adorable, I had to stop myself from chuckling.

"First, I'll have you know that bloggers can make a living wage, and I'd thank you kindly not to insult the industry that happens to spread the word about your books."

Properly scolded, I nodded. "I meant no offense—"

"And second, I don't *need* your money, Mr. Bane. My father invented the Slap Chop," she said with her nose in the air.

All instinct to laugh stopped dead, then rose like a tornado. "Your... what?"

Her rosy cheeks splotched at the edges. "He invented the Slap Chop. The ShamWow. Egglettes. A dozen other household innovations you can find at Bed, Bath, and Beyond."

I coughed to cover sputtering laughter as she continued.

"So, while I appreciate your offer, I do not require payment. A good reference would suffice."

I smoothed my face in earnest. "I...I'm sorry, Amelia. I didn't intend to insult you. I just didn't want you to feel taken advantage of. So, no...you don't need my money. I'm almost positive your dad's net worth is triple mine."

"Closer to quintuple. And thank you." She opened her notebook and smiled at me, pen at the ready. "Where should we start?"

"And that's my cue." Theo headed for the door. "Good luck, Amelia," he said with a smirk identical to mine. "You're gonna need it."

I shook my head. "I'd like to say he won't always be such a shit, but it'd be a lie."

She chuckled as I reached for the stack of papers on my coffee table.

I sorted through them aimlessly as I spoke. "I'm in a bind, Amelia. My manuscript is past due, and I have very little to show for. Just this."

I handed her the stack of shitty manuscripts, and she took them curiously.

Her brows furrowed as she flipped through them. "None of these are even a complete act."

"No, they are not, which is why I need your help. If you're interested, I'd like you to read this trash pile and tell me if you think any of it is salvageable. I'm wondering if there's a way to combine some of them to fully bake an idea. Hell, I'd take half-baked. These aren't even batter."

Her eyes scanned the pages as she thumbed through them, skimming the synopsis on the fronts. "How far behind deadline are you?"

"Far enough that my editor has crawled up my ass and made a nest."

One of her brows rose. "That sounds uncomfortable."

"You have no idea."

Another laugh. She tucked a bit of hair behind her ear, pen hooked in her fingers. "All right, I can do that. When do you want to meet again?"

"As soon as you can. As soon as you're ready."

She nodded. "Is tomorrow okay?"

I eyed her. "You can read all this and mark it up by tomorrow?"

One small shoulder rose and fell in a shrug. "Sure. I have to work on my piece for the signing yesterday, but it shouldn't be a problem."

I felt the weight lift from my shoulders. It'd piled on so gradually, I hadn't even noticed it was there. "That would be phenomenal. Message me in the morning and let me know when you can come over."

She nodded, her cheeks flushing. I swear, a gentle breeze could bring Amelia Hall to a full blush. The thought made me wonder if I could actually make her blush so hard, she fainted.

"Any initial thoughts?" I fished shamelessly.

She frowned. "Ah, no. I don't want to say anything until I've read them."

I tried not to pout. "No thoughts? None? Not even a tiny little baby thought?"

Her nose wrinkled.

"Come on, Amelia," I said smoothly, doing my best to persuade her. "Don't you know writers have insatiable egos? If you don't give me a little something, I'll be thinking about it at three a.m. in the heat of a staring contest with my ceiling."

"Well, I like the idea of the post-apocalyptic one, but I'm also prone to this one. The one with the dragon quest." She flipped through them. "All your heroes are male."

"*Heroes* usually are," I joked.

Amelia shook her head, rolling her eyes. "Your protagonists, I mean. Have you ever thought of writing a female lead?"

"Never," I answered without hesitation.

"Why not?" She frowned, her sweet bottom lip poking out. She meant it to look hard, but nothing about her was hard. Not a single thing.

"Because I'm not a woman, and I don't want to offend them."

"That's like saying you can't write diversity because you're white."

One of my brows arched as I gave her a look. "Tell me, has anyone ever reviewed your reviews? Because, when a white guy writes women and diversity, everyone who wanted it from them says, *But not like that.*"

Her brows drew together. "Well…no one has reviewed my reviews. Not exactly. But…I don't know if you've ever been to Goodbooks, but that place is a battlefield. I've been in my fair share of internet arguments over books before, sometimes in the comments of my own reviews."

A dry laugh escaped me. "Oh, I've been to that website—once. I'm no masochist. I much prefer to ignore people who hate me."

"Except me."

"Yes, except you, but you insist you don't hate me. So at least we have that." I caught my earned smile and put it in my pocket. "You weren't posting reviews with Liz Lemon eye-rolling GIFs just to get a rise out of people. You took the time to put together thoughtful feedback that was absolutely true. To be honest, those reviews sometimes hurt worse."

Her frown relaxed, softening with something akin to guilt. "They do?"

I nodded. "Because they press our soft spots, the bruises we have, the blind spots in our process."

Understanding flickered behind her eyes.

"Anyway, it was Theo who first found you. When I was with Simpson and Schubert, he always made sure they sent you advanced copies. You're one of my top bloggers. Your reviews sell my books. And I'm hoping your perspective and insight can help save the next one."

With that, her face melted into empathy, smiling with sincerity. "I hope I can help, too. It's actually something I love—helping people. I majored in English and considered going into elementary education."

I pictured her standing in front of a kindergarten class, and the thought warmed me up from the middle. "Why didn't you?"

She laughed. "I can barely speak to strangers, and I typically avoid public, except under strict circumstances."

"Like what?"

"Well…" She thought for a second. "It has to be somewhere I really want to go. Like the swing club where my friend plays or a movie I'm dying to see. Or the bar my friends and I go to every week. That's another thing. I *have* to have a buffer. Usually, that consists of my friends."

"No boyfriend?"

Her cheeks were smudged with color again. "That whole not-talking-to-strangers thing kind of puts a damper on the dating thing. But I'm working on it."

I laughed, wondering what kind of guy she liked, wondering what kind of guy could take Amelia Hall home. "You don't seem to have trouble talking to me."

She doodled on her page, her eyes on the paper. "I was scared to death at the bookstore. If I didn't want this job with *Times* so badly, I would have told Janessa to go fuck herself."

Laughter burst out of me at the unexpected swear from her mouth.

"But this is an important step for me. I blog because I love books and I love authors, and I want to connect readers with them. I want to help spread the word. I enjoy being a part of other people's success. So I decided recently that I'd like to try to get an internship editing with a publisher. I could use all the practice I've gained doing developmental edits, combine it with my English degree, and get a job to help *find* authors to share with the world. It's everything I want to do, all wrapped up in one pretty little job."

Her innocence about the industry was so endearing, I didn't have the heart to tell her that it was far more about what an editor could sell than what they loved. But that didn't stop me from answering honestly.

"I think you'll be great."

"Not if I can't get out of my shell. My therapist tells me I'm not a lost cause, but days like yesterday leave me wondering if it's worth it. It'd be so much easier to stay inside and order groceries online."

"You don't seem nervous now."

"Well, it must be working then, because I am." Her nose scrunched again for a nanosecond. "It gets easier the more I'm around someone and the less people are in the room. I was more nervous the second before my knuckles hit your door than I was when the door opened."

A dozen questions rose in my mind, but before I could find an appropriate one, she said, "So, tomorrow then?"

I packed my thoughts away for later. "The deadline waits for no man."

She shifted in her seat, her flush still present and eyes touched with worry. Her nerves visibly changed her, and that change was instantaneous. "I…I did need to t-talk to you about something, Mr. Bane. Thomas."

I sat back on the couch, smirking. "Tommy."

"Tommy," she said, testing the word. "I…I wanted to tell you I might have mentioned our… arrangement to Janessa, my boss."

I sobered immediately. And she must have seen it on my face because when she spoke again, it was hurried and rambling.

"I…it was before your brother sent the NDA. I didn't know. I should have known, but I didn't really think, and I wanted you to know she knows. I'm sorry."

I tried to smile, but the expression was wooden. Janessa Hughes had sicced more than a few reporters at me, including Vivienne Thorne. But my fortune-telling gut took one look at Amelia and knew.

She would never be a stooge for Janessa. The very fact that she'd told me she'd spoken to Janessa was one of a dozen points that whispered that Amelia was honest, trustworthy. Most of those points were undefinable, nothing more than a feeling. But I knew to trust it.

"It's okay, Amelia. And thank you for telling me. But you won't be able to speak to her about it again."

She relaxed, her shoulders softening with her face. "Yes, of course. I wouldn't dream of it. Truthfully, I'm thankful I have an excuse to keep her off my back."

"Why's that?" I asked, my guts tightening.

"Oh, nothing," she hedged. "She was just very interested in you. Her and half of America." She laughed gently.

I was instantly uncomfortable. "What'd she say?" I asked, trying to keep the emotion out of my voice.

It must have worked. She was unfazed and smiling. "God, she told me, if I wrote a story about you, got dirt on you for an exposé, she could get me a job editing at a Big Five. Can you believe that?" She chuckled, shaking her head.

"Yes, actually, I can."

Her smile fell. "I hope you know I'd never…I mean, the second she suggested it, all I could think was, *No*. I could never be dishonest."

"Too moral?"

"No. I'm a *terrible* liar."

A laugh huffed out of me. "That's not at all surprising. Your blush spells it out in cursive."

That flush rose at the mention of it.

"I appreciate your respect of my privacy, Amelia. God knows nobody else does," I said as I stood, torn between the desire to keep her there and the instinct not to tell her too much.

NDA or no NDA, people talked. Suing her would be no consolation for the betrayal, and it certainly wouldn't undo any damage done.

Disappointment flashed across her brow at my move to dismiss her, which strangely made me feel better. I found that I liked thinking she wanted to stay, too.

I ignored the fleeting thought that she only wanted to stay because she wanted to pry.

Paranoia—common side effect of getting fucked over. And over. And over.

Amelia packed her notebook and pen away and stood. I thought her body language indicated she was going to step toward the door, so I walked around the coffee table to follow her. But she stopped, reaching into another pocket of her bag with so much concentration, it seemed whatever she was looking for required the full capacity of her brain.

By the time I stopped myself, it was almost too late. I was in her space again, close enough to see the individual hairs on her head and the burst of silver in her irises when she looked up at me.

For a moment, we were caught. Awareness hummed across my skin, in the air between us as she looked up at me, and I looked down at her. I could kiss her. The way her eyes flicked to my lips and hung there, I thought she'd let me.

I almost did. If one more second had passed before my door opened, I would have.

"*Gus, wait!*"

Those two words were the only warning I had, and they weren't nearly enough to do a goddamn thing to stop what happened next.

My seventy-pound golden retriever thundered into the room, his nails clacking noisily on the hardwood, his face open and happy, tongue lolling as he bounded toward us. There was no time to shift us, to move Amelia out of the way. All I could do was brace for impact.

Gus jumped like the ill-mannered bastard he was, his paws aiming for my chest. But I was facing Amelia.

Which meant he had to go through her.

He slammed into us, his wiggling, hairy body sandwiching Amelia between us, and down we went. I wrapped my arms around her, shifting to land us on the couch with a squeal from Amelia and an *oof* out of me.

Gus just slobbered.

He jumped on the couch, standing all over us so he could get to my face, which he licked with panting, humid gusto. Amelia was still squealing, squealing and giggling, curled into my chest with her arms over her face.

"Goddammit, Gus!" I batted him away, and he met the challenge by trying to get at me around my arms. "Down! Get the fuck down!"

His tail wagged harder.

"*Augustus*!" I said, his full name a command he didn't ignore.

Not that he was afraid of me. He jumped off the couch like we'd bored him, wagging his tail as he trotted back to the entryway where he'd left his tennis balls. He picked them both up, one lodged so deep in his throat, it was a wonder he didn't choke.

"Oh my God, Mr. Bane, I am so sorry," my dog walker, Amanda, panted. "He can't even handle coming home to you."

I barely heard her. I was too busy cataloging the feel of Amelia lying on top of me. She unwrapped her head from her arms, eyeing Gus warily as he dropped the outermost ball in his mouth and spent several seconds attempting to pick it up again in his overfull mouth.

Then she looked down at me, her eyes wide and mouth in a little O as her face lit fire.

I swear, the color made her eyes look like slivers of sea glass.

I was smirking. I didn't care.

She put her small hands on my chest and pushed herself to sit, sliding off my lap with regrettable swiftness. "I...I am so...I'm sorry. I—"

"No, it's me who's sorry," I said as she stood, and I followed, keeping distance between us. For all of our sakes.

"No, it's *me* who's sorry," Amanda insisted. "I tried to hang on to him, but I think even if I had, he'd have dragged me all the way into the room with him."

I strode into the entryway where Gus had lain down, still fooling with his tennis balls. "You're a bad fucking boy, Augustus."

He looked up at me with his big, dopey eyes and barked. The tennis balls fell out of his mouth, and he was on his feet in a flash, gathering them up again.

I shook my head, turning to Amelia. "Are you all right? You're not hurt?"

She shook her head back, her eyes darting to Amanda. "I-I'm okay. Thanks. I'm sorry I … well, that I was just … you know, when we fell, and I …"

I chuckled. "Are you kidding? That was the highlight of my day. I should cook Gus a steak dinner."

At that, my curiosity was almost slaked. She blushed hard enough to teeter, steadying herself on the arm of the couch. And then, to my surprise, she laughed.

I watched her with interest, smiling uncertainly as I tried to figure out what was so funny. Her little face scrunched up, and one hand pressed her lips, the other her stomach.

"I mean, I'm funny, but I don't know if I'm *that* funny."

Another eruption of giggling broke out before she blew out a breath, her face flushed for a new reason—humor. When she caught her breath, she met my eyes and said, "Thomas Bane, you are ridiculous."

My brows flicked together. "Ridiculous good or ridiculous bad?"

But she shook her head, turning for the door. "Just absolutely ridiculous."

And inexplicably, I was a hundred percent certain that was a good thing.

fiers, counted them all ... ruined me. Those
have haunted me, ruined me. Those
my kingdom. I have walked through fire in search
elis that would save us, that would give me
kept them in coffers, counted them
for my pain. Those sins have haunted
claimed my kingdom. I have wal
is that would sav

The Smirk Factor

AMELIA

My entire walk home was spent processing one thought: *Did Thomas Bane almost kiss me?*

I thought the answer might be yes, as evidenced by the lapse in time when he'd stepped into my space, the way his eyes darkened to blackest ink, his lips parting just a little, just barely, just enough to send an inadvertent radio signal that practically screamed the word *kiss*.

The memory of his body underneath mine was its own separate catalog of details. He was huge, a beast of a man, hard as stone and hot to the touch. I meant that, too. He radiated heat like a power source. As if something vital and alive existed inside him that couldn't be contained by skin or muscle or bone, so it waved off of him and over me, intoxicating and arresting.

It was no wonder that he'd found fame. In fact, it seemed that he had been born to be adored, admired. Admonished. Everyone wanted to know everything about him, good or bad, true or false. If they really got their hands on him, the frenzy was so deep, they'd rip him apart like carrion. He was perhaps the most famous author at that moment in time simply because he'd been living in the public eye, making waves, making headlines for six years.

His gravitas was overwhelming under the best of circumstances, something about him so striking and imposing that it captured the attention of anyone and everyone who came in contact with him. When he walked into a room, you knew. You felt it, the tug, the draw, the allure of him too strong to resist.

And yet, he'd found a way to make me feel completely comfortable and at home. Well, maybe not completely, but that was as close as I got to comfort with a stranger. I'd forgotten for a minute who he was. The spell he put on people broke for a moment, and the man underneath was as real as I was.

But then he'd almost kissed me. And seconds later, I was sprawled on top of him with his arms around me. His very large, very strong, very masculine arms.

And with that, the spell was back, and I was reminded just how out of my element I was.

As I unlocked my front door, twenty thoughts were on my tongue, waiting to fly out the second I located my friends. But when I pushed the door open with hope all over my face, I found nothing but an empty brownstone.

I sighed, pulling my key out of the door and closing the noise of the city out behind me.

Claudius, my cat, strutted down the stairs with his eyes on me and mouth stretching in a meow as if to rebuff the insult at the implication that I was alone. I picked him up when he got close enough, holding him to my chest.

"I love you, but you give terrible advice."

He meowed again, and if I spoke cat, I was pretty sure it would have translated to, *Fuck you.*

The house was so quiet. Too quiet. Someone should have been home—Rin studying, Val relaxing before heading to work, Katherine…well, Katherine was still at the library. But Rin was probably at Court's or the museum. Val was at Sam's.

If Katherine went out to dinner with a guy instead of coming home to relieve me of my thoughts, I really might go ahead and pitch myself off the roof.

Everyone was moving on. Growing up. Finding love.

For eight years, the four of us had been an inseparable unit. We'd met freshman year of college as assigned suitemates, and when Val had sat us all down with cheap liquor and made us get drunk together, we'd forged a bond that carried us into our adult lives.

Deep down, I'd always known our time together was temporary. Because life was fluid, ever changing, never the same for long. It was a string of seasons, good times and bad, happy and sad, one after the other.

But above that deep-down knowledge was the naive hope that we'd somehow stay together forever.

It'd be so much easier than what I was facing now, which was loneliness. Katherine was next to find love, I was sure. And where would that leave me? Alone in my parents' brownstone with nothing and no one to truly call my own.

Claudius nipped at my finger, and I yelped in surprise.

"Except you. You're the only man I need in my life," I assured him.

He purred, ignoring my lie.

We walked into the kitchen, and I set him down next to his food dish. The kitchen was beautiful, one of my favorite rooms in the house, stocked with all the amenities any of us could want. Particularly me, given my propensity for baking.

I smiled. Baking. That would make me feel better.

I began to gather ingredients, grateful I'd gotten fresh blueberries with my last order. Lemon-blueberry muffins would set the world—and my mood—to rights.

My parents had purchased the house as an investment, gutted it, and offered it to me and my friends to live in. The library was extensive, our rooms bright and open, all the details of the old Victorian kept intact, just spruced up. The tall windows. The thick molding. The exposed brick.

I loved this place. But it was far too big for me alone, no matter how many cats I decided to adopt. And someday, I'd have to leave.

Discontent settled in my stomach.

I wondered where I'd go, what I'd do. Home to South Dakota wasn't an option even though I missed my parents. New York was my home far more than my actual home.

No, I couldn't leave the city. Maybe I'd just downsize. Dad would try to insist I stay. But standing there in the kitchen in the big, empty house, I knew I couldn't. My loneliness echoed in all the empty rooms.

I sighed and reached for a lemon to zest, reprimanding myself for being such a baby and reminding myself that I'd already shifted in the direction of my ambitions. Someday, I'd be sitting in an office, telling an author I wanted their story. Someday, I'd be brave and bold, just like Rin had been when she started working at the museum or like Val when she'd decided to ask Sam out. We all had something we wanted, something we wanted to change. And now, it was my turn.

That would take all my energy anyway. I'd be fine alone, too busy to care.

I patted myself on the back, feeling great. I could *so* be alone. I didn't *need* anyone.

A key slipped into the front door, and when it opened, Katherine strode in, weighted down with bags.

"Oh, thank God," I breathed, dropping everything in my hands carelessly on the countertop. I hurried around the island, wiping my hands on my apron and rushing Katherine.

Her eyes widened when I flung myself at her, hugging her with all my strength, her arms pinned to her sides. She stiffened in surprise.

"I'm so glad you're home." It was almost a whine.

"You don't say."

I let her go, beaming. "How was your day?" I asked as I took one of her bags. It was heavier than I'd expected, and I lurched so I didn't fall over. "God, what's in here, dumbbells?"

"Books. I'm putting together a class at the library and needed to source some material."

I oofed as I lugged the bag to the couch. "*Some* material, not *all* the material."

She set the other bag next to the one I'd taken, glancing into the kitchen. "What are you cooking?"

"Muffins. Wanna help?"

"Not really. But I'll sit with you, as it seems you have something you want to talk about."

My face softened, eyes watery and wide. "Would you?" The question was a sad little quiver.

The corners of her lips flicked in her version of a comforting smile. "Sure. Now, tell me what happened."

My shoulders slumped as I dragged myself back into the kitchen. She sat across from me as I picked up the lemon again.

"Do you…do you ever wonder what will happen to us? I mean, once Rin and Val move out."

She frowned. "I just assumed we'd keep living here. Together. Is that not the case?"

"No, of course it is," I assured her. "I just mean…well, you'll find someone too, I'm sure. And where will that leave me? Alone with no one but Claudius to talk to."

I heard a mewl from the living room and rolled my eyes.

"I doubt I'll find anyone, Amelia. I'm not warm or friendly. I'm too honest. I don't have feelings and don't understand them. I don't even have a cat to keep me company when *you* find someone and move on."

I snorted. "Please. That would mean I actually spoke to a man. There's a higher likelihood of you developing a desire to hug someone."

She shrugged one shoulder. "You talked to Thomas Bane today, didn't you?"

My cheeks warmed. "That doesn't count. He's not interested in me. Although…"

Katherine waited, one brow climbing slowly. When I kept zesting rather than speak, she prompted, "Although what?"

"Well…I think maybe…" I made a noise. "It's too stupid. I'm sure I imagined it."

"Imagined what?"

My nose wrinkled. "He sort of…well, I thought for a second maybe…maybe he was going to kiss me."

At that, her face opened in shock, which was an impressive animation for her. "Thomas Bane. Thomas Bane almost *kissed you*?"

"I know. I know! It's ridiculous. I had to have imagined it. I'm not even sure what those signals *are*."

"They're actually quite natural. A firing of nerves and a surge of brain chemicals. Did you know there are nerves in the tip of your nose that can detect another person's nose so you can kiss in the dark? They literally reach for each other like magnets, positive to negative. Kissing is…it's like a litmus test for a relationship. You can tell if the chemistry is right. And if it's not, it's your body's way of warning you. Sometimes, it's that simple—an instinct based on pheromones and micro-expressions to indicate compatibility. Your body knows things your mind doesn't, and chemistry is the first test. Arguably, the most important one."

It was my turn to frown. "It couldn't be possible for Thomas Bane to be attracted to me."

"And why not? You're loving, generous, beautiful. You're small, which triggers a protection instinct that dates back to the dawn of man. You are the kindest, purest of us all. If he wasn't attracted to you, I'd say he was a heartless asshole and that you should run."

My face softened. "Katherine, you really think that?"

Another careless shrug. "It's science. Maybe I'm biased because I love you, but that's the truth." Before I could comment, she continued. "So he almost kissed you? Did you faint?"

A laugh popped out of me. "I might have if he'd actually done it, but we were interrupted by his dog."

Her brow quirked. "Is that really the end of the story?"

Another laugh. "He knocked us down. I ended up sprawled on top of Thomas Bane on the couch."

"That sounds even more interesting than the almost-kiss."

"I don't think I've ever been so embarrassed. Like, where do you put your hands?"

"Oh, I could think of a place or two."

"I think I might have inadvertently brushed a few of those places. Anyway, I'm sure he almost-kisses every girl who crosses his path. And I'm even surer I'm at the bottom of his list. He dates girls like Aurora Park and Olivia Nash and Marley Monroe. Tall, beautiful, leggy, famous women who are charming and lovely and can speak to strangers. Not girls who show up in a blouse with cats on it."

"What would you have done if he'd kissed you?"

"After I went into cardiac arrest?"

"Yes, after that."

"Well, assuming I didn't come back as a ghost…" I paused. "I actually don't know."

Her eyes narrowed. "Did you *want* him to kiss you?"

I opened my mouth to answer with a resounding *yes*. But I closed it again, my brows drawing together as I considered it.

"No, I don't think I did," I finally answered.

Those narrowed eyes tightened even more in either assessment or confusion. Both maybe. "Why?" she asked simply.

I frowned. "Well, because. I don't want my first kiss to be with a random guy on a random couch."

"Nothing about him is random. He's *Thomas Bane*."

"That almost makes it worse. I bet he passes out kisses like religious tracts."

Katherine snickered.

"I mean, don't get me wrong. I don't need a parade or anything. But I'd at least like it to be with someone I was in a ... *thing* with."

"A relationship thing?"

I shrugged. "Dating at least. Or even just *a* date. I mean, is it too much to ask for dinner first? It doesn't feel like too much to ask."

"No, that's not too much to ask," she conceded.

"Plus, we work together. I don't know how to just run around kissing people without rules or boundaries. I like him, but I don't want to like him like that. I don't want him to think of me like that. It's just too much pressure," I said with the shake of my head. "Best to keep things professional."

"I'm just saying, I don't think you should rule it out. I bet he's a good kisser. And it's a scientific fact that men who smirk excel at cunnilingus."

"That is not a scientific fact."

She shrugged. "It should be. I read it in a romance novel, and it's maybe one of the truest things ever written."

"In all your worldly experience?" I teased, brow arched.

She mirrored me. "I've collected more data than you."

"Most eighth graders have collected more data than me."

A laugh shot past her lips.

"Anyway, I'm sure I imagined it. I'm nothing to him, just a means to an end. I've got his manuscripts, and we're meeting tomorrow to go over them."

"And when he kisses you—"

"He's not going to kiss me, Katherine! Ugh, don't even put that into the universe." I set down the lemon and zester to give her a look. "It's hard enough to do this—talk to him, put myself out there—without being worried he's going to kiss me and confuse things even more. I have a job to do, and that's all I'm planning on doing. Not only will my therapist approve, but my résumé will be so shiny and pretty with Thomas Bane's name on it."

"Your lips would shine with his name on them, too."

I rolled my eyes. "You are the worst, you know that?"

She smiled, a thin curl of her lips. "I know. But I'm usually right."

"Are not," I lied, telling myself like a fool that it was the truth.

ive me
ers, counted them in
have haunted me, ruined me. Those
my kingdom. I have walked through fire in search of
ic that would save us, that would give me
kept them in coffers, counted them in
for my pain. Those sins have haunted me.
claimed my kingdom. I have walked
ic that would sa

Dumpster Fire

TOMMY

"**So, what did you think?**" I asked the next morning, trying not to sound too eager.

Amelia didn't answer right away. I watched her unpack her bag, eyeing the stack of manuscripts now tagged with screaming neon-colored sticky tabs. I imagined that they annotated every failure.

I swallowed my bile.

"Well," she finally started, setting her notebook and pen on top of the stack, "I can see why you haven't been able to finish any of them."

"Mmm," I hummed noncommittally, wanting her to tell me the truth before I decided to light the whole stack on fire.

She took a steadying breath and picked up said stack of trash. "Your writing is impeccable—that's a given—but none of them quite make sense. If it's not the stories—which, for the most part aren't fully formed—it's the characters. They're missing something…the… *oomph*. The spark. The thing that makes them real."

I nodded. Once again, she was right.

"But each of them has a distinctive quality. I could feel what you latched on to. Like in this one," she said, sliding one out for inspection, "it was your heroine. She's the most real thing in the entire piece. Or this one." She pulled out my mpreg werewolf story. "It was the dynamics of the pack. I could feel your inspiration, but you never quite grabbed it. To be honest, I think this one is your strongest story. But... well, I don't think you can turn in a commercial novel about male pregnancy in werewolves, can you?"

"I'm a hundred percent sure Steven would fire me on the spot."

She sighed, returning the manuscripts to their graveyard. "Right."

"So what do I do? Can I use any of this?"

The look on her face said it all. "You want the honest truth?"

"It's why I asked for your help in the first place."

Amelia paused, watching me as if to make sure I was ready for the answer I'd already known I was going to get. "None of this will work. I thought there might be a way to... I don't know... combine them, like you suggested. But I looked for a thread to pull and... well, there's just nothing."

I drew a long, steady breath through my nose and considered all the ways I could dispose of the manuscripts. Fire seemed too obvious. Paper shredder was pedestrian. Garbage disposal? That would probably be harder than it would be satisfying. I could tear it all into confetti and throw it off the Brooklyn Bridge, but I'd probably get fined for littering. Maybe I'd let Gus eat it. He'd eat anything. And together, we could deposit all the shit I'd written with the shit he'd eaten exactly where it belonged—the dump.

"Okay," I said after a solid minute. "What do we do?"

She let loose a worried sigh, her eyes moving from mine to the stack of papers. "There has to be something else. Some other idea, something in the back of your mind or in a long-forgotten, dusty drawer."

"This is it." I swept a hand at the pile. "Every idea I had is here."

Her bottom lip slipped between her teeth. "There has to be something. Is there anything going on in your life that you could fictionalize? Something from your past?"

Internally, I shrank from the question. Externally, my chest puffed, my spine straightening. "Maybe. Let's talk world building, universe, canon. I haven't written about elves in years. I've been thinking about going that direction again. I blame a recent replay of *Witcher*."

Before I could explain what *Witcher* was, she nodded and said, "I get that. The elves in that story are brilliant. *Siri and the Elder Blood*? That story is just too good. I'm still not over it."

"You play *Witcher*?" I asked in disbelief.

"No," she answered on a laugh. "I read the books."

I nodded, my universe righting itself. "The elven ruins are my favorite. They always are, no matter the game or book. It's the mystery of them, I think. Where they came from. Where they've all gone. How their power manifested. It's fascinating."

She smiled, reaching into her bag. "Well, there's our thread to pull." When her laptop rested on her thighs and her fingers tapped the keyboard, she said, "Let's research."

I reached for my laptop too, but rather than open it where I was, I moved to the other couch to sit next to her. She stiffened, her fingers stilling for a moment.

I couldn't help but smile. If I could sit thigh-to-thigh with her without being a creep, I would. Because watching Amelia Hall squirm was becoming my new favorite pastime.

"All right," I said, stretching my legs and propping my feet on the coffee table, "where do we start?"

"How about Nordic myth? Russian? Something obscure. Or we could go classic archetype. Chosen one. The ace. Knight in shining armor? Rogue with a heart of gold?" She paused. "Anything zinging?"

"Is it too early to start drinking?"

A soft laugh. "Not if it has champagne or tomato juice in it."

I sighed, collecting my hair and twisting it into a knot. "I don't know if I'm ready to character develop."

"Okay," she said, her tone nothing but encouraging. "Let's look at old cathedrals." Her fingers tapped, and with a few clicks, she gasped. "Oh, Tommy, look!"

The way she'd said my name—like it had been born on her tongue—hit me in a strange, foreign place in my chest. I leaned over just as much to look at her screen as to get closer to her.

She was scrolling through Google images at photos of the Glasgow Cathedral, and the second I saw them, I got why she'd gasped. Sweeping ceilings and gothic arches in rows so tight, they looked like an illusion, a study in geometry and symmetry. Stained glass and thick pillars. It had all the pieces of a palace, a place of beauty and worship and art and soul.

"That's perfect, Amelia. Save that," I said softly before returning regrettably to my own machine.

She smiled at her screen, and for a minute, we were quiet. She was comfortable, already at ease around me.

I was openly grateful that her therapist had foisted exposure therapy at her. That she'd been exposed to *me*.

That I'd been exposed to her.

Years of fake relationships had left me largely in the company of models and actresses and socialites. Years of friends with benefits and empty relationships. I hadn't wanted more. Even now, I didn't want more. Because *more* meant that whatever I felt, whatever I wanted, would be chucked to the media like a prime rib and devoured without care. And in all the years since I'd stepped stupidly into the public eye, I'd never met anyone quite like her. *Normal* girls weren't something I had access to anymore.

Not that Amelia was normal. She was something entirely other, sparking my curiosity and wonder. Was she a novelty? A trinket to put in my pocket? I was attracted to her, that much was painfully clear. But what was the nature of that feeling?

I couldn't tell you. All I knew was that I was intrigued by the girl sitting on my couch, doing her very best not to cave under the weight of my presence.

I was a lot, I knew. In fact, my charm was a weapon I wielded at every opportunity. A weapon, and a shield. But I didn't want to woo her.

Well, I wanted to woo her. But that wasn't all I wanted. I didn't want to dazzle her or blind her.

I wanted her to see me. And that was maybe the worst idea I'd ever had.

"So, tell me, how'd a girl like you get to be so shy?"

She turned to look at me with surprise in her eyes. "How'd a guy like you get to be so brash?"

"Years of practice."

Her lips curled in a smile. "Same. And like I said, I don't *want* to be like this. I want to be able to walk into a room like Janessa Hughes—completely unafraid and ready for anything thrown at me."

"You shouldn't want to be anything like Janessa," I said, unable to keep the disdain from my voice. "And she's not as brave as you think. She's just as afraid as you or me or anybody. Her fears might be different from yours, but that doesn't mean they're not there."

The thought seemed to strike her. "I…I haven't really thought of it that way."

"If I had to guess, I'd say she's afraid of becoming obsolete. Irrelevant. She's afraid to lose her power, and that makes her desperate."

"What about you? What are you afraid of?"

Such a simple question. I was afraid for the pain my mother had yet to endure from her illness. I was afraid of losing my money, my means, and returning to the Bronx with my tail between my legs. I was afraid of many things, things I didn't want anyone to know. Especially not someone who could turn my life, my pain, into fodder for the gossip cannon.

But looking into Amelia's open face, her silvery eyes touched only with honesty and concern, I had to fight the instinct to tell her the truth.

The thought settled cold and sharp in my stomach.

So I smirked at her, enjoying the bloom of color on her cheeks. "Spiders."

A laugh shot out of her. "Oh my God. No you aren't."

I held up my hands, palms up. "Honest. Theo used to put them on my pillow when he found them, and no lie, I'd scream like a girl. Still do. Once, he actually had someone lend him a pet tarantula. I pulled back my covers, and there she was, beady eyes and hairy legs and pincers like this." I pinched my thumb and forefinger together. A shudder wracked down my back. "He's lucky I didn't smash the thing. Have you not seen the video?"

"There's a video?" Shamelessly, she turned to her computer and started searching the internet.

"My brother is an asshole. It went viral, like, five years ago."

She clicked the video, and I cringed as it started to play. I watched myself walk up to my bed, flip the covers, and jump backward with inhuman speed and a height I'd never been able to replicate. All to the soundtrack of my horror—a scream so high, I sounded like a teenage girl.

The loudest, bawdiest, hiccuping laughter ripped out of Amelia, the sound as incongruent as my screaming on YouTube. She was laughing so hard she could barely breathe, restarting the video the second it was finished. And then again as tears streamed down her face.

When she restarted it for the fourth time, I snatched her

computer and snapped it shut. "All right, that's enough of that."

She didn't even protest, just sat back on the couch holding her belly. "I...I can't. That's too good. Too, too good." Bubbling laughter spilled out of her again before she seemed to get herself under control. "I'm sorry. I don't mean to laugh. It's just that—"

She started giggling again, her face scrunched up. Another tear squeezed out of her eyes as she got ahold of herself, blowing out a controlled breath.

"That is one of my comedic weaknesses."

"People running from spiders?"

"No, men screaming like little girls." The sentence ended in a squeak and another fit. "That, and people running into glass doors. They never see it coming!" She dissolved again, which had me chuckling along with her.

"Mine's pranks. I swear, the ones where they prank people in the shower with the never-ending shampoo. Have you seen those?"

"Nuh-uh," she said, shaking her head and still trying to stop laughing.

"Here, watch this," I said, turning to my laptop. I passed it to her as the montage began to play, already feeling the hysteria of her giggles and the anticipation of the video overtaking me.

There was a guy in a shower at a beach, rinsing out his hair. And just when he had it almost clean, someone would squirt more into his hair without him knowing. Within thirty seconds, the guy was freaking out, panicking as he scrubbed his head, screaming, *It won't come out! SHAMPOOOOOOOO!* as he slapped his head like a monkey.

I couldn't stop laughing.

Amelia shook her head, smiling and laughing but gently. "That is *so mean*!"

"He...he can't—" I giggled. "Look! He can't get it out and—" Laughter shot out of me. "God, I would break somebody's nose if they did that to me."

"Well, a friendly heads-up: don't ever prank me, or I might break *your* nose."

I turned my laughter on her. "Pretty sure your tiny fist wouldn't tenderize a steak, never mind break my nose."

She folded her arms and put on a tough look, which made her look about as dangerous as a box of kittens. "Who says I'd use my fist?"

"You hiding a baseball bat somewhere, Melia?" I asked, leaning closer like I was inspecting her.

But once I was in her space, everything slowed, stilled. My eyes fixed on her lips. Would they be sweet? Gentle? Giving? Would they be everything she was?

I needed to know.

Her eyes widened as I drew closer, determined to find out. A puff of breath left those lips of hers and brushed mine, tingling with anticipation.

And to my deepest disappointment, she leaned back, scooting away from me.

Her cheeks flushed crimson. "*Oh!*" she breathed. "I...I don't... I'm not..."

My frown was spectacular. I leaned back, put in my place as she found her voice.

"I-I'm sorry, Tommy. But this is a business relationship, and it's too important to me to...to...mess up with...*that*." She gestured to all of me.

I swallowed hard, shaking my head. "No, please don't apologize. I didn't mean to make you uncomfortable. I didn't even intend to kiss you. I just...couldn't seem to help myself." I shifted, putting space between us. I handed her laptop over. "Don't worry. It won't happen again," I promised, meaning every word. "I'm sorry, Amelia."

"Thank you," she said, relaxing visibly.

And as we settled back into the couch, I tried to tell myself it was fine. It didn't matter. She didn't want me, and I hadn't realized until she rebuffed me how badly I wanted her. But it would never have worked anyway.

She was right.

And that was fine.

Perfectly fine, I told myself, ignoring the sting of the lie.

Brother's Keeper

TOMMY

"**Gus is my new hero,**" I said, punctuating the statement with a sip of my whiskey.

Theo chuckled once through his nose. "That dog is a fucking menace."

"Menace implies he has some sort of foresight or premeditation. He's too dumb to be a menace."

That earned me another laugh, this one with teeth.

"And anyway, you wouldn't call him a menace if he'd bumped a pretty girl into *you*."

"You're right. I probably would have fed him a hamburger as positive reinforcement."

"Maybe we could train him. Make him your wingman. God knows you need help finding women."

He made a face. "When do I have time to meet women? I'm too busy keeping you outta trouble."

"Psh, please. I've been a goddamn joy and a delight."

His face flattened, lips in a sardonic line.

"Really, Teddy—how could I get into trouble with a prison guard like you on duty?"

He rolled his eyes, but he was laughing, that asshole.

We were hitched to the bar at Jackson's—a momentary hotspot in SoHo—for Genevieve Larou's book release party, which meant the joint was packed wall to wall with publishers, editors, models, actors, and the clinging unknowns who'd finagled invitations and wanted to be seen.

If Genevieve wasn't such a good friend and if Blackbird hadn't insisted I be there, I would have passed. But Gen had just hit *New York Today's* bestseller list with a comedic memoir all about her career as a runway model, and in truth, she *was* a good friend. Most my exes were.

Plus, it *was* a chance to be seen. A *Page Six* feature wouldn't be the worst thing for book sales. Given my lack of new releases, my sales graph looked like the heartbeat of someone being defibrillated.

"So," Theo started, shifting on his stool to face me, "when's Little Miss Sunshine coming over again?"

"Tomorrow. She's already read all the pages I sent. Can you believe that?"

"I can a hundred percent believe that. I bet they were annotated and highlighted."

I laughed. "They had a million aggressive sticky tabs on the pages. It looked like a neon hate rainbow."

"Somehow, I'm not surprised. She doesn't seem like the type to dog-ear anything."

"Definitely not. I was kinda hoping they had cats on them or something. The neon-green ones were screaming insults at me."

"Cats, huh?"

"Always with the cats. Yesterday, the collar of her shirt looked like a cat wrapped around her neck."

He frowned. "That sounds weird."

"It was actually really cute. *She's* really cute." I shook my head. "It really is a shame she's a cat person."

One of his brows rose. "Why, because that'd stop you?"

"Nah. But we could never get married—Gus would never survive. He's too gentle for feline sensibilities."

That time, when Theo laughed, it was bawdy and loud and shocking out of his strict mouth. "You. Married? That is fucking hilarious."

I found myself smirking, pleased he'd taken the bait. "I know. Nobody'd ever put up with my shit long-term anyway."

"Oh, don't sell yourself short," Genevieve said from my elbow.

She was just as beautiful as always—tall, sleek, enviable jawline and cheekbones, big eyes and wide mouth. Her dress was short enough that if she took a full stride, the entire bar would be able to determine her waxing preferences.

She laid her hand on my shoulder and leaned in to press her cheek to mine. My hand moved to her waist.

"Hey there, handsome," she said through a smile.

"Heya, Gen. Congrats on *New York Today*."

When she backed away, her hand stayed put, her hips leaning toward me. "Thanks, Tommy. I'm glad you came." She glanced over my shoulder. "Hi, Theo."

Theo raised his glass. "Gen."

"Are you two having fun over here by yourselves?"

"Teddy won't let me leave the bar," I said petulantly.

Theo rolled his eyes. "Please. Somebody's gotta keep you out of trouble. Chaining him to a chair's my best bet."

Genevieve laughed. "You let me know how that works out for you, Theo." She turned back to me, crimson lips together in a smile as she toyed with the collar of my leather jacket. "You look good,

Tommy. You doing okay?"

I nodded, squeezing her small waist. "You don't look so bad yourself. And I've never been better."

Her brow climbed, and she glanced at Theo again. "That true?"

Theo snorted. "Ask him when his book will be finished."

My face flattened. "It'll get done."

She shook her head. "That bad, huh?"

I laughed. "It's like you guys have never met me. It'll get done."

She chuckled. "Always does."

I gave Theo a look. "See? Gen believes."

Theo made a noncommittal sound and took a sip of his drink.

Genevieve's voice lowered, her smile fading. "And how's your mom?"

I smiled. "She's good, Gen. Thanks for asking."

"Give her my love," she said before straightening up and putting on her show-stopping smile. "Come here—take a picture with me."

She hooked her arm in mine as I stood, and one of a fleet of photographers wound his way over and pointed his lens at us.

The flash burst in our vision, and we took a moment to hug. We kissed on the cheek again, exchanging those pedestrian phrases one said when one didn't know what to say or when others were listening. That flash burst fast enough to give somebody a seizure.

"Have fun tonight, Tommy. Don't get into any trouble."

I smirked down at her. "Why'd you think I brought Teddy?"

She laughed, shaking her head as she let me go. "See you later."

"Bye, Gen."

She strode through the crowd, which parted for her like the Red Sea, photographer in her wake. And when I looked around, there were at least a dozen cell phone cameras pointed at me.

So I took a second to offer my best smolder-smirk before taking a seat next to my brother again. My editor caught my eye from across the bar and raised his glass. Steven had all the no-nonsense affectation of a judge, which I supposed in a way he was. As one of the top editors at Blackbird, such was his right.

I nodded back, tipping my glass to him in answer.

Theo sighed in that way he did, a judgmental exhale, heavy with skepticism. "I really hope Amelia can help you."

"She already has. She told me everything I had was the driveling nonsense I'd known it was. I've got a few ideas moving around. Just waiting on something to stick."

A female squealed my name from behind me, and I turned with my best fake smile on. It was a damn good fake smile, one she bought completely as she gushed, blushing. I reminded her to breathe while we took a picture, asked her to tag me, and sent her on her way.

When I was seated again, Theo sighed, shaking his head. "Doesn't this ever get tedious?"

"A little, sure. It's all a pony show, just part of the gig. If I didn't like being seen, I never woulda built my brand on the backs of models and pop singers."

Another snort. "I just pictured Marley giving you a piggyback."

"She'd fold like a lawn chair," I said on a laugh. "Look—you know if I could quit the life, I would. But this? Putting myself in the gossip columns to get attention when I was young and stupid? That was my mistake."

"Our mistake," he amended.

"It seemed like such a good idea at the time, didn't it?"

"Can't say it didn't work."

I sighed. "It's like the mob. The only way to get out is to move to France like Johnny Depp."

"Or Italy like Sting."

"I heard you can shake down his olive trees during harvest season. For admission price."

Theo snorted a laugh. "You'd better keep Amelia on the low. Talk about folding like a lawn chair. I don't think she could handle the spotlight."

I frowned. "I dunno. I think she's tougher than she looks."

He made the universal face for *come the fuck on*. "Tommy, she could barely hold eye contact with either of us."

"Have you seen us?"

He ignored me. "I guarantee if some asshole shoved a wide-angle lens in her face, she'd have an epileptic fit."

"Well, the flashes *are* really bright."

He rolled his eyes. "Glad you didn't miss the point."

"Don't worry," I assured him. "I'm not gonna let them get to her. I won't let anybody hurt her. She's so little, so delicate. My brain keeps screaming that she's breakable. Did you notice?"

"Notice what?"

"How *small* she is? Even her hands are tiny, but her fingers are long. I don't even know how that's possible."

He was still making that face.

"I mean, I guess it's her fingers. They're longer than her palms, so it gives the illusion that they're long in general. Pretty sure one of her hands would fit on my palm. Like in *Beauty and the Beast* when he holds her hand and it's just a wrist disappearing into his big, hairy fist."

He added blinking to the face. "Did you just compare yourself to a Disney movie?"

I shrugged. "What's it to you, asshole?"

A pause. "You've given this a lot of thought."

"I like her. She's interesting, different. And she treats *me* different. I always feel like chum in the water, but for once, she makes *me* feel like a shark. She doesn't want a piece of me, doesn't care about the life. Her intentions are pure." I shook my head. "You know how rare it is to find someone like that. Someone who isn't a vampire. I don't feel drained after she leaves. I feel ... filled up."

"You're not gonna sleep with her, are you?"

The sound I made was similar to an air leak but wetter. "No. And anyway, she told me she wasn't interested."

The sting of that particular rejection rankled. I shifted in my seat to counteract it.

He eyed me, indicating he believed a grand total of none of that. But before I could defend myself, someone bumped into me, spilling my drink on my shirt.

I turned, brows drawn and ready to school somebody in manners, but the girl I found there kicked in another instinct altogether.

She was small, eyes big and brown, skin dark and smooth. But her cheeks flushed when she saw me, her eyes tight with concern.

"Oh my God, I'm so sorry," she said, grabbing a couple of cocktail napkins to dab at my shirt.

"What the fuck?" the guy in the suit behind her slurred, oblivious to me as he reached for her arm. "I bought you two drinks. What do you mean you're not interested?"

I pushed back from the bar, my eyes on the place where his meathook was wrapped around her slender bicep. My jaw clenched so tight, I thought I might pull a tendon.

"Tommy," Theo warned, standing with me and squaring up.

"Don't worry. I'm cool," I said, unable to look away.

The girl dislodged her arm from his hand. "I ... I'm sorry."

The suit laughed, his eyes hard and glinting. "Sorry? You're *sorry*? I just wasted half an hour and forty bucks for you to tell me you're not interested? Then pay for your own fuckin' drinks, cocktease."

I stepped between them, putting her behind me. "Hey, man. How's it going?"

He jerked his chin at me. "Oh, look. It's pretty boy Bane. What are you gonna do, clock me?" He leaned into my face. "Oh, wait. You *can't*. Isn't that right, *pretty boy*?"

In a grand show of will, I smirked, gripping the surge of rage in my chest. "Come on, how about I buy you another drink?"

"What I need is a time machine so I can pick another bitch to spend my cash on." He leaned around me to make eye contact with her. "One who follows through."

"You know, I have a better idea." I reached for my wallet, opening it up to thumb through the bills. I offered him a hundred, folded in my fingers. "This should cover her drinks and your cab fare. Come on, I'll help you catch one." I grabbed his upper arm to steer him out, but he thrashed away from me.

He listed, but I kept him upright by my grip on his arm. "You assholes are all alike," he said. "*Pretty boys* throwing money around, models and milkin' guys for drinks and then not putting out. It's bullshit—that's what it is. Why the fuck aren't you on *my* side?"

My anger tightened with my grip, my voice low with quiet menace. "Because I'm not a sorry piece of shit who can't take no for an answer. She doesn't owe you one fucking thing. I don't care how many drinks you bought her. Maybe she thought you were all right and then figured out you were a fucking creep. Who knows? But she doesn't want to go home with you. So take this"—I shoved the money into his front pocket—"and go home. Alone."

His face twisted. And in almost the same motion, he wrenched away from me, cocked his fist, and let it fly.

The hook caught me on the jaw, snapping my head to the side. Nothing else moved other than my heart, which hit double time in an effort to pump a surge of adrenaline through me. Slowly, I brought my head around to look at him as he gaped at me. The crowd around us held their breath.

And with a smile, I clenched my fist, wound up, and returned the favor.

offers, counted them in ... ruined me. Those
have haunted me, ruined me. Those
my kingdom. I have walked through fire in search
relics that would save us, that would give me
ave ... kept them in coffers, counted them
... for my pain. Those sins have haunted
... claimed my kingdom. I have wal
... is that would sav

Booked

AMELIA

I *was still rubbing the sleep* from my eyes when I saw Thomas Bane's mug shot.

My lungs stilled, full of the air drawn on a gasp.

I scanned the Twitterstorm, trying to parse what I was seeing.

Despite the fluorescent lighting, the orange jumpsuit, and the gap in his grin where one of his front teeth used to be, he was still absolutely, ridiculously gorgeous.

My eyes touched every corner of that photograph. His shining black hair. His dark, stubbly beard. His twinkling eyes, black as sin, one ringed in a sick shade of purple, the lid fat and watering. His nose, red and swollen. His gap-toothed smile, like he didn't have a care in the world.

Like he hadn't been *arrested.*

Twitter was on fire. The hashtag *toothlessthomas* was trending, and though many of the top tweets were news outlets recounting composed of clever one-liners about how stupidly hot he was, even missing a goddamn front tooth.

No, somehow, the damage to his face made him even more attractive.

That picture was everywhere. *Everywhere.* Not just gossip outlets, but even CNN and Fox had jumped on the bandwagon. He'd been arrested for assault at a publisher event in SoHo where one of the many models he used to date was having a launch party for her book. The articles were calling him a delinquent, an unconscionable beast, a menace.

And they were calling for his head.

Dread bubbled up in my stomach at the realization of just how much trouble he might be in. A fight at an industry event with his reputation and the publicity nightmare splattered all over the internet? That spelled trouble with a capital T to start and an *oh fuck* at the end.

I wondered if he was still in jail and brushed away the errant thought that if he was, we'd need to reschedule our meeting.

I took a breath. I let it out. I stared at my phone with my heart clanging and his mischievous, dark eyes sparking from my screen. It was a look that said, *I'm not even sorry about it.*

That made him hotter, too.

I flipped off my comforter. Claudius lifted his head, watching me with only mild interest as I chugged out of the room in search of someone who could help me make sense of things.

Katherine glanced up from her Raisin Bran and took me in. "You okay?"

"Uh-uh. Look." I shoved my phone at her.

She took it, her eyes widening fractionally. "Oh my God. He's... what happened to his tooth?"

"It was knocked out in a bar fight."

She nodded. "Very masculine. I bet his testosterone production is off the charts."

"I hardly think that's relevant."

"Really, look at all that hair. Factor in his aggression…" She paused. "His libido is probably gluttonous. No wonder he's had so many girlfriends."

"Ugh." I snatched my phone back. "I wonder what happened."

"The news doesn't say?"

"The news doesn't say what?" Val's sleepy voice yawned from behind me.

"How *this* happened," I said, thrusting my phone in her direction.

She blinked, her brows coming together in confusion. "He looks like he got put through a wood chipper, and he's *still* gorgeous. He's an alien," she said, handing my phone back to me. "What happened?"

"We were just speculating." I took a seat next to Katherine at the island as Val moved for the coffeepot. "The news outlets were vague. TMZ said eyewitnesses told them the other guy hit Tommy first, not that the fact absolves him."

"Did you just call *Thomas Bane* Tommy?" Val said with a smirk, handing me a cup of coffee.

I gave her a look. "That's what everyone else calls him."

"There are unwritten social rules that would absolve *Tommy* from blame," Katherine said. "Street rules would say, *Talk shit, get hit.* Legally, he was defending himself."

My face pinched with worry. "I hope he doesn't get in trouble with his publisher."

Val's smile fell. "Do you really think that could happen?"

"He's been in a lot of trouble ever since the Nazi rally."

Katherine snorted. "Things you never want to say about a guy you're involved with."

"We're not *involved*. We have a business arrangement. That's all."

A male voice said from the direction of the stairwell, "Is that what they're calling it these days?"

Val lit up, and Katherine and I turned to find Sam strolling into the living room in a T-shirt and sleep pants, scratching the back of his neck.

I groaned. "You guys are the worst. There's nothing between Tommy and me."

Katherine pinned me with a look. "He almost kissed you."

The flush on my cheeks tingled painfully. "Actually, yesterday he *did* try."

"*Involved,*" Katherine insisted with sharp eyes.

Val gaped.

"It was nothing. I swear. Just a … a fleeting moment. Misunderstood signals. He doesn't *really* want to kiss me."

"He literally tried to," Katherine reminded me. "*Literally.*"

Val still gaped.

I snorted a laugh. "Why would *Thomas Bane* actually want to kiss *me*?"

Katherine rolled her eyes. "Because you're smart and funny and impossible to hate. And beautiful, too."

My face flattened. "He was at Genevieve Larou's party. You know, the *literal* supermodel he used to date? *She* is beautiful. *I* am perfectly average."

Sam sidled up next to Val across from us. "None of you know how pretty you are. It's astounding really."

Val laughed and tucked into his side. "Must be nice to know how handsome you are."

He frowned. "That's not what I mean. I don't think I'm handsome."

All three of us made faces at him.

He rolled his eyes. "I mean, I know I'm not hideous or anything, but I'm not … I don't know. Entitled."

"It actually makes you hotter," Katherine offered.

Sam smirked. "Thanks. So what happened with Thomas Bane that has all of you up and gossiping so early in the morning?"

"Aside from him trying to kiss Amelia?" Katherine asked snidely.

One of Sam's brows—the notched one—rose.

"Show him," Katherine commanded, jerking her chin at me as she picked up her spoon.

I sighed, opening up my phone. I handed him the device, and he scrolled.

"Well, how about that? Did you see these pictures of the fight?"

I popped out of my chair and snatched my phone from his hand, scrolling through. Katherine leaned in.

Half a dozen photos of the fight had broken. Tommy was taller than the other guy by at least six inches, almost making the fight unfair. Almost. The guy had gotten a few punches in—there was a photo with the bottom half of Tommy's face covered in gore from his nose and tooth.

Tommy with one big fist full of the guy's shirt and the other cocked to fire.

Tommy being pulled off the guy by four others, including Theo. *Four*, like they were taking down an elephant.

Tommy's face twisted up in a combination of excitement and rage, beautiful and terrible.

In all of the photos was a girl with dark skin and wide eyes, her hands pressed to her mouth in horror. I didn't miss that she was behind him, and in one photo, it almost looked like he was shielding her. Protecting her.

"Maybe someone stepped on his shoe," Katherine offered. "If they were expensive, he'd probably be mad."

"Or maybe someone insulted him," Val added. "Or his brother."

I shook my head. "I think he was protecting her," I said, turning my phone around and zooming in on her.

Sam leaned in to look, the levity in his face turning grave. "I think you might be right. Can I offer some unsolicited advice?"

I nodded.

"Take it from a reformed player—this guy is big league. We can smell each other from a mile away, and this guy? He's trouble. Just be careful, all right, Amelia? I'd hate to end up in jail with him for breaking his nose again."

It started as a giggle, bubbling out of me without warning. And the giggle turned into a laugh that turned into a cackle that hiccuped with a snort.

Sam watched me warily.

"Sam," I said, trying to catch my breath and school the condescension from my voice, "you have nothing to worry about. Literally nothing. At all. Ever."

But he didn't seem relieved, and he didn't smile. "Well, on the off chance that I'm wrong"—he bent a little like he was whispering to Val—"*and I'm not wrong*—I'll owe you a full apology. Meanwhile, just promise me you'll keep an eye on him."

"Yeah," I said through a giggle, "okay, Sam. I'll make sure to protect my virtue from *Thomas Bane*." I broke into a small fit before wiping an errant tear away. "I'm going over there for a meeting this afternoon. Or at least I think I am. If he wants to talk after his"—I gestured at my phone—"incarceration. I'll get the scoop and report back tonight, then we'll know for sure what happened. Agent Amelia, on the case."

I gave them all a salute, and they laughed. Well, except for Sam. He just watched me like he knew a secret I didn't, shaking his head with a knowing smile on his face.

And I shook my head back at him, a hundred percent certain that whatever he thought was wrong.

coffers, counted them in ex-**. ** Those
have haunted me, ruined me. Those
** my kiordom. I have walked through fire in search
relic that would save us, that would give me **
kept them in coffers, counted them
** for my pain. Those sins have haunted
claimed my kiordom. I have wal
** that would sa

Hail Mary

TOMMY

"**Y**ou got fired." *Theo hovered* over me like the Grim Reaper, his face drawn and eyes hard. "I cannot believe you fucking did that."

"I'd do it again, too." I adjusted the ice pack on my face so it covered not only my eye, but my cheek and jaw, hoping it would keep the swelling in my mouth to a minimum. My tongue tested the recently installed tooth, surprised by the stony deadness of the thing as the local anesthesia wore off.

"Well, that's part of the problem, isn't it?"

"Fuck that guy. He hit me!"

"You're like douchebag catnip. It's like they seek you out."

"Come on, Theo. You were there. You know the truth, and you would have stood up for her, too, if I hadn't first."

"Yeah, well, *I'm* not the one whose ass is on the line, am I?"

"I mean, technically my ass *is* your ass. So…"

He made a face. "You think this is a joke?"

I pushed myself up to sit, ignoring the throb at the base of my neck where a persistent headache had been lurking. Theo had practically followed me into the shower when I washed the jail off of me, barking like a rabid dog.

"Of course it's not a joke," I said soberly. "But what was I supposed to do? I did the right thing even though I know I broke the rules—"

"You breached your contract," he shot. "And now, you don't have a fucking job."

I clenched my teeth and winced, forgetting my tooth and jaw and the rest of my aching face. "You called Steven?"

"Yeah, I fucking called Steven and pretended to be you so I could figure out how bad it was."

I paused for a beat. "There has to be something we can do. Something I can do."

He let out a noisy sigh and dragged his hand through his short black hair. "I think you've done enough."

Theo turned to the sound of shuffling from behind him, and silently, we watched our mother enter the room. Her dark eyes were wide and heavy with concern.

"Hey, honey," she said with a small smile. "How ya feelin'?"

"Been better," I admitted.

She cupped my jaw gently when she approached, searched my banged up face. "How's your tooth?"

I forced a grin to display the whole row. "Practically perfect."

She sighed and clutched the arm of the couch, turning to sit. I held her elbow to brace her.

"Well," she started, "what did they say, Teddy?"

He ran a hand over his mouth and chin and sighed again. "They dropped him."

The room went still and silent. I think all our hearts stopped beating—Ma's from the news and mine and Theo's from worrying for her.

"There has to be something I can do," I said again, reaching for my phone. I pulled open my contacts and called Steven, putting it on speaker so Ma and Theo could hear.

Ring.

Steven, my editor, currently owned me. They could sue me for advance money. They could sue me for worse than that. Six months behind was nothing, but given my other bullshit? I'd been on my last leg when I hobbled into the contract. Never mind now.

Ring.

My agent was going to kill me for going around him, but my sense of urgency had created an emergency that couldn't wait. I had to do something, and I had to do it *now.*

Ring.

I looked at Ma, her eyes brimming with tears and brow furrowed in concern, then at Theo, who looked like he hadn't slept at all. Between bailing me out and coordinating with the celebrity oral surgeon we'd probably paid a wildly inflated fee for speed and discretion, he probably hadn't.

Ring.

"Tommy," Steven answered in lieu of a greeting, my name flat and weighted with frustration.

"Hey, Steven. Listen, I wanted to talk to you—"

"What's left to talk about? You got fired, Tommy."

I paused long enough to swallow. "I know I fucked up—"

"Fucked up? You brawled at one of our own events, right in front of God and the press and everyone. It was hard enough to get approval to take you on in the first place, and that was under the promise of the cash cow that accompanies your name. But for *us* to get paid, we need a book. All you've given us is a publicity nightmare that's had our entire floor in crisis mode all day. You have held up a grand total of *zero* part of our bargain. And after last night's antics, there's not a damn thing I can do but call this what it is. Finished."

I dragged a hand down my face, wincing against the pain in my mouth. "Tell me how to fix this, Steven. Tell me what to do, and I'll do it."

A heavy sigh filled the room. "Tommy, there's no way you can turn the *Titanic* around. And even if you could, I don't have a manuscript to sell."

"What if I told you I could get you a manuscript in a few weeks?"

A pause. "I'd still say your image is a problem for my entire department."

"And what if I told you I could turn that around, too?"

Now, a laugh. "I'd say you're full of shit, Tommy. Listen—"

"I mean it, Steven. Give me one month. One month to fix my image. One month to get you a complete manuscript. If I could do that in four weeks, would you be willing to give me one last shot?"

When he paused again, it was long and thick with his thoughts. The creak of his chair sounded as he shifted in his seat. "A complete turnaround. No models. No pop stars. No more Bad Boy Bane. I'd need you to be a fucking saint, Tommy. Obscene donations. Saving the children. Kissing the babies. Oprah-endorsed, good-guy public reform. If you can do *that*? I'd not only reinstate your contract, but I'd throw an extra zero on the end."

I drew a painful breath, my brows knit together in determination. "You know I was trying to save that girl from that son of a bitch."

"I know. I was there. But it doesn't matter. The only thing that matters is what they think. And the only thing that matters to me is that manuscript you owe me. But they're not going to sell it if you're not squeaky fucking clean." Another creak of his chair as I imagined him leaning back. "Four weeks. Consider yourself on the most severe probation of your life. Call me in twenty-four hours and let me know what you're going to do. Show me you're committed to this with a gesture so grand, you can see it from space."

I nodded. "I won't let you down."

That earned me a disbelieving laugh. "We'll see."

The line disconnected without a parting word.

The three of us shared a pregnant look. Theo's eyes shifted to Ma, and so did mine. I reached for her hand, trembling and small in her lap.

Because this was the real fear, the reason for everything. I had to take care of her. She'd done *everything* to take care of us.

I swallowed hard. "All right, now—what kind of publicity stunt will be strong enough to turn this around?"

Theo's shoulders sagged, his eyes ringed with gray from stress and lack of sleep. Because of me. "I don't know, Tommy. I don't know what it'll take to fix this."

Ma turned her hand under mine, clasping mine palm to palm. "They used to tell famous men who needed an image overhaul to join the military or get married. Rock Hudson married his agent's secretary when whispers about his sexuality caught fire. Too bad your agent's assistant is already married," she joked.

Theo and I exchanged a charged glance, the gears behind our eyes whirring and clicking in synchronicity.

Married. *That* was something I hadn't done before. But who could it be? No models, no actresses. I needed someone I could trust, a counterbalance to my image, someone to make me look good. Someone sweet, innocent, virtuous. Someone like—

Ma's smile fell. "Oh, no."

"I know a girl who could save my book *and* my reputation."

Theo's eyes widened. "Oh, *no.*"

But I smiled, hope igniting in my chest along with a psychic tingle of rightness in my guts. "Oh, *yes.* Think about it. Think about it for just one second."

He did. I saw his resignation and felt a subsequent surge of triumph.

"You heard Steven. No romp with a Victoria's Secret model is going to save me. I've gotta go big. Like, married big. The gossip columns will go *insane*. It's the best I've got—they want to know who I'm dating, who I'm with? What if I give them a *wedding*?"

"When Steven said commitment, I don't think he meant *that* kind of commitment," Ma said, her face drawn.

"Picture it," I started, gripping the reins on my enthusiasm. "Thomas Bane meets shy, sweet, awkward book blogger. She's the little white lamb to his big, bad wolf. The light to his dark. The sweet to his salty. She smiles and kisses the babies with him. She's innocence embodied. Their romance is fast and fierce, and swiftly, they marry. Pictures all over the internet. Her sweet face over a stockpot of soup in a homeless shelter. And while we junket, we work on my story, which we were already going to be doing every day. She could save me. She could save all of us."

Theo frowned, even as he agreed. "She's the quintessential good girl. And the story…you dating the Egglette heiress, the gentle, unassuming book blogger who hates your books? I mean, we can sell that. We can sell it hard. But…" He pinched the bridge of his nose, his eyes clamped shut. "Can she even speak over a whisper? Could she appear in public without having a coronary?"

I smirked. "Maybe she'll swoon. So long as I catch her, she'll be fine. Plus, think of the photo ops."

He gave me a look. "And how the fuck do you plan on convincing her to *marry you*?"

My cavalier smile faded. "My charm and good looks?"

Theo's look somehow flattened and hardened simultaneously.

I drew a heavy breath and twisted my hair back so I could think. "She doesn't need the money, but, man, I wish she did. She's trying to…well, get out of her shell. I can help her with that. She wants to be a fiction editor. I wonder if I could get her a job with a publisher. Not that any of them are impressed with me right now." I swiped a hand over my mouth, thinking through my connections at the Big Five and crossing every name off the list as soon as it came to mind.

"There's an option," Theo said, his voice worn.

Ma waited expectantly. Theo looked like he was about to detonate a bomb if he cut the wrong wire.

"What, Teddy? What is it?" Ma asked.

"You're not gonna like it," he said definitively.

My eyes narrowed. "Why don't you tell us and we can decide together."

He steeled himself. "You told me Janessa offered her an editing internship in exchange for a story on you. That's the only bait you've got."

"She wants the story," Ma said, her voice trembling and small. "Tommy, you've gotta give it to her."

Theo and I protested simultaneously and in decibels that rendered us almost inaudible.

Ma shook her head, holding her hand up for us to hush. "I mean it. For years, you've kept everything quiet, played it close to the vest. Give her your story. *Our* story. She has an open mic at the newspaper, and you know what? The story will help save *you*, too."

I shook my head right back at her. "No. Putting my love life on display is easy—none of that is real. Pretending to be what they want me to be? It's not *real*. But they don't get *me*. They don't get you. I won't do it. I won't fucking do it."

"But what if you *have* to?" she asked. "Tommy, I love you for protecting me. I love you for taking care of me. But there's something else."

I waited, not sure I wanted to know what she would say.

"One day, I'll be much worse off than I am now. One day after that, I'll be gone. And if they know, they'll ask you about your pain all the time. They'll make you revisit it for themselves, for money, for the masses. It's easier, keeping it a secret. But maybe I don't want to be kept a secret anymore. Maybe I want to meet your friends. Maybe I want to get out, enjoy my life while I can, however I can."

"You really feel like that, Ma?" I asked quietly.

"I do. And I know you don't want to use me for sympathy. But they want to know *you*, not just the image you give them. They want what's real. And, baby, if they knew who you were, who you *really* were, they could only love you. Would you do it for me? Would you do it if I asked?"

I covered her hands with mine, leaned in closer, searched her face. "Ma, do you understand what you're asking? Do you understand what it'll really mean? They'll use our misfortune to sell magazines and newspapers. I can't do that to you. I won't."

"I don't think you have a choice," Ma said. "Give the girl the story her boss wants, so she can have the job she wants. It's the simplest solution to all of this."

"She's right," Theo added.

I swiveled my head to pin him with a glare.

He took a seat on the edge of the coffee table, looking more tired than I'd ever seen him. "It could convince Amelia to help you, and it *would* help your image to have an editorial. You could have someone write it sympathetically, not like some garbage Vivienne Thorne would publish. Amelia would write the truth. The real Thomas Bane. Just good ole Tommy Banowski from the Bronx. Doing what he can to take care of his ma as she suffers through Parkinson's."

"You'd use Ma that way?" I spat. "I can't even believe I'm fucking hearing this."

"You think I want to?" he shot back. "If you'd kept yourself in line, we wouldn't have to. But what the fuck else can we do?"

"Kept myself in line? Jesus, you act like I *am* a menace. That guy fucking hit *me*."

"And you hit him back like your fucking job wasn't on the line. That's your problem. You don't fucking think. You just *do*."

"Enough!" Ma yelled, though her gusto dissolved as she hunched, coughing.

My arm wound around her, and Theo knelt at her feet, our faces turned to hers.

She held up a hand, her head bowed as she caught her breath. "Please, don't fight," she croaked.

I squeezed her. "Sorry, Ma."

"Don't say you're sorry either. Just say you'll do it. Ask the girl if she'll help you. Offer her the story everyone wants. Save yourself, Tommy. Please, I'm begging you."

And there was nothing left to do. So I nodded, swallowing to try to open up my tight throat.

It didn't work.

"You'll do it?" she asked, her face full of hope.

And I tried to smile. "I'll do it."

Theo and I caught each other's eyes, and I swore I could read his mind.

His thoughts echoed mine.

I hope this fucking works.

Ambush

AMELIA

My hands, resting still and cold in my lap, felt like someone else's.

Tommy and his brother watched me silently. Expectantly. And in the air between us all was the last word that had left Thomas Bane's ridiculous lips.

Married.

That was what he'd said.

"*We should get married.*"

It had been the absolute last thing I ever thought he'd say to me. I'd have been less surprised if he'd suggested a bank robbery or a possible hit.

But, no. He'd suggested we get married. And now, he and his brother wore matching expressions of hope and expectation as they waited for my answer.

I couldn't seem to find my voice. My tongue was slow and stupid, sitting incompetently in my mouth.

"I … did you just … *married*?" I blinked, unable to parse the word.

Tommy's lips were set in a determined line, but the very edges curled up, as if he couldn't help but smile. "It's crazy, I know. And the truth is, Amelia … I'm at your mercy. There's not much I can offer you that you don't already have. Or things I don't think you want, like fame. But I can offer you the story Janessa wants. You can get the job you want."

I shook my head, still trying to make sure I was in fact awake and not dreaming.

"I know it's … extreme—"

A laugh shot out of me, unbidden.

A smile brushed his ridiculous lips. "But this way, everyone wins. I give you my story. Janessa gets you a job. And more than that, you want to be able to speak to strangers? Well, I've got the most intense exposure therapy known to man—the public eye. But you won't be alone. You'll have *me*."

I must have looked skeptical. I felt like I was maybe having an aneurism.

"I can show you how to be brave. To be confident. I'll cannonball into the deep end with you and show you how to swim. You won't be afraid to speak in public once I'm through with you. You won't be afraid of anything."

Somehow, I doubted that promise. But the allure was alive and well, glimmering in my future.

"And I can offer you my story. Janessa has been angling for it for years. Reporters have done their damnedest to worm their way into my life for the sake of finding out. If you give her the story, I know she can help you get the job you want."

My heart ached, not only at his rightness, but at the implication that he'd been deceived, misled. Cheated.

And then another thought crossed my mind. "You would trust me with this?"

At that, he smiled. "I do trust you. Call it a hunch."

I shook my head, glancing down at my dead mannequin hands. "This is the most insane thing to ever happen to me. I don't think … I mean, I don't know if I can—"

Theo cleared his throat. "Before you say no, just consider it. Hear Tommy out, okay?"

I took a deep breath in an attempt to steel myself. Calm myself. Get some footing.

It didn't work.

Theo didn't wait for an answer, only nodded once, shared a look with his brother, and excused himself.

The door clicked closed, and Tommy and I were alone.

He took a seat on the coffee table, his shoulders low and brow drawn. His mask slipped, revealing a glimpse of the worried, beaten man who rested beneath. And as my heart broke for him, he took my hands.

Awareness zinged through me, and those previously wooden hands were a wonderland of feeling. The heat of his skin. The curves of his palms. The length of his fingers as they closed around mine.

"Amelia," he started, his voice low and his eyes on our hands, "I realize what I'm asking of you, and I'm sorry. But this is the simplest, fastest way to save my career. I've done it before. Did you know?"

He was so warm, his hands like a furnace. Sweat blossomed in my palms.

"D-done what?"

"Dated women for publicity. Models mostly. Marley Monroe. Everyone I've ever been seen with in public has been for show."

My lungs pinched painfully. "No. Really?" I breathed.

He nodded. "I … I don't trust many people. I'll give them a show, dance around, give them something to talk about. But that's not real.

That's why it's easy to lie. This, with you and me, is a business deal. An exchange. You've already offered to help me with the story, and for that, I'm indebted to you. But that won't matter if I have no job. I'm behind by half a year—which wouldn't have been so bad had I not already been in the doghouse—and in order for me to keep this contract, the book has to be turned in four weeks from today. Four weeks. And you've read what I have, which is fuckall."

The tiniest laugh huffed out of my nose ignoring the sting of rejection that I wasn't the kind of girl who could ever be with a man like Thomas Bane. This was merely a business deal and a proposition of friendship, nothing more.

"I need your help. And not just me." He swallowed, inspecting my hand in his, his thumb shifting absently against my knuckles, as if he were mapping their topography. "My...my mom has Parkinson's, and I take care of her. Part of my story is *her* story." His voice grew gravelly, breaking off at the end. He wouldn't meet my eyes. "You asked me yesterday what I was afraid of. This—this is what I'm afraid of. I'm afraid of what will happen to her. I'm afraid I'll lose my career. I'm afraid I'll lose it all. And where will that leave her?"

"I...I didn't know, Tommy. I'm so sorry." The words were almost a whisper, spoken against the ache in my chest.

"Nobody knows," he said with a shake of his head. "But this goes beyond me. Everyone thinks I'm this delinquent, but all I've ever done is the right thing. I just do the right thing the wrong way. I stick my nose where it doesn't belong, and I end up in trouble."

"The rally?"

His eyes flicked to mine, a smile tugging at one corner of his lips. "I stumbled into it, drunk. Had no idea what it was until I talked to some fucking bigot who ended up getting his skinhead skull cracked. Started a brawl that ended up with all of us in jail."

"And last night...it had something to do with that girl in the photos, didn't it?"

Something warmed his face, sparked behind his eyes. Appreciation? Understanding? I wasn't sure, but it made me feel like saying yes to anything he asked me.

"Yes, it had to do with that girl. The guy was shaking her down after she refused him. I tried to give him cash and put him in a cab. Instead of taking the offer, he made one of his own. With his fist." He looked back to our hands, shaking his head. "I can't say I wouldn't do it again. Maybe Theo's right. Maybe I'm hopeless."

I shifted my hand in his so I could grasp it. "I don't think you're hopeless, Tommy."

When he looked up, his eyes were black and bottomless, and in their depths, I saw his hope, his fear, his desire.

"If I marry you, if I write the article and pretend to be your…" I couldn't say the word. "Pretend to be married…married to *you*…" I took a breath. "If I do this, it will help you?"

"It will save me."

I nodded. "So…I would live here with you. We would work on the book, and around that, we'd make appearances together. My privacy will be stripped, my life made public."

He nodded, his face impossibly sad.

"Will I have to be someone I'm not?"

At that, he brightened. "Not a chance."

I shook my head, as if it were possible to clear it. "Why not find a model? Someone accustomed to this sort of thing? I…I don't know if I can be in front of people like that. I don't know if I can speak or… or…" My cheeks caught fire, my heart thumping painfully. I felt like I might faint. "I don't know if I can do this."

"No model can save me. I need an angel. I need *you*."

The pain and desperation and truth in his voice slipped over me, through me, twisted around my heart and took root. His fate rested in my hands, in my answer. The fate of his mother rested there too, the fate of his career, of the stories he had left to tell.

The truth I found between our clasped hands was infinite.

This was all much bigger than me.

Could I give one year of my life to save a man's career and family? A man I not only respected, but thought I could truly like and be friends with. I didn't know how he could sell that he was in love with a girl like me, but I supposed that was more the job of hair and makeup than him and me.

One year.

One year as Thomas Bane's wife.

So many things could be worse, and my life, at that moment, was lacking a single obstacle to prevent me from agreeing. I had no boyfriend, no prospects, no social life to speak of beyond my friends, who had already begun moving on. More and more, I was alone. My life was something of a blank canvas, and he was handing me a brush.

And he was right. He could help me. Exposure therapy at its most extreme. And the credits of working on his story, coupled with pleasing Janessa with the article she wanted, would be brilliant for my résumé.

In one year, I could have everything I dreamed of.

His eyes whispered, *Help me, save me. It can only be you.*

So I smiled, squeezed his hands, and said, "I'll do it."

His face broke open like sunshine through a thunderhead, and with a whoop, he leaped to his feet, scooping me up like I was nothing.

I squealed, laughing as he spun us, my arms clamped around his neck. He smelled divine, the scent of him clinging to me as tightly as his arms around me. He buried his face in my neck, kissing it gently, absently before setting me on the ground.

I felt the ghost of his lips long after they were gone.

He looked down at me, grinning like a boy, his arms still around me. Mine had come unhooked when he set me down, though we were so close, my hands rested on his chest with nowhere else to go.

"We leave today for Vegas. I'll have Theo—"

I froze, locked to the ground. "*Today*?"

A sheepish look passed over his face and hung there. "Today. I promised Steven I'd commit to a plan tomorrow, and we've got to get started on the story as soon as possible. Plus, we've got to get contracts drawn up and signed before you tell anyone about this."

I swallowed. "Not my parents? Not my friends?"

He shook his head. "Not until we get the details sorted. We can't risk the truth leaking, not now. Not until we've established the story. Otherwise, it's all for naught."

I sat heavily on the couch. "Oh. Okay."

He knelt down and took my hands in his again, pausing for a long moment. "Amelia, are you sure you want to do this?"

My smile was genuine, as overwhelmed as I was. "I'm sure. Sure as I can be," I amended on a laugh.

His sigh was both audible and relieved. "Okay. I'll have Theo grab us first-class tickets for the next flight out."

"Oh, if you want, we can take the jet."

He stilled. "*The* jet?"

My cheeks flamed. "W-well, yes. We have a jet at Newark so I can fly home to see my parents whenever I want. We can take that. I just have to give James a two-hour lead."

He paused, still processing. "You are too good for me in all ways, Amelia Hall."

I laughed, unable to speak. Me. Too good for Thomas Bane.

I'd officially stepped into the twilight zone.

Tommy folded me into his arms, laughing as he pressed a kiss on the top of my head, his joy thoughtless and wild. God, him and those lips. I ignored the fleeting thought that I should be concerned with those lips in a more real way.

"Theo will have our room set up, the chapel booked, and the media alerted. I'll have a crew there to get you ready for the ceremony, dresses to choose from, just need to know your measurements."

I tried to take a breath and couldn't, only in part because of his arms as they squeezed me like a balloon string in a strong wind.

"I…I hope I can do this," I said.

He leaned back to look at me, cupped my face in his hands, smiled with more relief and joy than I could ever describe. But I felt it in my marrow.

"You can do this, Amelia. I'll hold your hand every step of the way. All you have to do is smile and wave and put up with me. I'll take care of the rest."

I nodded, swallowed, and smiled. Because like a fool, I believed him completely.

With my agreement, he wrapped me up again, squeezed me somehow tighter than he had yet. And with his cheek resting on my crown, he whispered words that settled into my heart, maybe forever.

"*Thank you.*"

ive me... counted them in ... rained me. Those...
...have haunted me, rained me... fire in search of
... my kingdom. I have walked through fire in search of
...ic that would save us, that would give me...
... kept them in cuffers, counted them in
... for my pain. Those sins have haunted me,
... claimed my kingdom. I have walked
...ic that would sa...

Sky High

TOMMY

"**O**h my God, there's a bedroom."

It was maybe the closest to a squeal as I'd ever gotten. I couldn't help it. As I bounced through the fuselage of the Egglette jet, I had no chill. None. Zero.

Amelia watched on, amused.

I bounded into the bedroom with my eyes bugging and a grin splitting my face. The room was narrow but with comfortable space around the bed and nightstands. Everything was the color of champagne. I plopped down on the foot of the mattress and bounced as if to test its durability.

I waggled my brows at her. "Seems sturdy."

Her cheeks flushed as she laughed, eyes rolling. "You are so ridiculous."

I flopped flat on my back, arms out like I was going to make a snow angel. "I have always wanted one of these."

"How come you've never gotten one?"

"I'm rich, but I'm not *private jet* rich." I sat, my gaze sweeping over the room. I resisted the urge to open and close the blackout blinds. "I mean, technically, I *could* afford it, but I don't want to be jet-poor."

She chuckled.

"I'm more interested in investing. Planning for the future, which, as you can see, is tenuous and largely out of my control."

"I'm not saying that guy didn't have it coming, but I don't know if I'd say that was out of your control."

"You're not wrong. You're good at being not-wrong."

"You mean I'm *right*." She smiled sideways at me.

"If you say so." I bounced on the mattress again a couple times before getting up. "Is the bar stocked?" I asked, more out of curiosity than anything.

"It is. There's usually a flight attendant too, but I figured the less people who saw us, the better."

The captain popped his head in and told us to take our seats. I wondered briefly if he'd let me come sit next to him in the cockpit and almost lost all composure at the prospect.

Instead of pouncing the captain like a six-year-old kid, I moved for the bar. "What's your poison?"

"Oh, anything is fine," she said as she sat in a tan leather captain's chair.

"Scotch it is," I joked, figuring she drank drinks with tildes. Pink drinks with umbrellas. Booze that was more schnapps and sugar than liquor and loose inhibitions.

"I'll take mine neat, please."

My face swiveled to gawk, but she didn't see. She had opened the window shade and was peering across the tarmac.

"Well, how about that?" I said to myself.

But she turned, unsurprised by my surprise. "What, a girl can't enjoy a glass of scotch unless she's an extrovert? Or wears pencil skirts? Or is a CEO?"

I shook my head, smirking as I picked up the two-thousand-dollar bottle of Gordon & MacPhail. "Not at all. It's just..." I chuckled. "No, you're right. I just assumed that because you're so... *you* that you were innocent to things like scotch and cigars."

Her nose wrinkled. "I haven't smoked a cigar—they smell terrible. I'm not interested enough in looking cool to smoke."

The high corner of my lips rose a notch higher. "I used to smoke like a chimney. Camel Wides." I handed her a crystal glass and took the seat facing her.

"Do you miss it?"

"Only when I'm editing." I took a sip, enjoying the smooth warmth as it slid through my chest. "I quit a few years ago when Ma was diagnosed. All of a sudden, doing something that could give me cancer felt like an actual risk. Not the lie our immortal brains tell us."

"The lie?"

"That it won't happen to us." I glanced out the window so she wouldn't see *me*. "So, we should get our plan together."

Her face, which had softened and opened with sadness, snapped into action. "Should I get a pen?"

"Nah, I think we can remember between the two of us."

She nodded, taking a sip of her drink. She didn't even flinch, the little badass.

"So," I started, "when we get to Vegas, I've got a hair and makeup crew waiting for you. They've got clothes for tonight and through tomorrow. Theo's got a photographer for the chapel and a couple of paparazzi on call. They'll shoot us from a distance as we come in and out of the hotel and the chapel. And Theo will meet us at the chapel at seven."

She nodded again, this time slower.

"When we get back to New York, we'll need to be seen at least a couple times a week. Dinners are easy. Photographers aren't allowed in, so we'll only have to deal with them in and out. Theo will start working on appearances for photo ops and charity donations once tonight is behind us."

"How much are we donating?"

"We?" I asked without thinking. We. As in *us*. Because we'd be married in a few hours.

She frowned. "Well, yes. I thought we'd pitch in together."

The hot spark of warmth in my chest wasn't from the scotch, and it wasn't because I'd forgotten she was rich, even as I sat in her father's private jet. It was because she'd just assumed she'd take financial part in the whole charade.

"I couldn't ask you to do that. It's bad enough that I've commandeered your life for a year."

"But what if I want to?"

I blinked. "I mean…"

"You said we could donate to charities I wanted. So I'd like to propose matching your donations, dollar for dollar."

I shook my head at her, stunned. "Why would you want the financial burden? You're doing *me* a favor. Please, let me do this for you."

"It's not a burden. And plus, it'll look great in print, won't it? Another reason our marriage is for love: I don't need your money." Her smile was wily, her eyes sparking with mischief. "Do I have to insist?"

I gave her a dubious look.

"I'm sure Theo will agree if you won't."

That did it. I rolled my eyes. "Fine, I give."

"Good." She smiled, but the expression fell almost immediately. "I…I'm not sure how to…I don't know. How to do makeup and dress for this. It's one thing to put on a little mascara. It's another thing to have to be camera ready."

"Will you let me take care of that for you? I have connections.

A personal shopper. Bea's the closest thing to a psychic I've ever met—she could take one look at you and build an entire wardrobe that suited you better than what you would have chosen for yourself. And she works with hair and makeup artists. Would you … would that make you feel more comfortable?"

She sighed, smiling. "That would take a huge pressure off. Thank you, Tommy."

Amelia was pleased, relieved. I found I liked being the reason.

"It's no trouble."

"So dinners, charity events, ribbon cutting, that sort of thing, right?"

"Right. And the rest of the time, we'll be working on the manuscript."

"Have any ideas?" She took another sip of her whiskey as we taxied to the runway.

I huffed a laugh. "Been a little busy with this." I gestured to my bruised-up face. "And now, this." I swept a hand at her. "We'll get started in a couple days once we get you moved in and settled."

A flash of fear sparked behind her eyes.

"Theo's coordinating getting the house ready for you. They're moving me into the other bedroom on the main floor so you can have the master."

Surprise widened her eyes.

She made to speak, but I cut her off. "It's the only bedroom with an attached bathroom, and I want you to have as much privacy as possible."

"But … that's your room. You can't move rooms for me."

I chuckled. "You're *marrying* me. Trust me, the very least I can do is move rooms."

She pouted at that but didn't protest.

"I've got an interior designer already working on it."

Amelia shook her head. "How in the world is it possible that all this could happen so quickly?"

"Easy." I leaned forward a little. "Money."

"Well, sure," she said on a laugh, "but don't these people have anything better to do than cater to you at the drop of a hat?"

One shoulder rose in a shrug. "I'm sure. But I pay a premium for their readiness. It probably helps that I'm easy."

She snorted a laugh.

"In that I let them do pretty much whatever they want, creatively."

"This is just so strange."

"We're in your jet, Amelia. What's so strange about me having a room decorated for you in twenty-four hours?"

She squirmed, her nose crinkling. "I don't know. We're wealthy, yes. But we weren't always wealthy. And we've never been...I don't know. New York wealthy."

"I haven't always been wealthy either," I said, inspecting my glass to feign indifference at the admission. "I grew up poor as poor gets."

Her face smoothed. "Did you?"

I nodded. "Ma worked three jobs. One full-time at the factory and two part-time—one at a diner, one as a seamstress. It was all she could do to keep the lights on and food on the table. It was at her sewing machine that she first realized she was sick. She couldn't thread the needle or keep her hands steady enough to guide fabric straight."

"Oh, Tommy. I'm sorry," she said without pity. "And your dad?"

"Left when Theo and I were kids." My chest hollowed out, my anger long cooled to ash. "Somehow, Ma still found time to make paper chains for Christmas. Our stockings were always full. There was always food on the table, and our shoes never had holes in them. We were warm, cared for, loved by her. And that sacrifice took the best years of her life. Parkinson's took the rest."

Amelia clutched the crystal glass in her hand. I didn't want her to have to try to think of something to say because those things people plucked out of the air to offer in those moments were always flat, empty.

But before I could speak, she did.

"Tommy, I'm so happy she has you."

Earnest. Honest. Unexpected. Not only her words, but Amelia herself.

"I'm just thankful I found a way to take care of her like I have. Bartending wasn't gonna cut it," I said on a chuckle. "I had no skills to speak of. But I'm resourceful. And Ma always said I could talk my way out of anything."

She laughed, her cheeks high and rosy.

"When I wrote my first couple chapters and showed her, she was floored. Know what she said?"

"What?"

"'*I guess I'm not surprised. You're such a good talker.*'"

Another laugh, this one more open, sweeter, a laugh from her heart.

"Between that and my overactive imagination, I guess it really wasn't a surprise to anyone. I was more surprised that somebody actually wanted to pay me for it."

"Well, I'm glad they did. And I'm glad you're caring for your mom the way you are. She's just so lucky to have you, just as lucky as you are to have her."

"If you'd asked her how lucky she felt when I was in high school, she might have had a different answer," I joked.

But Amelia said, "Oh, I bet she wouldn't have."

And once again, Amelia was right.

I switched gears, bringing us back to the task at hand—our impending nuptials.

"Theo sent me with all the papers," I said, setting down my drink and reaching into my bag for the folder of legal documents.

She sobered, taking them. One by one, she took the stapled packets out and flipped through them.

"If you need a lawyer to look them over for you, let me know, and

I'll have someone at the hotel to help decipher them."

"Oh, that's all right. I think I can suss it out. And anyway, I trust you. As long as the prenup goes both ways, we should be fine."

"It does," I said, smiling. "The disclosure contract is flexible and vague, but the gist of it is that you're bound to keep up the pretense of our marriage until we're divorced. After that, you'll be able to publish the article, subject matter to be determined."

"I had an idea about that. What if it was titled 'My Year with Thomas Bane'? It could be a great angle for the editorial, include a bit about your past, about working with you. About who you are, the man I'll come to know."

"That's genius, Amelia. Let's pitch it to Janessa in a few days."

She squirmed. "We're going to tell her?"

"It's the only way to get her to promise to get you the job, and it'll buy us some time. Otherwise, she'll be on us like a stain."

"All right," she said, though she didn't look convinced.

So I reached for her hand, feeling the fine bones under my palm. "Don't worry, Amelia. I've got this. I've got you."

And when she smiled, her fears seemed to fade. And I felt like a conqueror for banishing them.

The plane whirred as we picked up speed, my stomach lurching when the wheels left the ground. Up and away we went, the city stretching up in the distance and our future stretched out before us.

And watching the wonder on Amelia's face as she peered out the window, a comfort settled over me, the rightness that came with a decision made wisely.

There was no one I'd rather be hitched to, for better or for worse.

Chapel O' What?

AMELIA

I *never thought my first kiss* would be on my wedding day.

I should have been more worried about the fact that I was about to marry a virtual stranger as I waited beyond the doors of the chapel, clutching a bouquet of pale pink roses. I should have been more concerned with impending fame, the shock of becoming a public figure, or—perhaps most importantly—the logistics of pretending to be in love with a man I didn't know.

But in that moment, I was far more preoccupied with the kiss waiting at the end of the aisle.

I took a breath, pressing my free hand to the bodice of my dress, catching a glimpse of myself in the floor-length mirrors flanking the white wooden doors of the chapel.

Tommy had a crew of people waiting in the suite for us, as promised. The personal shopper had brought almost three-dozen dresses, long and short, tight and flowing, white and ivory and every shade in between. But the second I'd seen this one, I'd known it was the one.

The color was a creamy, dreamy champagne—white I'd decided to reserve for my *real* wedding—the skirts composed of layer after layer after layer of tulle. The topmost was adorned with delicate lace in a pattern that trailed off the bodice like wisteria. The tea-length hem was trimmed with eyelash lace, the waist bound with a thin ribbon, the bodice fitted with a sweetheart neckline. But the lace kept going, capping my shoulders, the neckline wide, framing my collarbone and neck.

I looked like a bride from a fifties magazine, especially once my hair had been coiffed and makeup had been applied.

My fair hair had been brushed and waved and shined until it gleamed, slipping over my shoulders in a style matching the dress, echoing an era long ago. False eyelashes made my already too big eyes so much bigger. And my lips were red as blood. I'd brought the tube I'd gotten with my friends, a pact we'd all made to be bold and brave. To date, I'd only worn it to dress up for the swing club we frequented with Val and her boyfriend.

I wished again that my friends were there, but they didn't even know it was happening, not yet. Their absence was probably for the best. It already felt too real. This way, I could easily remind myself that it was all fake anyway.

I wore my lipstick in solidarity, and I liked to think they would have been proud.

I certainly never thought I'd wear it on my wedding day. But it was a costume, a mask. The girl in the mirror was blissfully in love with Thomas Bane. That girl was beautiful, as if someone had taken *me* and, with some magic and makeup, made me a caricature, a bigger, brighter, bolder version of myself.

I wasn't even sure I knew who that girl in the mirror was. But when my hand moved from my stomach to the bouquet, hers did, too.

She was me, but I wasn't sure if I was her.

Theo entered the silent marble room, smoothing his tie, walking lightly. But the sound of his footfalls were deafening all the same. On his face was an expression of gracious pity.

"Are you ready?"

"Absolutely not," I said on a meager laugh.

He offered me a smile and his arm. "He's scared, too."

One of my brows climbed. "Isn't he an old pro?" I asked, slipping my clammy hand into the crook of his elbow.

"Not at this. Never this. It's one thing to date a model. It's another to get married. If he wasn't desperate, he never would have asked this of you."

"If he wasn't desperate, I wouldn't have agreed."

He looked down at me, his face so like his brother's—utterly ridiculous on all levels. "Tommy will be good to you. He's far more concerned with your virtue than he is his own. We're…we're just so grateful for you, Amelia. Thank you."

"I just hope it helps."

He covered my hand with his and squeezed. "It will. Now, let's go get you hitched."

My eyes fixed on the seam of the doors as "Clair de Lune" began to play.

ABCs—acknowledge, breathe, connect, I thought, acknowledging that this was crazy. Breathing like there wasn't enough oxygen in the room. Connecting the dots between real and pretend to draw a fine, delicate line.

The moment the doors opened, I found myself caught in a slipstream, aware only on the fringes of my mind.

The chapel was beautiful, with a soaring ceiling topped with peaked glass panes like a greenhouse. The walls were covered in ivy, the chairs wooden and elegantly rustic, the room bathed in brassy light from Edison bulbs stretched across the space. And at the end of the marble aisle, under an archway of ivy dotted with fairy lights, was Thomas Bane.

I floated down the pathway, tethered to the earth by Theo's steady arm, my eyes locked on Tommy, and his locked on me. He was resplendent in a suit as black as his hair and beard, as deep as his eyes. It was cut to perfection—the line of his shoulders sharp, the breadth of his chest and the narrowness of his waist accentuated by a single fastened button.

Those eyes, fathomless and magnetic, were trained on me as I drifted toward him like a specter, voiceless and anchorless. He grew before me until he filled every sense. He was all I could see, the total of my vision, filled to every corner with his herculean frame. The scent of him, clean and crisp—oranges and a hint of some spice, clover perhaps—slipped over me. Theo took my bouquet, and Tommy's hands reached for mine, closed them in his until they disappeared. And when he spoke, it was the coup de grâce that threatened to end me completely, the rumbling resonance of his words vibrating through me like a tuning fork.

"You're beautiful, Amelia."

Earnest and reverent were those words, stealing all my wits, all my fears.

My eyes cast down, my gaze landing on our hands, my cheeks aflame as I whispered, "Thank you."

Time stretched and sped under that ivy arch, my ears ringing and mind spinning as the officiant spoke. And in flickers of awareness, the girl in the mirror promised to love and cherish Thomas Bane, in sickness and health, till death did they part. She looked up into his ridiculous, beautiful, banged-up face, golden under the fairy lights as he held her hands so tenderly and slipped a ring the size of a small meteor onto her third finger, trembling left hand, and said words like *love* and *honor* and *forever*.

And the girl in the mirror did the same.

My hands rested in his as the officiant closed the ceremony, and electric warmth spread from my rib cage out. My eyes were on his. His were on the officiant. And then the words were said, the words that could be my undoing.

"By the power vested in me, I now pronounce you man and wife. You may kiss your bride."

He turned to me with a smile, shifting everything—his body, the universe—his big hands slipping into my hair, cupping my neck, thumbs on my cheeks. The warmth of his body radiated through his beautiful suit, through the lace of my dress. And I closed my eyes, felt his breath on my parted, waiting lips only a heartbeat before his lips pressed to mine.

The shock of sensation from the point of contact shot my lungs open in a draw of breath that breathed *him*. How could his lips be both hard and soft? How could they demand and submit in the same motion? How did he taste so sweet, so male, so succulent? How could it be that, with the simple brush of his mouth against mine, I could find myself boneless and breathless in his arms?

I had no answers. I had no thoughts of the past or the future, of my fate or the world, or anything beyond Thomas Bane's lips and hands and arms.

The kiss ended, catching me unaware—I lurched forward fractionally at the loss of his matching force. My lids peeled open to find him smiling down at me, his smile sideways and roguish.

I smiled back, drunk and reeling from nothing other than his presence.

He took my hand and hooked it on his arm, ushering me down the aisle. I hadn't even noticed several photographers. The sight of them sobered me.

It wasn't real. I knew it. I did. It was just that it *felt* so very real. The dress. The flowers. The chapel. Tommy. Part of me, the part that still believed in fairy tales, felt a deep, aching, irrational loss that it wasn't.

I wondered in earnest if our pretense wouldn't blur the lines between us.

But it was too late to wonder, too late to back away. Because the pen was in my hand, scrawling my name on a marriage certificate. A contract, legally binding me to the man at my side.

And as I watched him sign as I had, I begged my heart to let my head handle the arrangement. My head would build the fences, the boundaries. It would maintain the separation.

I only hoped my heart would listen.

Challenge Accepted

TOMMY

stood at the bar in our suite before two crystal glasses and a
bottle of scotch, wondering just what I'd gotten myself into.

The lights were low, the vast majority of illumination coming
from the wall of floor-to-ceiling windows that overlooked the Bellagio's
fountain and the strip beyond. And Amelia took a seat on the couch
somewhere behind me in a whisper of tulle and a quiet sigh.

I'd been in dozens of fake relationships, tens of public fights and
breakups, and even a handful of *accidental* public hookups in the
name of publicity. But never had I considered involving someone
who didn't benefit mutually from the deal.

My offer to her didn't seem like enough, not in exchange for what
she'd done for me.

The thought made me feel like a crook, which set a blazing
instinct to protect her flaming in my ribs. She'd entrusted me with
her care and safety, and that was not a responsibility I took lightly.

Watching her walk down the aisle, the picture of loveliness, of absolute chaste purity, of sweet innocence…she had disarmed me, stripped me to the bolts. It was inexplicable. I told myself it was merely the illusion of it all—the dress, the chapel, the words spoken that bound us together. There was some magic in those words. Once spoken, they'd invoked a bond I felt in the very depth of my heart, something unshakable, some sorcery or spell cast that entwined her fate with mine.

I brushed the thought aside as I poured the scotch, picked up the glasses, and turned to face my bride.

Her eyes were on her phone and fingers as she typed. So I set her drink on the table in front of her and took the armchair.

Amelia glanced up, her eyes colored with trepidation and relief, a strange and beautiful combination on her. She picked up her glass and cupped it in her hands.

I brought mine up, leaning toward her. "To Mrs. Bane. May she withstand Mr. Bane."

She laughed, a sweet, soft sound, bringing her glass to mine. They clinked. We drank.

I nodded to her phone as I sat back in the armchair. "Message your friends?"

She nodded, worrying her bottom lip. "I told them I'd explain everything tomorrow when we go by to get my things."

"The story breaks in the morning. I wanted to give you tonight at least to get accustomed to everything."

This time when she laughed, it was sardonic. "I don't know how much it'll help, but I appreciate that." She watched me for a second. "What do you think will happen?"

"Well, for starters, I think your blog is going to crash. Your Twitter will be barraged with tags and mentions and DMs, probably more than you could get through in a lifetime. Instagram will blow up. Your picture—*our* picture—will be on gossip magazine covers and website home pages. Tomorrow morning, everyone's eyes will be on you."

"Right." She swallowed once, drew herself up a little straighter, and brought her drink to her lips. I expected her to take a small sip.

She downed the entire thing.

I extended my hand for the empty vessel with a smirk, and she placed it in my hand, coughing once, daintily. I stood to refill her.

"Promise me you'll at least stay offline tomorrow," I said, pouring a finger of scotch into the glass with the creased red-crescent lip print.

"All right. I promise."

When I turned again, she was standing, walking toward the windows. She was illuminated, the lights from below throwing a halo around her golden hair, brushing the edges of her dress. She was so lovely, the lines of her body, the notch of her waist, the delicate bones of her arms and curves of her legs.

So unbelievably lovely.

An angel in white, come to save me.

I stopped when I reached her side and offered her the drink I'd poured. She took it gratefully, bringing it to her pretty lips for a sip this time. And I shamelessly cataloged the beauty of her porcelain face, a doll, too perfect to be real.

Her eyes were on the fountain below, which for the moment was still and dark. "I've never been to Vegas before."

"Never?"

"Never. I don't gamble, and I don't really party. So many people in one place freaks me out. But I have to admit, it's so beautiful at night like this."

I checked my watch. "Wait a couple of minutes until the fountain goes off."

She looked down at the strip, avoiding my eyes. "I don't think I've ever been so scared in my life."

A jolt of guilt shot through me, settling in my chest. "What scares you most?" I asked quietly.

"Is *everything* a sufficient answer?"

"Sure is."

She sighed. "I don't know how to pretend. Everyone will know I'm a fake, a phony. I'll ruin the whole thing and end up hurting you worse when they realize it's all for show." She looked up at me, her eyes tight with worry and shining with tears.

"Just follow my lead," I said with a gentle smile, turning to face her. "We should come up with a signal."

"A signal?"

"Mmhmm, or a safe word. You say the word, and I'll get us out of there. Like, *unforgivable sin*."

She laughed, the tension in her shoulders easing. "Not exactly something to work into casual conversation."

I smiled. "I suppose that's fair." I searched her face for a moment, my gaze coming to rest on her lips. "How about, *I need to touch up my lipstick*?"

The color rose in her cheeks again like a barometer for her feelings. "Oh, I don't wear this very often."

"Think you'll wear it when we're on camera?"

"Hair and makeup, right? Will I have a choice?"

I frowned. "Of course you'll have a choice."

Amelia sighed, the sound resigned. "I'll wear it, and that's a perfect signal."

"And how about a nonverbal signal? Three squeezes means, *Get me out of here*."

Another laugh, a soft, pretty sound. "Three squeezes of what?"

I found myself smiling again. "Anything you can reach."

She shook her head, but her smile hadn't faded. "How do you pretend like this all the time?"

One shoulder rolled in a shrug. "It's not so hard. The first time is the hardest. But we'll find a rhythm, a groove." I watched her for a breath, calculating the best way to say it. "There's a good way to break the ice, but I'm not sure you'd be interested."

"I dunno. I'd be willing to try just about anything if it'd make me feel more confident," she joked, taking a sip of her drink.

"Well, we could make out."

She choked on her scotch, breaking into a coughing fit with her lips pursed to keep the liquor in place.

I took her drink, depositing it on the nearby end table next to mine. Her hand fisted over her mouth as she tried to catch her breath through her seizing esophagus.

"You okay?" I asked, unable to put away my smile. I cupped her elbow with one hand and her cheek in the other.

"I'm fine," she croaked, clearing her throat.

"Told you that you wouldn't be interested. You told me as much the other day." I ignored the sting of that rejection, which had been following me around for days.

She blinked up at me. I hadn't let her go. I should have let her go. It was just that I really didn't want to.

"I-I…well, did the chapel not count?" Her fine brows drew together in confusion.

I chuckled. "A chaste kiss in a Vegas chapel in front of cameras? No, Amelia. That didn't count. It barely counted as a real kiss."

"Oh," she breathed, her cheek warming under my palm.

Something in the quality of her voice struck me like a bell.

"Did you think that counted as a real kiss?" I asked carefully.

"Well…I suppose I wouldn't know. That was my first one."

For a long moment, I stood there, holding Amelia, looking into her open, innocent face as the sum of my awareness shrank to a pinpoint in my chest.

I couldn't have heard her right.

It was impossible.

Unthinkable.

Unbelievable.

A single laugh shot out of me.

She frowned.

I frowned back. "You…you can't…you mean to say you've…" I stopped myself, gathered my wits. "That kiss in the chapel was your first kiss?"

She nodded into my palm.

Shock rose in my chest, followed by guilt and an unexpected feeling of ownership and possession. It was no wonder she'd refused my advances. I'd almost kissed her without care, without realizing. I'd almost taken her first in a way that would have been criminal.

"Please tell me how that's possible."

She opened her mouth to speak but closed it again. Gears whirred and clicked behind her eyes for a moment before she finally spoke. "I've never had a boyfriend. No one's ever even tried to kiss me."

"Impossible," I hissed.

Her face crumbled. "You don't believe me?"

My jaw clenched. "Of course I believe you. I just can't believe no man would have tried." My eyes widened at another realization, a realization that sent a tingling numbness down my arms and to my fingertips. "Amelia," I said quietly, my anxiety barely tamped down, "does that mean you've never…"

Her big eyes were so wide, they almost overtook her face. She couldn't speak. She shook her head instead.

My heart stopped. "You're a virgin?"

Those crimson lips of hers pursed. She nodded.

I let her go like she was fresh out of the oven and stepped back. It was just one step, but her shoulders curved at the loss, her arms winding around her small waist.

I ran a hand over my mouth, unable to comprehend the reality I'd just been handed.

"I-I'm sorry," she stammered. "I didn't think—"

"Don't apologize," I interjected. "Please, don't apologize for that."

Something dawned on her, breaking her face open with a gasp.

"Oh. Oh my God." Her hands flew to her lips, her eyes ringed with white. "Tommy, I…" Her cheeks flushed deep scarlet.

"What?" I asked gently, though my mind was scrambling for what else she could drop on me.

"I have…" She shook her head, seeming to try to gather her thoughts. "I'm a *virgin*. As in *clinically*."

It took a long, silent second for me to understand what she meant. "Oh," I said. It was the only coherent thought I had.

She drew a breath and launched into a stammering spiral. "Oh God. *Oh God.* I can't believe… I mean, I didn't even think… but what if… I mean, is it even legal if I'm a virgin when we get divorced? Are there consummation laws? And what if… what if I date someone else, and he realizes, and *ohmygod*, what if he tells people? Will I have to have him sign an NDA on my virginity? What if—"

I cut her off, moved to touch her arm. "Let's not worry about that right now. Okay?"

She blinked at me so rapidly, it could have been Morse code. "O-okay."

For a moment, I watched her. "Can I ask you a… *personal* question?"

"More personal than my hymen?" she joked dryly.

I chuckled. "No, I don't think so." Another pause. "Do you… do you *want* to be a virgin?"

More blinking. A dangerously bright blush. "Of course not." Her little face twisted in offense. "I hope you're not suggesting that… that you… *throw me a bone*."

A laugh burst out of me.

Somehow, that offense twisted tighter. "You know what I mean, Thomas Bane. I don't need a sexual handout, thank you very much."

"I didn't say you did. I don't hate the idea, but no…that's not what I was suggesting. I was only curious."

The twist eased, but only marginally. "I've waited this long. And that's not to say I'm holding out for marriage—"

We shared a look and laughed.

"I mean, a *real* marriage. But I at least want it to be with someone I care about. Call me old fashioned, but there it is."

I shook my head and shifted into her. "I don't think it's old fashioned."

Her face turned up to mine as I invaded her space.

One hand slipped into her glossy hair. The other palmed the curve of her hip, urging her closer to me. "There's only one thing left to address."

Her eyes were liquid silver, searching mine.

"A wrong needs to be set right."

Her brows stitched together in confusion.

But before she could speak, I leaned in and pulled her into me in the same motion, pressing my lips to hers just as the fountain below us shot to life.

Lips, tentative and unpracticed, stiff against mine for only a second.

And then those lips were mine.

They softened, supple and sweet, testing mine, tasting mine. I swept the seam of her mouth with my tongue—a request. And her lips parted to let me in. Her arms threaded around my neck, a humming moan from the base of her throat that I could taste. Those arms squeezed, pulling me closer, her face angling to open her mouth wider, to delve deeper into my mouth with pleasure and illumination, as if she'd discovered something vital, something necessary to her.

She kissed *me*, thoroughly and without hesitation or shame. She kissed me with enthusiasm I matched with my own, taking a long, sweet moment to touch her face, her hair, her arms, her waist— every safe place I could. And all the while, I surveyed each place we touched, acquainted myself with what my fingers and lips could taste.

She seemed to find herself, to my sadness. The kiss slowed, then stopped, her lips breaking from mine. I pressed my forehead to hers for a moment, reeling. My hands rested on her hips, her body pressed against mine, her arms still hanging from my neck. The fountain burst in waves, the lights shifting, coloring her pale skin.

"Now I can rest easy," I said, my voice gravel and fire, "now that you've been kissed properly."

And with that, I let her go and turned, stepping to the end table to retrieve our drinks, the picture of calm collectiveness. I smirked and smoldered at her to cover the crack in my foundation that kiss had rent.

That was not the kiss of a girl who was not interested.

With the knowledge of her inexperience, I understood her refusal had nothing to do with me. She needed to be wooed, to be loved. She needed to feel safe, needed to be cared for.

And those were all things I could provide.

I handed her her drink, my eyes lighting on her swollen lips, hoping to God she'd change her mind about me.

I didn't know if I'd truly rest until she did.

An idea sprang in my mind, warmed by the scotch and the prospect of possessing such a creature as the one before me. I'd been around long enough to know exactly what the feelings I had for her meant. I knew the power of the chemistry between us.

With time, I knew could care for her very much. I also knew with a tingling in my guts that she would protect me with the fierceness that I would protect her. In that, we were equals.

And with that, we were partners.

I only had to discover if she could care for me, too.

And that was a challenge I found I'd already accepted.

Hymenology

AMELIA

My phone buzzed in my lap.

Again.

I sighed, leaning back in the leather seat of the Mercedes. We were in what felt like a soundproof bubble, the noise of the city nonexistent as we crossed into Manhattan from Newark. The only sounds were the soft, quiet music floating from the speakers and the buzzing vibration of my damnable phone.

Tommy smirked at me. "Your friends don't quit, do they?"

"Well, I did run off and get married to an infamous bachelor without telling them. You'd be worried, too."

"I wouldn't be worried. I'd be murderous."

I chuckled, shaking my head. My eyes caught the sparkling diamond on my finger, the surface as wide as the pad of the finger where it rested. I could practically see my bewildered reflection in the facets.

Ridiculous, just like everything else about him.

He ran his hands through his gorgeous mane, his fingers digging ruts as he pulled it into an unintentionally artful knot at his nape. I watched shamelessly, my gaze hooking on the wide gold band that bound him to me.

A surge of false ownership and extravagant fantasy rose in my chest. I put it out with a hissing chill of admonishment.

Thomas Bane would never be mine, which was a good thing. A man like him would only break my heart.

He had nothing to lose.

I, on the other hand, could lose it all.

I pursed my lips at a sudden flash of memory—the kiss. Not the kiss in the chapel because, as he'd proven, that kiss hadn't been a kiss at all.

I wasn't quite sure how he'd done it. Not the kiss itself—clearly, he had much experience in that department—but the way he'd stripped me bare of my inhibitions. It hadn't been conscious, I didn't think, but something elemental, as if the mixture of whatever essence stirred in his lungs infected me the moment he exhaled.

Something in me had come unfettered. And damn him for letting it loose.

I wasn't sure how I'd ever bottle it back up.

As mad as I'd been when I thought he was about to suggest deflowering me, my heart had snagged on his admission that the idea was appealing. In fact, I'd considered retracting the statement not only right then, but in the bathtub alone that night and for several hours as I lay in the massive bed alone, staring up at the crystal chandelier.

The sight of him raking his wedding band through his hair had me thinking about it again.

But I put those feelings away in a Tupperware box and pressed the lid until all the air hissed out. Nothing—literally nothing in the entire world—could be more ridiculous than me sleeping with

Thomas Bane, America's bad boy.

There was, of course, the issue of my hymen being firmly intact.

I was sure our marriage would be called a sham, and rightly so, but if we parted ways and I was with another man, the other man would know. And if he knew, he might tell someone. For all purposes, our relationship had to appear real. And any straight woman with a heartbeat would sleep with Thomas Bane the second they got the green light.

Well, except me.

I picked up my phone to distract myself, scrolling through the group text and source of all that buzzing.

Val: PLEASE TELL ME YOU HAVE SEEN INSTAGRAM.

Rin: That's nothing compared to the article on People's website. There's a whole spread.

Val: OMG, that kiss. THE KISS. HOW EVEN? I swear to God, I'm going to have a conniption fit if you don't get your bony ass home and spill every goddamn detail in your brain.

Katherine: I don't think she's kidding. Her blood pressure has to be dangerously high given the color of her face.

I chuckled and fired off an answer. *I'm on my way. We should be there in a few.*

Val: WE? As in THOMAS BANE IS COMING TO OUR HOUSE?

Sort of, I answered. *He's dropping me off so we can talk. The movers will be by in a couple of hours.*

My phone exploded with responses. Val sent twelve messages, each with a single word to compose a single dramatic sentence dotted with the word *fuck* for emphasis. The tone of all three of their explosions was the same: *What do you mean, moving?*

My nose wrinkled as I inhaled noisily through it. *I'm married. I can't keep living with you guys.*

Their responses devolved to emojis. Well, except Katherine.

Katherine: Well, that makes sense. But I hate it.

I smiled, but the gesture was thick with grief. *I know. Me too. I'll explain in a bit.*

Val: Please hurry. I really need a hug, and Katherine keeps running away from me.

At that, I laughed, though tears stung the corners of my eyes.

Tommy was watching me, and I tried to compose myself, setting my phone back in my lap, facedown.

"You okay?" he asked gently.

I smiled and met his eyes, blinking to clear my vision. "I am. I...I've never lived with anyone but them and my parents."

He nodded. "You scared?"

"I just hope you're a good roommate," I hedged. "You don't leave all your dirty dishes in the sink or clip your toenails in the living room, do you?"

"Nope. I'm a model roommate. Gus, on the other hand, is a nightmare."

I laughed, but the sound died in my throat. "Oh God. I didn't even think..."

He frowned. "Think what?"

"I have a cat. Can I bring him?"

The sigh he drew and released stretched his chest to capacity. In that moment, I knew he was going to say no, and I was going to have a panic attack in the backseat of a Mercedes.

Fake marriage? No bigs. Losing my cat? Beyond the pale.

But to my relief, he said, "Of course. I just hope he's not an asshole."

I smiled. "Oh, thank you. He's not, I promise. No more than Gus, I'm sure."

That earned me a laugh.

"He won't be a bother, I promise."

"What's his name?"

"Claudius."

His smile tilted. "Claudius and Augustus, kings among men."

"Couple of Roman gentlemen."

"Except Claudius Caesar was weak and sickly, and Augustus was actually named after the Willy Wonka character."

I cackled. I couldn't help it. "You named your dog after Augustus Gloop?"

"He's a glutton, always has been. When he was a puppy, he'd eat until he was sick. Yacked up every dinner until I figured out just how much to feed him. Plus, our old dog was Sir William Wonka, the third—Bill for short. Seemed fitting to keep it in canon."

"I mean, how could you not? Mike Teavee is just pedestrian, and Charlie Bucket's too obvious."

"Gus's about as smart as an empty bucket, and he has as much energy as Grandpa Joe when he gets his greedy fingers on the Golden Ticket."

I chuckled, but when we turned onto my street, my insides flinched with anticipation and an ominous flash of awareness.

It was change I felt, and the reality of that change—explaining what I'd gotten myself into, the packing of my things, the act of saying goodbye to my friends—hit me like a freight train loaded with gunpowder.

Tommy reached for my hand, startling me. But when I looked into his eyes, I found compassion and understanding. His hand, broad and strong, squeezed mine.

I tried to smile. I tried to breathe. I tried to ignore the bite of the unfamiliar wedding ring on my finger and the glint of light on his.

It was madness. All of it. And it was too late to change my mind.

Even if it hadn't been, I didn't know that I would have chosen differently.

The driver pulled up to the curb and hopped out, dashing around to open my door, leaving Tommy and me alone.

"I'll be back in an hour. The movers will be here just after." He watched me for a beat. "Is there anything else I can do?" His thumb shifted against the knobby bone of my wrist, inexplicably comforting me.

"Thank you, Tommy. I'll be fine, just have to figure out how to explain everything to them."

He nodded. "Theo has all their NDAs, so don't worry about the story. Just talk to them. Lean on them. You've been handling everything so well. Maybe too well," he joked.

"Trust me, I'm panicking on the inside."

He chuckled, but when he really looked at me, his smile faded. But not with sadness or discontent. His lips parted, his dark eyes flicking to my mouth. Neither of us breathed.

The door popped open, and we popped apart.

The driver extended his hand, and I took it, my brain lagging and fumbling and trying to sort out if we'd been about to kiss again.

I made a mental note to stay out of closed spaces with Thomas Bane.

Once on the curb, I thanked the driver, who moved to retrieve a weekend bag full of clothes that weren't mine from the trunk. Tommy leaned into the open doorframe, smiling that ridiculous smile of his as he jerked his chin behind me.

"Tell your friends I said hi."

Confused, I turned to look at the brownstone, catching the movement of curtains closing, followed by the sound of thundering footsteps as they barreled down the stairs.

I accepted my bag, clutching it by the handles in front of me, my eyes on Tommy as the driver closed his door. His hand rose, long fingers flicking blithely, the motion barely visible through the dark tinted glass, but I saw it all the same.

With a painfully deep breath, I turned and marched up the steps of my brownstone, prepared to face the battle that waited behind the old oak door.

The door flew open before I reached the top, and Val rushed out, nearly tackling me with a crushing hug.

I laughed, thankful she had ahold of me—I nearly tipped over from the force.

"I cannot believe you!" she scolded with a wavering voice. "Married? Married! And we weren't there!"

I hung on to her as best I could with the leather weekend bag between us. "I know. I wish you had been. It was the most terrifying thing I've ever done."

She leaned back to look at me with tenderness and worry. "Come on. We need every goddamn detail." With that, she grabbed my hand and towed me inside.

Katherine pushed the door shut. Rin took my bag and hugged me, pressing her cheek to mine. For a moment, no one spoke, and with Rin hanging on to me like she was, I felt the prick of tears again.

"I'm making tea," Katherine announced. "This seems like the right moment for tea."

I chuckled through the burn in my throat, and we followed Katherine into the kitchen.

Val machine-gunned questions the whole way. "What happened yesterday? How did he ask you to do this? Did you have sex? Oh my God, please tell me you didn't have sex with him yet because if you did, the fabric of my universe is gonna tear, and I don't know if I'll recover."

I shook my head, smiling as I sat at the island bar. "No, we didn't have sex. The whole thing is for show."

Each of them froze—Katherine with her hand on the teakettle, Rin standing next to me, Val mid-step on the other side of the island. Their faces swung in my direction.

"Explain," Katherine commanded.

All three of them had been otherwise rendered speechless.

"Well," I started, folding my swampy hands on the cool granite, "Tommy's in trouble. His publisher fired him, but he wiggled his way into a Hail Mary. He's been tasked with rebuilding his reputation, and nothing short of sainthood will do. So, here's our story." I straightened up and recited, "Tommy and I met at the book signing, as documented on social media. We began a whirlwind affair that landed us in Vegas, taking vows. I am his angelic, altruistic counterbalance, the person to put reins on the wild beast and domesticate him. We'll be appearing publicly at events all over the city, supporting all my favorite charities and causes. We're publicly reforming him. And I'm the face of the campaign."

When I paused long enough to indicate I was finished, the three of them broke into conversation at once. Val's was of the disbelieving variety. Rin's full of comfort and compassion. And Katherine pointed out everything that could go wrong. I couldn't really hear her over the noise, but I caught enough to be sure of that much at least.

I flinched from the barrage, and Rin put a hand on Val's shoulder, staying her. Katherine followed suit. They waited for Rin's lead.

"I think our first concern is about how you're going to survive public appearances, given that you haven't been to the dentist in years because you couldn't call and make an appointment."

I frowned. "I have very sensitive teeth, Rin, and I will have you know that my dental hygiene is impeccable."

Val's brows knit together. "*My* first concern is regarding the fact that you're a *virgin*. A married virgin."

"I'm with Val," Katherine said with a nod in her direction.

Rin sighed.

"Well, my therapist wanted me to do three things that scared me this week. I feel like I overachieved."

Val rolled her eyes. "I don't think she meant to get *married*."

"Probably not," I conceded, "but we've been working on exposure therapy. This is the ultimate exposure, isn't it?"

A snort from Val's direction. "I guess that's one way to look at it."

I shook my head. "There are so many reasons to do this. Writing the story will land me my dream job, but that's just one part of it. Tommy needs my help. He could lose everything—his career, his income. Plus, he takes care of his mom. She…she has Parkinson's."

Their faces softened in unison.

I let out a weighted breath. "I'm going to be working with him on his book, which is due in a few weeks. I can help him save his career with the manuscript, and by being part of a narrative for the media, I can save him. And maybe he can save me, too. I wanted to be brave? Well, he's offering that. I can give Janessa the story and use my editing credits helping Tommy, coupled with what will be my newfound freedom from my shyness, and get a job with a publisher, just like I wanted. Everyone wins."

"How long?" Rin asked softly.

"A year," I answered in equal decibel.

For a moment, we were all quiet.

"It's not like I'm doing anything else with my time," I continued. "If I don't do this, if I don't push myself, I'll never grow. I'll never change. I'll be alone forever. Tommy has offered me a way out, and I'm taking it."

The teakettle whistled, easing the tension with distraction.

Rin covered my hand with hers. "Put that way, it's hard to feel anything but proud of you."

"I agree," Katherine said as she poured. "I didn't consider that this could be an advancement for you. Getting married was bold. Maybe a bit of an overcorrection, but I'm proud of you, too."

Val folded her arms, but she was smiling. "I'm still wondering what you're going to do about your hymen."

Laughter barked out of us.

"Are you sure you still have one?" Katherine asked.

"Oh, I'm sure," I said wryly.

"Listen, getting tutored in sex and dating was the best thing to ever happen to me. That's basically what you're doing, right? Are you going to have sex with him? Let him teach you the ways of the world?" Val asked with a waggle of brows.

My cheeks warmed. "Of course not."

They gave me a dubious look.

"I'll admit," I started when no one spoke, "he's probably the perfect male specimen, but I refuse to sleep with a man I'm not *with*. I want the first time to be special and with a man I care about."

Katherine's face flattened. "Oh, special like your first kiss? You know, the one splashed all over *Page Six*?"

I rolled my eyes. "That's different. That was fake." I kept the kiss that happened *after* the wedding to myself. "If I sleep with him, won't I fall in love with him? Isn't that a thing that happens with virgins? I'll get my heart-feelings all mixed up with my vagina-feelings and end up getting hurt simply because I don't know the difference between the two."

Katherine eyed me. "Who's to say he won't fall for you?"

I rolled my eyes. "Don't be ridiculous. We have nothing in common."

"Untrue," Katherine said flatly. "You love books, and you're both writers."

"I write blog posts, not fiction, and love of books isn't enough to make people fall in love."

Val reached for her phone. "Relationships have been built on less. Plus, that chapel kiss looked a hundred percent authentic." She swiped, typed, and turned her phone in display.

I threw my hands in front of me and closed my eyes. "Ahh! I

swore I wouldn't look!"

Val huffed and batted my hands away, thrusting her screen into my space. "Oh, stop it. Just look at this."

I cracked one lid, then the other, leaning in with rising wonder and emotion.

There we were, Tommy and me under the ivy arch, hands joined, him in his inky-black suit and me in the floating lace and tulle I'd decided I loved very much. The light was soft and golden, the shadows deep.

But what struck me most—in truth, it emptied my lungs and lit a fire in my heart—was our faces, his turned down, mine turned up. We gazed at each other like lovers. I could see our nerves, see our hopes and fears. I knew the truth of those emotions, the root of them. But to anyone else, we would have looked lovesick and full of bliss, our fear strictly the swiftness of our marriage.

She swiped, showing me the photo of the kiss, and I nearly slid out of my chair and melted into a puddle in the floor.

His hands holding my face, his lips capturing mine, my body against his. I was in his arms, my face soft, everything about me submitting to him. The way he held me was as one might hold something delicate and precious, something to protect and to cherish. I could recall every single sensation, but coupling that with the vision of us was too much to bear.

When I sighed again, it was full of wishes and dreams for a future that didn't exist. It was perfect, the picture of what I'd dreamed of since I was a little girl. A fairy tale, romantic and utterly fabricated.

"There's no danger of either of us falling in love," I said with certainty.

Katherine made a derisive noise.

"Okay, there's no danger of *him* falling in love. He's been in dozens of pretend relationships. He knows exactly how to sell his feelings. They're not real. He's had more practice than any of us have had in *real* relationships."

"I mean, that's not saying much," Val said. "But kissing him in public? Pretending to be married? Sam and I pretended to date. But the funny thing about that is that you can't really pretend. At some point, you're just dating. Or, in your case, *married.*"

"Well, right, but if we're only doing all *that* in public, it'll be fine. You and Sam were different—you were both so into each other. It was plain as day. But *Thomas Bane* could never be attracted to me in a serious way."

At that, Val turned the full weight of her gaze on me. "Please tell me you're kidding. Not only are you a goddamn catch, but I'd like to remind you that I never in a million years believed that Sam could want me."

I shrugged it off. "I'll be fine, I promise. I just have to keep the fake feelings separate from the real ones."

"In all your worldly experience?" Katherine asked plainly. "How will you know which is what?"

"I won't. Which is why I'll need you three. Tommy and I entering into any relationship that isn't strictly platonic would be a mistake. I'm yoked to him for a year, and getting tangled up with him would only make things harder."

Val smirked. "Oh, I'm sure getting tangled up with Thomas Bane would make it *so hard.*"

I shook my head, laughing. "And anyway, I'll have a full year to figure out what to do about my hymen."

"You're *absolutely* sure it's still intact?" Katherine asked before stating the obvious in that matter-of-fact way of hers. "Not having a hymen isn't a test of virginity, but having one is definitely a sign that you *are.*"

Val made a face at her.

"I'm sure," I said. "My gyno asked me if I wanted her to break it. I should have said yes, which I guess I still could."

"Or you could have your *husband* break it for you," Val said.

I rolled my eyes. "Mine's apparently indestructible. It has proven immune to super-plus tampons, speculums, and roller coasters. And, I mean, it's not like I haven't—*you know*—myself, but I can't use, like…internal toys or…*ugh*, God." My cheeks were so hot, they hurt. I pressed my palms to them in an effort to cool them off. "This is so embarrassing."

"Maybe you could take up horseback riding," Katherine suggested.

"Or bobsledding," Rin added helpfully.

"Or that snowmobile game at Dave and Buster's," Val said with a nod.

We all gave her a look.

"What?" she asked no one, blushing. "It's like sitting on a vibrator for ten minutes. I don't know what man invented it, but bless him."

I laughed and picked up my mug for a sip.

They say that when a woman gets engaged, she becomes left-handed. Although I'd skipped that phase entirely and jumped straight to married, I found the sentiment was still true. And as the coffee cup rose to my lips, three pairs of eyes caught the gargantuan stone and followed its path.

"Jesus Christ," Val breathed, her eyes widening. "Is that thing real?"

I lowered the cup and laughed. "I'm no jeweler, but I doubt it's fake. I assume when his brother picked it out, he asked for the *completely outrageous* package. We're hoping *Page Six* does a feature on it."

"Gimme," Val said, extending her hand for mine.

I obliged, and the three of them leaned in close enough for their heads to almost touch. The bright light over the island lit it up like a lighthouse.

"That is beautiful," Rin whispered.

"That's a Harry Winston," Katherine said, shifting it under the light. "A custom. Three and a half carat, emerald cut. This ring probably cost over a hundred thousand dollars."

None of us breathed except Katherine, who went on inspecting it with businesslike practicality.

"How in the world could you know that?" Val asked.

Katherine shrugged. "I know a few things about engagement rings, and I have a photographic memory."

Val's brows quirked. "But—"

"I hope he has insurance for this," Katherine said. I couldn't tell if she was evading or detached. Maybe both. "And I hope you get to keep it when you're divorced."

We laughed. What else could we do? It was all too insane for anything but hysteria.

In a year, I'd be a divorced virgin. Thomas Bane would be a thing of my past.

I ignored the shocking pang of sadness in my chest at the thought. Maybe we would remain friends. He could move on, find a real wife, and make a real life for himself. And as for me? The best I could imagine was that my shell would be broken, and I could take the first steps to building a life of my own.

I only hoped he'd help me get there.

ers, counted them in suffers. Those
have haunted me. rained me. Those
my kingdom. I have walked through fire in search of
ic that would save us. that would give me the
kept them in suffers, counted them in
for my pain. Those sins have haunted me.
claimed my kingdom. I have walked
ic that would sav

The Duke & the Jester

TOMMY

The box of books in my hands probably weighed more than Amelia.

I set it on top of a stack in her room. Stack was probably an understatement—almost all the spare space around her bed was occupied by boxes on boxes of books.

When I turned around, pressing my hand to the small of my back, Amelia was in the doorframe, heels together, cat crate in her hands and a smile on her face.

"I'm not sure where you'll put anything else, but there's all your books."

"What else do I need?" she said cheerfully, her little smile rising on one side.

"Thirty-two boxes of books. *Thirty. Two.*" I glanced at the wall of bookshelves, then at the boxes, and back to the shelves again. "No way are those all gonna fit. I'll order you some more for the other

Her cheeks flushed prettily. "My hero."

"I don't think I've ever seen so many books in one place outside of a library or bookstore in my life. Did you really need to bring *all* of them with you?"

Her face scrunched up like she was angry, but it was too adorable to be menacing. "I take it back. You're a villain after all."

I held my hands up in surrender, smile on my face and heart tha-dumming against my ribs. "I only meant that it's just a year. You didn't have to bring every book you own."

She made a face. "Please, these are only my favorites."

I narrowed my eyes at her, then at the boxes, doing some quick and dirty math. "You're kidding."

"I'm not. My office at home is still mostly full. And that's not even counting my library in my parents' basement."

"And here I thought I liked books."

She chuckled, stepping into the room to set the crate on the bed. "They're my best friends," she said simply. "I can't leave them."

I leaned against one of the sturdier stacks, hitching a leg on the top. "I get that. I just had no idea you've read *that* many books."

She busied herself with the crate, unlatching it and reaching inside as she spoke. "Oh, I've been a reader ever since I could read. I…I didn't have many friends before college. I didn't play outside, and I barely spoke at school. I ate lunches in the library with a book, usually a new one every day. It's all I did really. Eat, sleep, and read."

For a moment, she clutched her orange tabby cat in her arms, peering into his face. I saw her ten years younger, sitting silently in a library, eating a sandwich. I imagined her with her nose in a book, walking the halls of a nondescript high school, bracketed by rows of lockers and a cacophony of sound and motion, mostly caused by beefcakes in letterman jackets and cheerleaders. I imagined that she'd never been seen and very seriously doubted she'd ever been heard.

"Why didn't you speak much?" I asked, too curious to be polite. She was my wife after all.

She seemed to concentrate a little harder on a thorough scratching of Claudius's neck. His eyes were almost closed, his face the very picture of ecstasy. "When I was little, I had a speech impediment. I couldn't pronounce Rs or Ls for that matter. The kids...well, they made fun of me. My second grade teacher even teased me, called me in front of the class to read for what she called *practice*. It only made things worse—they snickered their way through every reading. That was the year I quit speaking unless absolutely necessary."

A flash of anger shot through me like wildfire. "Did your parents have that miserable cow fired?"

She offered a small smile. "Oh, no. My parents are...eccentric at best. They are passive, submissive, kindhearted saints with a deep love of math, physics, and imagination. But they would never confront anyone. They did move me to a private school after that though."

"Was that better? Easier?"

She laughed. "I take it you've never been to private school."

"Not in a million years. I didn't even go to college."

Her smile faded, but her face was wondrous. "Really?"

"Really. If I'd gotten suspended once more in high school, I wouldn't have even graduated. My mom worked her fingers to the bone to keep the lights on, so there was no college fund. My grades were terrible—all those suspensions didn't help—so there was no option for a scholarship. No one to cosign a student loan. I probably could have gotten some financial aid, but..." I opted for a shrug rather than finish the thought.

Her face was sad and open but without pity. Only compassion. "What did you do?"

"Got a job as a bartender. I've always loved to read—not like you, but you're superhuman." I gestured to the stacks.

She chuckled.

"And…I don't know. I came up with the idea for *Jack of all Hades* on the subway one day and came home to write longhand on a yellow legal pad. Took me three months to save up to buy a laptop. First agent I queried picked me up and got me a deal. And the rest is history."

"You've achieved so much," she said earnestly. "You've done so much."

I snorted a laugh and brought my hands up in display of the room. "A regular old Cinderfella. Wanna know another secret?"

She smiled and nodded. Claudius's tail flicked and curled around her waist.

I cleared my throat and unleashed the Bronx. "I've been hidin' my accent for comin' on ten yeahs." I stuck my hand in her direction. "Niceta meetcha. Name's Tahmmy Banowski, straight outta da Bronx. Mount Eden, which is lessa paradise den you'd think."

Her eyes widened and lips parted in an O, though the edges curled just a touch. "Oh my God. That's amazing."

"Glad you're impressed, sweethaht," I said with a smirk, packing it away again. "I didn't want anybody to know where I came from. Didn't want anybody to know my past."

"Is it…did something bad happen to you?"

I shook my head. "Nah, nothing that interesting. I just worked hard to get out of that life that it was easy to create a new identity. That, and I didn't want to sell out my ma. I didn't want to sell *my* story. I'd rather make one up. It's what I'm best at anyway. So, I get it. Not wanting to speak. Not wanting people to judge you for the way you sounded."

She drew a breath, her eyes wide and sparkling. That gorgeous color rose in her cheeks, and I clenched my fingers to stop the tingling wish to touch her.

Before either of us could speak, Gus ambled in, shaggy tail

wagging, tennis balls lodged in his mouth. He completely ignored me, pausing a few cautious feet away from Amelia.

He went still from snout to tail, his eyes locked on the feline in Amelia's arms. The cat, in turn, stared back, the tip of his tail flicking wickedly. The air was thick with anticipation—I think everyone held their breath, except the cat. Clearly he was the emperor of us all—everything hinged on his response.

He leaped lazily from her arms, and Gus lowered his front half in a snap and a thump of his paws on the rug, ass in the air and ears perked.

Claudius pranced around Gus, his tail a question mark as he inspected the dog, whose tail had begun to wag tentatively. His tennis balls were all but forgotten, rolling across the room toward Amelia's feet.

In Gus-speak, this was mammoth in meaning.

The dog's nose was low, his eyes big and hopeful. His nostrils flared in pulses as he caught the scent of the pious cat. Claudius stopped, eyeing him with the aloofness of a duke for a protracted moment.

And then he walked away, completely uninterested, tail high as he strutted out the door to survey his new domain.

Gus sprang into motion, scrambling to grab his tennis balls before chasing after the cat, trying to get his attention. The balls slipped, and Gus panted around them, bouncing behind the most disinterested cat on the planet.

Amelia laughed. "I think Gus wants to play."

"And I think Claudius doesn't even know he exists."

"Well, at least they're not fighting. I don't know if Gus would survive."

"I assure you, he would not."

Gus started barking, and we bolted out to save him from the cat. But instead of that kerfuffle, we found my mother kneeling down to pet Gus, who was attempting to lick her face off.

"That's a good boy," she cooed, stretching her neck in a vain attempt at avoiding the onslaught of his tongue. "You're such a good boy."

"Heya, Ma," I said as I approached, bending to hold her arm with one hand cupping her elbow, the other waiting palm up for hers.

She took the offer, putting her weight on me as I helped her up.

"We were gonna come down," I scolded.

"I know, but my son has a new wife, and I didn't want to wait to meet her." She smiled, shifting to look around me. "Hello, Amelia. I'm Sarah."

She offered her trembling hand, and Amelia stepped up and took it in both of hers.

Ma beamed her approval, and Amelia matched her enthusiasm.

"Oh, it's so nice to meet you."

"You too. My God, you are the sweetest thing. Come sit with me." She took a step toward the living room with her arm in mine. "Tommy, make your ma and your bride some tea, honey."

I smiled down at her. "Anything you want."

The smudges under her eyes and tightness of her lids betrayed her exhaustion.

I lowered my voice. "You shouldn't have walked up here."

"I know, I know," she said like a kid getting told to clean their room. But she hung onto my arm in a way that admitted her agreement.

I deposited Ma on the couch, and Amelia took a seat next to her, hands folded neatly in her lap and face light and happy. She didn't look at all nervous, I noted.

The knowledge left me smiling a little wider as I busied myself making tea.

I couldn't quite hear them from across the room, especially once the kettle got going, but they were smiling, nodding, laughing together. I found myself curious to know what they were saying. It was probably about me, I ventured, which both pleased me and made me anxious.

I willed the teakettle to work faster.

The second the Darjeeling was steeping, I grabbed the mugs and strode into the room, depositing the vessels in front of each woman. They were the two most important women in my life—the one who I would do anything for and the one who held our fate in her small, soft hands.

I sat on the couch perpendicular to them.

"Oh, Tommy's lost more teeth than just the one immortalized in the papers."

"Ma, nobody reads the papers anymore."

She waved a hand at me. "Don't be smart," she said before turning back to Amelia. "Oh, you shoulda seen him. He had more black eyes than the population of rats in the subway. I think he was beat up in every school picture he ever took."

"You shoulda seen the other guy."

They laughed, and Ma shook her head. "Spent a small fortune on meat tenderizer in my day."

"Preparation H worked better, all told," I said.

"Makes me glad we couldn't afford steaks. You'da ruined them all with your face."

Amelia laughed. "Does that actually work?"

"Nah," I answered. "But it feels nice. Anyway, all those black eyes coulda been worse."

Amelia's brows flicked together. I smirked.

"I coulda been the cow."

That earned me a laugh out of the both of them.

"Trouble," Ma said, shaking her head at me. "This one's always been trouble. Teddy's always been the easy one. It's strange, you know. They look the same after all. But they're night and day. Teddy's the brains, and Tommy's the brawn."

"Hey, Ma, watch it. You're gonna give me a complex."

She gave me a look but otherwise ignored me. "Teddy tempers

his brother's fire, and Tommy pushes his brother out of his fences. Balance—that's what it is. But my Tommy has always found trouble. Always had a reason for finding it. He's got a…" She looked to me to finish her sentence, the topic one we'd been talking about for twenty years.

"Moral code."

She nodded, smiling with endearing pride. "Moral code. He was a playground superhero, sticking up for the little guys. A rebel *with* a cause." Ma sighed and shared a look with Amelia. "A regular old James Dean but without the angst."

"Or the headstone," I added.

Ma laughed. "And thank goodness for that. I dunno what I'd do without him." She watched Amelia for a moment and reached for her hand. "I want to thank you for what you're doing for us. For Tommy. I don't know how we'll ever repay you."

"I'm just glad I can help," Amelia said gently. "And I hope we can pull it off," she added with a laugh. "Honestly, he couldn't have picked a worse wife."

As my mother argued the point, I watched on.

The only thought, one I couldn't collect myself enough to speak, was how wrong she was. She was perfect. Kind and gentle. Soft and pure. Honest and true.

Everything I wasn't.

She was the angel to my devil. And I'd do my damnedest not to drag her down with me.

Judgy McGuff

AMELIA

A **little while later, Tommy handed** me a stack of Lisa Kleypas novels with a judgmental look on his face.

"I'm amending my statement from earlier. I've never seen so much *romance* in one place, maybe ever."

I rolled my eyes at him, moving to my historical bookcase. I set Lisa on one of the eye-level shelves—a place of honor on any book lover's bookcase. "You've never been to Wasted Words?"

When I turned, he was frowning with his arms buried in a box. "Been where?"

"Wasted Words. It's half romance and half comics with a bar in the middle?" I watched him expectantly.

He shrugged, eyes on his haul as it rose from the box. "Nope."

I sighed. "We should go. I'm actually working on a piece about it for the *Times*. Anyway, they have a—ugh, stop looking at my books like that." I took the stack from his hands like he'd defiled them.

"Like what?" He looked so confused. It would have been adorable if his lack of awareness wasn't so annoying.

"Like they offend you." I turned for my shelves again, my hands clutching the stack protectively.

A small laugh from behind me, just a derisive puff of sound. "My sensibilities aren't *that* delicate."

"*You* were judging."

He paused, though I heard him shuffling in another box. "It's just that…well, don't get me wrong, but I've never read a romance I liked."

I placed a book on the shelf with a sharp snick. "Then you haven't read a good one."

A snort. "That's a presumptuous canned response."

I felt my face screw up as it warmed. "Please don't tell me you're one of those literary snobs who thumbs their nose at genre fiction. You *write* genre fiction, for God's sake."

"It's not that," he volleyed. I heard him stand, his voice moving closer as he spoke. "They're just…predictable."

I rolled my eyes so hard, my frontal lobe waved at me. "You write fantasy."

He sidled up next to me, his arms full of novels. His stupid, ridiculous, elitist smirk sat proudly on his face. "It's not the same."

"Isn't it?" I snatched the top book off his pile. "The formula's the same. The beats are the same. Romance is fantasy, too. But instead of a quest for a magical relic, it's a quest for happiness. For love. How's that any different?"

He watched me take the books and set them where they belonged. I might have used more force than was entirely necessary.

"I guess I never thought of it that way. Maybe it's that the stakes are so low."

I barked a laugh and swiped another book from his hands. "That's a matter of perspective, sir." I scanned my shelves for my worn copy of *Lord of Scoundrels* by Loretta Chase, finding the yellow-paged tome with the curled edges. I set it on top of the dwindling stack with a stern look. I hoped for stern at least. "Read that."

He shifted the books to hold them with one hand so he could pick up the novel. He gave the cover a dubious look—a thickly muscled Marquess Dain held Jessica in the clutch, her raven hair spread around her on a bed of autumnal gardenias. His eyes met mine with an amused flick of his brow.

"That, *Thomas*, is the definitive romance, a classic display of all the reasons we read the genre. I'll have you know that Stephen King said that writing romance is one of the hardest things any writer can do."

"Well, if Steve said so, I guess it has to be true."

"Don't mock me. Read that," I said again, nodding to the stack. "Tell me I'm right later. Consider it research."

He chuckled, tucking the book under his arm as I took the last of his stack. "Whatever you say, coach."

A smile teased my lips. "Lording over you is kind of nice."

Tommy made a dismissive sound. "Don't get too used to it." He moved the empty box to the hallway. "We should go to dinner tonight."

My hand froze midair, the book suspended on its track for my shelf. "Hmm?" I hummed, not knowing what else to say.

He couldn't mean in public. I wasn't ready for public.

Over the tear and pop of tape as he opened another box, he said, "Trial run. We're going to have to get out in public soon. Dinner will be a great icebreaker." I must have looked as hesitant as I felt because he continued, "Really, it's not so bad with the paparazzi. Two minutes in, two minutes out. If even. We'll pick a hot spot, one of the places people go to get seen. Carmine's? How do you feel about Italian?"

"The same way I feel about *Lord of Scoundrels*," I joked to cover my nerves. *Exposure therapy. Might as well start now.*

He laughed. "And it's casual, so we don't have to get too done up. It'll be good—the iron's hot. Everybody's watching." He paused. "You stayed off social today, right?"

I nodded, turning to face him. "Val showed me a picture of the chapel. I tried to stop her, but...well, she's not easily stopped when she's trying to make a point."

"Good. Stay off until tomorrow at least. Longer, if you can stand it."

I worried my bottom lip between my teeth as he pulled out his phone. "Is it...is it bad?"

His dark eyes flicked to mine, his lips—so full and pouty—tugged up on one side. "No. It's definitely not bad."

I relaxed, smiling back.

"Everything's going as planned. Better than planned, really. They love you. Everybody's scrambling to find out anything they can."

"There's not much to tell."

"Be grateful for that. How are your parents holding up?" He was still typing.

I wondered what he was doing but answered him rather than ask. "Fine, I think. As far as they know, we're happily in love. They were surprised. No," I corrected, "they were shocked. But happily shocked. They never said so, but I have a feeling they'd thought I'd be alone forever." I laughed, though the sound was admittedly pathetic. "I probably will. But at least this is a step in the right direction."

Tommy looked up at me then, his eyes tight and black as midnight. His jaw flexed, setting those gorgeous lips of his in a flat line. Well, as flat as they could get, full as they were. "You won't end up alone," he said with all the certainty of a clairvoyant.

I shook my head, smiling in a way I hoped wasn't patronizing. "If you say so."

"I say so," he commanded, turning back to his phone.

I tried not to consider the possession in his voice when he'd said it, clearing my throat and changing the subject. "You're not making me another marriage deal already, are you?"

"No. I'm texting Theo to get us a reservation. Hair and makeup will be here in a bit, along with Bea. Have you looked in the closet?"

I glanced in the direction of the door I assumed to be the closet. It was the only one I hadn't been in—the other door led to my private bathroom. "No. I think I was more concerned with my books."

"Unsurprising," he teased, jerking his head in that direction. "Go look."

I was inexplicably nervous as I crossed the room. I couldn't imagine what was inside. Spandex and platform heels? Contoured mini dresses in jewel tones? Because if that was what he wanted me to wear, I worried I might actually cry on the spot.

He stopped what he was doing, hanging a meaty arm with a sculpted elbow on the edge of the bed to watch me. Really, even his stupid elbow was ridiculous, a smooth knob surrounded by ropes and cords of muscle.

I felt like I was opening a birthday present with the recipient waiting with expectancy for my reaction. There was no way out of it. My worry over disappointing him with my own disappointment was fierce, gripping my guts. My hand was sweaty as I reached for the doorknob.

When I opened the door, a light came on autonomously, illuminating the room and my shocked face.

I said room because it was bigger than most bedrooms in Manhattan. A small chandelier hung in the center of the ceiling, framed by floral plaster molding, shining its twinkling crystal light on three walls of clothes, shoes, handbags, and drawers.

My mouth hung open, my eyes bulging as I crossed the threshold, heading for the hanging clothes for inspection. My hands brushed a gauzy chiffon sleeve in wonder. Because surely this couldn't be real.

The clothes were beautiful—and expensive, I wagered—and

somehow, magically, they were exactly my style. Everything was tailored and modern, touched with a hint of quirk and whimsy. A Peter Pan collar here. A print covered in cats there. Bright and light and wispy. Pretty and sweet and romantic.

Maybe he was clairvoyant after all.

There were casual clothes and dressy clothes and elegant, sparkling evening clothes. There were heels and sneakers, sweaters and button-downs. Jewelry and purses and—I gasped—sweatpants. Three drawers full of sweatpants, leggings, and loungewear.

My fingers brushed my lips, and I turned, finding Tommy leaning on the doorjamb, hands in his pockets and smile so pleased.

"You got me sweatpants," I said, staving off tears.

"I told Bea you'd want something without zippers to work in. Do you like it?" he asked, the question and his eyes touched with uncertainty and hope.

I flew across the space and threw myself into him with barely enough warning for him to brace himself. I wanted to grab him around the neck, but his neck was out of reach. Instead, my arms snaked around his waist, my face nestled in the hollow between and just under his pectorals. His chest was so expansive, that niche nestled my head as if one had been carved from the other. I felt his heart brushing my cheek with every beat.

"Thank you," I whispered, my voice trembling against the emotion I'd thought was tamped down and under control.

His arms wrapped around me, caging me, separating me from the rest of the world. His hand was so big, it splayed from my spine to hook around my hip. "You're welcome," he said softly, like he'd heard the truth. Like he knew it had little to do with sweatpants.

Nothing really.

It was just that the sweatpants were what had finally broken me.

The reality of the last twenty-four hours swept over me like a tidal wave. As deeply as I believed in my reasons, the depth of the situation hadn't really hit me, not until just then, all because of a drawer of sweatpants.

I was married to a stranger. A stranger who cared enough to fill up a closet with things he thought would make me happy. A stranger who held me like he wasn't a stranger at all.

I couldn't stop my tears, and I didn't try. And Tommy didn't ask any questions, didn't offer me any platitudes. He just held me there in the doorway of a ridiculous closet, swaying with ridiculous gentleness, kissing my crown with ridiculous tenderness.

Which was exactly what I needed, and he had known it before even I did.

Erotic Elbow

AMELIA

"**W**hat do you think?" *Bea* asked, stepping out from between me and the mirror at my vanity.

The vanity was gorgeous, a gilded mirror over a quartz countertop set in my huge bathroom. The surface had been set up with shelves and drawers and slots stuffed to the gills with makeup, makeup that touted brand names I'd never even considered buying.

Really, I was too intimidated to purchase Chanel *anything*. It wasn't the cost. It was walking up to the counter in Bloomingdale's and not knowing what I was doing, what I needed, what I wanted. It was facing the counter girls in sleek black dresses, hair and makeup impeccable, and me without a clue what to say or do.

When Val had dragged us all into Sephora months ago and forced us to find and purchase our perfect shade of red, I'd been petrified— scared silent and so out of my element, I could have been standing on the Wall Street trading floor among screaming traders with a million dollars on the line. I never wore makeup aside from a touch of mascara or the occasional costume makeup my friends would put on me to go to the swing club where Sam played. And because of my gross lack of practice and skill, buying makeup was beyond the scope of my capabilities.

Hell, buying clothes was even beyond me. It was the exact reason I did all my shopping online.

But thanks to Bea, I didn't have to pick out a single thing or apply a stitch of makeup myself.

My reflection blinked back at me. The makeup artist, who also happened to be an aesthetician, had put a set of eyelash extensions on me, and the effect was breathtaking. They looked *real*, except thicker and longer, lush and dark and lovely. My makeup was natural—the darkening of my brows, a creamy foundation, a splash of blush combined to take me to Amelia-plus level. It was me—I could see that plainly—but me with a little oomph.

The only thing *not* natural were my lips, painted the same shade of red I'd been bestowed with by a makeup artist on that fated day at Sephora. Val and Rin had used that lipstick as a leapfrog into the women they wanted to be, the biggest and hardest part of that being having the stones to put it on.

Until my wedding, I hadn't either. But that was easier. It was just like wearing it to the swing club—there, it was a costume. Fake. A mask.

It was a mask I'd wear for a whole year.

The makeup artist said it was perfect for me, asking me for the color's name—Loud and Clear.

"These eyelashes are the best thing to ever happen to me," I said with all the reverence of a nun on Christmas Eve.

She laughed. "Kiss your mascara goodbye and say hello to *I woke up like this* selfies for Instagram."

My cheeks flushed a shade deeper. "I've never posted a selfie on

Instagram before."

Her smile fell. "Wait, really?"

One shoulder twitched a shrug. "I bookstagram. Most of my pictures are of books."

"You're Mrs. Bane now. The internet is clamoring for you already." I sighed. "That's what I hear."

"You haven't seen?"

"Tommy won't let me look until tomorrow."

When she smiled again, it was with fondness. "I'm telling you, you've picked a good one."

I did my best to give her an equal smile, but something in my chest pinched at her words. "Oh, no—I'm the lucky one. He picked me." I slipped out of the chair and smoothed my dress.

"God," she said with a shake of her head, her auburn bob swinging, "that color is incredible with your skin tone."

I glanced at my reflection again. The dress was cobalt velvet, the neck high, the sleeves long, and the hem brushing my calves. But the detailing on the shoulders and bodice was what made it truly spectacular—large-scale vines crept down, their ends punctuated by red, white, and peach flowers, the petals broad and open.

"It's perfect, Bea. I don't know how you did all this, how you knew what to choose."

She leaned toward me, smiling conspiratorially. "Well, you know I'm a witch, right?"

I must have looked like I believed her because she laughed.

"I had Tommy describe the outfits he'd seen you in, and I stalked your blog to get a sense of your aesthetic—not only in colors, but in the pictures you've taken. It was easy really. Especially when he told me about the cat shirt you wore the other day to see him."

"You're good," I said with a shake of my head.

She shrugged. "Just part of the job. I mean, it could be worse.

Who wouldn't want to shop for a living?"

"Me, for one. Unless I could do it all online."

I turned a bit in the mirror. My hair had been blown out and sprayed with something that smelled so good my mouth watered when the hairstylist sprayed it. And whatever that stuff was, it made my hair shine and gleam like a movie star.

"Are you sure this isn't too fancy for Carmine's?" I frowned at my reflection.

Bea stepped behind me, cupping my upper arms and smiling at me in the mirror. "It's your first appearance. This is a beautiful dress for dinner, and it's not too fancy for Carmine's. People will be there in either jeans or suits."

"Will Tommy be in jeans?"

She winked, squeezing my arms. "Nope."

The thought relieved me, then intrigued me. The memory of him in that suit last night filled my mind with visions, my rib cage heat, and set a tingling to somewhere else, too.

A knock sounded on my bedroom door.

My heart knocked on my ribs in answer.

I hurried to the door—in heels no less. I should have won some sort of prize for not breaking an ankle.

When I pulled it open, the smell of oranges and spice rode the currents of air, stirring my hair, invading my senses. Though not more than the sight of him.

He was a god, too tall to be mortal, his shoulders too broad to be human. And his smile, a sideways tilt of his lips, was too charming to be real. But my body knew he was real, could feel the heat of his body like curling fingers reaching for the heat of me.

The high corner of his mouth slipped when he saw me, fading to match the soft wonder in his eyes.

For a moment, we soaked up the sight of each other. His hair—

as glossy and black as pitch, the exact opposite to the paleness of mine—brushed his shoulders, curling in decadent waves. His shirt, crisp and white, structured to highlight the breadth of his shoulders, the curves of his biceps, his ridiculous, sexual elbow. His narrow waist, circled by a leather belt, his pants a cobalt blue that neared the shade of my dress.

I smiled.

Up his lips went again. "We match."

Our clothes, I clarified. He meant our clothes, not *us.*

"We can thank Bea for that, I'm sure," I said.

He offered his arm, smoothing his skinny navy tie as I hooked my hand in the crook of his erotic elbow.

An unbidden laugh chuffed out of me. I tried unsuccessfully to cover it with a cough.

Tommy glanced down at me, one brow arched. "Something amusing?"

I pursed my lips like I'd been caught in a lie. "It's just that…" I couldn't find it in me to finish the thought.

"It's just that…" he echoed, waiting.

"It… it's just that…" I paused. "Did you know even your elbow is hot?"

He blinked once, his face frozen for a split second before he burst into laughter.

Heat stung my cheeks. I thought it might be the good kind of laughter and not the mocking kind, but I'd never been good at deciphering the difference between the two.

Tommy started walking, bringing me with him, given that my hand was locked in the vise of that stupid, hot elbow, which also happened to be inhumanly strong.

"You know," he started as we headed for the door, ignoring Gus as he bounded around like a jackrabbit, "I've caught myself watching your hands, thinking about how sexy they are."

My face swiveled, and I stared at him like he'd grown an extra head or four. "My hands?" I said stupidly.

He glanced at me, amused. "Your hands." He opened the door, and we descended the stone steps. "They're so small, so delicate. Sometimes, I wonder what they'd look like...full."

At that, my blush flared so intensely, I saw spots. "I...they...I mean..." I stammered, finally landing on a noncommittal, "Huh."

A black Mercedes waited at the curb with the driver at the open door. Tommy transferred me into the car by way of my hedonistic hand. The door closed with a thump, leaving me alone for long enough to press the back of my hand to my forehead and consider how fucking hot it was in there. Maybe it was my dress, a virtual furnace. Or maybe it was just that the driver had, in an effort to warm the car up, turned it into an inferno.

But when Tommy slipped in next to me with smoldering eyes and that damnable smile, I realized it was just him.

"So, can we go back to when you said you thought I was sexy?" he asked.

Just like that, the tension snapped with our laughter.

"You're the one who said you wanted me to...to...fill my tiny hands with...well, you didn't say what, but I have my guesses."

He snickered. "Well, you want to make out with my elbow."

My nose wrinkled, but I was still laughing. "You wouldn't even be able to feel it."

"What do you mean?"

"You know that thing kids do? Dare somebody to lick someone else's elbow when they're not looking?"

His face screwed up in confusion. "Is that what kids do in the suburbs? If that happened at my high school, it'd end with somebody losing teeth. Probably the one with the wayward tongue."

I rolled my eyes. "My point is, you can't feel it. Your elbow is one of the least sensitive parts of your body, like your heel or your knee."

"Okay, first—knees can be very sensitive."

"It's thick, wrinkly skin over a joint. It's not sensitive," I said, so sure of my rightness that I sounded petulant.

"I'll prove it," he countered, his voice as deep and velvety as my dress.

Before I could ask what he was going to do, he was doing it. His hands—so big that they were far more like paws than hands— reached for the hem of my dress, the tips of his fingers rasping the skin of my shin. A tingle shot all the way up my thigh at the contact.

He slipped the hem up my shin to expose my knee. Goosebumps raced down my calf. I watched with fascination as his fingertips came to a point, brushed the center of my kneecap, and opened up, spreading out with feather-lightness that set my skin on fire.

"Oh," I breathed, anticipating more, waiting for his hand to trail higher, to tease my tingling skin into a flame.

But he only chuckled and set my skirt to rights. "See? Told you."

I tried to gather my wits, which had been strewn all over the floor of the car like a busted pearl necklace. But for the life of me, I couldn't understand why he was uncuffing one sleeve and hitching it up past that goddamn manly knob he called an elbow.

"Your turn."

My eyes dropped to the naked joint, then back to his eyes, which glinted with something dark and brilliant. "My turn to what?"

"Prove it." He turned his gaze to the city beyond the window and thrust his elbow in my direction.

For a second, I just stared at it, inspecting the topography of ropy muscle, the flat line of his ulna, the divots where muscle gave way to bone and tendon that comprised the man—machine? Gallic prince? barbarian warrior?—who sat next to me.

I couldn't see his mouth, but I could see the curve of his cheek and the crinkle at the corner of his eyes that indicated he was smiling. He wiggled his elbow back and forth.

"Come on. It won't bite."

I swallowed hard.

It's just an elbow. It's not sexual. It's not anything. Look, he's not even looking! And I bet my bottom dollar that he won't back down. You wanna be brave? Lick his elbow, you big baby.

At that, I took a breath. Ignored the painful chugging of my heart. And then, I bent, parted my lips, extended my tongue. My breath bounced off of him and back at me in the second before I brought my tongue to the rough skin of his elbow.

I shot back from him like an arrow, cursing myself for a zillion things and him for at least a dozen. First and foremost was that even his stupid, sexy elbow tasted good.

I made a mental note to ask him what kind of lotion he used.

His laughter filled the cab of the car, his eyes cataloging me as I sat bolt upright, hands folded in my lap, neck long as a giraffe and nose in the air.

But he was only amused, that wily smile of his lighting up his face.

"I told you," I said archly, staring at the headrest of the passenger seat in front of me. "You can't feel it."

"Who said I didn't?"

My head snapped around to frown at him. "You didn't."

He bobbed his head side to side like he was weighing things out. "I didn't feel you lick it—"

"Ha! I knew it!" I crowed.

"But I *did* feel your breath just before you did it. I knew it was coming. And when it was done, the wet spot was cold." He rubbed the spot absently before flipping his cuff and sliding it down his arm, taking my view of his flesh with him.

"So I was right."

Tommy shrugged, buttoning his sleeve with long, blunt fingers. "So was I."

I rolled my eyes, both irritated and charmed, that ass.

He changed the subject. "Still nervous?"

"Surprisingly, yes. Your elbow antics are no match for my anxiety, sir."

A soft chuckle. "And here I thought I was doing so well." He settled back into the seat, sleeve back in place. "There will be a handful of photographers outside of the restaurant. They shouldn't get *too* close, but with the internet blowing up like it has been, who knows."

I took a long, silent breath.

His hand slipped over mine and squeezed. "Don't worry. Just hang on to me. I won't let them get to you. You won't have to speak to anyone."

I nodded but said nothing. The weight and warmth of his hand was a comfort I didn't want to lose. It felt like an anchor, a tether, something to keep me from acting on my flight impulse.

To my surprise, he didn't retract his hand. Instead, his thumb shifted against the knob of my wrist bone.

"People will take our picture inside, but they'll be more discreet. Well, hopefully. I can't tell you how many times I've signed a takeout box at Carmine's. It's a tourist trap, but the food's good," he said on a laugh. "Mostly, it'll be phones. The staff will be respectful at least."

I hadn't stopped nodding like a bobblehead. "All right."

He watched me for a moment. "I say this because we'll be *on*. People will be watching us." Another pause. "Are you ready for that?"

I met his dark eyes. "For people to watch me? As long as I don't have to talk to them, I think I'll be okay."

A smile flickered on his lips. "Smile, nod, hang on to my arm. I'll answer for us. And if it gets to be too much—"

"I've got to freshen up my lipstick."

"Or a triple squeeze."

"Or that. Whatever I can grab, right?"

He chuckled. "I'll make sure my elbow is within reach at all times." His smile faded into something closer to uncertainty, almost…*timidity.* "Is it okay for me to touch you?"

My heart held its breath for a beat before doubling up. "I…um…"

"Hold your hand," he clarified, that ghost of a smile back. "Hold you close. Touch your leg, your waist. Kiss you."

At that, my heart actually fainted for a second. "Ah…well…I mean…we *are* married. I…I guess as long as there's no tongue, it's fine."

I caught a shadow of disappointment in his eyes, but then it was gone. "Fair enough."

The car rolled to a stop at the mouth of the awning. A handful of guys with cameras around their necks loitered just away from the entrance, their curious faces turning to the car in unison. A valet hurried toward us.

Exposure therapy. This was the first, maybe the biggest step I'd take, and I had no idea what to expect, only that I was nervous as all hell. Maybe I'd trip and fall. Maybe my shoe would break. Costume malfunction. Walking malfunction. Heart malfunction.

Acknowledge. Breathe. Connect.

I turned my hand in Tommy's and clutched his palm to ground me, my eyes out the window and heart fluttering.

"Don't worry. I've got you," he said quietly, squeezing once before popping open his door.

He ran around the car, heading off the valet, who smiled broadly and shook his hand.

The camera guys were already shooting, cameras pointed at Tommy like AKs, moving toward him like a front line in a battle.

He opened the door, putting his gigantic body between me and the paparazzi. They were calling his name, asking him questions.

Tommy offered his hand. His eyes offered comfort, protection. Trust.

So I slipped my fingers into his palm and braced myself to exit the vehicle and step onto the sidewalk.

Onto the stage.

The second they saw me, their voices rose, the flashes firing so fast, I was momentarily blinded.

And on the wind was my name in a chorus.

We were a blur of motion and consciousness as Tommy pulled me into his side, wrapped an iron arm around me, and steered us toward the door. His legs were so long, his stride covering the ground I would make in two, but he swept me with him, my thoughts too obscure and fast to catch a single one.

"Amelia! Mrs. Bane! Amelia Hall! How was Vegas? Show us your ring!"

My breath was shallow, my fingers tingling.

He looked down at me as we hurried. "Imagine me naked, if it helps."

"You mean, imagine *them* naked?" I muttered, dragging my eyes from the flashing cameras to glance up at him.

His smile tilted. "Oh, no. Me. Elbows and all."

I kicked my head back and laughed, the din and crush of people that had come out of nowhere, all yelling our names, almost disappeared. It was just me and Tommy and his arms and his smile and those eyes so full of humor and mischief.

And before I had time to consider what that meant, the brass door opened at the hand of the valet, and we were inside.

As the door thumped closed, he pulled me to a stop, and the noise snapped off, leaving us in the calm, comparative quiet of the restaurant lobby.

Tommy smiled down at me.

"I did it," I breathed in disbelief.

"I never had a doubt in my mind," he said gently. "Need to check your lipstick?"

Lips together, I smiled as a zing of adrenaline shoot through me. "Nope. It's perfectly in place."

He pressed a kiss to my forehead and snagged my hand, towing me to the host stand with him.

My heart clanged in my ribs while he gave the hostess our name.

If you'd told me even yesterday morning that I'd be in full set makeup, running into a restaurant with Thomas Bane as we were accosted by paparazzi, you would have had to commit me for a fit of histrionics. But here I was, listening to the deep rumble of his voice, holding his hand like a lifeline.

It was all because of him. I was quickly learning that it was impossible not to feel safe in Tommy's care.

Beyond all reason, I was standing in the restaurant with the comforting hum of patrons muffled by the lush red carpet under my feet and Tommy holding my hand like it was the most natural thing.

I tried not to consider that his was the first hand I'd held since it didn't count anyway.

It was good practice at least.

Fake and not fake. Real and pretend. It was real, and it wasn't. The kiss in the chapel and the kiss *after* the chapel. Tommy's hand and mine. The rings on our fingers.

I was already confused, and it'd only been twenty-four hours. I squirmed against the discomfort of that realization.

The hostess seemed unaffected by Tommy, though her eyes flicked curiously to me, indicating she knew exactly who we were. But she was the picture of discretion as she led us through the restaurant and to a table.

Literally in the middle of the room.

The staff might have been discreet, but the patrons were not. I felt everyone's eyes on us as Tommy pulled out my chair. The tables were crowded together, the couple next to us gawking. The woman's phone was positioned in such a way that I was positive she was taking a picture.

Tommy leaned in, buried his face in my hair behind my ear, and said, "You're gorgeous."

My gaze dropped to my lap, my cheeks aflame, my lips smiling. He laid a small kiss behind my ear, and I mourned that I couldn't feel his lips against my skin for my hair.

The table was set for four, but rather than sit across from me, he took the seat to my side, effectively blocking the camera lady from view.

He shot me a knowing smile as he unfurled his napkin and set it in his lap. "So, what's your poison?" he asked, picking up the menu.

I flipped mine open and skimmed it. "I'm not picky at all. In fact, I don't think I've ever had an Italian dish I didn't like."

"Even eggplant?"

I shrugged. "I love eggplant."

"But it's so...slimy." His nose wrinkled up.

"So are mushrooms, but I like those, too."

An endearing shudder wracked through him.

"Okay, so nothing slimy," I said, smiling.

"How about veal?"

It was my turn to wrinkle my face. "I'm morally averse to the idea of eating a baby cow."

He looked pleased, like I'd passed a test. "One that's never even stood or walked a step. It's cruel, really."

I imagined I looked pleased, too. For a split second, I imagined him bursting into some evil farm conglomerate to save all the wobbly baby cows. Something in the region of my uterus quivered at the thought.

But he wasn't watching me salivate over him. Or maybe he was and figured I was thinking about lasagna.

"The chicken scarpariello is my favorite," he said. "It's family style, so unless we want enough left over to eat for three days, we should probably share. If that's okay with you," he added.

"That sounds perfect. Should we get extra for Theo and your mom?"

This time when he smiled, it wasn't big or wide or amused. It was small, genuine, touched. And it lit him up from the inside. "Good idea. We can take them a slab of lasagna and some tiramisu. Ma might faint from joy. Wine okay?"

"Whatever you want."

That soft smile curled slyly. "Careful what you promise, Amelia."

The waiter appeared, mercifully saving me from having to respond. Tommy ordered for us, and we passed our menus over.

When we were alone again, he shifted—not only turning to face me, but leaning toward me. He took my hand from where it rested on the table, turning it over in his. With his other hand, he traced the lines of my palm.

A tingling zip ran up my arm.

"We have a lot of things to figure out," he said.

"L-like what?"

"Well, for starters, Theo is up my ass wondering what charities you want to contribute to. He's got to get started setting up appearances and events, and it's making him jumpy to have so many loose ends."

I watched him as his giant index finger trailed my love line, which was deep and long and curled all the way off the end of my palm before fading.

I didn't realize I hadn't responded until he asked, "So, what do you think? What should we donate to?"

"Well, I haven't thought about it too much. Something with reading. Reading and children. Libraries?"

"I can have Theo find some options, if you don't have one. What else? Have any animals you'd like to save?"

My face melted. "God, Katherine sent me this video of sea lions that were shot but not killed, climbing up on the ice to die, and I've had nightmares about it ever since. This is why I never leave my house. Humans are cruel creatures."

"I have to agree."

Tommy and I turned to the feminine voice to find an equally feminine and poised Vivienne Thorne.

I'd always thought she was the picture of beauty and power, her body lithe and feline, her eyes sharp and shrewd. She was a journalist for *New York Today*, her articles were always airtight, brilliantly composed, and exposed the subject matter down to its marrow. Like when she'd uncovered that golfer's trillion affairs or the takedown of one of America's sweethearts by airing all the sordid details of her drug addiction.

I had the sinking feeling that I was about to be the object of her scrutiny.

The air around Tommy tightened. "Funny seeing you here, Viv." It was almost an accusation.

She shrugged elegantly. "Please, Tommy. It was a happy accident." Vivienne turned her icy gaze on me and extended a hand, her lips slithering into a smile. "We haven't met. I'm Vivienne Thorne."

I smiled, flustered and starstruck and certain somehow that everything I said would be used against me. "A-Amelia Hall."

Her hand was cold and firm as she shook mine. "Bane."

I blinked. "I'm sorry?"

"Your name is Amelia *Bane*, isn't it?"

A painful flush tingled in my cheeks. "Y-yes, of course."

Tommy transferred my hand to his free one and squeezed it, gripping the back of my chair with the other. "We haven't exactly had time to get to the Social Security office," he said with a charming smile and a devil-may-care tone, but I could feel the tension on his skin against mine.

"Yes, you probably have't. Your little surprise marriage is causing such a stir. Must be a full time job to keep up with," she said with a smile as easy as Tommy's, her voice light. But snaking through the undercurrent was accusation and malice.

The hairs on the back of my neck sparked, drawing to attention.

"I knew the second I met Amelia that she would become vital to me. Why wait once you know?"

The conviction in his voice struck me so deeply, my heart reverberated like a bell.

He squeezed my hand again.

Vivienne laughed. "You've always been a fantastic actor. You fooled me once." Her eyes shifted to blatantly gauge my reaction.

I did my very best to hide my shock over learning Tommy had been with Vivienne Thorne. Judging by her smile, I did a lackluster job of it.

"Takes a snake to know a snake," he said, the humor in his voice gone. "Now, if you'll excuse us—"

"Oh, come on, Tommy," she said on a laugh. "I heard a rumor that Blackbird dropped you, but you made a deal to get back in. And within hours, you married a book blogger from the *Times* that nobody's ever heard of? There's coincidence, and there's contrived."

Tommy's face hardened, the shadow passing behind his eyes foreboding. "If you'll *excuse* us," he repeated with force, "my *wife* and I are trying to enjoy our night. You can direct all questions and unfounded accusations to Theo. He'll answer without using words like *nosy, bitch,* and *mind your own fucking business.*"

That smile she wore only deepened in its certainty. "Of course," she said, turning to me. "It's a pleasure to meet you, *Mrs. Bane.* I'm sure I'll be seeing both of you soon."

Tommy watched her walk away with a look as fiery as it was cold as granite. But I watched him, my palms breaking out in a clammy sweat.

"She knows," I said under my breath.

He turned his attention to me, brows drawn. "She doesn't know anything for sure," he said, leaning closer, releasing my hand to capture my chin in his thumb and forefinger. "It was why she was over here, trying to shake us down. She's jealous. You have the gig she wanted, the story she wanted."

"B-but she doesn't know that."

"No, but she assumes, and that assumption will drive her to be a fucking nuisance. Vivienne has an active imagination and too much ambition for her own good."

I peered into the depths of his russet eyes. "Did...did you date her?"

A laugh huffed out of his nose. "No, we didn't date. We met at an industry event, had too much to drink, and ended up tumbling into bed in what I thought was a chance encounter."

"But it wasn't?" I asked quietly.

"I assumed not after I caught her trying to break into my laptop when she thought I was sleeping. That was the first and last time I took anybody home without a signed contract."

"Oh," I said stupidly, not knowing what else to say. Especially with him close enough to see the slivers of brown and burgundy in those dark eyes of his.

His lips smiled. "Don't let her get to you. I won't let her hurt you, Amelia. I got her fired once. I can get her fired again." He must have read my indecision because his smile faded. "Do you trust me?"

I drew a quiet breath and answered honestly and inexplicably, "I do."

"Good. Because I promised to honor and cherish you, and that's what I intend to do." He paused, his gaze smoldering, his eyes shifting darker, pupils widening to swallow what little color existed in his irises.

"I'm going to kiss you, Amelia Bane." The possession, the raw heat in his voice as he said my name lit a simmering fire low in my belly.

My permission was given in an exhale, a shift into him, a parting of my lips as my body said yes before my brain could even consider his words.

He claimed my consent with his lips, the kiss as chaste as it was searing.

And with that, I lost the will to care whether or not Vivienne was right. He might be the best actor in the world.

When his lips were on mine, I couldn't find it in me to care.

offers, counted them in coffers. Those sins
have haunted me, ruined me. Those
my kingdom. I have walked through fire in search
relic that would save us. that would give me the
ave kept them in coffers, counted them
for my pain. Those sins have haunted
claimed my kingdom. I have wal
that would sav

A Deal's a Deal

TOMMY

Janessa's pen scratched on the paper.

When she looked up, it was with a shark smile. "Mind telling me what all this is about?" she asked, handing the NDA to Theo.

Amelia shifted in her seat next to me, her discomfort humming across the space between us. I reached for her hand in her lap.

Janessa followed the motion with interest.

"We'd like to offer you a story," I said, squeezing Amelia's hand.

"I'm all ears."

Theo took over. "Amelia will be writing an editorial about Thomas Bane to be published in a year. If you want it, it's yours."

"What's the angle?" she asked.

"'My Year with Thomas Bane.' An editorial to cover all the things you've been trying to find out about my brother—not only about his past, but his relationships and family. We'll willingly offer the story, but while your input will be welcomed, the story will be written our way. If you can agree to those terms and you're interested, we're offering it to you first. And in exchange, you will ensure Amelia gets a job at a top New York publishing house."

Assessing eyes scanned the three of us. "I assumed this was a stunt, but this is more than I could have hoped for. Will you admit in the article that the marriage was fake?"

I chimed in, "We'll let you know when we decide. I'd like to call a truce. With the volunteering of my story, I want your promise you'll otherwise leave me alone. No more reporters. No more prying. I'll feed you what you want, but it'll be on my terms. And you will get Amelia the job she wants. Deal?"

She smiled. "Deal. We will take the story you give us, and Amelia can take her pick of a Big Five house. I have connections at all of them. What if we do the piece in parts? One for each month of the year, the perspective of your life through the eyes of sweet, unassuming Amelia Hall. The fame. The famous exes. The truth of your history. Will we finally learn about your mother?"

A sharp, hot flare of aversion whipped through me at even the mention of Ma. "You will."

Theo nodded. "I like the idea of a monthly piece. It could serve as almost an episodic. Expand the piece's life."

I turned to Amelia. "What do you think?"

When she met my gaze, it was as if we were having a private conversation. "I think it's brilliant. The first one could be the wedding. People seem to be interested in the details, and I already have so much material."

Janessa watched the exchange before speaking. "Would you consider releasing the pieces sooner? If we decide not to spill the beans about the fact that it's all for show?" Before I could refuse, she kept talking. "Dropping the story sooner will drum up more interest. You're all anyone can talk about, for now at least."

My eyes narrowed. "We'll consider it," I hedged. "And if you play your cards right, we'll offer you other exclusive content."

Her smile widened.

"But you *will* behave yourself, or we're taking it to *New York Today*. Is that clear?"

"Crystal," she said as she stood. "Let's keep an open dialogue about direction, and I'll keep an eye out for the contract outlining the details. We're looking forward to learning all about you, Mr. Bane."

She offered a hand, which I took, the shake singular, firm, unbreakable. It was a handshake that promised more than words had.

I wasn't naive enough to believe that promise would ever have my best interest at heart.

But that was where Amelia would step in, bridge the gap. Tell my story in a way that would be honest, heartfelt. True.

I hoped at least.

Control the narrative.

And if the whole ordeal helped save my career and build Amelia's, we'd both win.

Janessa shook Amelia's hand, then Theo's. And seconds later, we were striding out of the newspaper offices with everyone's eyes on us.

None of us spoke as we rode the elevator down or walked through the noisy lobby, heavy with traffic. Amelia's hand was in mine, clammy and cool. I wanted to hold her, to nestle her under my arm, wrap my arm around her shoulders. I wanted to be a human shield, deflecting anything—gaze, question, or otherwise—they might fire at her.

It wasn't until we were in the cab that she sighed, sagging against me like she was exhausted.

"You okay?"

She drew a long breath. "I think so. She scares the shit out of me, Tommy."

"Me too," I offered.

She shifted to look at me with disbelief. "Really? I never would have guessed. You were kinda scary in there, too," she said on a chuckle.

"The thing is, we have the upper hand. We have the story. And until we give her what she wants, she's at our mercy. I'd like to hold that off as long as we can. No sense in being shackled to her before we absolutely have to."

"So no early articles?"

Theo shook his head. "I'm with Tommy. Let's keep an eye on her so she doesn't come at us sideways. Best thing we can do is hold her off. Maintain control."

Amelia's brow furrowed. "Are we really in control?"

I wrapped an arm around her like I'd wanted to. "We are. We have her exactly where we need her, and the ball is in our court."

She didn't look convinced.

"Trust me," I urged gently. "We are in control. She will do what we want, exactly how we want. And nothing is going to stop us."

When she smiled, I saw her relief.

And when I looked inside myself, I saw just how thin my promise was.

offers, counted them a... ...
have haunted me. ruined me. Those ...
my kingdom. I have walked through fire in search
relic that would save us, that would give me ...
ave ... kept them in coffers, counted them
... for my pain. Those sins have haunted
... claimed my kingdom. I have wal...
...e that would sav...

Money Where Your Mouth Is

AMELIA

"**O** kay, are you sure you're ready?" Tommy asked, hesitant from head to heel.

I steeled myself, meeting his eyes with courage I tried to tell myself was real. "As ready as I'll ever be."

He reached for my hand. "Just tell me if you need to stop, okay? I don't want you to get hurt."

I had no idea the pain that was about to be inflicted on me, but I nodded, grateful for his comfort. "Thank you, Tommy."

"Don't thank me yet," he said on a chuckle as he handed me my laptop.

I took a deep breath and rested the machine in my lap, sitting back on the couch as I flipped it open.

Tommy sat close enough to feel the heat rolling off of him so hard, I could almost tell the topography of his muscles by the waves that hit me. And I could almost hear his thoughts as he watched me navigate to Twitter.

A tingle that was fire and ice crawled across my skin like spiders.

My account was a fucking shitstorm of mentions and DMs. In the thirty-six hours since we'd gotten married, I had gained just over a million followers.

One. Million. Followers.

My tiny, stunned brain could not comprehend that number. I stared at it like it might change if I blinked.

It didn't.

I opened my notifications, which was the mistake of my life.

At the top was a mention from *Us Weekly* of their cover.

Their cover that happened to have *me* on it.

Not just me, of course. Me and Tommy, one of the pictures from our wedding night, the one of us staring into each other's eyes like we were lovesick. Inset were a few other pictures, including one of us running into the restaurant last night.

I realized distantly that my mouth was hanging open. "How…"

"They move fast," he answered my unspoken question gently.

I scrolled down. *People* magazine. *TMZ. The Goddamn Today Show.* Oprah had congratulated us on our marriage. *Page Six. Daily Mail. Entertainment Weekly. Glamour. Vogue.* All featured pictures from the wedding, discussion of my dress. My past. My family. My friends. There was even a triptych of sneaky paparazzi photos of Sam and Val, arm in arm in the Village, Court and Rin at The Met, and Katherine behind her desk at the New York Public Library.

My vision dimmed by way of dark tendrils that pulsed with my heartbeat as I scrolled. I realized that was the only sound I could hear—the rushing thunder of my pulse in my ears. I then noticed with clinical detachment that my chest felt like a bomb had gone off in my rib cage, and I couldn't get enough air, not with the shallow sips that my locked ribs would allow.

"Okay, that's enough for today," Tommy said with authority, swiping my computer off my lap and closing it with a snap.

My hands lay uselessly in my lap, cold and numb. He took them, shifting to put himself in my line of vision as I stared through a spot across the room.

"Amelia?" My name was a tender, worried string of syllables on his tongue. "Fuck, I knew it was too soon for this," he muttered. "Please, say something."

I blinked, bringing my eyes back to focus. "Oprah offered felicitations."

"I know," he said, relaxing only by a hair.

My hands weren't visible, locked somewhere in his broad palms and fingers.

"Oprah. *Oprah.* She's following me on Twitter now. Did you know that? Oprah Fucking Winfrey."

"Maybe she'll want you to help recommend books for her book club," he joked.

I almost fainted at that. One million followers had nothing on being part of Oprah's Book Club team.

At my lack of humor, he sobered again. "Okay, everything is going to be okay. Do you want me to put Theo on your social so he can filter through everything for you?"

"I...Theo?" I frowned, trying to figure out if he was speaking English. "Um...ah, n-no. Not right now, thank you."

He didn't look pleased, but he didn't fight me. "I know it doesn't feel like it, but I swear, you'll get used to it. It just changes how you use social media. Consider DMs a thing of the past. Ignore your notifications and turn them off on your phone. Post and walk away. Otherwise, it will absorb every minute of your life, free or not."

I tried to swallow, but my mouth was sticky and dry.

He eyed me, bending down to get to my eye-level. "Are you all right? You're so pale."

A tired smile tugged at my lips. "You say that like it's news, Tommy."

He ignored the joke. "What do you usually do to calm down? De-stress?"

"Bubble bath, book, and sometimes baking."

"The trifecta of Bs," he said, almost smiling. "I'd ask you if you had a book to read, but since I carried *thirty-two* boxes into your room yesterday, I feel like you've got options."

The tension in my shoulders eased when I laughed, the shock waning. I wondered what percentage of that could be attributed to the warmth and comfort of his hands enveloping mine.

"Aren't I supposed to be reading for you?" I asked.

"Trust me, if I had something for you to read, I'd foist it on you with more insistence than I did our marriage."

"Too bad you don't write romance, or I'd beg you shamelessly for it."

At that, his smile turned salacious. "I don't hate the idea of you begging me shamelessly for anything."

I tried to cover the surging fluster with a roll of my eyes.

"And anyway, I *could* write romance. I just *don't*."

"You say that like it's easy."

He shrugged like an arrogant jerk. "Romance *is* easy. Paint-by-number. Kiss here. Conflict there. It's got beats just like any genre fiction."

My frown turned into a full-blown scowl, and I removed my hands from his in order to fold them across my chest petulantly. "I call bullshit."

He chuckled. "I can't even handle it when you swear. You're like a little bunny rabbit with a filthy mouth."

"Stop hedging," I shot, poking him in the chest. "Why don't you put your money where your mouth is, *Mr. Bane*? Write me something to read in the tub."

Now he was frowning too, and I tried not to gloat when I caught a flicker of doubt in his eyes. "Need I remind you, *Mrs. Bane*, that I'm on a deadline for a fantasy that is definitely *not* meant to be romance?"

I shrugged like that was his problem and not mine, ignoring the fact that he'd called me by my married name. "Make it work. Maybe it'll unjam something in your brain. I want a romance. I want tension and angst and sparks. I want kisses and squirming and longing."

Tommy's bravado rose with one corner of his lips. "All right, *wife*. You're on."

He stuck out the meathook he called a hand for a shake, and I took it, squeezing it hard.

I bet he barely felt it, the mutant.

Tommy grabbed his laptop and sat back on the couch, propping his feet on the coffee table. "What are you going to do while I write?"

"Bake," I answered without thinking.

"Bake what?"

"Everything," I said cheerfully as I hauled myself off the couch and wandered into his massive kitchen in search of baking supplies.

TOMMY

Come on, man. It's just a stupid romance. You can do this in your sleep, I assured myself firmly enough to believe it.

Amelia bustled around the kitchen as I opened a new document. A certain brand of hope filled me at the prospect of something *new*, the kind one only found in imagining outcomes that hadn't yet happened. Truth was, once the document was open and that stupid fucking cursor blinked scornfully at me, my brain emptied itself of all thoughts.

My gaze drifted back to Amelia. I only saw her ass as she leaned into the pantry, emerging with her arms full of flower, spices, and several cans of something I couldn't make out from where I sat.

Her face was alight, her hair up and cheeks rosy as the pile on the island grew.

"Do you mind if I turn on music?" she asked over the rattling of baking sheets.

"Not at all. I actually prefer it."

"Oh!" She carried the stack of muffin pans and cookie sheets to the island along with a bag of chocolate chips she'd scrounged up from who knew where. "Well, why don't you put yours on then? That way it won't distract you."

"All right." I pulled my phone out of my pocket, smiling as I connected to my living room speaker.

Wu-Tang Clan came on first in my shuffle, and I was just about to change it, certain the angelic little fairy in my kitchen would be somehow offended. But then she started rapping along with Raekwon to "C.R.E.A.M."

If we hadn't already been married, I would have proposed on the spot.

"I don't know if I'm more surprised that you're into Wu-Tang or that you know all the words to 'C.R.E.A.M.'"

Amelia laughed. "Rin loves them. We lean on Wu-Tang when we have bad days. Nothing pumps you up quite like Method Man, you know?"

"I do know," I said on a chuckle.

She bopped around the kitchen, collecting more supplies—bowls, bread pans, spoons. To be honest, I didn't even know where half of it had come from and made a mental note to send my interior decorator a fruit basket for hooking me up so thoroughly.

I looked back to the judgmental cursor and felt my mind shift, clicking into the track that led straight into my imagination.

My thoughts wandered through a repository of mythical creatures, finding footing in the classic fantasy bracket. Besides being my current interest, elves seemed to be the most romantic option, beautiful and elite with aristocratic rules that could provide conflict, especially if he were royalty.

I should name him.

I pulled open a list of Gaelic names and skimmed through. *Conlan, Deren, Elwynn… Wynn.*

I smiled to myself and jotted down some notes. *Wynn Morain, heir to the throne. High priestess prophecy that his father will die, and the throne will be lost. Relic needed. Stone? Book? Spirit?*

My attention shifted to Amelia, still rapping in the kitchen, though she seemed to have foraged for everything she needed and had begun measuring and mixing. Her big eyes were turned down, her hair piled on her head. Her nose was nothing but a button on her small face, an apostrophe between wide eyes and a small, luscious mouth. She looked like a sprite. Give her some wings, and she'd be the spit of Tinker Bell but with a far better disposition.

Nothing but a sweet fairy, making sweets in my kitchen.

And that was when the idea hit me like a Louisville slugger to the face.

My notes soon became too long to be considered notes, morphing without intention to a fully formed idea, like Athena popping out of Zeus's head, sword in hand and ready to take over.

Words—glorious, luscious, effortless words—poured out of me. Words that I'd thought had abandoned me, leaving me empty and without purpose.

But they hadn't. They'd only been sleeping, lying dormant,

waiting for something worthy to call upon them.

The story sprawled out, my mind stretching and yawning, my fingers flying. The words came too fast, too quick for my mind to relay to clumsy, out-of-shape fingers. But I didn't care about the typos or the missing punctuation I was certain had unknowingly made their way in.

I felt like a conduit, a vehicle. And before I realized how long had passed, I'd written three chapters.

I blinked at the screen, taking a look at the word count. I'd written nearly seven thousand words, which was roughly seven percent of a first draft.

And in ...

I checked the clock.

Three hours.

That can't be right. I rubbed my eyes, highlighting the text to recount the words. It had to be a glitch, an error. I'd never written that much in three hours, especially not at the beginning of a novel when I didn't know the world or characters or story. But there it was again, without error.

I glanced to the kitchen, feeling like I'd lost time, my knees aching from the long stretch on the coffee table, my neck stiff as I scanned for Amelia without finding her. But just as I began to list the places she might be, she popped up from behind the island with a tray of cookies in hand. The oven door thumped closed behind her, closed by her foot I figured, as her hands were full.

She smiled when she saw me looking at her. "How's it going?"

"I just wrote three chapters."

Her mouth popped open. "You're kidding. I mean, you looked like you were in the zone but ... *three* chapters?"

"Uh-huh," I answered, smirking.

Amelia had set the cookie sheet down and clapped, the sound

muffled by her oven mitts. "You did it! Send it to my Kindle."

Fear snaked through my guts, but I turned back to my laptop and did it anyway.

Maybe it wasn't any good. She'd probably hate it. I had no idea what she'd think, but chances were, it was a bust.

I closed my laptop with a snick and set it on the coffee table like it was covered in anthrax. When I stood, my knees popped, and my back screamed when it straightened after slouching on the couch for hours.

My smile found its way back onto my face. It had been years since I'd gotten so lost in what I was writing. I lifted my arms, clasping them over my head in a stretch as I walked into the kitchen. The island was covered in baked goods—cranberry muffins, two loaves of pumpkin bread, and a tray of cookies. Amelia had been transferring what looked to be the last batch onto a cooling sheet.

I say *had been* because she'd stopped midair, cookie resting on a metal spatula and her eyes locked on the sliver of bare skin over the waistband of my jeans, exposed by my arching back.

Not gonna lie. That was almost better than my word count.

She shook her head as if to clear it and brought the waiting cookie to the rack. Her eyes were glued to her hands. I decided not to tease her about the color of her cheeks, which was somewhere between the peach towel draped over her shoulder to the cranberries in those muffins.

"Well, you've been busy," I said, reaching for a muffin. "Where the hell did you find all of this?"

"In your pantry. Flour, sugar, baking soda, and powder. Chocolate chips, a can of pumpkin mix, a bag of dried cranberries. Didn't you know it was there?"

"No idea," I said, unwrapping the muffin, salivating furiously.

Her face quirked as she gave me a look. "Do you not grocery shop?"

"Nope. Theo has groceries delivered every week. I don't even put them away." I took a bite, and an unbidden groan climbed up my throat and surrounded the morsel of muffin. The tang of cranberry and orange filled my mouth. "Humuguh, Melia," I mumbled around the bite, opening my mouth to shove more in. "Disha 'mazing."

She smiled, lips together and eyes shining with pride. "Thanks. I used to make these with my mom. Though, honestly, it's so much easier not having to use her mixer."

I swallowed. "Why? Was it old?" I asked before stuffing what was left of the muffin in my gaping maw before reaching for another.

"No, it was one of her inventions, and it never worked right. If the motor didn't burn out, the beaters would clank and groan and ruin the dough. I'd rather use a spoon, but she never got it. *'Why use your own energy when a machine could do it for you?'*"

I huffed a laugh and took a bite. "Pretty sure that's the opening line to at least four Asimov novels."

She giggled and walked the cookie sheet to the sink. Everything she'd used—other than that and the spatula—was neatly lined up and upside down on a drying mat that I also hadn't known I owned. "So, tell me about your story."

"Nope. You're gonna have to read it for yourself and find out." I polished off the muffin, sucking the crumbs off my thumb.

"Ooh, going in blind. I like that," she said as she washed.

I crumpled up my wrappers, debating on a third muffin. But somehow, I rediscovered my willpower and tossed the wrappers in the trash.

The kitchen was so clean, especially considering all she'd baked while I was in the vortex, that the crumbs I'd shed while mannerlessly eating her muffins stood out like the clumsy mess it was. I scraped them off the quartz with the meat of my hand, cupping them gingerly as I made my way to the trash can and dusted them in.

"Feeling calmer?" I asked, leaning against the counter next to her, watching her dry the pan.

"Much. But I decided you were right."

My smile tilted. "Oh? I love being right."

She laughed and rolled her eyes. "I think I'll stay off social for the next week or so."

"Good idea. You ready for your bath?"

She stepped around me to put the tray in the drawer under the oven. "I don't know if I still need it. I feel so much better."

And she looked better, happier, when she straightened up and met my eyes. Her smile was so pretty, her cheeks a dusty rose. A smudge of flour made a track across her little nose.

I chuckled and thoughtlessly stepped into her, cupped her small face and brushed her nose with my thumb. "I think maybe it's not a bad idea."

She was still and stunned, caught. Her eyes locked on to mine, her lips parted. I didn't think she was breathing.

It was anticipation, crackling on her skin like static.

And God, I wanted to give her what she wanted.

But instead, I snagged her hand and towed her into her room, then her bathroom. The claw-foot tub sat in the corner, eating up the space like a glutton in the disproportionately large room. I reached for the ivory handles and started the water, testing the temperature before plugging the tub.

"I had Bea get you some of those…fizzy bath thingies. My mom loves those things. Let me see if I can find them." I rummaged through baskets on the teak shelf, crowing when I found the one I had been looking for. "There's all kinds of stuff, some oils and these fizzy things and bubble bath I think, too. Here," I said, offering the basket to her with a smile.

She took it, beaming. "Oh, I love these."

"I'll let Bea know."

She reached for my hand, propping the basket on her hip. "No, thank you, Tommy. She wouldn't have gotten them without you asking, and I appreciate that so much."

My face heated up, and I couldn't stop smiling. "Tell you what. Pay me back by not hating my story."

She laughed, releasing my hand. "No promises. Now, scoot. I'm gonna read and soak. Go eat some more muffins, and I'll be out in a bit."

I nodded and scooted out of there like she'd told me, closing her door gently behind me.

The moment it was shut, my brain freaked out.

First item of business: grab my laptop.

Second: relocate to the island.

Third: shove a cookie in my mouth.

Fourth: read over what I'd written.

My first thought as I stress-ate was that it could have been way worse. I edited as I went, tweaking sentences, all the while thinking about what she would think when she read each passage. Would she have liked it better written like this? Would she hate Wynn? Would she get what I'd done? Would she think it was as empty and vapid as everything else I'd written? Would she hate Aislinn?

Would she know Aislinn was her?

Would she know that the story was ours?

The first time I read through it, I was frantic and skimming and finding everything wrong. The second time I read it, I calmed down a little, though my stomach ached, gnawing painfully on itself, and only in part for the half-dozen warm cookies I'd devoured.

It was after that second read-through that I really started wigging out.

It began with pacing. Elevated to me standing outside her door, alternating between poised fist and ear to the door. Ended with me calling myself a baby and pouring a glass of scotch to prove that I did in fact have some sense of self-control.

I tried to stay away from the cookies. That was probably the hardest part of all.

I finished the scotch and once again lost my cool—I was midstride on the path for her door just as it swung open.

Amelia shot out of the doorway and across the room, her hair twisted up in a fluffy white towel and her small body swathed in a bathrobe so big, I wondered if she could bring her arms flush to her sides.

But her face was alight with disbelief, her smile split wide. "Tommy!" she called as she flew toward me.

"What?" I said cautiously and not without my own disbelief.

She stopped just inside my personal space, and I had to stop myself from reaching for her.

"It's amazing."

"What?" I said again, squinting like I hadn't heard her right.

"It. Is. *Amazing*." Her hands clasped, and she clutched them to her chest like a cartoon character. "Wynn is perfect—powerful, dark, but oh my God, his one-liners had me rolling. And Aislinn... she was plucked right out of her acolyte position and yoked to him, thrown into the limelight. It... it's *us*, isn't it? You're Wynn, and I'm Aislinn, except you wrote this tension that's just... *gah*. I'm dying. Dying! You have to write more. When are you going to write more?"

I was still squinting at her, waiting for the *but*. None came.

"Are you... are you serious?" I asked. "You actually *like* it?"

"Like it?" she huffed. "I *love* it. Tommy, you did it! You fucking did it!" She was giggling, giggling and bouncing, her smiling cheeks as red and shiny as a cherry from the heat of her bath and her excitement.

When I started to laugh with her, she threw herself into my arms. I caught her around the waist and stood straight, lifting her feet off the ground, squeezing her tight.

"I can't believe it," I said into the towel around her head.

"I can," she said, still laughing.

Her arms relaxed, and I let her down to find her smirking at me.

"Now, go write me some more."

The Fine Line

TOMMY

I **whipped the tennis ball with** as much force as I could, laughing when Gus took off like a shot, a blur of blond fur in hot pursuit of the slobbery green ball.

"He's practically airborne," Amelia said on a chuckle.

I smiled down at her. She sat on a red plaid in Washington Square Park, a shock of white on the deep crimson—white wool coat, white knit hat, blonde, blonde hair, and cheeks rosy and high. The arch stood proudly in the distance, the fountain still and quiet for the winter, the square packed with people.

We'd been walking through the park every day for the last week when the weather permitted, and always at the same time. The routine had bred a slight following of paparazzi, though they hung around the fringes, relying on wide-angle lenses. It gave us at least a modicum of privacy, though the regular joes who visited the park weren't always as discreet.

But today, we'd been largely left alone. Amelia smiled up at me.

the sight of her so picturesque I reached for my phone.

"Pretend like you're reading," I said, opening my camera.

She laughed, but obliged, and I moved around until I got her framed up. One shot—that was all it took.

Amelia was that perfect.

"Did you get it?" she asked.

I was already texting it to her.

"'Gram that," was my answer.

She picked up her phone and inspected the photo. "You are the best thing to ever happen to my Instagram, you know that?"

"Well, I guess we're even then," I said as Gus approached.

"Like your Instagram needed help," she volleyed on a laugh.

"You're the best thing to happen to me."

Neither of us had time to speak before Gus skidded to a halt at my feet, dropping the ball with a bark.

I chucked it, and Gus spun on his paws, taking off again.

"Are you all caught up on reviews?" I asked, changing the subject.

Thankfully, she let me. "I am. I finished a review this morning, and I'll have the last book on my list finished tonight, if we read instead of watch TV."

"Deal. Jessica and Dain are about to get married in *Lord of Scoundrels,* and if they don't bone soon, I might actually die."

She shook her head with a laugh. "Ready to tell me I was right yet?"

I shrugged. "Eventually."

"Well, fortunately, I'm a patient woman."

"God knows that's the truth. You married me, didn't you?"

Another laugh. "I'm so glad I'll have all my commitments out of the way. It hasn't been easy, reading for my blog and the paper *and* helping you. I'll be glad for a break."

"I've been monopolizing you. I'm sorry."

"Oh, don't be. I much prefer working with you. To be honest, I'm a little burned out. It's hard when you're not reading for fun anymore. When it's a job, it…changes things."

"Man, I know how that feels. I miss the days when writing was pure, fearless. Expectations change things." I nodded to her Kindle in her lap, the case closed. She'd been reading my manuscript. "Finished already?"

"Mmhmm," she hummed, looking down at her hands as she absently fiddled with the device.

Instantly, I was frowning. She'd just read everything I'd written today, and I knew immediately that whatever the news was, it wasn't good.

"All right. Let's have it," I said to the thundering of Gus's paws as he approached. I reached for the ball in his mouth, grateful I had something to do while she crushed all my hopes and dreams.

"It's…good."

"What a glowing endorsement." I chuffed a laugh, muscling the ball from Gus's jaw, so I could throw it, putting all the heat I could on the pitch. The neon ball sailed away in an epic arch.

"It's just…" She paused, unfazed by my butthurt sarcasm. "It really is good. But it's missing something. It's…it's like you're holding back. I don't understand how they *feel*. I mean, they're on their way to the dwarf city, Aislinn was just attacked by Deirdre's minions—God, I *hate* her—and the action is great. He protects her, saves her, even as she saves *him*. It's her spell that blows them all up—which was fantastic, by the way. It's *good*. I just don't…I don't *feel* it. Their connection is superficial, but there's more there. I…I can't put my finger on it," she said half to herself.

"I suck at romance." I watched Gus as he hauled ass back to me. He was finally slowing down though, and I hoped he only had a couple pitches left in him before he was finally worn out.

"You don't suck at romance. But you have to change your

perspective. You have to peel back the layers."

I frowned. "I don't understand what there is to peel. He likes her, feels responsible for her, thinks she's beautiful and smart. He respects her. That's all there is to it."

"That's why you have to dig. Push into them, into the uncomfortable places of their characters. It's not about what you think they'll do or what you think the reader will want. What motivates them? What do they *want*? What lie are they telling themselves? What's the lie they believe?"

The thought struck me, stilled me. "He wants her," I said simply, my throat tightening painfully at the realization in my own heart. "He's tired of the pretense, tired of holding back how he feels. His lie? It's that he's in control. But is anyone ever in control of their hearts?"

Her eyes were bright and wide, peering up at me with absolute innocence. "That's perfect. Then could this scene be the moment he realizes it?"

Gus careened into me, nudging me off-kilter. And I took the excuse to tumble down onto the plaid with Amelia, Gus hysterically licking me, then Amelia, then me—whomever he could get his tongue on. Amelia squealed, hands in front of her to try to block his access.

I wedged myself between them, putting Gus at my back. And then I laid her down, shielding her, caging her.

She smiled, unafraid, unabashed, just happily gazing at me as if it were the most natural thing. As if it weren't fake.

I'd only just realized the truth of the matter.

I'd insisted on these daily walks because they were my favorite part of the day.

She thought it was pretend.

She didn't know this was the only time when I *didn't* have to pretend.

Here, I was free to touch her, to kiss her, to lay her down in the grass and make her laugh. I could hold her hand here. Here, I didn't have to wish. I didn't have to long for her.

Here, I could have her.

Her hands were on my chest, then my jaw, her eyes darkening, smoldering. Because she knew I needed to kiss her just as well as I knew she wanted me to.

I'd never put a move on her when we were alone, never even brought it up. I hadn't realized just how badly I wanted to, how desperately I missed moments like this when we were alone.

Could this be the moment he realizes it? she'd asked.

"I don't know how he hasn't realized it before," I answered.

Recognition passed behind her eyes the second before I kissed her, tasted the sweetness of her, the long, languid flex and relax of her lips and mine, of my tongue and hers.

I wanted her. I wanted more.

I just had to figure out how to tell her.

AMELIA

Conversation flowed around me, the dinner table as lively as always. Theo's lasagna sat in the center of the table, Tommy at my elbow, his mom and Theo across from us, just like every night. I'd adopted my seat at the dinner table where we ate when we didn't go out.

Everything was the same, except Tommy.

His familiar dark eyes were charged, sparking with a fire I didn't understand. Something had changed, and I'd felt it from the moment he kissed me in the park that afternoon.

We'd been talking about the book one minute, and the next had given me the distinct feeling we weren't talking about the book at all. It'd felt like he was talking about him. About us.

And I had no idea what to make of that.

It couldn't have meant what I thought it meant. He was just being Tommy, the charming, cavalier cad he always was.

I redrew the line in the sand between what was real and what was fake.

Theo kicked his head back and laughed. "Jesus, Billy Kowalski always had it comin'. He couldn't keep his mouth shut for anything."

Tommy chuckled. "He thought he was safe behind his toadies. Little did he know."

"When he broke Charlie Wilson's glasses, I thought you were gonna flip," Theo said with the shake of his head. "Poor kid."

"I know. Who would pick on a kid like Charlie? He couldn't have weighed more than eighty pounds."

"Nah, I meant Billy. You broke his arm in two places."

"And you broke his nose," Tommy added.

Theo shrugged. "I wasn't gonna let you take on that whole pack of shits by yourself."

Sarah shook her head, but her smile was doting. "Nobody in the neighborhood would mess with the Banowski boys. When they were back to back with their fists up, nobody was getting through them. They were the first boys in their class to hit a growth spurt. They were pushing six feet and had Adam's apples the size of a baby fist the summer before ninth grade."

The thought of Tommy and Theo standing inside a circle of thugs sent a little thrill through me. "You two are quite the pair," I said on a laugh.

"Always have been," Theo said.

"Nobody else I'd rather fight the good fight with. We're a team. Theo always has answers."

"Even though you hate them."

"I don't always hate them."

Theo gave him a look.

"All right, I usually hate them, but you're always right."

"I dunno," he said soberly. "I regret suggesting we set you up with Olivia. If we hadn't kicked you off in the tabloids, maybe things would be easier now."

"Or maybe they wouldn't," Tommy added. "It's been good for me and bad."

"Have you ever thought about getting out?" I asked.

The twins shared a glance.

"Tommy tried once," Theo admitted.

A shadow passed over Tommy's face. "Starving them only made them hungrier. Two months in, and somebody broke into my house. A week later, a crowd spotted Theo, thought he was me, and mobbed him. They broke his arm. That was the last time I tried."

"I'm so sorry," I said softly, sorry I'd asked.

But Tommy's lips tilted in a smile. "I learned my lesson and got back in line. Can't fight the gossips. You gotta feed them, keep them happy. Otherwise, you're swinging blind in a losing fight."

Sarah sighed. "Gossip might be the end of us all. When their dad left, I got my fair share. The boys, too. Tommy almost got kicked out of junior high for popping a kid in the mouth in the cafeteria line for suggesting I had a ... *night job*."

Tommy's jaw clamped, the muscles at the corners flexing as he ground his teeth. "Anybody who calls my mother a whore would be lucky to walk away with just a fat lip. He'd be lucky to walk away at all."

With a shake of her head, Sarah said, "It wasn't true though. Why not let him think what he wanted?"

Tommy's eyes narrowed, and he leaned forward an inch that felt like a mile. "There are two things in this world I can't abide: liars and people who believe the lies."

"Even at personal detriment, we know," Theo added. His gaze

shifted to me. "He has a deep sense of right and wrong, black and white. And when those lines get crossed, there's rarely any going back."

Tommy frowned. "I don't think it's unreasonable to expect people to be honest."

"Things aren't always black and white though," Theo argued.

"Maybe not for you."

"See?" Theo said with a smirk. "There's no reasoning with him. You're a saint for putting up with him, Amelia."

"Oh, it's not all that bad," I teased.

"That's because you are inherently honest," Tommy said. "It's one of the many reasons I married you."

There it was again, that zing of electricity, the tremor of change. We all chuckled, brushing the joke away as just that—a joke.

But I couldn't shake the feeling that there was more to it, some undercurrent of truth, too vague to pinpoint, too obscure to snag.

I had to be imagining it. It was a daydream, a wish, a desire I couldn't feed. Because nothing could be more foolish than letting myself believe that Thomas Bane could actually want plain old, boring old me.

I might be naive, but I wasn't born yesterday.

Faux No

TOMMY

The speech I'd prepared echoed off the walls of the McGraw Rotunda in the New York Public Library, the faces of attendees rapt and focused wholly on me.

Well, for the most part.

I couldn't help but note each one that was turned to Amelia, who sat next to Theo in the chairs just off the podium, hands folded neatly in her lap. Her face was turned to me, her smile serene and proud and absolutely lovely.

We'd been married for almost two weeks, and in that time, I'd crushed nearly fifty thousand words. The story had been coming fiercely, swiftly, and with a healthy helping of discussion. Amelia read everything as I went, offering her advice and changes, arguing her points with fire and determination I never would have expected from her when I first met her.

But if I'd learned one thing, it was that Amelia had opinions, and

So long as the recipient wasn't a stranger.

Our days had slipped into a comfortable routine. Write in the mornings. Walk Gus. Edit in the afternoons. Dinner at a hot spot or with Ma and Theo. Evenings spent curled up on the couch, reading together.

Work had become *easy*. After a year devoid of ideas, the surge of productivity was addictive. Every day, I would write, and she'd sit next to me, editing. When I got stuck, she'd unstick me. When I thought I had everything wrapped in a neat little bow, she'd untie it. And when I had my plot straight, she'd throw a kink in it that would inevitably make it stronger, better, *more.*

In short, Amelia was magic.

Steven agreed. I'd sent him the first five chapters, sure he'd tell me it was garbage, too romance-driven. Amelia and I had done a lot of work to make sure the plot was more of a driving force to the romance, but the romance was strong. Aislinn and Wynn were fire—complementing each other and challenging each other in a way I found not only refreshing, but familiar.

The metaphor for my relationship with my fake wife was undeniable, the two of us chained together by fate as equally as by choice.

We spent every waking moment together, from our first cup of coffee until we said goodnight. We'd worn side-by-side divots in the couch with our asses. We'd walk Gus through Washington Square after lunch for brainstorming sessions almost every day.

I'd developed a sick habit—one that fed my growing desire to tell her how I felt—of scrolling social every morning, first thing. I'd lie there in bed in the quiet morning and smile at my screen at the photos of us, the articles, the speculation. *In Touch* had a poll going as to when she'd get pregnant, and *Us Weekly* had an article devoted to what we should name our fictional child.

I'd been in fake relationships for almost a decade, one after another after another. Most of the time, we hooked up, but it was more out of convenience, safety, and a way to help us sell our affection publicly. Some—like Genevieve—became friends, confidants. But never had I truly opened up, and never had I given myself over.

A few weeks with Amelia, and I was finding the allure of her impossible to resist.

I resented being caged with her at home, the moments when I wanted to touch her and couldn't. There, I found myself tugging at the restraints, always looking for a reason to show her affection. Being in public with her was so much easier, somehow more real to me. Here, I could show her how I felt without crossing any boundaries. We had agreed to it in advance, consent given, and I took the action without a second thought.

I'd tried in earnest to convince myself that it was the proximity that left me wishing for more. She was *safe*, honest and kind, innocent and beautiful. Her help was motivated just as much by her compassion as it was for herself, a saint immortalized in the novel I was writing.

Maybe it was that Wynn was falling for Aislinn desperately, fiercely. Maybe art was imitating life. Or maybe life was imitating art.

When I factored it all together, there was only one answer: the way I felt about Amelia went far beyond a business partner.

Most people didn't want to make out with their business partners.

Beyond that, the stunt had worked. Blackbird was thoroughly pleased with the turn in my image. Book sales were up, and bad press was down. Everyone wanted to know about Amelia, about our relationship, clamoring for photographs and digging for the real story. I'd become a reformed scoundrel, and the media was attributing the change to Amelia.

They weren't wrong.

Theo had been very, very busy. And Amelia had decided to forego social media for the time being—thank God. If she lost her purity and innocence to the media, I didn't know what I'd do, but I imagined it would involve gasoline and a felony.

As my speech came to a close, I glanced back at Amelia, smiling at her with fondness I didn't have to fake as I addressed her as *my wife* and talked about our mutual passion for reading and early literacy. I scanned the faces, making sure to pass over Vivienne Thorne without making eye contact, which unquestionably drove her insane.

When I thanked them, they clapped and stood, more in an effort to disperse rather than give me an ovation.

Questions began, and though it wasn't officially a junket, I was prepared.

I was also prepared for the questions to have everything to do with Amelia.

I skipped Vivienne three times, fielding superficial questions about our wedding and how I'd proposed. I was going to skip her again, but she stood and spoke out of turn in the lull, pad in hand and recorder going in her pocket, I was sure.

"Mr. Bane, do you have any response to the claims that your marriage is a publicity stunt to salvage your career?"

Tension zapped between Amelia and me, the two of us so in tune, we nearly had a full conversation through the connection.

But I gave Vivienne my most charming smile and said, "I'd say that they've never met Amelia. Anyone who knows her also knows she's far too good for me. I'm just lucky she wasn't snapped up already because she's as vital to me as air, water, and scotch."

A wave of chuckling rolled over the crowd.

Vivienne smiled humorlessly. "This isn't your first fake relationship though. Is it, Mr. Bane?"

My smile fell, hardening with my brow and eyes. "That speculative claim is old and worn out, Ms. Thorne, and an insult to my wife. I'd call you heartless, but that would imply you to had a heart to begin with. Having read your exposés, I think we can all agree you don't.

Next question," I said, breaking eye contact and dismissing her in the same motion.

Begrudgingly, she sat as I listened to and answered a question about my next release, which eased my heart from the snakebite Vivienne had left. And a few minutes later, Theo stepped up, indicating my time was up.

I said goodbye to another round of applause and traded places with my brother, who took a few more questions.

I only had one objective—Amelia.

She smiled bravely, though her eyes sparked with fear and anxiety. She was isolated by the barrier of space and propriety that barred anyone from hassling her. But that barrier was thin, and I suspected Vivienne had punched a gaping hole in it.

I extended my hand, and as soon as hers rested in the curve of mine, I tugged it gently. When she stood, I wound an arm around her waist and pressed a kiss to her flaxen hair.

It was far more for her than the crowd.

My relief was tangible at the contact, the lines gone, wiped away.

I longed to hold her like this where no one could see.

She made to shift away from me, but I held on to her. She looked up at me, a curious smile tugging at her lips as the conversation went on around us, the attention on Theo.

Her small hand rested on my chest. I felt the warmth of it through my tailored shirt.

"What?" she asked quietly, her brow flickering with intrigue and amusement.

"I was just thinking how good we are together."

She chuckled, rolling her eyes. "You and me and our curated relationship?"

"Mmhmm," I hummed, glancing at her smiling lips, deciding I needed to taste them while I had the chance. "Smile for the cameras."

I caught her bottom lip in mine, kissed her tenderly, cataloged everything—her small body melting into mine, the feel of her waist under one palm and her cheek in the other, the scent of her silky hair that brushed my knuckles.

When I broke the kiss, her eyes stayed closed, not opening until a sigh slipped out of her. And even then, her lids were heavy, drunk from the kiss.

Lips together, I smiled sideways at her. "Careful, people will think we're in love." I twitched my head to the crowd, who was still occupied with Theo.

Her cheeks flamed, but she laughed openly.

I tried not to pout. "Would that be the worst thing?"

Another roll of her eyes, though she was still laughing. She leaned back, but I didn't relax my grip, and her hands moved to my biceps. "Tommy, you're ridiculous."

"You say that a lot," I said, working to keep the salt out of my tone.

"Well, it's true. Do you take anything seriously?"

She was joking. But it pressed a bruise on my heart.

"I take a lot of things seriously," I said quietly, the words heavy with meaning. "Writing. My family. You."

Her smile faded for a heartbeat but flashed back as she laughed again, swatting my arm. "Stop messing with me."

"Who says I'm messing with you?"

Her eyes widened, then blinked. "What are you talking about? We would never work, you and me."

"Why not?" I asked earnestly, thumbing the pale satin ribbon tied around her slender waist, not sure I wanted the answer.

"W-well … *because*," she answered as if that single word explained everything.

"Because why?"

"Because it's a terrible idea, Tommy. I … I don't know how to date, and starting now would be … would be … *irresponsible.* There's no separation, no boundaries of space. We live together, work together. It's just too complicated."

"I don't believe that."

She was laughing again. My ego shuddered.

"Tommy, stop goofing around."

"Admit it, Melia. We're good together."

"You are a mess."

"I know I am. And you balance me."

"Babysit you."

I shrugged. "Same thing. And I make you brave."

She chuckled. "That's true."

I pulled her closer, bringing her hips and thighs flush against me. "I like making you laugh, and I like seeing us together all over the internet. I like holding your hand. Touching you. Kissing you."

That officially got her attention. Her smile fell, and this time, I had a feeling it wasn't coming back without the help of another kiss.

"Tommy…that's…we can't. That's *crazy.*"

"Is it?" I asked, still holding her face, searching her eyes. "We're good together. Admit it to me."

The color rose in her cheeks again, warming my palm. "No, I will not, sir," she said on a breathy laugh, proving me wrong about her smile. "Now, kiss me once more for the cameras, and let's go have lunch. I'm starving."

A realization set a fierce fire of disbelief in my guts.

She didn't believe me.

She didn't think I was serious.

She couldn't imagine that she was my last thought before I slipped off to sleep and the first thought when I woke. That her smile, her touch, her laughter and opinions and approval were the impetus of my entire day. Every day.

She didn't believe me.

And I was going to convince her of the truth.

The challenge rose in my chest along with a determined smile of my own. "Oh, I'll kiss you all right. And I know you want me."

"And how do you know that?"

"Because of this."

I pressed my lips to hers once again, my intention singular—to dissolve her will and melt her into a puddle of submission. And I did what I'd set out to do. I branded her with my lips, spoke the truth without the necessity of words, the kiss searing.

Our chemistry was undeniable, as hard as she might try to convince me otherwise. This was an area where my expertise became gospel.

And my kiss left her soft and willing in my arms.

I'd forgotten we were in the middle of a library with a seated audience until they broke out clapping and whistling.

Amelia broke the kiss with a pop and an owlish glance at the crowd. I only smirked, offering a bow, hanging on to my wife so she didn't hit the deck—her knees were useless. I could feel their trembling all the way up her spine.

Theo shook his head at us but smiled. Vivienne stared with enough heat, I was certain she was attempting to napalm us with her brain.

And I felt like the king of New York Fucking City.

Because I was right about Amelia and me. And I meant to prove it to her.

Made in the Bronx

AMELIA

Claudius rumbled in my arms the next morning, his head tucked under my chin. I drew back my bedroom curtains with a sleepy smile on my face.

Snow fell in swirling eddies against the backdrop of brownstones, floating down between anemic branches of the oak outside my window. It was beautiful and silent, the bends and curves of the tree catching snowflakes. The sidewalk and street were blanketed in white, the sight idyllic and temporary. Two hours from now, there would be nothing but gray mounds of sludge. But for now, it was serene and peaceful.

My bedroom door creaked open behind me, and I turned to find Gus trotting in with a floppy bear in his mouth. At least, I thought it was a bear. It had no eyes, one ear was missing, and it was short one arm. The other dangled off its shoulder, waving gently as Gus slowed to an amble.

"Hey, buddy," I cooed, which triggered a violent wagging of his tail

He nosed me hard enough to nearly knock me over.

Claudius glanced down at Gus apathetically as the dog chuffed and snorted around his bear, tail swishing.

I kissed Claudius's furry head and deposited him on the bed. Gus flung his front paws on the mattress, ears perked and eyes eager, but Claudius only flicked his tail and hopped away, leapfrogging up various articles of furniture until he was perched on top of a bookshelf, looking down at us imperiously.

Gus seemed disappointed but followed me into the kitchen, forgetting Claudius almost instantly when he spotted his tennis balls. He bounded over to them and began the task of trying to fit a tennis ball in around his bear.

I shook my head, smiling at him as I made my way to the coffee pot. It was already full, and my mug sat next to it, waiting to be filled.

My smile stretched wider. I filled up my cup, only just noting the sound of Tommy's running shower.

I still found myself surprised that he'd given me his room, but that was the kind of man Tommy was. Fiercely loyal. Compassionate and giving. When it came to the people he cared for, he would do anything to ensure their happiness and comfort even if it meant sacrificing his own.

So he showered in the guest bathroom and left me the big soaker tub in the master. Upstairs were more bedrooms and his office, which he hadn't worked in since I'd been there. Instead, we spent all our time in the living room and kitchen, working side by side, eating side by side.

We'd slipped into our routine so naturally, I hadn't had time to feel a shred of doubt or warning. Everything about him was easy. His smile, our conversation, cohabitating. He even made being in front of people and cameras easy—he was a human shield, his purpose singular. To protect me.

It was spoken in every action.

We're good together, I heard him say in my mind.

My cheeks warmed at the memory of the kiss he'd proven his point with yesterday.

He wasn't wrong. We *were* good together, and that thought was as terrifying and disastrous than I had the heart to entertain.

Tommy was… *Tommy*. He was bold and brave and brash. He was confidence and certainty. He was experienced and evocative.

He was so far above me, on another planet, another plane. As much as I trusted him, I knew on some level that I was a novelty. A little tchotchke to smile at and hold under the light and admire.

We'd become friends. I knew he cared for me. But his suggestion, his admission that he wanted more—more kisses, more touching, just *more*—was unnerving. And not because I didn't want that, too. But because we were in a bubble, a protected space of him and me and nothing else. I was a shiny new toy. I was safe. I was a lot of things, including his *wife*, but I wasn't capable of being his girlfriend.

A laugh huffed out of me at the irony. And my heart lurched at the reminder of the truth.

None of this was real.

I turned to the island, leaning against it to look into the living room. Gus was still trying to unhinge his jaw in an effort to fit every toy he owned in his eager mouth, and I watched him, amused.

My phone buzzed from the pocket of my robe, and I reached for it, hoping it was my friends. When I saw Janessa's name on my screen, all hope sank and soured.

Let me know when you can come in next week. Want to talk about your assignment.

My nose wrinkled up like cellophane.

We hadn't seen each other since the meeting we all had after the wedding, though not for Janessa's lack of trying. She'd been getting more aggressive. This time, she hadn't even asked. She'd commanded.

And I had zero good feelings about the impending meeting. It wouldn't be so bad if Tommy could come with me. But she wanted me. Alone.

None of it boded well for me—or for Tommy, if I were being honest.

I caught myself frowning and sighed, smoothing my face. I was sure I was worrying over nothing. Janessa had been fully briefed and agreed to Tommy's terms. She probably just wanted to talk through a proposal or outline or something. Normal, edit-y things.

Gus barked in frustration at the second tennis ball, the sound muffled by his bear.

"You are so silly," I said, shaking my head at him.

He perked up, turning to me like he'd forgotten I was there. I was just about to call him over when the hall bathroom door opened, consequently stopping the earth's orbit and flinging me into space for lack of gravity.

Thomas Bane stepped out of the doorway in slow motion, propelled by a cloud of steam that licked at his glistening body like it wanted to taste him. His hair was black, wet, curling and dripping in rivulets down the planes and valleys of his expansive chest and abs and narrow hips. He had that thing, the trough of muscle bracketing his hips that caught sluicing water and carried it in an angle that would eventually reach that unknown terrain beneath his towel. I saw the ghost of that terrain, the long, cylindrical bulge that was substantial enough to clearly state its presence, even through the thick towel.

He smirked, dragging his hand through his wet hair. I salivated, watching droplets of water roll down his forearm and collect on the tip of his erotic elbow.

"You're up," he said.

I blinked, not knowing when I'd set my coffee down or how

many minutes—hours? years?—had passed in the time I spent ogling his body.

He sauntered into the room like he wasn't basically naked. I tried unsuccessfully not to stare at his knees, the place where his ropy thigh connected, the angular muscles of his calves, the curve of his ankle, the broad pad of his foot.

He was perfectly proportioned. Michelangelo would have carved him twenty feet tall, and women would have worshipped at his perfect feet.

Gus bounced when he saw Tommy, his toys forgotten. And when Gus took off running, Tommy stopped, eyes widening and hands splayed in front of him.

"Gus, *no*," he commanded.

To no one's surprise, Gus did not listen. He barked once, snagged the hem of Tommy's towel, and whipped it off him in a single tug that exposed every inch of skin on Thomas Bane's ridiculous body.

Thank God my coffee was already on the counter. I'd have gotten third-degree burns.

For a split second, Tommy was frozen there in all his natural glory, poised to run after his dog, his face drawn and eyes locked on the sweet, disobedient dog. He wasn't paying any attention to me.

I, however, gave him my full and undivided consideration.

His thighs were a mass of muscle so hard and defined, the tops were planes that came to a notch at his knee and a point where it met his hip. My eyes caught that trough that had before disappeared and followed it where it pointed—straight to the thatch of dark hair and the member nestled there.

The very thick, very long, mostly limp member.

If I stared at it a second longer, I was going to faint—my vision was already dim, my pulse pumping so hard, I could feel it in my neck, at the back of which a cold sweat had broken.

But he shifted to run after Gus, who was galloping away, trailing the towel behind him.

"Dammit, Gus! Gimme that!"

Then it was the back of him I saw, his hair, the streaming water rolling down all the curves of his shoulders, his back, the valley of his spine, and down to the most perfect ass I'd ever seen in real life.

Well, the *only* ass I'd ever seen in real life that wasn't my own, and even that I couldn't get a good look at without a mirror.

Seriously, that ass. That perfectly sculpted ass, round and tight and curved in the sides, shifting from one side to the other as he ran after the damn dog. My gaze caught a tattoo on one ass cheek, and I squinted at it, trying to make it out.

Tommy bent to snag the end of the towel—I caught sight of his sack and almost dissolved through the floor in an acidic puddle of embarrassment—but when he pulled, Gus spun around, ass in the air and tail wagging as he growled, pulling back.

A string of obscenities left Tommy's mouth, but I was still gaping and staring at his ass. I realized that I was laughing. It sounded like someone else in a different room.

I wondered if this was how it felt to have a stroke.

Tommy was locked in an epic battle of will with Gus, the towel taut and caught in Tommy's massive fists. He pulled hand over hand, eliminating the distance so he could grab Gus by the jaw, clamp his fingers in the soft spots, and squeeze.

Gus opened up, panting so wide, he looked like he was smiling. And then he bounded away, heading for his bear again like he'd already forgotten the whole ordeal.

Tommy's face was hard, his eyes still on the dog, towel in hand as he walked across the room again.

He almost reached the kitchen when he seemed to remember I was there.

I was staring at his dick.

"How's the view?" he asked.

And when I looked up at him, his smirk was so smoldering hot that I gripped the countertop, grateful for its cool comfort.

I resisted the urge to press my flaming cheek to it and close my eyes.

"I…oh God, I…I'm sorry…I just—"

Tommy laughed, a comforting sound that filled the room, easing my mortification.

Him covering his junk helped. I couldn't think with it flopping around like that.

"Don't be sorry," he said. "Just promise me tomorrow you'll come out for coffee in your towel so Gus can return the favor."

I groaned and covered my face with my hands, which was a mistake. Burned on the backs of my eyelids was the vision of Tommy's dick.

My eyes shot open when my hands dropped, my lips pursed so tight, they were pinned hard between my teeth.

A flicker of concern flashed behind Tommy's eyes, but he was still smirking, that bastard. "You okay?"

"Mmhmm."

"You sure?"

"Mmhmm."

For a second, he watched me. "Melia…have you ever seen a naked man before?"

"Mmhmm. Loads," I answered with numb lips.

One dark eyebrow arched. "Loads, huh?"

"I watch porn like any other red-blooded American," I said with bravado I didn't feel.

He laughed with an astute certainty that he knew something I didn't. "Not quite the same as flesh and blood though, is it?"

I shrugged and picked up my coffee. "If you've seen one, you've seen them all."

Mischief. Mischief and meaning skated off his skin and reached for me. "Oh, I don't think that's true at all." His voice was low and raspy and thick with intention.

An awkward, nervous laugh bubbled out of me, and I used the moment to change the subject, tangentially at least. "I have to admit, I didn't peg you for a tattoo-on-the-ass kind of guy."

He let me shift the conversation, but something in his smile told me he wasn't letting it go.

I thought he was going to explain himself, but instead, he turned around and dropped his towel enough to expose that imposing, mathematically perfect muscle. It was close enough to touch, but I clutched my coffee mug like a lifeline, leaning forward to get a better look.

Tattooed in a typewriter font on the sculpted globe of his ass were the words *Made in the Bronx.*

Laughter bubbled out of me, and Tommy glanced over his shoulder with that ridiculous sideways smile of his before returning the towel to its rightful place around his waist.

"What?" he asked. "It's true."

I rolled my eyes, though I was still giggling. "I'm sure your mother is proud."

He shrugged one gorgeously naked shoulder. "She's always proud. And I'm always trying to make her proud."

"Even with your USDA ass tattoo?"

"Sure. It's part of who I am, part of my past. I didn't want to forget where I came from, and I think that *is* something that makes Ma happy."

God, I didn't know how he did that. How he could be this pillar of flesh and stone and beauty that set me on fire like he did and make my heart ache and long and yearn in ways I'd only found in fiction.

My smile softened. "Well, when you put it like that, I think you might be right."

"I have my moments," he said with a hotshot wink that was too fucking sexy.

It wasn't even fair.

On that, he turned for his bedroom, rustling Gus's ears when he passed. And I watched him all the way, shaking my head over my coffee.

Because, boy, did the Bronx ever turn out some winners.

Homemade Dynamite

AMELIA

"**If he's a grower and** show-er, you are in so much trouble," Val said on a laugh.

I groaned, but Rin and Katherine shared in the laughter at my expense. We sat at our favorite table at our favorite bar for the first time since I'd gotten married. It felt like a lifetime ago, a different girl, a different universe.

"I find it interesting it wasn't completely limp," Katherine said. "I can only assume it was because he liked that you were watching him exit the shower."

"Pretty sure anyone with a pulse would have watched him exit the shower like a thirsty, thirsty perv." I picked up my drink and sighed. "It's just *not fair*. How am I supposed to withstand that?"

Katherine shrugged. "Don't."

I snorted a laugh. "That's funny."

Confusion pinched her brow. "Why?"

"Because Tommy is homemade dynamite—unstable, lethal, and

with unknown potency. He'd blow me to smithereens."

Val snickered. "I bet he would."

I rolled my eyes. "Please. My vagina would have no idea what to do with him."

"Well," Rin started, "he said he likes you, didn't he? That he… that he wants to date you? Kinda?"

"He said we were good together, and honestly? We are. We work well together. We never fight. We're constantly laughing. When he kisses me, all the planets start moving backward and the stars flip upside down. But how in the world am I—Amelia Hall—"

"Bane," Katherine corrected.

I rolled my eyes. "—Amelia *Bane*, virgin and mute and utter know-nothing, supposed to agree to letting a man like Tommy through the gate?"

Katherine was too serious to be serious. "If by gate you mean your vagina, it's really just a matter of unlocking your knees so he can get to it."

Rin and Val broke into laughter.

My face flattened. "I meant to my *heart*."

She shrugged. "Heart, vagina—they're basically the same thing."

I ignored her. "His idea of *good together* could be one of a million things, and none of them bode well for me. He would eat me alive, whole, in one bite."

Katherine made a face like she was about to crack a joke.

I pointed at her. "Quiet, you. I mean it. I am *way* out of my league here." My eyes fell to my drink, and my heart twisted in my chest. "I'm having a very hard time keeping the line between Thomas and Amelia Bane, public oddity, and Tommy and Melia, business partners and buddies, in place. I can barely even *see* the line anymore. I keep trying to draw it in the sand, but the wind just blows it away again. Poof." I exploded my fist to illustrate.

"I'd say to just make out with him, that it's not like you're getting married, but…" Val said, smirking.

"I know. Even if I wanted to make out with him…" I paused, correcting myself. "Even *though* I want to, it's just a bad idea. A bad, horrible, terrible idea."

At that moment, we turned to the sound of a stranger calling my name, weaving around tables toward us. But before she could reach us, the two brick walls Tommy had sent with me stood from the table in front of us, arms folded. She bounced off them like a ping pong ball.

Rin shook her head. "This is so weird."

"Tell me about it."

Val frowned. "Sam and I saw a guy taking our picture with a camera lens the length of my forearm yesterday. If you Google any of us, there are now paparazzi pictures and mentions in *Us Weekly*."

"You seem to be adjusting well," Katherine stated. "You don't really look nervous at all, not like usual."

With a sigh, I smiled. "Tommy's like my security blanket. Nothing can touch me when he's there. I'm pretty sure if someone tried, he'd go berserk and separate someone's head from their body."

"But Tommy's not here, and you're"—Katherine assessed me—"confident."

"Fake it till you make it, right?" I said. "The more I pretend and the more I'm around people, the less scary it is. Exposure therapy for the win."

"Have you been online much, Amelia?" Rin asked. "I keep seeing your posts on Instagram but only book-related stuff."

"Not to scroll, no. All I do is post and then bolt. I never hang around. It's just too much. But to be honest, being offline is so refreshing. I didn't realize how obsessive I was about social until I couldn't check it anymore."

"I don't even know how you do that," Val said.

"Tommy deleted everything but Instagram from my phone, and he turned off the notifications for that. It's been surprisingly easy. We've been posting all our fake-personal stuff on Tommy's."

"Oh, we know," Katherine said. "We've been stalking his feed."

Rin melted next to me. "The story he posted with you guys baking? Oh my God."

"When you smashed that cookie in his face, I almost died," Val said dreamily. "Even Sam was all gooey about it."

I laughed. "Tommy is the best. We spend literally every waking moment together, and never once have I been annoyed or needed space. I…" I sighed, the sound heavy and forlorn. "I don't even know if I can face the truth."

"The truth of what?" Rin asked gently.

I didn't meet her eyes. I locked my gaze on the ice cubes in my drink and said the words aloud that I'd been avoiding for days. Weeks. Since the first time I met him.

"That I like him. That I want him to want me. That I want him to kiss me as much as it terrifies me that he will."

"You kiss all the time," Katherine noted. "The two of you in a lip-lock populates an entire Instagram."

"That's different. That's *fake.*"

Her face flattened. "How many times are you going to fake kiss before it becomes real?"

"Oh, I don't know, but I think I might have reached that limit," I said miserably. "Why did he have to tell me he wanted more? I wish he'd just kept it to himself. Because now that I know how he feels, I'm even more confused. How can I say no? How can I say *yes*?" A shake of my head, my eyes still cast down. "This was the arrangement, and I'm well aware of what I'm capable of. I would gladly make out with him in the safety of public where it's fake. But opening the door to be together in private is a step too far. I don't know *how* to do that, what it would even mean. And I guarantee I would end up hurt. Besides, we have so much work to do. If something happened, if we fought or broke up or... I don't know. If I left now..."

"He'd write it on his own," Katherine finished, ever the pragmatist. "I'm only suggesting that things are already moving in that direction. Why not go for it?"

Heat rose in my cheeks again, this time in defense. "Because I'm scared. Because I don't know what's real and fake anymore. I don't know how to feel or what to do or how to answer him, because if I know Tommy at all, he's not going to just let it go. I'm caught in the limbo of expectation. Tommy's pressuring me—"

My friends sat straighter, the air tightening.

"Not like that," I assured them. "If I really told him no, he'd leave me alone. But that's the trick. Because I don't *want* him to leave me alone. But I need him to. I'm stuck. Stuck and screwed and not screwed because I'm a stupid virgin."

I huffed, picked up my drink, and set it down before taking a sip.

"I have never been so sorry to be this inexperienced. If I had any experience at all, I wouldn't hesitate. Well, not much at least," I amended. "But there's no way to do this without putting my heart in a slingshot and firing it into the Grand Canyon." I made a splat sound with my mouth.

Rin took my hand, her face soft. "I get it. I really do. But Val and I have both been where you are—scared, unsure, and up against something that seems insurmountable. We took a chance even though it was scary. And *you* helped convince us to jump. I think we should return the favor."

"This is different," I said.

"Is it?" Rin pressed.

Val flashed a smile, stuffing her hand into her bag. When it reappeared, it was with her tube of Heartbreaker in hand. She clapped the flat end down on the table like a gavel.

I rolled my eyes. "Oh God."

"I hereby call a meeting of the Red Lipstick Coalition to order. We promised to be brave, Amelia. To be bold. You've got your lipstick on right now. Don't you dare betray it."

I put on my most magnificent frown.

"You like Tommy," she noted, "and he likes you. You have chemistry. You're friends. You're *married*, Amelia. And Tommy cares about you. He wouldn't have told you if he didn't mean it, would he?"

"No," I answered softly.

"No, he wouldn't," Val agreed. "Most girls got their first kiss behind a temporary building in middle school. Most girls lost their virginity to a tuba player with acne in the back of a truck. Tommy is offering you the ultimate—a beautiful, rich, kind, funny, *experienced* man to be your first *everything*. So you might get hurt. That is the sad, unavoidable truth. But if that were a reason not to give your heart to a man, neither Rin nor I would have found love."

Katherine nodded. "Has Tommy given you a reason to think he doesn't mean what he says? Any reason to think he wouldn't be honest and true when it comes to you?"

"No." My heart ached and twisted against the admission. "He wants to cherish me, just like he promised. He wants to protect me, just like he does with everyone he cares about."

Rin turned to me, her eyes full of encouragement and hope. "Amelia, don't do anything you don't want to do. But don't be afraid of what you *do* want. Talk to Tommy. If he wants more than just the physical, then maybe you should consider it. Because that seems to be what you want too, isn't it?"

My bottom lip slipped between my teeth. I didn't want to answer.

Katherine gave me a nod. "You are one of the best judges of character I have ever known," she said with conviction—which for

Katherine meant a slight inflection in her typically flat voice. "Trust that. If he wants you to admit your feelings, maybe you should."

At the thought, I felt the urge to fold in on myself until I disappeared.

"And if you decide not to get physical with Tommy," Val said, "we got you a little something. Consider it a belated wedding gift."

She pulled a white box wrapped in silver ribbon out from the bench seat and slid it across the table to me.

For a split second, I was excited—maybe it was fancy wine glasses or a pour-over coffeemaker. But then I registered their faces, which were rigid as they tried to stifle laughter, and my ass clenched tight enough to make me an inch taller.

I pulled the tail of the bow, cursing them in my mind. For a split second, my hands rested on the lid of the box, and my head shook at the three of them.

"Oh my God, open it!" Val finally squealed.

I drew a noisy breath and held it, lifting the lid of the box.

For one stunned second, I stared at the veiny purple dildo, wondering if it was ten inches or a full foot of silicone dick. And then I slapped the lid back on and tried not to sink out of the booth and under the table.

They laughed, those bitches.

"You are all so lucky I love you," I said, folding my arms across my chest.

Val cackled. "Not as much as you're gonna love Donny Dong."

I groaned. "You did not name it. You didn't."

"*I* didn't," she insisted, hand pressed to her chest. "Sexbangers. com did."

I swiped the box and put it in the booth next to me, ignoring the gargantuan cock as it thumped the inside of the box. "What the hell am I supposed to do with this?"

"Well," Val said seriously, "so you take it like this—" She gestured.

I died right there on the spot. "Oh my *God*."

Rin laughed. "Leave her alone, guys."

"Thank you," I mumbled.

She offered a comforting smile, and I returned it, wanting to stick my tongue out at Katherine and Val.

Rin took my hands. "Talk to Tommy. Maybe there's another option between the two of you."

"And if not, Donny will take good care of you," Katherine said.

Our laughter was loud enough to garner looks from a few surrounding tables. And there, in the company of my friends with a big purple dick in a box sitting next to me, I found it hard to be afraid.

I just hoped I could hang on to the feeling.

And I hoped that when I gave Tommy my heart, I wouldn't lose it forever.

Donny Dong

TOMMY

Gus popped to his feet and took off for the door before Amelia's key slipped into the lock.

I smiled, closing my computer as she worked her way through the door around Gus, her voice high and happy as she greeted him.

"Hey," I called, hauling myself off the couch. "How was girls' night?"

"Good," she said, shaking the snow off her coat over the mat before hanging it up. She'd set a box on the bench, wrapped in a silver bow.

"What's in the box?" I asked as I strode over.

Her face turned a painful shade of red. She swiped it off the bench and clutched it to her chest, her crimson lips flat. "Nothing."

I laughed, folding my arms across my chest in challenge. "Nothing, huh?"

"Nothing at all," she said evasively, nose in the air as she tried to scoot past me.

I snagged her around the waist, eliciting a yelp. I pulled her into my body, her back to my front, and twiddled my fingers in her ribs.

An eruption of giggling bubbled out of her between protests. My free hand found the base of the box.

"Come on, Melia, lemme see."

"Ah! No! Stop it—*ahhhhahaha*!" She squealed and squeaked and wriggled against me.

I almost forgot about the box completely for a second.

"What's in the box?" I asked, inching my tickling hand higher.

"Nothing! Ah! Tommy, oh my God, *stop*!" She laughed the words, defying the laws of speech.

"Not until you gimme the box," I answered, curling around her to bury my face in her neck.

"Oh!" she gasped around giggles, arching her back.

The surprise had the desired effect. Her hand relaxed long enough for me to yank the box free.

"Aha!" I crowed, whipping the box away from her and into the air where she couldn't reach it.

She spun around. Her eyes shot wide, irises ringed with white like a spooked horse. "Tommy, gimme that. *Gimme*!" She jumped for it, scrabbling at my arm.

"There's no way I'm not finding out what's inside of this. You should have told me it was tampons or footie pajamas or something."

She groaned, her face tight and flushed with mortification.

"Hmm, what could it be?" I said as I turned for the kitchen. Her hands were all over me, and that in itself brought its own satisfaction. "What could have you so worked up, Melia? Maybe it's an—*oof*!"

I lurched as she jumped on my back like a monkey, one arm around my neck tight enough to crush my larynx, the other reaching for the box. I didn't have time to jerk it away. Her fingers caught the lid. The box tumbled out of my hands and hit the ground, the lid flying off in a somersault.

The contents rolled out and bumped into my bare foot.

We froze, staring down at the purple silicone dick, the cacophony of sound and motion gone instantly. Her heart was beating so hard, I could feel the thump of it against my spine. Her breath was shallow in my ear.

I burst out laughing, hinging at the waist to prop my hand on my thigh. Amelia let go of my neck and slid off my back. But when she stepped around me and her hand entered my field of vision, I snapped to action and swiped the dildo before she could get her little hands on it.

"Tommy," she groaned. "Give that back!"

I turned to face her, making a show of inspecting the rubber cock with both hands and my full attention. "Twelve whole inches. This might set some unrealistic expectations."

"Oh my God," she said from behind her hands.

"I mean, Jesus. This thing is like an Easton." I grabbed it just above the balls and swung it like a baseball bat, clucking my tongue with a pop like I'd cracked a homer.

Another groan. Her face was so red, her eyes sparkled like diamonds.

I smirked shamelessly and spun it like a helicopter in front of my hips. "That is some serious heat Stevie Schlong is packing."

"Donny," she squeaked.

My brows knit together, and I glanced from her to the purple cock. "Donny?"

"Donny Dong, not Stevie Schlong."

"You *named* it?"

"I didn't," she huffed, lunging for it. "Sexbangers.com did."

I laughed, holding it over my head. It flopped uselessly around. "Him or me, Melia? Take your pick."

"Him," she said without hesitation, jumping for it. "Now, *give it!*"

"Donny Dong with the floppy schlong, diddled Amelia till it didn't feel wrong."

"Ugh, you are *the* worst, Thomas Bane!" Her face scrunched up in anger, and she stepped back, propping her hands on her hips. "It was a gift. I did not ask for it or buy it. I wanted a pour-over, not a dick! And certainly not a dick *that* big." She flung a hand in its direction. "I don't think that'll even fit into a single orifice in my body."

I inspected it thoughtfully for a second, then held it out, closed one eye, and measured it against her torso. "Hmm, you might be tasting plastic for a week if you get it all the way in."

Her brows were so close together, there was nothing but a single angry crease between them. "You are awful."

I pretended I hadn't heard her and took a step toward her. "But you know something?"

She didn't budge.

I didn't waver. My eyes were on the cock, and my cock was thinking about her. "You can take more than you think."

Her eyes were hard, but I didn't miss the flicker of desire behind them.

I shrugged and offered the purple dong, which she swiped from my palm and tucked comically under her arm.

"I'm sorry for teasing you," I said.

Her annoyance eased only marginally.

"But that was the highlight of my week."

She let out a weighted sigh, but she was smiling.

I considered that a win.

"I got you something," I said, nodding behind her. "It's in your bedroom. I mean, it's not a footlong or anything, but I hope you like it anyway."

She rolled her eyes and marched toward her bedroom. I followed, smiling like an asshole.

"It's on your bed."

She humphed, not slowing until she was near the foot of her bed where a large, flat white box waited.

I leaned against the doorjamb and folded my arms with a smile on my face. She tossed a curious look over her shoulder, and I jerked my chin at the box.

"Go on. Need me to hold your dick for you?"

She rolled her eyes and set it down on her bed. I found myself disappointed she hadn't gripped it like a spear and chucked it at me.

But I forgot about Donny almost immediately when her fingers hooked the lid and pulled.

Her gasp was small and sweet, her hand reaching in to stroke the red velvet cloak. "Tommy, this is gorgeous. What's it for?"

I pushed off the doorframe and strode over, hitching a leg on the edge of the bed, opposite her. "It's Aurora Park's birthday—"

"The Victoria's Secret model you used to date?"

"Fake date," I corrected. "And yes. There's a charity event tonight that she sold tickets for. All proceeds go to the purchase of new books for the library. Everyone is supposed to dress up like storybook characters. Bea got this together super last minute. She'll be here to help get you ready soon, if you want to go."

Amelia opened the cloak and picked up the black bodysuit underneath. She held it up and cocked an eyebrow at me. "Where's the rest of it?"

"Oh, did I forget to mention it's a *lingerie* costume party?"

Her face flattened. "Tommy…"

"I was going to decline, but the thought of you in lingerie was too much to resist."

Color smudged her cheeks.

I chuckled and reached into the box, unpacking everything so she could see. "I told Bea to make sure you'd be comfortable." I gestured to the bodysuit. "Black with red piping, a little red bow for around your waist." I set it down. "Opaque thigh-highs." I flicked the red satin ribbon that would tie them. "The only skin anyone will see is a sliver of your chest and this." I snagged her chin in my thumb and forefinger, relishing in her smile. "Your cape even has sleeves and a long red tie. Try it on."

I grabbed it and stood, and she stood with me. I unfurled the velvet cloak, sweeping it over her small shoulders. She slipped her arms into the wide sleeves as I tied the thick velvet fastener in a knotted bow, leaving the tails dangling almost down to her thighs. And then I brought the broad hood over her head.

She looked up at me with uncertain blue eyes, her blonde hair loose and shining against the deep red of her cape. The cut of the cape was brilliant, sweeping the ground, ruffling like liquid. The hood was so big, and it draped gorgeously. The smaller layer that doubled over her shoulders opened up to frame her breasts and waist in the most perfect of proportions.

"What do you think?" I asked quietly.

"I think I can't believe I'm about to go to a nightclub in underwear."

I laughed, arranging her cloak so I didn't have to stop touching her. "So I did good?"

She smiled, her cheeks rosy. "You did good, Tommy. Little Red Riding Hood, right?"

"Yup."

Her smile lifted on one side. "Are you the Big Bad Wolf or the hunter?"

"Guess."

She laughed. "My, what big teeth you have."

I hunched my shoulders, drawing my face closer to hers, my smile wicked. "All the better to eat you with, my dear."

Her chin tipped as she giggled. My hand had fallen to her waist, and by its own will was pulling her closer.

But she didn't pull away. She leaned into me, her hand braced on my chest.

"At some point, you're going to acknowledge this," I said with quiet meaning.

Her smile faded, but her lips parted, her lashes swept up and eyes willing. "This what?"

"*This*," I echoed, tightening my grip on her waist. "I'm tired of pretending I don't want to kiss you." My eyes were on her lips. The words were absent, murmured from my heart. "I want to kiss you whenever I want and whenever you want me to. But I won't. Not until you're ready."

Lashes flashed. Breath stilled. Lips parted, waiting.

"Tommy…"

The tone of the word hooked my heart. I couldn't tell if it was with permission or denial. So I didn't let her finish.

Instead, I gave her a smoldering smile and kissed her nose.

"Don't worry. You'll see it soon enough." I let her go and took a step back. "And in the meantime, I'll be waiting."

She chuckled like I was kidding, her eyes sweeping the ceiling and smile relieved or disappointed—I couldn't tell. And I gave her a wink and left my heart in there with her when I walked away.

Big Bad Wolf

AMELIA

We stepped out of the Mercedes to chaos.

I couldn't see anything for the flashes, couldn't think straight for the screaming of our names. But Tommy had me solidly against him, sweeping me into the club, my red cloak snapping behind us.

My legs felt a trillion miles long—which was funny, considering I barely cleared five feet. The combination of the thigh-highs and patent leather mid-calf boots with the fact that I was wearing nothing else but underwear and a cape had me feeling brash and badass and utterly unstoppable.

And here I thought I'd be self-conscious. But I wasn't.

On Tommy's arm, I didn't know how I could.

Bea had done me up with the works—winged liner, ruby-red lips, my hair shining, tumbling out of my hood in gleaming Hollywood waves. I looked like an innocent dominatrix. And oddly, I didn't hate

When I saw my reflection in the mirror earlier, I almost chickened out.

Charity, I'd told myself. *Books! A party for books—there's nothing bad about that. This is what the young and beautiful do. They put on their underwear like it's outerwear and get publicly drunk. Think about the photo ops. Think about Tommy.*

To be honest, I'd worn sluttier costumes than this at Halloween.

Okay, that was a lie. The closest I'd gotten was a square dancer. But there had been some very risqué knee going on with that one, and in this, you couldn't even see my knees at all.

The thought had made me feel better even though I didn't know that I'd ever looked so…sexy. But the truth was, I was nervous, uncomfortable—not because of how I looked, but because I knew people would be looking at me. And I wasn't sure they'd like what they saw.

Until Tommy whisked me out of the car. And I realized I had nothing to worry about, not one little thing.

Tommy's naked arm was around my waist, covered in goosebumps, and his nipples were tight and hard from the freezing temperature.

It was a lingerie party after all. But given the fact that lingerie wasn't really a thing for men, he'd gone with *mostly naked*. His jeans were black as his hair and fitted to his gorgeous thighs and calves, the band hanging low enough on his waist to see that V. And trust me when I say everyone saw that V. Even the bouncer took a second to stare in curious wonder at the depth of the valley as we hurried inside. His feet were clad in his combat boots I'd come to love, half untied and tongue gaping like he'd just thrown them on and headed out the door. Which was exactly what he'd done.

But on his head and slung over his shoulders was a wolfskin, the mouth of the beast capping his head, his dark hair spilling out and brushing his shoulders. The legs and paws hung down his chest, the hind legs and tail down his back.

He looked savage, like a warrior from another time, another place. Another existence, where he'd clutched a knife made of obsidian to take what he wanted and to protect what was his.

The wolfskin was a fake—there was a moment after I'd gathered my wits from the sight of the wild, primal man I'd married and looked into the glass eyes of the wolf with anguish. But Tommy had shown me the underside, which was fake leather, the fur synthetic.

And thank God for that. I'd almost burst into tears at the thought that it wasn't.

Inside, the club was thumping, the bass so deep and loud, I could feel the waves pass through me, thrumming my bones and flesh in pleasant pulses.

Through the mostly naked crowd we wove, Tommy first and me in the wake created by his massive body. Every face followed us, cataloging everything, but my heart was beating too hard and fast for me to pay them any mind. I just wanted to get out of the crush of the crowd, and Tommy knew it, too. Up the stairs we went, to a balcony of booths and tables beyond a velvet rope and a stern brick in a suit who nodded to us as we passed.

The entire space seemed to be devoted to the party we were attending. From corner to corner were people in costume.

Correction: immortal goddesses and demigods in costume. They were too beautiful to be human.

I recognized a dozen models, scanned the faces of two dozen more who, if they weren't models, should be. There were at least four actors who'd been in major motion pictures and a handful of Billboard Top 100 musicians, and that was just counting the ones I could see. At least a third of the party had another human wrapped around them like a stole.

Aurora Park squealed from across the room and ran—*ran* in platform heels that gained her at least eight inches of height—toward us. Tommy didn't let me go, but he put himself between us in case she was going to jump for it. The way she was swinging her drink around, the insides sloshing dangerously as she hauled ass across the room, I figured she'd been partying for some time.

"Oh my *God*, Tommy! You look *amazing*!" She flung herself into him and planted a big old kiss on his cheek.

He peeled her off, and once she was stable, he let her go and reached for me, tucking me into his side.

Her face stretched into an O as she *awww*ed at us.

"Rory, this is Amelia Bane, my wife."

She smiled so genuinely, I decided I didn't want to trip her when she walked away after all. She flung herself at me this time, grabbing me around the shoulders for a crushing hug.

"Amelia, I am *so fucking happy* to finally meet you!" She twisted me with every syllable of *so fucking happy*, and I couldn't help but giggle. She leaned back to look at me. "God, you are the cutest fucking thing in the entire world. And look at you two together!" She shook her head at us, smiling proudly. "You two are *dapper as fuck*."

Tommy pulled me back into his side. "Happy birthday, Rory."

"Thank you," she said on a curtsy. "Guess who I am?" She held up her hands and did a twirl. Her teddy was black and royal blue, a red capelet on her shoulders and a red ribbon in her black hair. Her legs were clad in thigh-highs the color of a daffodil. The rear of her getup was sheer with a red satin bow just over her ass, the tails hanging down to almost hide her crack.

Almost.

"Snow White!" I cheered. "That is *fantastic*."

She hooked an arm over my shoulder and smirked at Tommy. "I like her."

"Me too," Tommy said, smirking back.

"Come on," she said, pulling us as she pointed with her drink to the crowd. "Let's get you guys some drinks."

We made it all the way to the bar before she got distracted and flitted off, leaving us alone again.

I sighed and smiled up at Tommy. "Aurora Park thinks I'm cute."

He laughed. "You're not cute, Melia. You're hot."

I blushed and rolled my eyes. "I can get behind cute. Adorable even. But hot is a level I will never achieve."

His dark eyes glinted, his brows lowering, drawing together. But that pouty, sideways smile stretched. He pulled me into him and held me against his body. Heat waved off his naked chest like a furnace.

"That's where you're wrong. Never in my life have I ever wanted someone like I want you."

I opened my mouth to speak, but he kissed me instead, swallowing my objection. He took advantage of the shadows and the crowd, kissing me deeply, telegraphing things he'd said and things he felt, things I didn't believe until he kissed me like that.

He made me feel as beautiful as he'd said I was.

My arms were wound around his neck, my hips pressed into his, and my back arched away as he dipped me gently. And then he broke the kiss, though he didn't let me go. Instead, he smiled at me, his eyes hot as coals.

"Believe me now?"

My tongue was useless now that he was done with it. So I nodded.

He chuckled and set me to rights before towing me to the bar to get a drink.

I'd never been so grateful for liquor in my life.

We wandered around the party for the span of a couple of drinks, at which point, my bladder made its size known.

I squeezed Tommy's bicep, which probably felt like a butterfly kiss to him. But it got his attention all the same. He lowered his ear to my lips so I could tell him what I needed.

"I'm gonna go freshen up my lipstick."

He frowned and turned to me. "Are you okay?"

"Yes," I said on a laugh. "I really am going to fix my face and pee."

He relaxed, smiling. "All right. Hurry back," he said, kissing me swiftly before letting me go.

I felt like a princess or royalty or some kind of badass as I floated to the bathroom and into a stall. I had a brief moment of terror as I wondered how the fuck I was going to get out of my costume on my own, but once my cape was hanging safely on the hook on the back of the door, I figured it out.

My relief was palpable. The thought of Tommy helping me undress was only slightly less mortifying than the thought of Aurora Park jammed in a bathroom stall with me. Assuming she could still see well enough to undress me.

It took slightly longer to put it all back together than it had to disassemble, but before too long, I was exiting the stall with a content smile.

Which instantly hit the black tiled floor when I saw the woman standing at the sink.

Vivienne Thorne smiled shrewdly at me in the mirror. "Hello, Mrs. Bane."

"Vivienne," I said tightly, carrying myself to the sink next to her. "Aren't you just everywhere these days?"

She shrugged a naked shoulder. She was dressed as a French maid—Lumiere's feather duster in *Beauty and the Beast* was my best guess—her costume consisting of a white Chantilly lace apron, a little lacy hat, garters, and cheeky panties. That was it. In the harsh fluorescent light, I could see the shadow of her nipples through the delicate lace and hated that they were perfectly pink and round and pert in the center of her stupid boobs.

"I make it a point to be everywhere my story is."

Adrenaline shot through me. I turned on the water, grateful that it was warm. My hands were ice. "I don't know what you're talking about, Vivienne."

"Sure you do," she said like I was a child. "I knew Tommy would be at Aurora's birthday, so of course I got a ticket." She assessed me. "I've got to admit, you've got that scared bunny look down pat. You're both good—even *I* almost believe it."

My teeth clamped together and squeezed until my jaw hurt.

She laughed, the sound beautiful and cruel. "The second I crack you open, everyone will know the whole thing is a sham, just like all Tommy's relationships."

My hands fell, my brows drawing together, my heart thundering in a surge of protectiveness and bravery. "Why are you doing this to him? To us?"

Her smile fell, her eyes steely and jaw set. "Because Tommy was a failure that stripped me of the things I wanted, and I intend to correct that mistake. Just as I intend to prove your marriage is fake. Really, I should be thanking you. You two are going to get me my job back at the *Times*. So smile for the cameras and watch your back." She pushed off the counter and leaned into me. "See you around, *Mrs. Bane*." Vivienne backed off, smiling coolly at me.

I couldn't speak. Or swallow. Or stop washing my trembling hands. Not until the bathroom door closed behind her.

I let out a shuddering sigh and turned off the faucet, reaching for the paper towels. I couldn't feel the tips of my fingers, they were so cold, and I only had one thought.

Escape.

I'd find Tommy. I'd code-word the shit out of this, and we would go home where it was safe and quiet. Where we didn't have to pretend.

I whipped open the door and bolted out, but when I turned the corner, I slammed into a big, broad, naked chest that smelled like oranges and cloves and *Tommy*.

"Hey," he said on a gentle laugh. But when he met my eyes, everything about him sobered. "What's wrong? What happened?"

I opened my mouth to speak, but my tongue was still so fat and useless. "Vivienne," I finally breathed.

He darkened like a thunderhead, pulling me into him, holding my face, searching my eyes. "Are you all right? What did she say?"

I shook my head, and his hands rode the motion.

A few people stopped nearby, watching us for signs of commotion. I could feel their eyes, the anticipation in the air.

"Come with me," he commanded.

My hand disappeared into his, and I followed him to the VIP dance floor. We were isolated there in the crowd, surrounded by people and noise and bodies, the music electronic and sensual, not too fast, just the right tempo to move to.

His hands found my hips, then his hips found my hips. We swayed, our bodies rolling to the beat. I was surrounded by him.

I was safe with his hands on my body, safe with his eyes locked on mine.

He bent, brought his lips first to my neck, then to my jaw. "I won't let her hurt you," he said.

"She's not going to stop until she blows this story, our secret. She wants to prove it's fake, and she will not let it go until she does," I said, my lips to his ear, my arms around his neck. "She'll unravel everything."

"Well, we know the truth." The words brushed the shell of my ear.

"What do you mean?"

He backed away so I could see his face, so I could see every line, every plane, every angle. So I could know with certainty that what he was about to say was honest.

"It isn't fake, not anymore. Not for me."

The band on my lungs was so tight, I couldn't breathe.

"You have become necessary to me in all ways. The worst part of my day is saying goodnight, and the best part is waking up to you. No," he corrected with a shake of his head, "the best part of my day is when we leave the house and I can touch you. I live for the kisses I'm granted and the warmth of your hand in mine. That's the only time it feels real—when we're faking it. I'm tired of pretending, Amelia."

I cupped his jaw, the scruff of his stubble scratching my palm. "I'm scared," I said softly. "I...I don't know how to do this."

He covered my hand with his. "I know, and I don't either. Not when it's real. I don't trust anybody, Amelia. I never have. Not until you."

"But why, Tommy? Why me?"

"Because you want to protect me like I need to protect you." He paused. "Am I right?"

"Yes," I breathed.

His grip tightened, his voice rough. "And you want me like I want you. You don't want to pretend. You want it to be real, this. What's between us."

I hung on to him with all my strength, which waned as all my power shifted to my heart. "Yes," I whispered.

Something in him broke open and poured out. He held my face in his palms, his eyes on mine with such intensity, I could see nothing else.

"Do you trust me?"

"More than anyone."

"Can I have you?"

Four devastating words, and my will crumbled into dust. "Only if I can have you, too."

A smile—a bright, brilliant smile—flashed across his face, relief spilling over him, over me, into me.

And then he kissed me, and gravity shifted into him.

I thought that I'd been kissed by him. I thought I'd known the power of such a thing, a meeting of lips, of tongues, a mingling of breath. A rush of desire and anticipation.

But that had been nothing compared to this kiss.

Slowly, deeply, his lips moved, drawing mine into his mouth to taste them, to own them, to know them. His tongue brushed mine, tangling, curling in languid motion that said one word, over and over, without ever speaking.

Yes.

It was the yes of his heart and the yes of mine, the plea of our bodies that twisted around each other in both submission and command.

It was too soon that his lips closed, his forehead pressing mine, our breath heavy and mingling. I couldn't open my eyes, couldn't find my footing, couldn't think about anything beyond the places where we touched.

And then he grabbed my hand and smiled.

"We're leaving. Now."

Kablooey

AMELIA

I **couldn't stop kissing Tommy.**

Not in the car, curled up in his lap like a purring cat. Not as we blindly climbed the stairs. Not when he opened the door and I almost fell into the entryway. Not when he kicked the door closed with his boot.

He leaned against the door, legs wide so I could fit between them, the never-ending kiss slow and lazy, an unhurried exploration by tongue and fingertip, by lips and palms.

Kissing Tommy was the most brilliant thing to ever happen to me.

One hand skated my waist, the other cupping my face, my body nestled between his legs and my hands resting on the hot, velvety skin of his solid chest.

I never wanted to stop kissing. Never ever, not for a million years.

Which was why I wore a full-blown pout when he broke away.

His lips were plump and pliant, swollen and smiling.

He chuckled, thumbing my bottom lip. "Because now we're home. Now we're alone."

My frown softened as I registered his meaning. "Oh," I said quietly.

"What do you want to do, Melia?"

I wound my arms around his neck. "Kiss you forever."

I pressed my lips to his to demonstrate, and for a long moment, that was all we did.

A laugh climbed his throat, exiting his nose and humming in the back of his mouth just before he broke away again. "Here? In the foyer?"

I tasted my bottom lip, which was slick and fat. "No, I suppose not." The words were tentative. I glanced behind me into the dim living room. "Where should we go?"

"It's up to you."

"Why is it up to me? You're the one with all the experience."

Another laugh through his nose. "That's exactly why it can't be me. Where do you feel good? Where do you feel safe?"

"Right here," I said with a smile, tightening my arms around his neck. He squeezed my waist, bringing me closer.

"In the foyer?" he said again with that damnable smirk on his face.

I laughed and kissed him, though nerves squeezed my guts with light fingers. "Is my room okay?" I hated the timidity in my voice.

But when Tommy's eyes softened, all I felt was comfort.

"Anything you want."

I pushed away and grabbed his hand. "Anything?"

"Anything at all," he said with absolute conviction as he followed me in the direction of my room.

Tommy's door was open, and Gus's head popped up from Tommy's unmade bed. One ear was flipped inside out, and his blinking eyes were only half open.

"Some watchdog," Tommy said on a chuckle.

I was trying too hard not to freak out to respond.

I led him into my dark room and let his hand go at the foot of my bed. My heart thumped painfully in my chest as I moved to the nightstand to turn on a lamp.

When I turned to face him again, he was draping his wolfskin on my armchair. The light kissed every curve of his bare skin, the shadows running in deep rivers in the valleys of his body. I ached to slip into the darkness of him as equally as I feared it.

He met my eyes, saw my fear, slowly stepped toward me. "I make no demands," he said, the words low and soothing.

He stopped when he was close. So close, I had to tip my chin up to see his face. To see the hard line of his jaw, brushed with dark stubble. His lips, full and dusky and wide. His brow, dark and low. His eyes, endless and black, devoid of light. They shifted to his fingertips as they grasped the tails of my cloak's tie, which whispered as he tugged, the velvet slipping against itself.

"All I want is you," he whispered.

He clasped the collar and lifted the cape away. Goosebumps pricked my bare shoulders as he tossed it on the bench at the foot of my bed. But the second his hands, so wide and hot, cupped my shoulders and skimmed down my bare arms, the goosebumps set fire and smoothed.

Tommy didn't kiss me, and for a brief, irrational moment, I thought it was hesitation. But I looked into his eyes and saw the truth.

It was permission he sought. And the realization deepened my trust in him like roots twining around my heart.

So I gave him all the permission in the world.

First in my kiss, a deep, long kiss coupled with noisy breaths and roaming hands. Then with my body as I shifted backward, telling him where I wanted to be.

In my bed.

His arm laced around the small of my back, his free hand bracing us on the bed as he laid us down, hovering over me, the kiss never breaking. My body twisted toward him, anticipating his weight, wanting it desperately, but instead, he stretched out beside me, kicking off his shoes with a one-two thump on the floor.

Our legs scissored together, my hips reaching for him, my lips open for him, my hands thirsty for him. I didn't question anything, not what my body wanted, not the shift and roll of my hips, not the deep ache between my thighs. The fulcrum of that ache found the hard ridge of flesh in his pants and dragged the long length.

A soft moan slipped out of me.

His breath was labored, his hand gripping my hip so hard, it hurt.

I broke the kiss, stopped my hips, felt the throb of my body, clutching empty space that wanted to be filled.

He brushed my hair back, cupped my neck. "You okay?"

"I...I'm sorry. I don't know w-what's the matter with me."

A smile tugged at his lips. "Nothing. Not one thing."

"It's just...I've never..."

"I know."

"But I..." My body thrummed, and my hips shifted, satisfied by the pressure they found.

Tommy's eyes darkened, smile fading. "I know." He pulled my hip, grinding me into him again.

I sighed, then pursed my lips and moaned again. "God, I feel...I feel...I think I could..." Again, my hips rolled, and his rose to meet me. The friction. I needed that friction, couldn't stop needing it. "Oh God," I gasped, feeling the tightness, the heat of my orgasm building.

At the sound, he shifted fractionally, separating us. "Melia," he murmured, reaching for my face. "Can I...can I touch you?"

My hips were already shimmying for him again. "Mmm," I hummed. "Please...I think I'll die if you don't."

At that, he chuckled. If I wasn't a writhing mess, I might have been embarrassed. But in that moment, I didn't give a fuck what he did so long as he touched me.

His hand, so big and warm, slid from my jaw and traced the curve of my neck as he kissed me, pressing me into the bed, flat on my back. His thigh—that thick, broad muscle—slid between my legs and nestled where they joined, his hips and hard cock pressed into my side.

It was the only place of awareness on my entire body until his thumb grazed my nipple, the shock of connection shooting to that aching point between my legs.

My thighs clamped around his. His tongue searched the depths of my mouth. My heart flung itself at my breastbone. I could feel my pulse in every place we touched.

His hand kept moving, trailing down my stomach, resting on my hip, tracing the hem of my bodysuit around to the tender, tingling skin so high on my thigh.

I reached for his wrist to brace myself as he slid his hand between us and cupped my sex through the fabric of my bodysuit, fingertip pressed to the dip and palm squeezing my aching clit.

I gasped, back arching, kiss breaking, eyes slamming shut. He nosed my temple, hand shifting in a grind that set me on fire from my very core. His middle finger stroked the line before fitting between my swollen lips.

My hips bucked, but he didn't let me go. I was pinned to the bed by his leg, his thigh adding weight and pressure behind his hand.

My face pinched, my hands scrabbling, one slipping into his hair and squeezing without knowledge of my strength, the other opening and closing in the sheets.

"I..." I gasped at the ceiling, chest heaving, hips wild. "I'm gonna—*oh*!"

He kissed my neck, my ear, his tongue slipping out, the softest groan puffing against my skin as his hand squeezed.

My body seized, stopped, started with a burst radiating from my center, pulsing around nothing and against everything, the relief palpating, the yes whispering, his lips lingering. And when I could breathe, he kissed me, fierce and deep, a hard press of his mouth on mine, a determined thrust of his tongue as his hand kept moving, moving like it was another part of him fucking me.

But when my desire faded, something filled its place.

Shame at my innocence.

I broke the kiss and curled into him, hiding my face as I tried to gain composure. I was so stupid, a stupid girl so inexperienced, I'd come with all my clothes on.

Even if I *was* wearing lingerie.

That hand that had just brushed my detonator skated my hip, then my ribs before slipping into my hair. He pressed a kiss to my crown.

"I'm sorry," I said, sounding so small and miserable.

"Sorry?" he asked, and I thought he might be smiling. "Why are you sorry?"

"B-because I…God, you must think I'm so lame." My throat tightened, burning against tears.

He leaned back to look at me, but I burrowed into his chest.

"Melia," he urged. "Look at me."

I shook my head.

"Please?"

I sniffled, blinking back embarrassed tears. "I'm sorry," I said again.

"Stop it. That was *hot*."

I stilled, now blinking in confusion. I looked up at him. "What?"

He was smiling that ridiculous smile of his, his eyes hot and hair falling around his face. "You wanted me that much, *so* much. Don't you know how bad I want you after that?"

A surprised laugh burst out of me. But I sobered when I

remembered the rocket in his pants. "Oh…should I…do you need me to…" I glanced down at the alluded-to member, straining against the confines of his pants.

He chuckled. "No, I don't need you to anything. Not until you can think about it without that look on your face."

"What look?" I tried to smooth my face, but he laughed, catching my chin in his fingers.

"That one. You look like somebody just told you you've got to eat monkey brains."

I barely had time to laugh before he kissed me.

It was an unhurried stretch and flex of lips, the languid slip of his tongue into my mouth. The satisfaction I'd found began to burn away as he set me on fire again. Our bodies came together, our breaths mingling and loud. For a little while, he made up the sum total of my thoughts. But my mind began to wander, wondering what was next. What else? Would he leave and go sleep in his room? Or would he stay here all night and kiss me like this? Would we sleep? Or would we…

My stomach clenched, though not with aversion—with anticipation. I decided something then and brought my lips together, leaning back so I could see him.

His lids were heavy, his ebony lashes long and sweeping as he looked down at me with a look I could only define as adoring.

My rib cage filled with something warm and tingling. I smiled. "Will you…will you sleep with me?" When his lips angled higher, I added, "I mean, like actual sleep, not like *sleep*, sleep with me, although if you want to keep kissing, I really, really want to keep kissing, too. I just don't know if that's too much or if it'll make…I don't know. Are you…frustrated?"

He angled his face like he was inspecting mine, his smile small and amused. "I'm a big boy, Melia. I possess nearly bottomless self-control—don't worry about me. I can wait. Okay?"

I sighed, the tension in my body easing with the exhale. "Okay."

"And yes, I'll sleep with you. But not *sleep*, sleep."

I chuckled.

"I'm glad you asked," he added quietly. "I didn't want to leave."

My insides liquefied. My hand cupped his neck and pulled, bringing him down for another kiss. His hand rested on my ass almost passively. I imagined him giving it a squeeze, and my thighs clenched involuntarily.

I had never been so horny in my life. Of course, I'd never had Thomas Bane's hand on my ass or the python in his pants pressed against my stomach.

First time for everything.

When I broke away, I said, "Come on, let's get ready for bed. I've got to get out of these thigh-highs."

He smirked. "Yeah, you do." His hand slipped from my ass to my thigh, his big fingers fiddling with the crimson satin ribbon. "Can I?" he asked gently.

There was legitimately no way to say no. I nodded like a dummy.

His eyes shifted to my thigh, his tongue sweeping over that pouty bottom lip of his, drawing it into his mouth.

I rolled onto my back, leaving my hand on his shoulder as he turned his attention to my legs. But he sat, pulling one leg over his thigh. His fingers hooked my bootlace, slipped in the crisscross, and tugged to loosen them. My heel rested in his palm as he squeezed and pulled, discarding the shoe with a thump.

Every nerve reached for him as his fingers approached the ribbon.

"I've been thinking about this all night," he said half to himself. "I've wanted to untie these since you walked out of your room in them."

With a whisper of satin, the bow unfurled. His fingers slid between the black silk and my skin, his thumbs hooking the edge. He dragged the stocking down the length of my leg, his hand riding every curve, skin to skin, all the way down to my ankle, my heel, the arch of my foot.

With almost absent reverence, he held my foot in one hand, cupped the back of my knee in the other, followed the line of my leg back up to my thigh, where he shifted to press a kiss.

That kiss fanned the fire in me, a fire that grew to an almost unbearable heat.

To my disappointment, he didn't linger. He reached for my other leg and repeated the process. When my legs were naked, he pulled them into his lap, knees together and bent, hips turned gently in his direction. He studied the lines of them with eyes and fingertips.

I wanted him to kiss my thigh again. I wanted him to keep kissing until his face was between my legs.

The thought shocked and excited me, the vision of his face buried in my heat, of my thighs slung over his broad shoulders. I tried to imagine what it would feel like and couldn't.

I desperately wanted to.

"Tommy," I whispered, and the word was a plea.

He met my eyes, leaned over me, capturing me in his arms, clutching me to his chest. "Yes?" he answered, close enough for his word to brush my lips.

"I...I don't know how to...how to tell you what...how to say that..."

"Just tell me. Just say it. The answer is yes."

Relief and courage rose in my chest. I drew a painful breath against tight ribs and let it out. "I want you to touch me. Really touch me. I want you to kiss me. Kiss me everywhere."

Everything about him darkened, heated up until he was crackling, his hand gripping my hip. "Melia..." The way he said my name, like I'd be his deliverance and his undoing.

I knew the feeling with exact certainty.

"Please," I whispered, terrified and desperate.

His hand moved to my face, his broad thumb tracing my jaw all the way up to the curve near my ear.

"Tell me if it's too much," he finally said, his voice rough and rumbling.

"It won't be," I whispered and pulled him down to me, my lips reaching for his like they needed him.

That kiss branded me with intention, with gentle demand, with the promise of his care and protection.

He kissed me until I was wriggling against him, my body hot as a struck match. Only then did he let my lips go, his hands forging a path that his mouth followed. First down my neck, brushing my naked collarbone. His fingertips traced the curve of my breast before nestling it in his palm. And then were his lips. A brush of tongue against the soft flesh above my bodice. His hands moving to the zipper at my ribs as his mouth closed over my peaked nipple through the cotton of the bodysuit.

A shock of cold air brushed the newly exposed skin of my ribs. It was too much feeling—the heat of his mouth on my breast, the chill of my exposed skin, the ache between my legs, the weight of his body against mine. I was a slave to sensation.

He shifted again, bringing his lips to mine for a kiss, a kiss meant to soothe, to warn me as his hand slipped into the V of open zipper to cup the back of my ribs, his fingers squeezing my back, testing my comfort.

To answer without words, I slipped my hand into his hair, my legs threading through his, my hips twisting to meet him.

It was the encouragement he needed. His hand shifted, skimming up my back, knuckles trailing back down. And then his fingers hooked in the bodice and peeled it away.

He didn't break the kiss. I could feel him whispering comfort with his fingertips and lips against mine.

My breast filled his palm, and he squeezed, the pressure a perfect, delicious sensation that spurred the kiss deeper.

All I wanted was to wriggle out of this bodysuit and feel the heat of his skin against mine. The urge was inexplicable, as was the realization that I wasn't afraid. I was too hot and bothered for logic or pragmatism.

I wanted him. I wanted him with a deep, wild desire that overrode all else.

On the recognition, I was filled with boldness. I unwound my arms without breaking the kiss to tug at the gaping bodysuit.

Tommy took over, first taking my hand to drape it over his neck again, the kiss slow and deep and probing. And with one-handed deftness, he peeled the bodysuit away, exposing first my breasts, then my ribs, then the rest of me. Down my legs it slid. I brought them up to shorten the distance, not wanting him to stop kissing me, not wanting to see my nakedness for fear it would put out my desire.

My eyes remained pinned shut, and I existed only in touch. His hot, hard chest against my soft breasts, his arms a vise, his hands splayed across my back, our necks bent as we wound around each other, unable to get close enough. He twisted, putting me on my back, pressing me into the bed with his chest. His thigh had found its way between mine again, the rough denim of his jeans rasping the skin of my legs.

I wanted those gone, too. I wanted him as naked and willing as I was.

Logically, I knew I wasn't ready.

But he had me ready to damn logic.

His fingers skated down the curve of my waist and hip, thumbing the black lace of my G-string. He slipped his hand under the band to grab my ass again, this time giving it that epic squeeze I'd wished for. My hips ground into him in answer or request. Both.

He moaned into my mouth, dragging his hand lower, taking my panties with him. I shimmied my hips as they disappeared, too.

And I was naked. Naked and pressed against Tommy. Naked with his hand roaming my skin. Naked with his tongue tangling with mine, with his lips hard enough to make a seam.

I held his lips in place by way of my arms around his neck, certain that if he stopped kissing me, I'd lose my nerve.

And then his fingertips trailed up my thigh.

I stilled, panting through my nose, his lips slowing against mine, cautious, cajoling as his fingers moved higher. Higher, until they slipped between my legs to cup my sex, just as he had before.

Only now, there was nothing between us but a thatch of soft hair. Such as to say, there was nothing between us at all.

His palm pressed the aching tip of me, his fingers at the threshold of my core. The longest finger curled, brushing the slick line, parting swollen lips to make way.

I gasped, the velvety feeling of his finger stroking me arresting all thought, all function.

My eyes stayed closed, but the kiss had ended, leaving me gasping at the ceiling. I could feel him watching me and found I didn't care at all. A squeeze of his palm, a flex of his finger. It felt foreign, invasive in the most delectable way, and my core pulsed as if it wanted to draw him in.

My hips rolled and shifted, wanting the same.

His breath was labored, his fingertip testing me, teasing me, drawing lazy lines up and down, tracing the rippling flesh. It circled the dip, the place that ached so deeply for him.

I clasped his arm, just above his elbow, my nails digging into his skin, trying to hold him still so I could force that finger into me. But he couldn't be forced.

He was, however, coerced.

The very tip of his finger slipped into my heat.

I whispered, "*Yes*," to the sky, my hand sliding down his forearm and to the back of his hand. I pushed.

He pressed, sliding into me to the knuckle.

I mumbled something even I couldn't understand, my hips rocking and shifting and certain of what to do even though I wasn't.

Another squeeze of his palm, the slide of his finger out of me and in again. The brush of his lips against my cheekbone, jaw, ear. The buck and roll of my body. The heat of my desire cupped in his palm, at the tip of his finger.

The unexpected feeling of his tongue on my nipple, his humid breath, the gentle suck, and my lungs shot open. I curled around him, his head cradled in my arms, holding him to my breast, my orgasm building with every flick of his tongue and flex of his palm. And he knew I was close, knew with the pulse of my body, the thud of my heart, the pace of my breath, the plead on my tongue. The tingling heat crawled through me, up my body, to my neck, to my cheeks, into my lungs and my veins until it was too much, too hot, too deep, too tight.

With a flex and pulse, the heat expanded with tremoring force, ripping through me like lightning, snapping my spine off the bed. It was unlike anything I'd ever experienced, nothing compared to my own hand, nothing compared to the orgasm he'd given me before. This captured me in a way I couldn't understand, and I wondered in a fleeting burst how in the world I would survive actual sex and an orgasm by an actual cock.

But the thought left me as soon as it'd entered my mind, and I rode the orgasm back to myself on Tommy's hand.

I finally peeled open my eyelids to find him descending for a long, punishing kiss. I melted into him, my body soft and slack. When he backed away, I didn't let him go. He smiled down at me.

"You okay?" he asked.

"Mmhmm," I hummed sleepily. "Never been more okayer," I mumbled.

He chuckled and pressed a brief kiss to my lips. "What do you want to do now?"

"Sleep for a year."

Another chuckle. "I think we can manage that. Still want me to sleep in here?"

A shock of doubt sobered me. "U-unless you don't want to."

His arms tightened around me. "Oh, I want to. The very last thing I want to do is go sleep alone with you right here, so close."

"Well, you wouldn't exactly be alone. You've got Gus."

"Please, he's the king of bed hogs. Plus, he snores."

"How do you know I don't snore?" I asked on a laugh.

"Don't you know? I sneak in here and watch you sleep like that creepy vampire in *Twilight*." I must have looked freaked out because he added, "I'm kidding, Melia."

I sighed, relaxing. I hadn't even realized I'd locked up.

He kissed my nose. "I'm gonna go brush my teeth. Be right back."

With one more kiss, this one deep and pressing, he let me go and slid out of my bed.

It wasn't until his gorgeous back disappeared through my doorframe that I remembered I was completely naked.

I hurried out of bed, trying not to feel ashamed. I didn't know why—I wasn't particularly prude about nudity. I supposed I just hadn't been exposed to enough.

I snorted a laugh. I was plenty *exposed* now.

Into my closet I slipped, snagging a pair of pajamas that I clutched to my chest as I headed for my bathroom.

My reflection stopped me.

I barely recognized myself, a pale visage in the mirror, holding her pajamas over her breasts. It was that girl again, the one I'd seen before. The one married to Tommy. The beautiful girl with tousled hair and swollen lips, with long lashes and sparkling eyes.

I lowered my hands and looked at my body. Narrow shoulders. Small breasts, round and tipped with dusky pink. Notch of a waist, stomach soft in that feminine way, without definition, the curve under my belly gentle.

Who was this girl? I knew her, but not like the twin I'd thought she was. I knew her like a distant cousin, far off and largely unknown to me.

But I wanted to know her better. I wanted to be her.

No, I wanted her to be me. And I realized then that those two things weren't quite the same.

With a sigh, I cleaned myself up, washed my face and brushed my teeth, pulled on my pajamas and twisted up my hair. The reflection I saw on my way out was far more familiar, and I sighed, not quite sure how I felt about that.

I padded toward my room, stopping dead when I caught sight of Tommy.

He stood next to my bed with his back to me, arms stretched over his head and a yawn on his lips. His back was comprised of rolls and ridges like sand under a receding wave, his dark hair licking at his shoulders.

All he had on was a pair of black boxer briefs that hugged his ass like half the women in Manhattan would like to, present company included.

I swallowed hard and told my feet to move, which they did, carrying me toward the bed. Tommy turned when he saw me, that devastating smile on his face.

"Cupcake jammies? Color me jealous."

I glanced down, instantly regretting my choice. Not like I had anything sexier to wear. I tugged the hem of my shirt before crawling into bed opposite him.

"Don't get me wrong," he said, climbing in next to me. His body slid toward mine under the cool sheets, the heat of him reaching me first. "I could eat you up."

Before I could make a joke, he kissed me. We wound together like stripes on a candy cane.

He was like a furnace, heat radiating from him and across my skin, into my veins, firing up the space between my ribs like a wood-burning stove. When he broke away, I could feel the flush all over my body.

He smiled down at me, his face cast in shadows from the lamp behind him. "I hope you sleep well."

And as I curled up in his arms, I said that I would, knowing with absolute certainty it was going to be the best night's sleep of my life.

The Gauntlet

AMELIA

t was the worst night's sleep of my life.

Sleep had found me in sporadic bursts through the night. Because Tommy was hot. Hot as hell. Hot as a fucking oven in August.

Temperature-wise, too.

When I woke, I lay starfished on top of him, my flannel pants kicked off in the night and my top on the heap shortly after, leaving me in a cami bra and underwear. It'd been hard enough dislodging myself from his grip long enough to even get my clothes off. The second I wriggled away from him to kick a leg out from the covers, his arms would wind around my waist and pull me back into his chest. His face nuzzled into my hair. His boner pressed against my naked back.

I'd gotten no sleep, it was true.

But it was the best night of my life.

I'd thrown the covers off us but kept the sheet. And once I was out of the flannel, the heat of his body was welcomed.

At one point, I was half-asleep and dreaming of him, my ass

pressed into his hips. I was too groggy and turned on to fight the urge to nestle his length between my ass cheeks. He woke with a moan, kissing the back of my neck, his hand slipping between my legs, into my panties, into me until I came again.

I'd felt terribly guilty leaving him in the state he was in, which was still aggressively present and currently pressing my full bladder into my spine.

I rolled my neck and pressed a kiss to the broad disc of his chest, planning to roll off him and head to the bathroom, but his arms locked around me before I could. He rolled us over to our sides, slipping his hand into my hair and bringing his lips to mine.

For a split second, I worried about my breath, but the thought floated away as his tongue delved into my mouth. He didn't seem to mind. So I wrapped my arms around his neck and kissed him back with all I had in me.

When he broke away, he was smiling. "Did I take these off?"

I shook my head, smiling back. "If I hadn't, I'm afraid I might have actually spontaneously combusted."

"I run hot," he said with a chuckle.

"That's an understatement."

His smile faded, concern taking its place. "Did we...last night, did I...touch you again?"

I slipped my thigh between his to get my hips closer. "Boy, did you."

Tommy frowned, and I didn't know if I imagined his boner easing, which made *me* frown. "I'm sorry, Melia." He cupped my face. "I thought it was a dream."

"Why are you sorry? That was the best part about not sleeping last night."

A laugh left him, his worry fading.

An admission tickled my throat. "I...I was going to turn around and return the favor, but I chickened out."

"Well, as soon as you *don't* feel like a chicken about it, it'll be waiting."

My pelvis nudged his gigantic hardon. "This doesn't seem like it wants to wait."

He drew a breath through his nose, snagging my hip to pull me closer to him. "Oh, trust me. *This* wants you so bad, I'm surprised it didn't give it up last night. But a long, hot, soapy shower awaits. I'll take care of it."

I salivated at the thought of Tommy in the shower, surrounded by steam, covered in soap, hand on his cock and eyes clenched shut.

He must have read my mind, which was likely written all over my face, because he laughed and kissed me, covering me with his body, grinding his length into that spot, that place that wanted him. It was a match striking, and he knew just what to do. And I was so hot so instantly, I could have blown my top with three well-placed shifts of my hips.

Starved. I felt like I'd been starved my entire life and had just been offered a feast. A naked man-feast.

His lips came together, ending the kiss. "Come on. I want to get you off to Janessa's so I can get you back here."

"You have a lot of work to do today, mister. If Aislinn and Wynn don't get out of the dwarves' caves soon, your word count is going to blow to high heaven."

"I'll make you a deal," he said, the corner of his mouth climbing.

One of my brows rose.

"I don't get to kiss you until I hit word count."

I pouted. "I don't know if I like this game."

But he laughed. "I'm shooting to finish before you get back. And then I'm kissing you for hours."

I wet my lips in anticipation. "So I shouldn't hurry home?"

His grip tightened. "Oh, you should *definitely* hurry."

And he kissed me once more to impress exactly what I'd be missing while I was gone.

AN HOUR LATER, I WAS out the door and headed to Midtown where the *USA Times'* offices were. Our parting kiss had left me floating, tethered to the earth by nothing more than a piece of twine. But every block that brought me closer to Janessa tugged on that string, shortening the distance between me and the ground.

By the time I stepped into the elevator, my shoes weighed ten pounds apiece. The offices were busy, full of phones ringing, people chattering, reporters marching through mazes of cubicles. Everyone looked exhausted, but that was nothing new. I didn't think there was ever a moment where anyone's work was actually done.

Janessa's assistant waved me into her office, absorbed with whoever was chattering into her earpiece, never acknowledging me beyond eye contact and a few gestures.

When I entered the office, Janessa smiled at me from behind her desk, leaning back elegantly in her chair, so at ease. As if we were old friends.

"Amelia, it's good to see you. Please, sit."

"Thank you," I mumbled and took one of the chairs. The leather creaked as I sat.

"How's life as Mrs. Bane?"

A hot flush climbed my neck like the devil's fingertips. "Good. He's easy to be married to."

She chuckled. "I bet he is. And how's the story coming?" Some secondary question lingered under the spoken one, though I couldn't comprehend what it might be. "I expected an outline already, and your first month is due soon. I don't like being kept in the dark."

"I...we've been so busy working on the book, we haven't had much time for anything else. But I'm getting my outline together. Just need to circle back with Tommy on it."

She watched me for a moment. "I had some thoughts."

I nodded, reaching into my bag for my notepad and pen. "I'd love to hear them."

A smile curled her lips. It was not a friendly smile. "Excellent." She stood as she spoke, walking around to my side of her desk to hitch a leg on the surface. "I understand what he's looking for—a fluff piece. He wants a pretty little editorial to paint him as the sympathetic rogue, the good guy, the misunderstood scoundrel with the rags-to-riches story."

I frowned. That was exactly what he was.

"But there's more to him than that. And *that* is the story I want. I want the truth, Amelia. I want to know about the fake relationships before you." At my attempt to protest, she waved a hand. "Don't deny it. I already know it's true. But I want to know why, how, when. What did the other girls get out of it? Was anything real, or is everything we know about Thomas Bane a lie? Why have I never been able to find out anything about his mother? He's hiding something, and I want to know what it is. I don't want an editorial, Amelia. I want an exposé."

My pen never touched paper. I couldn't bear to write the words down. "Janessa, I don't know if I can do that."

Her head tilted, her eyes hard and calculating. She reminded me of a cobra with its eyes on its prey. "Oh, I think you can. It's just a question of whether or not you *will*."

My brain fired in six different directions, and all of them said no.

She spoke before I had to. "I have been after the truth under Thomas Bane's mask for years. A dozen good reporters have failed, but you have something they could never gain." She leaned in. "His trust."

Discomfort seized my guts—they crawled into themselves at the implication. I fought the urge to stand up, excuse myself, and bolt out of the building like it was on fire.

I couldn't do what she wanted. I wouldn't.

But I panicked all the same.

I swallowed hard, my mind reeling, an idea springing. "There must be a compromise to be made, some other way. If I can find another angle, will you consider it?"

"You can try. But I doubt you'll change my mind. I'd like you to think very long and hard about what it is you want, Amelia. Because the time might come that you have to choose—Tommy or your career."

A resounding howl of Tommy's name whistled in my chest. I was otherwise still and silent.

She stood, her tone instantly cheerful and light. "I for one can't wait to see what you come up with. You're an incredible writer with a bright future. I have high hopes for you, Mrs. Bane." She sat, smiling amiably at me, as if she hadn't just thrown down the gauntlet at my feet. "Any questions?"

"N-no. Thank you," I said, cursing myself for thanking her for anything. I slipped my unused notebook back in my bag and grabbed the strap, slinging it on my shoulder as I stood.

"I'll be in touch," she said, shifting her attention to her computer, effectively dismissing me.

I floated away, though this time I was caught in static, hovering in a fog of limbo.

I'd been right to be nervous about coming here, but the sad fact was that I should have known it would go this way. I should have known things had been too easy, that Janessa had been entirely too malleable. Until today. I was a rube, a greenhorn, a naive girl with stars in her eyes who honest to God thought people said what they meant and meant what they said.

Lies, lies, lies.

And the play Janessa had made put me in danger of losing more than I'd bargained for.

Because I would have to come up with a way to impress Janessa, or I'd be faced with making a sacrifice— Tommy or my career.

My only comfort was that I knew exactly what sacrifice I would make.

I wouldn't betray Tommy. Not for any job. Not for all the money. Not for anything.

TOMMY

I picked up my phone again, swiping Amelia's last message saying she was on her way home to check the time of her last message.

The two chapters I'd had to write had flown out of me in the time she was gone. Though it wasn't inspiration exactly. Not to say that I wasn't inspired. The last eighteen hours had woken something in me that I found seeping onto the pages, a deep, beautiful longing injected into the characters as they fought their way out of the burning city, dwarves at their back. When Aislinn fell by Ardukan's sword, the anguish Wynn felt had seized me, tightening my throat, detonating something in my chest, flinging shrapnel into my ribs.

It was good, the whole thing. Really good. Even my editor was impressed, which, given the circumstance, was really saying something.

Gus nearly hopped in my lap again, taunting me with his slobbery tennis ball. I dislodged it from his jaw and chucked it across the room. He bounded off after it without a care in the world beyond that ball.

I knew just how he felt.

I was the big, dumb dog, chasing Amelia down until I caught her. And now that I had her, I'd hang on to her with all the gusto and joy that Gus showed.

She was unlike any woman I'd ever known, innocent and untouched, brilliant and unexpectedly brash, honest and humble and braver than she knew.

She'd taken me on after all.

For years, the only women in my acquaintance were famous in some way or another, looking for publicity and press like I was. But Amelia was pure, her motivation a direct influence of her goodness. And I found myself craving that goodness, wanting to breathe it in and let it fill me up.

She was everything right in the world. And now she was mine.

Trust was such a complicated thing. I'd never given mine easily. Years of conditioning had left me suspicious of almost everyone I met. My dad had been a factor, though I didn't like to admit it. We'd been abandoned, left to fend for ourselves. *Ma* had been abandoned in ways we could never make up for. She'd been alone. Even now, she was alone, alone and sick. Never would she know true love, and the thought set a sick twisting in my stomach.

I'd figured love was for fools and dreamers. Giving your heart meant cutting a hole in your chest. And no one could be trusted with that offering. Time and time again, it'd been proven. Not that I'd been hurt. I'd have to give my heart to get hurt, and no one besides my mother and brother had ever been deemed worthy.

Until Amelia.

It was a sweet, reckless feeling to let her in. I didn't remember ever making a choice on the matter—she'd slipped into my heart so naturally, so easily. There were a hundred reasons why, but the truth was that I didn't believe Amelia had an unkind, cruel bone in her body. Not once had I wondered over her intentions. They were offered plainly and without hesitation.

It had never been a question in my mind. I trusted her implicitly, and that trust had grown every day, every minute.

The undeniable urge to protect her was reciprocated. She would fight for me just like I would fight for her. And that fierceness of feeling was all the insurance I needed.

Gus bounded back, launching himself into my lap, jaw working that ball and tail wagging hard. I grabbed his face and scruffed it, rubbing his ears and telling him what a good boy he was. His eyes closed with satisfaction.

I snatched his ball and flung it again, and he took off after it.

Visions of Amelia rose and fell like waves in my mind, slipping over me and sighing away. On my arm in that red cape and thigh-highs, smiling at Zayn Malik like she wasn't terrified. The fear in her eyes after Vivienne Fucking Thorne had cornered her in the bathroom. The feel of her in my arms on the dance floor, her body pressed against mine. The relief on her answer, on her yeses. The taste of her skin, the sweet softness of her, of every curve that had never been touched.

The treasure of her body, the gift of her self, was one that I would forever hold sacred.

But the moment that always stayed near the surface was when she'd said yes, her face open and hopeful and afraid. So afraid. But I'd meant what I'd said—I'd protect her with everything. Fuck a morality clause. If anybody laid a finger on her, they'd have to fucking lock me up anyway.

I kept my promises, and I believed she would, too. So I'd tell her all my secrets, knowing she'd protect them.

Gus was halfway back to me when the bolt on the door clicked. He skidded to a stop, turned on a dime, and took off for the door, reaching it just as it opened.

Amelia giggled, stumbling as she tried to absorb the force of impact, and I hopped to my feet, hurrying to help heel the incorrigible dog. He didn't listen, to no one's surprise, so I clamped my fist around his collar and yanked until she was free of him.

"Hey," I said, leaning down to kiss her briefly, holding the wriggling dog away from us as best I could. "How'd it go?"

She closed the door and sighed.

One of my brows rose. "That bad?"

Amelia shrugged out of her coat and hung it onto a hook with her bag. "You know, I always feel like I know what I'm doing until the second I walk into her office."

I chuckled. "I feel like that with my agent and editor all the time."

She didn't look comforted. I picked up Gus's bear, shook it around to get his full and undivided attention, and tossed it across the room.

I pulled her into my arms, held her head against my chest, kissed the top of her head, waited for her to relax. "Janessa is one of the most intimidating women I've ever known. I always get the sense she's talking out of both sides of her mouth."

Another sigh, and she melted into me. "I know. But I don't want to talk about her. I'll handle her."

My brow quirked, and for a split second, I wondered what exactly needed handling. A flash of fear shot through me. Could it be possible that something else was going on, something I couldn't see, didn't know?

I brushed the thought away. Amelia would never. If something were going on, she'd tell me.

She smiled. "What I *do* want to talk about is your word count."

"Crushed it."

She leaned back to look up at me, her lips pink and smiling. "Did you? I wasn't even gone that long."

I shrugged. "What can I say? I was inspired."

"You got them all the way out of the caves?"

"Well, almost. A plot twist worked its way in."

Her eyes widened. "Oh God. Do you have time for a plot twist? What is it? Did the fight end like you thought? Or did—"

I laughed. "I'm not telling. I've already sent the pages to your Kindle."

She groaned. "Dammit. I need answers, Tommy!" She shifted, reaching for her bag, but I didn't let her go.

"Later," I said, angling for a kiss. "Truth is, I finished fast so I could kiss you when you got home."

She gave up the fight, smiling sweetly as she wound her arms around my neck. "Oh?"

"Mmhmm," I hummed and did just that.

For the next hour, that was all I did—kiss Amelia, hold her.

And I lost myself in the currents of that trust and affection I'd found in her.

Shark Bait

AMELIA

I **hung on to Tommy's massive** arm, the rocks under my galoshes slick and uneven, but my smile was as smooth and genuine as it had ever been.

The crowd gathered around the sea lion exhibit at the Central Park Zoo was impressive, bubbling with energy. That energy didn't faze me.

Tommy made it so easy. He always took the lead, spoke for us when he knew I was uncomfortable or scared, made me laugh when things were tense. He seemed to know how I felt, the weeks of spending every second together connecting us with a familiar intensity. We could have full conversations in a glance or a well-placed squeeze.

But then, Tommy made everything easy.

He was my own personal magic feather, and I held on with all the faith and hope that I could fly if I believed hard enough.

It had been an entire week of nothing but him and me, of hours of kisses and laughter. I'd spent a week in his arms, with his scorching body in my bed. With his hands on me and mine on him. Well, on most of him. I still hadn't gathered the courage to fully handle what waited for me in his pants.

I'd started to worry he'd grow impatient. But he never did, not in the way that would pressure me or make demands. Only in the way that transcribed how deeply he wanted me.

Don't get me wrong. There had been touching. Lots of touching, stroking, and orgasms galore.

Mine under the pants.

His over the pants.

My frustration and urgency for his body, coupled with my pure and absolute trust in him, had come to outweigh my fear. Which was why I'd decided that tonight, I was going to try to go down on him.

I said *try* because the truth was that I was tiny all over—height, hands, vagina, and palate included. My mouth was tiny. And Tommy's dick was most definitely *not* tiny. I'd be lucky if I could get the crown alone into my mouth without gagging.

But I was armed with advice from my friends, distributed with enthusiasm at our last girls' night. I'd also found several extremely helpful articles on the internet, including one with exercises to curb my gag reflex that involved my fingers, a lot of heavy breathing, and only one accidental dry heave.

My foot slipped out from under me, but no one would have known—Tommy had me so tight, I might as well have been floating. I giggled, hanging on to his arm as my galoshes squeaked.

The trainer in front of us stopped, reaching into a basket hanging off her belt for a fish. The second her hand disappeared, three sea lions flew out of the water and onto the deck like they'd grown wings.

Water sloshed around our feet as they flopped and borked toward us. They were *huge*, nearly as tall as me. I suspected they weighed three times me, their bodies dense and slick and shining.

"I'd like you to meet our girls," the trainer said proudly. "Charlie, April, and Margaretta. Say hello, girls."

In unison, they hitched onto one flipper to wave at us.

Emotion squeezed my throat, stinging the corners of my eyes as I half laughed, half sobbed at the sight of them. My hands moved to my lips, and Tommy wrapped an arm around me.

The trainer tossed fish, gave commands, made hand motions, and with every one, the sea lions clapped and barked.

I hated zoos. The thought of so many animals raised in captivity like that just made me too sad, even though I loved seeing all the animals and learning about them. But those sea lions looked thrilled to be there—not only for the fish they caught midair, but for the crowd.

One jumped into the water in an arch I hadn't thought was possible for an animal that size, shooting through the water like a bullet for the big boulder in the center of the exhibit. Up to the top she flopped, did a handstand on her front fins, and backflipped into the water below. The crowd went nuts, and the sea lion knew it, zipping through the water to hop up on another rock by the glass wall where the people stood clapping and smiling. The showboat preened like a peacock.

The director of the zoo smiled from beside Tommy. "I can't thank you and your wife enough for your generous donation," he said, a bucket of fish under his arm. "We'll be able to do a lot of good with our conservation efforts, thanks to you two."

"Thank you for letting us crash your exhibit. I hope us being here doesn't disrupt the animals."

He laughed. "The girls are clearly distraught," he said, gesturing to the sea lions as they wove in and out of each other in the water, occasionally leaping out like dolphins. "And you brought a crowd with you. They told me we hit capacity at eleven this morning. Your announcement on your social media yesterday seems to have done the trick."

It was true. The zoo was packed, the sea lion exhibit so jammed with people that there was no way to get around the fixture. Someone called my name for the crowd, and I turned in that direction without even considering it with an instantaneous smile. I waved instinctively, searching for the face of the person who wanted to say hello.

A realization struck me like a lightning bolt.

I wasn't afraid.

Somehow, somewhere along the line, I'd stopped being afraid. Weeks of appearing in public, of camera flashes and my name being shouted and called out by strangers.

Weeks of the comfort and protection of Tommy's arms and smile, and I wasn't afraid.

Admittedly, the glass retaining wall helped.

I scanned the crowd, marveling at the sheer volume of people watching us with eager faces. A hundred phones and a couple dozen cameras were pointed at us. Some I recognized as paparazzi, some as press.

Including the dour, calculating Vivienne Thorne.

She was dressed in that deliberate way that sophisticated people did when trying to look casual. But everything about her was stiff and strict and discerning, including the heat on the glare she pinned us with.

I was so distracted by her, I didn't notice the trainer was speaking to me until a bucket of fish was thrust into my hands.

My attention snapped to her, then to the smelly bucket, then to the three beasts flopping their way toward me with hungry looks on their faces. I took a step back as Tommy took a step forward, putting himself between me and the sea lions, taking the bucket from me.

"Hey, girls," he cooed, tossing a fish at one of them.

She caught it in the air and swallowed it whole. His laughter rumbled, putting smiles on the faces of everyone in earshot, including the sea lions. They arfed, dappled skin gleaming as they hopped around.

Tommy took a step closer, firing fish into the air in succession, which they caught—*one, two, three*. The trainer made a hand gesture, and they dived backward into the water and swam a lap.

"Come here," she said, waving Tommy over to the edge. "You, too," she added, smiling at me.

We approached the edge, the cement graduating into the water like a beach. She waved us down to get on our haunches and handed us each a fish.

"Okay, take the fish like this. Hold it in between your fingers by the tail. Perfect," she said as we got the fish in place. "Now, extend your hand, and don't be scared!"

Adrenaline shot through me at the warning. Tommy and I shared a glance—mine concerned, his smirking and reassuring. My heart clanged when the sea lions turned and headed back toward us like a trio of three-hundred-pound bullets.

They slid up the incline, emerging from the water with a splash, mouths open and teeth flashing. And just when I thought I was about to get my hand chomped off by an animal I was passionately attempting to save, she plucked the fish from my fingers with delicate grace and swallowed it with an effortless gulp.

I turned to Tommy, laughing like a maniac and weirdly not trying to cry, but he wasn't paying attention to me.

He was getting slapped in the face by a sea lion.

Charlie had taken the fish like she was supposed to. What she apparently was *not* supposed to do was give Tommy a hug. She'd flung her massive body at him like she was trying to claim him for her own, knocking him backward into the icy shallow water.

Every woman in the crowd was Charlie in that moment.

Briefly, I panicked. Would she hurt him? Bite him? Drag him into the pool and drown him? Try to mate with him?

I mean, I wouldn't blame her for that either.

But my fear dissipated with Tommy's laughter, his hands in his face, palms out, Charlie's whiskers tickling him. And then she pressed her nuzzle to his lips in a lingering, deliberate kiss.

When she had her fill, she lifted her head and barked in succession like a laugh, waving at the crowd before turning back to Tommy. She nosed him—he was laughing so hard, he could barely breathe—kissed him on the cheek once more, and dived back into the water and away.

The crowd was a wave of laughter and clicking cameras. Tears streamed down my face as I stood, extending a hand to help him up. When he took it, I leaned back, bracing myself for his weight, but he tugged, pulling me down into him.

I squealed, giggling as he wiped his slippery face all over mine, trying to push him away, which was as fruitful as attempting to shove a brick wall. He buried his face in my neck, making chomping noises as water lapped at our legs.

His lips finally found mine, the kiss awkward, a little smelly, and broken by laughter.

The director and trainer helped us up, and I was thankful it had gotten a warmer, though we were still freezing. The trainer had the sea lions do a few more tricks, but the crowd was watching Tommy and me as we laughed through chattering teeth, wiping each other's faces, fixing each other's sopping jackets.

"I brought us clothes," he said, smiling down at me.

"Oh, so they warned you?"

He shrugged. "I had my suspicions."

I swatted his chest. "You could have warned *me*."

But he laughed. "No way. I was banking on that look on your face when you thought I was cheating on you with a sea lion."

"I was more concerned she was going to make a meal out of your face."

"Psh, please. Charlie and I have a complicated relationship built on mutual respect. She'd never eat my face. Now, I might worry she'd mistake other parts of me were a minnow."

"A minnow? Maybe a bull shark but *definitely* not a minnow."

That earned me a full-blown throaty laugh that chased away the chill and kept it gone.

AN HOUR LATER, WE WERE changed and shaking hands with the director again. Tommy had thrown his damp hair into a careless knot at the nape of his neck, and I stared at the exposed skin, the knot of his Adam's apple as he spoke.

I didn't think there was a single stitch of skin on his body that wasn't gorgeous, even his throat and the unassuming cords of his neck.

Ridiculous. Ri-goddamn-diculous.

We headed out of the office buildings, which were hidden in a quiet corner and away from the crowds. No one had seemed to follow us with the exception of a couple of photographers and Vivienne Thorne.

Tommy tensed when he saw her, pulling me closer. His arm around my shoulders was fiery iron.

We walked past her without acknowledgment.

Undeterred, she fell into step beside us. "Cute show. They're eating you two up."

"What do you want, Vivienne?" Tommy snapped without slowing our pace toward the exit.

"Oh, just wanted to say hello to the couple of the hour. The public can't get enough of the Banes these days. Press is clamoring for all the details, especially about Mrs. Bane. Seems there's not much to dig up."

"And you won't find anything past what we've already told you."

She laughed. "Oh, come on, Tommy. Nobody's that squeaky clean."

I worried my bottom lip, hanging on to Tommy.

He squeezed me once. *Don't worry,* the touch seemed to imply.

I would have laughed if I wasn't so uncomfortable.

"What are the odds," she started, "that sweet Amelia here has never had a boyfriend?"

I stiffened. She smiled. Tommy held me to him and picked up his pace.

"So a nobody blogger who's never had a boyfriend ends up with Tommy Bane in a whirlwind romance twenty-four hours after he got arrested. Just seems a bit of a stretch, doesn't it?"

"Well, lucky for us, we don't need to convince anyone of anything," Tommy shot.

"But what a story it would make if they found out the whole thing was a sham?"

"The fuck do I care what they think?" He gripped me tighter, holding me into his side like he wanted to absorb me.

"Oh, I think you care. In fact, I *know* you care."

"You don't know shit, Viv. You think you've got everything figured out. But what if you're wrong?"

She lifted one shoulder in a carefree shrug. "Truth is, nobody cares if I'm wrong, not if they get a good story about it. You know that better than anyone, don't you? Controlling the narrative is your favorite trick."

"Well, gee, looks like you've got all the answers. Now, if you'll excuse us, we have anywhere to be but here."

Vivienne ignored him, pinning me with a glare. "I know what

you're doing, Amelia. You think you're the only one Janessa has tasked with getting this story? Once upon a time, it was me."

Shock zipped down my spine. I glanced up at Tommy, who was firing daggers at her.

She laughed again, that cold, heartless sound. "Of course he didn't tell you. I lost my job because of that failure. But I have a feeling you'll do just fine, won't you, Amelia?"

In the wake of that shock was shame at her rightness. The story had landed in Janessa's lap, and like the opportunist she was, she'd snapped up the chance.

For a breath, I felt nothing beyond the futility of my situation. Janessa wanted the exposé, as she'd said. The one Vivienne had tried to get and dropped the ball on. Because Tommy was too smart for her.

But he trusted me.

My stomach rolled.

"It's always so nice to see you." His words were saccharine, dripping with sarcasm. "If you could do us both a favor and go to hell, that would be a real help."

We brushed through the exit. She didn't follow.

"It'll eventually come out, whether you want it to or not, Tommy. And I intend to be the one to pull the trigger."

Tommy shot a rude hand gesture over his shoulder without looking, hurrying us to the Mercedes. A few people paused, looked, whispered as we passed, but we were a blur of motion that didn't stop until he deposited me in the backseat.

A moment later, he slid in next to me, and the door closed with a thump.

He sighed his relief.

I inhaled against tight lungs.

He saw my discomfort immediately, his eyes tightening at the corners with worry.

"Hey," he said gently, pulling me across the bench seat and nearly into his lap. "Don't let her get to you." Tommy kissed my crown and held me for a handful of heartbeats. "She was only right about one thing."

Something in my chest twisted. "Oh?"

"Controlling the narrative. Right now, we've got control. And besides, Melia…there is nothing fake about this." Rumbling and earnest and quiet were his words.

I shifted to look up at him, tears stinging my eyes and nose.

God, he was beautiful, his wide lips and Roman nose and those dark, daunting eyes that smoldered with adoration and desire. And I felt like a thief.

Vivienne was right about more than that. The truth didn't matter. It only mattered what people thought.

It was the whole reason we'd gotten married in the first place.

I had to find a way out, and quitting was the thought that arrested me. I imagined Janessa's reaction, and dread lit fire in my guts.

She wouldn't let this go. She wouldn't let *Tommy* go. And if I didn't write the story, someone like Vivienne would. Someone who wouldn't protect him. They'd set him on fire and dance on his ashes.

It had to be me.

Control the narrative.

The urge to tell him overtook me, the words climbing my throat, resting on the tip of my tongue. But before I could speak, he kissed me.

His ardent lips were an anchor, tethering me to him for a long, lovely moment, one that hushed my thoughts and slowed my galloping heart.

When he broke the kiss, those lips were smiling down at me. "Let's shake her off. We've got work to do. You have two chapters to edit, and I have two to write." He settled back in the seat with a happy sigh. "I can't believe I'll be finished in less than a week. And it's all thanks to you, Melia."

I shook my head, glancing down. "Oh, I didn't do much."

He caught my chin and lifted my face to his. "You did everything. You gave me something to write about."

My brow quirked.

"Love," he said simply.

And then he kissed me again.

Love.

Could it be true? Could it be our future?

Could this be everything I'd hoped for? All that I wanted?

As he kissed me, as I searched my heart for the answers, I knew them. I'd known them long, long before.

I knew I could love Tommy.

I already did.

The admission spilled in my ribs, filled me with warmth and hope and relief and a spark of fear. Because with that admission, I had everything to lose.

I could lose him.

The second he sent his book to the editor, I'd tell him. We'd come up with a solution together, figure out how to handle Janessa, the exposé…everything.

The article was the least important thing to any of us. The book was what the publisher needed, and as long as he didn't hit any snags, that would be finished in a matter of days. But Janessa had the power to do more than take Tommy down. If I'd learned anything, it was that Tommy would be fine, no matter what.

But that article could break him and me. And that was something I found I could not let happen.

I couldn't lose him. And I wouldn't hurt him.

No matter what it would cost me.

offers, counted them ... ruined me. Those
have haunted me. ruined me. Those
... my kingdom. I have walked through fire in search
relic that would save us. that would give me ...
... kept them in coffers, counted them
... for my pain. Those sins have haunted
... claimed my kingdom. I have wa...
... that would sav...

But First

AMELIA

The kiss, which had been going for a full and steady hour, regretfully ended.

A forgotten movie played on the TV the next day, muted by Tommy. In lieu of *Lord of the Rings*, he'd turned on some guitar-driven indie music, stretched out on the couch, and spent what felt like a fleeting moment kissing me well and thoroughly.

Father John Misty sang about the Hollywood Cemetery while Arwen and Aragorn kissed in Rivendell, and my heart swelled until it ached. I rested my head on Tommy's chest and watched.

I choose a mortal life, she whispered, the sound unheard as she gave him her necklace, the Evenstar, along with her heart.

Tears stung my eyes, my throat clamping shut. Arwen and Aragorn always did that to me.

I wouldn't admit it with a gun to my head, but their love story was my favorite part of the books. And watching the movie, I always

Tommy's big hand smoothed my hair.

"They always get me, too," he said, the words rumbling in his cavernous chest.

I sniffled and shifted, folding my arms. I rested my chin on top as he propped up his head so he could see me better. "Well, aren't you a big old softie?"

He chuckled, adjusting the pillow behind his head. "I have a confession to make."

One of my brows rose. "Oh?"

He paused for a moment, gathering the words or the gumption—I couldn't be sure. "Writing romance is fucking hard."

A laugh shot out of me along with a sense of victory. "I can't believe you just admitted that."

"Don't tell anybody. I've got a rep to uphold."

"Not when it comes to romance, you don't."

He twiddled his fingers in my ribs, tickling me. I wriggled, squealing until he stopped.

"It really hit me reading *Lord of Scoundrels*. When I got to that scene where he unbuttoned her gloves...I realized it was maybe one of the most unexpectedly erotic things I'd ever read. And the follow-up thought was that I could never write tension like that."

My smile was so broad, it almost hurt. "Thomas Bane, you love romance."

"Who knew?"

"I did," I answered proudly. "You're writing it brilliantly."

"With you alternating between whipping me to finish and punching the story in the ass."

I chuckled. "I mean, I don't hate whipping you, and you have a pretty hard ass."

He smirked back. "We've been so focused on what I need to write that we've barely talked about what you need. Have you planned any more of the article for Janessa?"

I was instantly uncomfortable, my smile disappearing faster than rain in the desert. "No, not much. I figured we could talk about it after you get the book turned in."

He brushed my hair over my shoulder absently. "Well, I got my chapters finished for today, thanks to the *no kissing until the chapters are written* rule. And I got my kisses earned by those chapters. So what do you have so far? And what do you want to know?"

I hedged, "What do you want me to write about?"

He shrugged. "I dunno. Growing up in the Bronx. The trouble I always seem to find. Ma, all she did for us, the kind of woman she is. Her diagnosis—as much as I hate to put that out there."

"How is it that more people don't know about her illness? Or your background?"

"Well, Ma changed her name back to her maiden name when my dad left, and Theo and I legally changed our names to Bane when I started writing and we hatched the plan to get me seen. A couple of people have connected all the dots, but it's convoluted enough, and the records are all spread out. It's been surprisingly easy to keep everything under wraps."

I chuckled.

"Anyway, Ma doesn't leave the house much. Her nurses all sign secondary contracts, to take HIPAA a step further, and we hired a private company who works a lot with celebrities and is known for their discretion. Some people have figured out her name but nothing else about her. And honestly, the second Teddy gets word of someone sniffing around, he usually pays and gags them. If you Google her name, you won't find much of anything."

"And what about you? No one's selling yearbook photos of Tommy Banowski to *People* magazine?"

He laughed. "It happens. Usually when it does, I break up with

Marley Monroe or get a shoe thrown at me in front of The Polo Bar."

I shook my head, smiling. "Control the narrative?"

"The media is so easy to manipulate. A whisper of drama, and it's all anyone can talk about for three days. Everything that came before it is washed away with the tide." He swept his hand to illustrate. "The people who knew me have mostly been pegged, pinned, and hushed."

"It's so elaborate. So much work."

"Nah, it wasn't so bad. Truth is that where I'm from, there's a sort of…code. Snitches get stitches and all that. Plus, what could they know? I lived in the Bronx and almost got expelled twice a semester? Nobody'd be that surprised."

"Then why hide it?"

His smile faded as he drew in a breath. "Because I don't want their pity, Melia. I'm self-made, and I'm around simply because I've figured out how to work the media. That's all. I got them to pay attention to me because I was seen with the young and rich. That's how empty it all is. Every celebrity is a brand, and my brand is the devil-may-care breaker of hearts. It's a good story—the untamable rogue. Doesn't matter if it's true or not. Just gotta give 'em the old razzle-dazzle and let them do what they do—regurgitate it."

"Well, you *are* a rogue, but you've never capitalized on one other important fact."

"What's that?"

"You're a rogue with a heart of gold."

A laugh shot out of him, his square chin lifting. "I dunno about that. I've corrupted you completely and for the most selfish reason."

I was frowning. Really, I was pouting, but the honesty of the gesture annoyed me. "First, I came willingly—"

"You come willingly every night. Another way I've corrupted you."

I rolled my eyes. "And you *do* have a heart of gold. You keep who you really are away from the world."

"Because I don't trust them. Isn't it easier to keep the things I hold sacred away from them? They'll take the truth and twist it around to be whatever they want without a single care for what it *is*. And anyway, they get a version of me. Just not *all* of me."

For a moment, I let that sink in. "Even with the article, there's a level of control. An editorial. Have you thought about…about exposing anything?"

Now he was frowning, and that squirmy feeling in my stomach was back. I wished I could reel the question back in.

"What else should I expose?" he asked.

"Well," I started, my eyes moving to my fingers as they toyed with the button of his henley, "people are obsessed with your love life and the girls you dated. What about talking about why you dated them?"

His frown deepened, the crease between his eyes deep and dark. "Why the hell would I do that? Melia, I'd be in breach of a dozen contracts if I admitted anything." His eyes narrowed. "Why do you ask?"

I laughed nervously. His eyes tightened a millimeter more.

"Just curious how far you wanted to take it."

"Not that fucking far," he said without heat.

"Well, let's talk about it some more after the book is done. You've got the long, dark night coming. Your villains are in place. The end is near."

He relaxed under me, his frown easing. "I've just got to get through Wynn's declaration before I kill him."

"And then bring him back," I added pointedly.

Tommy sighed, his eyes rolling. "I mean, if I have to."

I gave him a look. "If you leave Aislinn in the ice palace to fend for herself against the Leviathan, I will never forgive you."

He pulled me closer, scooting me up his long body. "I wouldn't do that to you or to them. They're us after all, and I wouldn't leave you to face the Leviathan alone."

I cupped his jaw, searched his eyes. Felt my heart stretch and grow to make room for him. What I saw there in the depths of his eyes was more than I could name. But I found a truth, one that had been growing for some time. Since the beginning.

I was falling in love with my husband. And I had the undeniable feeling that he was falling in love with me, too.

"How in the world did you choose me, Tommy?" I said half to myself.

"There was no choice to be made." His big hand held my face, his own soft and searching. "I knew the second the universe put you in my path that you would change everything, and you have. Ignoring that gift would have been a grave mistake, one I don't think I could have made if I'd tried."

He pulled me down to him, kissing me before I could tell him that I knew how he felt, that I felt the same. That I didn't deserve someone so beautiful and kind, to have earned the trust of a man so guarded, a man who let everyone see him but let no one in. Against all logic, he wanted me, wanted to protect me, wanted to cherish me. He wanted to make me happy, and he did every day, every minute.

I only hoped I could do the same.

Our legs were scissored, my fingertips on his chest, my heart thudding and my lips against his. The impressive bulge in his pants was, well, *impressive* and apparent and right there for the taking.

I just had to get up the courage to actually take it.

With a twist and shift, Tommy was on his back, and my brain was shouting instructions like a drill sergeant.

Don't be a baby, Amelia. Get down there and put that dick in your mouth! That dick is the most patient dick in the whole world, and it deserves to get off. So look that penis in the eye and show it who's boss.

My hand moved tentatively down his chest.

Seriously, do it!

My fingers paused somewhere in the vicinity of his belly button.

Oh my God, unzip his pants, you big baby.

The vibration of his zipper zinged up my forearm.

Okay, okay. Now reach in there and touch it.

My fingertips brushed the hot, velvety skin of his crown, which could not be contained by such mortal devices as underwear.

Fuck, it's so big. I always forget how goddamn big *it is.*

Down his shaft my hand moved, eliciting a low, quiet moan from his throat and a flex of his hips. I tried to close my fingers around him, but my fingers didn't touch.

Sweet God, where the fuck am I going to put that? My jaw's gonna break. I'll choke to death. I'll—

Stop that! the drill sergeant barked. *You will put that dick in your mouth, and you will like it!*

I broke the kiss, trying not to panic, shifting to put my thighs between his, spreading his legs.

You're not going to choke. Tommy wouldn't let you choke, I told myself as I shimmied down his torso.

His hand was in my hair, his body perfectly still as I came face-to-face with the beast.

In the way of dicks—the comparison by way of YouPorn—his was gorgeous. Perfectly proportioned, smooth and pink, the ridge of his head thick and luscious.

Gorgeous.

And absolutely terrifying.

For a minute, I just stared at it, mute and blank. I blinked. I listened for direction from the drill sergeant, but all I heard was static.

"Melia," he said roughly. When I looked up the long line of his body, I found him smirking. "You've got that look on your face again."

I screwed my face up with determination. "No, I don't."

"No," he agreed, "*now*, you look like you want to assault it. Come here." He gripped my upper arms, hips shifting to shimmy down.

"But I want to," I whined. "I want to do it."

"You can. You will," he assured as he got underneath me well enough to twist, turning me over toward the couch. "But first," he started before bringing his lips to mine.

The kiss smoldered slow and hot with Tommy caging me into the couch. And for a good, long moment, that was all he did. Kiss me until the drill sergeant was drooling and my body was sweltering.

His leg slipped between mine. With a simple shift, he was on top of me. His hand on my thigh, guiding it open. The crowbar in his pants grinding against that part of me that wanted him so desperately.

And down he went.

The haze induced by his kisses left me useless and limp as he undressed me. First my sweater, shifted up my torso to hook over my breasts, which for a moment found their happy place in Tommy's palm. Then my sweater was gone, my hair spread all over the throw pillow. My bra disappeared in a poof, and my breasts reconfigured their happy place to Tommy's mouth.

That mouth was a place of holy worship.

His fingers hooked in the band of my leggings, snagging my panties with them. His mouth disappeared, leaving the hard peak of my nipple wet and tightening painfully against the cool air.

Naked, socks and all.

And there wasn't even a whisper of shame, not a thought in my mind beyond Tommy. What he was doing, what he was about to do. My trust in him left me unworried, unhurried, without pressure, without expectation.

I barely recognized myself.

He was kneeling next to the couch, my body twisted. One thigh over his shoulder. His lips low on my belly. The other thigh over his other shoulder. My fingers slipped into his hair, gathering it out of the way so I could see him. The dark crescents of his lashes. His big tan hands wrapped high around my pale thighs, the tips of his fingers tightening, pressing into my flesh. His lips, so full as he kissed with aching slowness, the trace of his tongue where I couldn't see. The reverence on his face as he licked a long line up the threshold of my body.

I sighed at the contact, the heat of his mouth setting the hot static in my chest skating across my skin. The sensation zipped and sizzled through me, licking at my awareness, which shrank to the point where his mouth latched to me.

I watched down the line of my body, my heaving breasts, my rolling stomach, my wild hips. His broad shoulders, his strong hands, his hot mouth and wicked tongue. His eyes opened, black as sin. And when they met mine, the hold I had on my body was lost.

The orgasm pulsed through me, seizing my heart, clenching my thighs, bucking my hips. But he held on, didn't stop, not as every brush of his tongue sent electric bursts down my hamstrings, up my clenching core, through my hammering heart, across my tingling lips as they drew breath after painful, noisy breath.

I came down in languid waves, my hips still shifting, Tommy's mouth still kissing, his eyes closed once more and his face touched with an expression I couldn't name, one that slipped into my heart and squeezed. It was a mixture of reverence and adoration, of determination and sincerity. It was a look that was unselfish in its attention, as if giving me pleasure was his pleasure. That, in the space where he was nestled, he found satisfaction that had nothing to do with him and everything to do with me.

His lips slowed, his tongue trailing unhurried curves and sweeps that traced the topography of my flesh. My face tilted as I watched him, my limbs languished, my fingers slipping lazily through his hair. He didn't stop until he was good and ready, and even then, he took his time kissing the inside of my thigh before looking up at me. His smile was sideways, but his eyes were dark with unslaked desire.

"C'mere," I mumbled, reaching for his face, rising to meet him as he crawled up my body.

Our lips connected, the tang of my sex on his lips triggering a flex of my core. My arms threaded around his neck, and I leaned back to lay us down again. But he held back, kept space between our hips, wouldn't rest the weight of his body on mine.

I bucked against his restraint, told him with my lips and tongue and hands that I didn't want gentle. I didn't want care.

I wanted him. All of him.

One hand held the back of his neck to keep him kissing me, and the other slipped over the curve of his shoulder and down his stomach, finding its way back into his pants.

He broke away with a hiss, his cock impossibly hard in my palm. "*Ah*," he breathed, thrusting into my fist.

"You distracted me," I said, my voice rough and quiet as I stroked him. "I wanted your cock in my mouth."

A pump of his hips in a rolling wave, a sound deep in his throat that was more a growl than a groan. "You've said that in my dreams for a fucking month."

All of my fears had been washed away with a sweep of his tongue and a heady orgasm, just as he'd intended. "Please?" I asked, looking up at his lips, my hands full of his cock.

The kiss he laid upon me was bruising, his hips flexing and rolling into my palms. Impatiently, I let him go to tug his pants and boxer briefs off the hard curve of his ass, the kiss not stopping as our blind hands freed him. Up the hem of his henley my fingers roamed, wanting his skin. Only then did he back away to kneel, knees planted in the couch as he reached over his shoulder and between his shoulder blades for a fistful of jersey. With a tug, his body was unveiled, his narrow waist and broad chest, the muscles shifting and stretching, bunching and smoothing. His hair tumbled out of the neck, his eyes finding mine the second they could.

I'd sat up unwittingly, my hands on his abs, his cock at my chest. I looked down as I reached for his base, the slit at the tip of his crown shining and slick. I realized distantly what that slickness was in the same instant the urge rose to taste it.

His fingers slipped into my hair, but I barely felt it. My eyes were locked on his cock, my tongue darting absently out of my mouth to wet my lips, my salivary glands on overdrive.

My lips parted, breath heavy, tongue extending the split second before I reached his cock.

Soft and hard, smooth and hot, the very tip of him slipping into my mouth. My tongue explored the notch under his crown, tasted the salt of his skin, felt the fullness of my mouth and heard the hiss of pleasure, the sting of my scalp as his fist tightened in my hair.

I backed away, closing my lips in a kiss when they reached the top, and opened my mouth again, sighing as I took him once more, testing my limits as I took him deeper.

Deep being a relative term. There was no level of relaxed or ready that would fit all of him in my mouth. But Tommy didn't seem to mind. His ass was clenched so rock hard, his body trembling as if his chains were about to snap. And when they did, he'd fuck my mouth until I choked.

Shockingly, the thought didn't scare me at all.

I took my time where I was, not sure what I was doing, only knowing that it felt good. And by the way Tommy was panting, hips locked in place, it seemed like it felt good to him, too.

I wanted all of him in all of me, the urge inexplicable and overwhelming. Deeper I went, my eyes watering and throat protesting, one hand stroking his base. The other had a grip on his stony ass. As I descended, I pulled him into me, forcing his hips to move. Forcing him to get deeper. Begging him to take what he wanted, not to hold back.

My hair was fisted in his big hand, the tail brushing my naked back. I could feel that he was close in the pulse up his cock, the shaft impossibly hard, the throb and the slick coat of cum in my throat. And incrementally, his hips unlocked. Little by little, he trusted my certainty, flexing gently as he learned how deep I could take it.

From gentle to easy. From easy to intent. From intent to hard.

I spurred him on, knowing he was there, right there, telling him with my hand on his ass to come, to let go, to do it. But he was still holding back.

I opened my eyes, looked up his body.

For a moment, time paused, my mind—jacked on adrenaline—took note of a sight I had never imagined and was completely overcome by.

I was at the mercy of a god, and he was at mine.

The ridges of his abs climbed his torso like a ladder, the rippling muscles over his ribs catching the light and casting shadows. His pecs, broad and wide, his peaked nipples. The curves of his shoulders and biceps, his forearm of the arm that had ahold of my hair.

But it was the expression on his face that once again struck me. Full lips parted in desire, the square of his jaw hard, the line of his nose strong. His brows, so dark and powerful, drawn together, shadowing his dark eyes, eyes that met mine with a plea and demand. His dark hair fell around his face, everything about him both shrouded and open. His face. His body. His heart.

I pulled him into me, deeper this time, my throat closing painfully, but I didn't stop.

He did.

In a chain of motion too fast to follow, he pulled out with an unexpected pop, and the place where his cock had been was replaced by his lips. My hand still gripped him, the other following suit, his length slick from my mouth and sliding between my palms. Two thrusts, and he swelled, and with a deep, controlled grunt, he came in hot bursts that streamed across my stomach and breasts. His forehead pressed to mine, his eyes pinned shut and breath noisy, hips pumping slower, slower still.

Our breaths mingled, his lips so close to mine that I could feel them, feel the tingle of anticipation just before they met. He kissed me with a depth that went beyond the reach of his tongue. He kissed me with more love and adoration than I'd thought could be relayed in a press of lips.

And I did my best to return every feeling.

Chemosignals Are Sexy

TOMMY

That vein in my forehead pulsed with every curl of the weights, my breath hissing as Mos Def rapped on about smashing Ms. Fat Booty's ass like an Idaho potato.

Theo watched on while I finished my reps, his arms folded, biceps fanned out. The suits he preferred masked some of his bulk. You'd never know he was so cut. Broad and big, sure. But Theo was more obsessed than I was, and his body showed it. Dude had like six percent body fat. I could see the ripples in his shoulders through his T-shirt. It was sick, really.

Truth was, Teddy never did anything halfway. He went all the way and made sure he was the best. I didn't even fight it. To be honest, the competition in the gym pushed me harder than I would have gone on my own.

I finished my reps and racked the weights, trading places with my brother.

"I can't believe you're dragging me to a jazz club tonight," he said as he picked up the weights, spending a second getting his posture just right before starting his set.

"Oh, come on. When'd you get to be such a killjoy?"

He side-eyed me rather than answer.

"Right. Always." I undid my hair and twisted it into a fresh knot. "Everyone will have a date but Katherine, so thanks for showing up. Plus, it'll be fun. A live band and swing dancing? Nobody can be unamused at a place like that, even a humorless suit like you."

He gave me a look in the mirror that said, *It's like you don't even know me.*

I huffed a laugh. "Honestly, it'll be nice to go out with Melia without the dog and pony show for once. Dance with her, get all dressed up."

He grunted, and I didn't know if it was some sort of a response or from the effort. Two curls ended his reps, and he set the bar back on the rack with a clink.

"You guys have gotten serious pretty fast."

I frowned at his tone. "Well, we are *married.*"

He rolled his eyes, but one corner of his mouth lifted. "I wasn't judging. Just noting."

I relaxed as we switched places again. "I can't help it. She's... she's a wish I didn't know I had. I didn't know what I'd been missing."

"I don't think you woulda found it with anyone but her. She's the last person I would have chosen for you, but she's the closest thing to perfect that I've ever seen. I've never witnessed anything like it, Tommy. The two of you float a little higher than the rest of us mortals."

"It feels like that," I admitted. "Like my entire universe has shrunk to her and me. I can't stand to do anything without her. Even this sucks." I picked up the bar, shooting my brother a smirk.

"Yeah, I miss you too, asshole."

I shut up for a second as Nas told us to get up off our asses like our seats were hot.

"I'm not surprised, not after seeing you two get together. I'm more surprised it took you so long."

My jaw clenched, muscles burning as I pounded out the rest of my reps, thinking about her, about how the last few weeks had changed everything. My life had been rearranged, and all the pieces had come back together with Amelia in the middle.

I racked the weights, huffing. "Took her longer than me."

"Can you blame her? You're a fucking mess."

"Nah, I couldn't blame her at all. Even now, I'm not sure what she's doing with me."

Theo laughed. "Me neither."

I sneered at him comically and chucked him in the shoulder harder than was necessary. "Ha-ha."

He took the hit without losing his smile. "Don't be modest, Tommy. It doesn't suit you."

"I mean it. I don't deserve someone so good, so kind. I don't deserve her. I don't deserve to be the one to corrupt something that innocent."

"Corruption implies you're tarnishing her, debasing her. You're not. You care too much about her to treat her with anything but reverence and respect." He picked up the weights, looking back to his reflection.

"It's more than that, Theo," I said quietly. "I love her."

His gaze snapped to mine, everything stilling.

"So much makes sense now that I have her. You hear men say they want to be a better man because of love. They say they've found purpose. She's become my whole world, Theo. I could mark my life by who I was before and after her."

Theo set down the weights and turned to face me, casually leaning against the wall to mask his shock. "You've never felt like this.

You've never even entertained the idea."

"It's because of her. No one has ever compared. I am devoted. That's the only way I know to explain. I am devoted to her completely, with everything I am. All I want in the entire world is to love her. To protect her. The thought of her pain guts me, Theo. All I want is her happiness, and if I don't have that, I've failed."

"Have you told her?"

"I haven't. Not yet. I…" I shook my head, collecting myself. "I'm afraid she won't take me seriously. She trusts me but not when it comes to how I feel. She thinks I can't be serious. She doesn't realize I've never been so fucking serious."

He nodded, a ghost of a smile on his face. "I'm happy for you, Tommy. And I don't think you should be afraid to tell her."

I scoffed. "Easy for you to say. She shot me down the first time I tried to tell her I wanted her. How will this be any different?"

"Because she trusts you," he said simply. "One of your best qualities? Loyalty. It's palpable, and your trust—once earned—is worth solid gold. Amelia knows that. And judging by the way she takes care of you, she loves you, too. You'll tell her when the time is right. But when that time comes, don't hesitate. She's not gonna laugh. She's not gonna reject you. She won't hurt you, Tommy."

My ribs expanded with a breath so deep it was almost painful. "I hope you're right," I said with a shake of my head.

At that, he laughed. "When the fuck am I ever wrong?"

"Oh, so now you're psychic?" I joked.

He pushed off the wall, leaning in to say, "Nah. Just smarter than you."

And that was a bigger comfort to me than he could have known. Because he was right about that, too, the bastard.

AMELIA

"I cannot actually believe you put a dick in your mouth."

Val leaned over her bathroom counter and pressed the lipstick to her lips.

"My jaw still hurts, and it's been twenty-four hours," I said on a laugh, wishing I were kidding. "There's a price to pay for enthusiasm, I guess."

"Worth it?" Rin asked.

"*So* worth it." The smile on my face was dreamy. My cheeks were as rosy as the red scarf in my hair. I wore it as a headband, twisted up and knotted on top.

We were all decked out for the club—Val in her favorite red dress, Rin in a black cap-sleeved crop top and high-waisted emerald skater skirt, Katherine in a topaz shirtdress, and me in black pedal pushers and a red polka-dot tailored shirt, cuffed at the elbows and knotted at the waist. The victory rolls were glorious, the hot pants flashing, and the lips were red, red, red.

"Honestly, though," I started, inspecting my reflection, "I'm kinda bummed he pulled out."

Rin smirked at me. "That's just because you don't know what he saved you from."

"Seriously," Val agreed. "As long as he's held off, if he'd blown in your mouth, jizz probably would have shot out of your nose."

I sputtered a laugh, my face hot and cheeks high.

"Definitely would have put a damper on the mood," Katherine said with a nod.

"God, you guys act like we don't fool around every night."

Katherine gave me a look in the mirror. "A hand job in his underwear isn't the same as giving him head."

I gave her a look right back. "No shit, Sherlock."

Val turned around, her face eager as she leaned on the counter. "Think you're gonna have sex soon?"

My smile was small, my eyes shifting to my hands. "I ... I hope so. I was thinking maybe tonight."

Squealing and clapping sounded from the peanut gallery. Well, except Katherine, but she was smirking, which was basically the same thing.

"Do you think you're ready?" Rin asked.

"Is anyone ever really ready in the sense that they're prepared?" I asked back.

"I don't think there's any way you could be prepared for a dick that big," Val noted.

"I mean, what if it's not even that big? It's the only dick I've ever seen. Maybe it's totally average, and I'm just being dramatic."

"You can't even close your hand around it," Val argued.

"Well, my hand *is* exceptionally small. And if the old measurement for men's hands and their dicks is true, then my vagina is exceptionally small, too. I'm a hundred percent sure I'm gonna feel like I'm getting split by a battle axe."

"I mean, at least you're prepared for it to suck," Katherine said.

"If he's gentle and gets you ready, it won't be so bad," Rin offered.

We all gave her a look.

She sighed.

"I just want to get the first time out of the way." I paused, frowning. "Wait—it does get easier, right?"

Val nodded. "It does. I mean, assuming he knows how to wield such a beast properly. Lube helps."

"Oh, good. We have that."

They turned surprised expressions on me.

I flushed. "What? It makes things all ... slippery and stuff."

A laugh barked out of Val. "Who even are you right now?"

"I'll have you know I am very worldly now, Val."

"One blow job, and all of a sudden she's an expert," she joked.

I giggled. "Logically, I know the first time is going to be the worst. I'll probably have an out-of-body experience and black out."

"God, I hope not," Katherine said.

"I know he'll be good though. I know he'll take care of me. I'd trust him with anything," I said simply.

It was a fact, a truth. He'd never do anything to hurt me, which was why it was so easy to give myself to him.

Rin beamed. "I'm just so happy for you, Amelia."

"Have you told him about Janessa yet?"

My smile faded. "Not until the book is done. He's so close. Janessa's fine for now. We're almost a year away from the article coming out. There's time," I said, still trying to convince myself that everything was in fact fine. "There has to be a way for both of them to get what they want. Tommy will know what to do. But that book has *got* to make it to his editor."

"Do you really think it would derail him that bad?" Katherine asked.

"Do I really want to find out? Because if it did, he could blow his last chance. It'll keep. I hate keeping it, but it'll keep."

"Unlike your virginity." Val snickered.

"Yup, my virginity has an expiration date, and the clock is up at midnight, just like Cinderella. Except instead of getting my pumpkin smashed, it'll be my vagina."

"Maybe you should get a little drunk," Katherine said helpfully. "You know, to numb it. Like drunk feet."

I squinted my eyes like I was confused, waiting on her to finish.

"Drunk feet...like when you wear pretty heels for an entire night out and realize when you can't walk the next day that your shoes weren't comfortable after all. Your feet were just numb. It's like that but with your vagina."

I laughed. "I'd rather not be drunk when I lose my virginity, but a little scotch probably wouldn't hurt."

"We're all so worried about your vagina," Rin said, "but nobody's asked about your heart."

"My heart is…ready, I think. There are so many reasons to love him. And however things work out, I don't think I'd change a single thing." I chuckled softly. "Easy to say right now when my life with him is a fairy tale. I just know he'd never do anything to hurt me. I don't know that there's a bigger sign than that."

"Love?" Rin whispered. "You love him?"

"I do," I answered, my heart somehow both filling up and squeezing tighter. "So much."

"Are you gonna tell him?" She took my hands, her eyes shining.

"I…I think I want to wait for him. Knowing is enough for now. It's still so new, you know? I want to give him time. And I definitely *don't* want to jump the gun."

Val sidled up next to Rin. "You love your husband, Amelia."

I laughed, sniffling against a deep burn in my nose. "How about that?"

When the doorbell rang, we jumped, laughing at ourselves, the four of us slipping into a brief hug before rushing down the stairs like it was prom.

Val whipped the door open in a whoosh that would have shifted her victory rolls had they not been hair-sprayed solid.

On the stoop was Court, bouquet of red roses in hand and a sideways smile on his impertinent lips. He was about as soft as a slab of marble, his jaw square and eyes steely. Until they met Rin's. Then they turned to hot embers.

The smallest pout brushed Val's lips. "Hello, Courtney."

"Valentina," he said, kissing her cheek as he passed.

"No suspenders tonight?" she teased.

He huffed a laugh and rolled his eyes. "Those suspenders are second only to that stupid fedora."

"Aw." Rin chuckled, stepping into Court to wrap her arms around his neck. "You're such a good sport."

"Only for you." He kissed her red lips softly.

Val peered through the open doorway, sticking her head out the threshold to look down the street. Her pout flipped at what she found, and she bolted down the stairs and down the sidewalk, jumping for Sam like a howler monkey.

He caught her with ease, spinning from the force, the red chiffon of her skirts lifting. To be honest, it looked like a swing move, as graceful as it was, her arms around his neck, her legs around his waist, lips crushed in a kiss worthy of some homage to immortalize it— statue, poster, billboard, linograph, *anything*.

I sighed dreamily.

"They're just too goddamn much," Katherine said from my shoulder as she leaned in with me to watch. I would have almost called her tone wistful. I mean, if not for the monotone.

It was my turn to scan, my gaze sweeping up and down the street, looking for a car or a set of twins too gorgeous to be human.

And then it was my turn to pout.

I ducked back in the door, followed by Sam and Val.

"Should we have a drink while we wait?" Court asked, already heading for the cabinet where we kept the booze.

"I guess," I sulked.

"Don't look so glum," Val said, bumping my hip. "He'll be here any minute."

"Ugh, I'm the worst," I muttered. "I can't be away from him for even a couple hours without whining about it."

"Hey, we know the feeling," Sam said with a wink and a smile.

Katherine made a face at all of us. "Brain chemicals are so bizarre."

Rin chuckled. "How so?"

"Well," she started, accepting the first drink from Court, "think about it. You meet a person, and your biology tells you whether or not you like them almost immediately, like a knee-jerk. It's not love at first sight. It's love at first *smell*. One brain sends chemosignals in the way of pheromones, and the other brain either accepts or rejects them. Insta-lust. Then attraction. Then attachment. Sex hormones, then dopamine, then oxytocin. And your brain gets addicted to those chemicals, and there's only one person who can give them to you. You guys are living proof."

"How romantic," Court deadpanned.

"Who needs romance when you have science?" Katherine shrugged and took a sip of her drink.

The doorbell rang, and I squealed, charging for the door. I whipped it open and practically launched myself at Tommy.

It felt like I hadn't seen him in a day. Stupid brain chemicals.

I jumped, and he bent to catch me, my arms hooking around his neck and my lips on his. His shirt collar was crisp under my hands, the satin back of his vest cool and slick under my fingers.

When he set me down and the kiss broke, he pressed another to my hair, just over my ear. "Missed you, too," he whispered.

I leaned around him. "Hey, Theo," I said with an immovable smile, my hand lost somewhere in Tommy's.

"Heya, Melia." He was gorgeous, too, his hair slick and shining, hands in the pockets of his slacks. Both he and Tommy wore tailored shirts cuffed above their identical sexual elbows.

Hot bastards.

"Come on in and meet everybody," I said, tugging Tommy into the house.

The collection of my favorite people in the world, dressed up in timeless clothes and brilliant smiles, set my heart fluttering. Sam leaning against the island, long and lean, his arm resting on the counter, hand hooked on Val's hip to keep her close. Court and Rin behind the island, drinks in their hands as they leaned into each other. Katherine on a stool, her legs crossed and smile dry and quirked with amusement.

I realized then that we wore matching expressions. As much as I admired all of them, they seemed to be assessing Tommy and me with the same love and sentimentality.

"Boys, meet Tommy and his brother, Theo."

Sam kicked off the island, extending his hand to Tommy. "Good to finally meet you. I'm Sam, and that's Court. We've heard all the good things."

Tommy smirked. "Lies, all of them. The only good thing I have going for me is Melia."

Sam's understanding and appreciation shone on his face, punctuated by the tilt of his lips.

Court nodded. "Need a drink?" Which was Court's way of saying, *You're in, but watch your ass.*

Tommy seemed to pick up on it and said, "Scotch, if you've got it." Which was Tommy's way of saying, *Yes, sir.*

Another curt nod of approval from Court, but a smile flickered on his lips.

"Theo, this is Val and Rin, and Katherine, your date."

Val and Rin waved their hellos, and Katherine slipped off the stool and strode over with businesslike purpose.

She stuck out her hand formally.

"Hello, Theodore. It's nice to meet you."

Theo took her hand with a smirk, but rather than pump it in a shake, he flipped it over and pressed a kiss to her knuckles. "Nice to meet you, Katherine."

The second his lips were gone, she jerked her hand back, discreetly rubbing it off on her thigh. "That's how the flu spreads, you know."

One of his brows rose, his smile still in place. "Well, I'd hate to be the cause of senseless virus-spreading. I'm sorry."

She nodded. "You're forgiven. I hope you like to dance."

"I do," he said, amused.

"And I hope you don't mind me leading."

His mouth opened to speak, but after a pause, he closed it again. His brows quirked in confusion.

"Katherine and I usually dance together," I clarified.

"Some people say I have control issues," she said with a shrug.

I laughed. "It keeps us from getting hit on, too."

"They think we're lesbians," she explained.

Laughter sputtered out of Tommy, and he laid a disbelieving look on me.

"Oh, don't look at me like that. Pretending to be a lesbian is easier than talking to strange men. Even when she kissed me in front of a hundred people."

His laughter stopped dead. "I thought you'd never been kissed."

I rolled my eyes. "That didn't count. There wasn't even any tongue."

A single, bawdy *ha!* erupted from Katherine.

Court made his way around the island with drinks in hand, passing them off to Tommy and Theo. Val raised her glass, and everyone grabbed theirs, following suit.

"To new friends and old. May we give the love we take and live the love we make."

Hear, hear, we called, taking our sips.

Tommy caught my eye, smiling with those ridiculous lips I loved.

And I had the unshakable feeling that he loved me too, lips and all.

counted them in
have haunted me, rained me, Those
my kingdom. I have walked through fire in search of
that would save us, that would give me
kept them in coffers, counted them in
for my pain. Those sins have haunted me,
claimed my kingdom. I have walked
that would sav

Sway

AMELIA

S***way was swinging.***

The club was a feast of sight and sound. Bodies bopped and bounced in waves under the golden Edison bulbs suspended at uneven heights over the parquet. The occasional feet in the air were like whitecaps, and the bounding music was the sound of the tide coming in.

I watched Tommy take it all in, seeing it all for the first time again through his eyes. Faces turned to us as we passed, though no more than usual. The bit of anonymity was a novelty.

The second we reached the dance floor, Sam grabbed Val around the waist and spun her into the crowd like a goddamn pro, the two of them triple-stepping and bouncing their way in circles as Sam whipped her around like she was nothing. And for a few minutes, we all just stood there on the edge of the crowd and watched them, cheering and whooping when he flipped her over his shoulder.

He pulled her close, the two of them locked in an embrace as they danced, laughing and talking and oblivious to the rest of us.

Court led Rin into the crowd and twirled her. When he launched into a triple-step, it was with less grace than Sam—I could practically hear him counting from where I stood—but it was with all of his heart and then some. Never in a million years would Court have learned to dance like this if it wasn't for the fact that he'd do anything to make her happy, even if it meant making an ass out of himself.

That in and of itself was perhaps the deepest declaration he could make.

Katherine grabbed Theo's hand and pulled him toward the crowd. Her eyes were big and bright, her smile as close to a grin as she ever came. I almost caught a sliver of teeth. Theo, on the other hand, looked mightily unsure of himself.

She stopped, turning to him. "All right, are you ready?"

Tommy laughed. "This oughta be good."

Theo took her hand, which was out and at the ready, but his other hand, which should have gone on her waist, seemed to find no home. He frowned.

"Put it on my shoulder," she said.

When he did, his palm swallowed the joint.

The dubious look on his face deepened.

We watched as she showed him how to triple-step, how to twist out. But when she tried to get him in a sweetheart hold—sorta like a prom pose, back to front, hands at the partner's waist—she couldn't get her arm over her head. He was too tall.

She frowned, her face pinched in irritation. "Well, that does it. You're going to have to lead."

"Oh, thank God," he sighed, switching their hands and laying his gigantic paw on her waist.

And then he took off, pulling her around the dance floor like he'd been doing it his whole life.

But the best part was Katherine's face. She looked like she'd been electrocuted, and the only thing she'd regained function of were her eyelids, which blinked like hummingbird wings.

Tommy and I burst into laughter. One of my arms was hooked around his waist, and my free hand was occupied, absently fiddling with buttons on his vest.

"Dance with me, Mrs. Bane," he said, taking my hand.

"It'd be my pleasure, Mr. Bane," I answered. "Do you know what you're doing as well as Theo does?"

"Let me tell you a little secret, Melia," he said around a smirk as he pulled me into him, bringing his lovely lips to my ears. "I'm a quick learner."

I laughed, not believing him.

Not until he spun me away and kicked us into a rock step.

I gaped, catching flies even worse than Katherine as he took me through every one of the moves he'd seen Katherine show Theo, and then he improvised. And by improvise, I meant that at one point, he actually picked me up and brought me into one hip, then the other, and thank God he told me what to do because at the last possible second, I kicked my legs open to straddle his waist.

The first thing I learned was that I much preferred dancing with Tommy than Katherine. The second—Tommy could probably throw me around like one of Gus's tennis balls. And the third?

Tommy was good at everything.

No, really. I had yet to witness him do anything half-assed. It made me want to force him to cross-stitch or take him golfing or something. Nobody was good at golf the first time.

But I'd bet my inheritance that he'd hit a hole in one.

The band brought the music down, bringing everyone cheek to cheek. Well, except us. My cheek rested in that divot between his pecs. His heart beat like a drum against my skin.

It was the kind of moment where everything in you stilled, when for one sweet second, you became fully and wholly present. I felt the warmth of his hand around mine, the press of his body against me, the heat of his skin, the rhythm of his heart. I noted it all—the place we stood swaying, the fact that a month ago, I'd never been kissed. I'd stood right here, swaying with Katherine in an effort to not feel alone.

But I hadn't realized then that I was very lonely. Not until I wasn't anymore.

I shifted so I could look up at him and was struck by the sight. How do you ever get used to someone so beautiful? And how was it possible that every day, that beauty grew? Every day brought the discovery of another reason to love him. And that deepened the way I saw him, the way I wanted him, and the way I wanted to show him how I felt.

There was only one threshold left to step through, one more door to walk through. I couldn't tell him I loved him, not yet. But I could show him.

He gazed down at me, turning us in slow circles under the golden lights that bronzed the angles of his face and cast shadows with every line.

His lips, so full and wide, rose on one side.

"Tommy," I started, my breath shallow and heart fluttering madly, licking my ribs. But I couldn't find the words, my tongue useless and throat tight.

That smile faltered. "What is it, Melia?" he asked so gently, so tenderly.

I swallowed, gripped by my feelings and my fears. But when I looked into the depths of his dark eyes, the sense of safety and sanctuary filled my heart, eased my mind.

"There's…there's something I wanted to say, but I…"

I glanced down, shaking my head. But only until his big hand cupped my jaw, lifting it so I'd meet his eyes again.

"Don't be afraid. You can tell me."

A smile touched my lips, thin as it was. "I know. I know I can.

That's the thing. I'd trust you with anything."

"With your books?" he asked, his smirk back in place.

"As long as you didn't dog-ear the pages."

"With Claudius?"

"Only if you didn't feed him like you do Gus."

A laugh. "Baking your grandma's coconut cake?"

"Oh no, never that. You'd burn the house down."

This time, when he laughed, he kissed me. And for a second, I lost myself there in his lips. But when he broke away, his face was serious, his eyes sincere.

"Tell me what's wrong so I can fix it."

I shook my head. "Everything's perfect, Tommy. Everything. You. Us. Tonight. Like I said, I'd trust you with anything. And there's one thing I've been wanting to give you for a while now, but I've been too afraid."

His dark eyes searched mine. "Your heart?"

"Oh, you already have that," I said softly.

Every hard edge to him softened, his body curling around me. "I have your heart?"

I chuckled, that muscle thumping painfully. "Yes, you do. I don't know when I gave it to you, but I don't think I want it back."

"You have mine, too. You have all of me, Amelia. And I don't want it back either, not if it means I can have you."

"You can have me," I breathed. "You can have all of me."

He stilled, the two of us a fixed point in a room of motion. "All of you?"

I nodded. "All of me. Tonight, Tommy."

He didn't smile. He didn't speak. He didn't ask questions or need clarification.

All he did was kiss me, kiss me with a hundred promises and a sigh drunk with love.

A Matter of Time

TOMMY

Tonight.

I held Amelia in my arms, held her in my heart, held the most precious thing I'd ever possessed in my hands and kissed her, hoping she knew how I loved her.

With the close of my lips, I broke the kiss, gazing down at the only girl I'd ever want. The realness of her, the truth and simple kindness of her heart, the gentle love she gave endlessly—all of her called to all of me. And there was no resisting that call even if I wanted to.

"Let's go home," I breathed, the words raspy and thick.

A small chuckle, a flush of her cheeks. "Already?"

With a smile, I amended, "Unless you want to stay. I can wait forever, Melia."

"Well, I can't," she said with a wicked smile, stepping back to take my hand. "Take me home."

"Anything you want," I promised.

Hand in hand, we made our way to everyone to say goodbye, the girls embracing and kissing cheeks, the guys shaking hands.

Theo got a hard look from me that said, *You're on your own,* which he accepted with a nod before twirling Katherine back onto the dance floor.

And with Amelia tucked into my side, we hurried out of the club.

The second we were in the cab, Amelia climbed into my lap, sitting sidesaddle so she could wrap her arms around my neck.

I took the opportunity to kiss that red lipstick off her lips until they were pink and swollen and naked, my hands on her small waist, on her face, on her back and arms and thigh. The air we shared was thick with anticipation, with intention. Hers with determination. Mine with control.

Because my control was the best chance for her comfort.

That long, lazy kiss didn't stop until the cab did. In a blur of motion, I paid the driver, exchanged some pleasantry that was instantly forgotten, and followed Amelia out of the passenger door. We hurried up the steps and into the apartment, first Amelia, then me.

I almost ran into her when I closed the door, my hands reaching for her shoulders to steady myself at the sudden stop.

Her hands were on her chest, her voice sweet. "Tommy, look."

I looked in the direction of her gaze to see Gus curled up on the rug in front of the fireplace. And nestled in the curl of his body was Claudius the cat, sound asleep.

I wound my arms around Amelia's waist, pressed a kiss into her hair as we watched on with smiles on our faces. She leaned back into me, her hands resting on mine.

"They love each other," she said softly.

"I suppose it was just a matter of time," I said half to myself and not at all about our pets.

She turned around in my arms and looked up at me in the dim light, her eyes silvery and soft. "I suppose it was," she echoed.

"Melia," I breathed, the space in my chest tight and hot and aching. "The world isn't a safe place—it never has been for me. It's full of greed, packed with liars, thick with thieves. And they will steal everything important to you, everything you love, even your hope. But you…you are everything they aren't. You *are* love, and you've shown me that love's not only possible. It's real."

My hands moved to her face, to hold her small jaw, to look into her shining eyes and say the words of my heart with lips that would only speak the truth.

"I love you, Amelia," I whispered in the quiet room. "I love you with all of me, from the depths of my heart, with fierceness I didn't know I possessed. I love you, Amelia. And I hope someday, you'll love me, too."

Her breath shuddered, her small hands on my chest. "But I already do."

My heart flung itself at her palm. "Do you?"

"I love you," she said. And those three little words shifted the total of my world into her hands.

I couldn't speak. There were no words to explain. No air in my lungs. But my heart was full, stretching and aching and unable to hold everything I felt.

So I kissed her and told her without the limitation of words. I showed her instead.

And I'd keep showing her as long as she let me.

Our bodies twisted together, the kiss deep and honest and bare. I bent to pick her up, cradling her in my arms, hers hooked around my neck as I walked us to her room.

When I set her down at the foot of her bed, she looked up at me, smiling. And when she looked at me like that, all I wanted to do was kiss her.

Instead, I smirked, settling for a kiss on her nose.

"Wait right here," I commanded.

Her brow flickered with uncertainty, but she said, "All right."

I rushed out of her room, and the second I was through her doorway and on my way to my room, a flash of fear tore through my chest.

I'd been dreading this moment almost as much as I'd been dreaming of it. There was no way I wasn't going to hurt her when I took what she was offering.

For women, sex with me wasn't always easy. It required patience, foreplay, and lube, and even then, plenty of *normal*-sized girls couldn't take it.

And Amelia was tiny. She was tiny *everywhere.*

I'd never had sex with a virgin, not even my first time, and as such, I had no small amount of anxiety about it happening with Amelia. We'd moved at her pace, but I knew as well as anyone that we'd eventually move in that direction. I could tell by the way her body responded to mine, in the hungry way her hips would move. I would have waited forever for her. But I'd prepared myself, knowing this would be so difficult for her. I didn't want to hurt her, not in any way.

In this case, I was afraid it was unavoidable.

All I could do was make it as painless as possible, and I'd prepared myself with Boy Scout thoroughness.

I opened my closet, reached for the box I'd stowed there, and headed back to her with my plan in hand and my heart chugging in my ribs.

She stood next to the bed with her back to me, her fingers buried in her hair as she pulled out bobby pins one by one. I set the box on the bed and moved for her.

She startled when I cupped her hip, chuckling softly.

"Can I?" I asked.

She glanced back at me, smiling. "Of course."

I slipped my fingers into her hair, searching for the pins. We were silent, lost comfortably in our thoughts. And with every clink of a pin against its mates on her nightstand, her golden hair fell, lock by lock, down her back.

When it was down, I reached into her hair to knead her scalp. As much metal as I'd pulled out of her hair, I figured she needed it.

I was rewarded with a long, happy sigh.

I kissed the back of her head. "Come here. I want to show you something."

She turned, her eyes finding the box on the bed. She climbed onto the mattress to sit in front of it. "What's this?" she asked.

"Well," I started, suddenly unsure how to explain. I paused. "Amelia, I don't want to hurt you."

Her face softened. "I know."

"When we started getting serious, I…I started worrying. About this. I've never…done *this* before."

One of her brows rose with her smile.

"I mean, I've done *this*, but I've never done…*virgin* this."

"Oh," she said, her cheeks flushing.

"So I got some stuff I think will help make it easier," I said, opening the box.

She leaned in to peer inside.

I reached in, fishing out the contents.

She reached in too, her hand reappearing with a tube of lube. "We already have lube," she said on a chuckle.

"I know, but this is more…it's just better," I hedged, flustered.

Her eyes bugged when she looked in, and this time, she held the tube in her hand. "Tommy…"

My brows drew together as I leaned over to see which one she'd picked up.

She turned it so I could see. "Please tell me this doesn't say *anal lube*."

An unbidden laugh bubbled out of me. "*No, no, no,*" I assured her as I took it. "It's thicker, and it has a numbing agent in it. Don't worry, Melia. I'm not touching your ass."

She sighed, relaxing.

"Yet," I added.

She rolled her eyes, swatting my arm.

"Anyway, there's some other stuff here. Ultra-thin condoms. Some stimulators, though I don't know if that will really help you. I figured I'd see what you wanted to use."

"Tommy," she said with a teasing smile, "did you make me a deflowering box?"

I rubbed the back of my neck. "I mean, when you put it like that, it sounds kind of creepy."

She laughed. "I don't think it's creepy at all. Look at all this," she said, picking up the tube of anal lube. "You got all of this because you were worried about me. That is the most thoughtful thing anyone's ever done for me."

"Well, I love you," I explained.

"I love you, too," she echoed, reaching for my face. "You're more worried than you are excited, aren't you?"

"I don't know if I'd say that," I admitted with a smile, angling for her lips.

"I trust you," she said. "Now, kiss me," she commanded.

And I did as she'd bidden.

She threaded her arms around my neck, pulled me into her, onto her, the box forgotten.

My plans to take things slow were overridden by Amelia, who apparently did *not* want to take her time. Her hands skated down my chest, first unbuttoning my vest, which I shucked and tossed blindly in the direction of the floor. Then her delicate fingers grabbed my shirt and tugged with unladylike gusto, unfurling my shirttails and unfastening the buttons of my shirt faster than I could have. With her enthusiasm, I was surprised she didn't just tear it open, flinging buttons all over the room.

And her enthusiasm fueled my own, although I took my time despite her rush, unbuttoning her shirt, untying the knot, slipping the fabric over her pale shoulders. Our shoes were kicked off, clumsily thunking against the ground. Before I even thought to take off her bra, my torso was naked, and her hand was snaking into my pants.

Her fingertips grazed my aching cock, and I hissed into her mouth, taking her wrists in my fist. I twisted us, pinning her into the bed with my body, holding her hands over her head with one of mine.

I broke the kiss and looked down at her, panting. "We've got all night, Melia."

Her hips rolled against mine. "I've waited all this time. I don't want to wait any longer."

"I know," I said against her lips. "And you won't. Trust me," I breathed.

"I do," she whispered.

And with that surrender, I kissed her.

Long and slow, I kissed her. Hot and deep, I kissed her. I kissed her until she was soft underneath me, her urgency gone, her body supple.

Only then did I move.

First, my hands, fingertips tasting her long neck, the ridge of her collarbone, the curve of her breast. Then, my lips, tasting every space my fingers had touched, spending a long, luxurious moment sampling her skin as my hands relieved her of her bra.

Her skin was snowy white, the tips brushed in pale pink. Everything about her was delicate, calling for the gentlest touch, the softest kiss. And I paid my homage to her body. Traced the swell. Closed my lips over the peaked tip. Sighed and hummed my appreciation as her arms cradled me to her, her hands slipping into my hair.

Down my hands moved, fingers unfastening her pants, sliding them off her hips and away, taking her panties with them.

For a moment, I did nothing but drink in the sight of her in the quiet light of her room. Her flaxen hair fanned out, framing her blushing face. Her eyes, silvery blue, pupils wide and lids low, drunk with lust, heavy with love. The quick rise and fall of her breasts. The curve of her waist and hips, the angle of her legs, knees together, turned to the side where I'd left them.

Never had I seen anything so beautiful.

Never would I witness something so real as the pale visage of my wife, waiting for me.

Her arms opened, and I filled them.

My skin was hot to the touch, flaming against hers as we kissed. The heat came from within, from deep in my chest, spreading through my veins, across my skin, reaching for her.

Our bodies locked together, a twist of limbs, scissored and shifting. Hips rolling. Hands searching. Mouths hot and open, lips a seam. And in that moment, I didn't want to go slow. I didn't want anything but to have her.

My hand skated down her body, to her ass, squeezing hard, opening her up. I swallowed her moan, my hand searching for her heat, fingertips skimming the threshold of her body, rewarding the shift of her hips with the slip of my finger into her body.

For weeks, we'd done this very thing, but nothing about this felt like before. Not the way she moved, the intent behind every flex of her hips, in the reach of her tongue, in the hunger in her fingertips as she trailed them down my chest. And I could feel that unbridled hunger in me, the finger buried in her telegraphing every sensation to my cock in vivid detail.

I'd held back all this time, conceding to take what she'd offered and nothing more. Even now, her body was an offering, one I would pay the veneration it deserved.

The space where she held me so tightly pulsed around my finger, drawing me deeper. Lazy circles of my thumb, tracing the peak of her sex, the rhythm of my hand matching the rhythm of her hips until she writhed under me. A gorgeous flush climbed her chest, her neck, the curves of her cheeks, her eyes pinned shut and sheets fisted in her hands.

"Not yet," I said, my voice fiery coals.

I released her. Brought my lips to the tight tip of one breast, teasing the peak until it was hard and reaching.

She mewled, her hands slipping into my hair, cradling me to her, her hips wild, seeking pressure, contact. Seeking me.

Down her body I kissed, licking a trail, sucking a path across her breasts, beyond the gentle swell of her stomach, to the place where her thighs met. Those thighs, milky white, velvety soft, the taste of her skin on my tongue. My eyes were barely open as my hands spread her legs to expose the rippling flesh, pink and swollen, waiting and ready.

My breath, hot on her core. My lips, wet and parted. Her body, there for my taking.

My lips descended, the scent of her triggering something deep and elemental in me. A brush of my tongue first, a velvety caress of a feather, and she gasped, the flinch of her thighs flexing my hips without intent. And my lips closed over the slick sweetness of her, latched to her body, drew her into my mouth with a gentle suck and sweep of my tongue.

A soft moan from her lips, her thighs drawing wider in her pleasure as the flat of my tongue dragged the length of her, circled around the swollen flesh, traced every valley, every peak, taking my time, taking every precious moment I wanted, content exactly where I was.

My index finger took the place of my tongue, stroking her,

spreading her. I slipped that finger into her heat, felt the pulse of her body as I swept my tongue against the heart of her sex. Curled to find the spot inside her that wasn't quite as silken as the rest, circled my fingertip against it.

Her hands gripped my hair like reins, her hips shifting in the rhythm she wanted—*needed*—and I matched her pace. The barrier of her body made way easily as a second finger joined the first, something I'd done so many times before, though nothing compared to what I was about to do. But I brushed the thought aside, turning the full power of my attention on the place where my lips lie, where my fingers reached, where her body squeezed and held. I listened to the sound of her heavy breath, of her muttered pleas.

I hummed my desire, traced the peak of her, teased it hotter until she burned. And with a flex that consumed her, toes to thighs to core to lungs, she came with a cry, with a shuddering pulse that galloped through her, that pulled me into her deeper, deeper with every surge.

She came down slowly, whimpering and stroking my hair, hips rolling, thighs shaking. But I stayed where I was, riding out the slow bursts of her body as they slipped away, kissing her tenderly.

She called my name, a whisper of sated desire, of longing and promises. And I was helpless to do anything but obey. So I went to her, moved up her body, lost myself in her lips, in her hands and arms, in the warmth of her body.

But tonight was not about that alone. She reminded me with her hands trailing down my body, hooking her fingers in the band of my slacks to push them over my ass and hips. I broke the kiss and held her eyes as I slipped out of my pants.

We'd never been fully naked together, and the sensation of her body, her hot skin against the length of my body triggered a deep awareness of every point we touched. Her thigh slipped between mine and rode the line of muscle to the top until our hips met. The warm valley between her legs was slick and hot against my thigh, and with a wave of her body, she stroked herself on the cord of muscle.

A groan climbed up my throat, my hand gripping her ass, my control thin. But it was there, separating our hips. Pressing her into the bed. Shifting to hover over her. Kissing her for a long moment to cool myself off without success.

I broke the kiss and sat, reaching for the forgotten box. As I rummaged through it, she sat, reaching for the anal lube with a knowing smile on her face. I resisted the urge to kiss that smile off it, as my fingers closed over the box of condoms.

But she stayed my hand, her smile slipping. "I...won't that hurt worse?" she asked tentatively.

"Maybe a little."

She shook her head. "I'm on birth control for my periods. And... you're *clean*, right?"

I nodded slowly. "Yes, but..."

Fear flashed behind her eyes. "I...if it'll hurt less, I think I'd rather not," she insisted meekly. "Okay?"

"All right," I agreed, unable to deny her anything, kissing her to tell her so.

I broke away to put the box on the bench at the foot of her bed. And when I turned back to her, the vision of her stopped my heart hard enough to smoke.

Her lids were heavy, her shoulders propped on the pillows, her eyes down, gaze resting on her hand. That small, fine hand, fingertips shining from the contents of the tube, tracing those fluttering lines of her body where my lips had just been. She met my eyes and slipped her middle finger into her body until it disappeared.

When my heart started again, it was with a painful thud and rush of blood, racing to my aching cock.

She sighed, her fingers slick, her breasts high and heaving. I leaned to the foot of the bed, reaching for another tube of lubrication without care as to what I picked up. I coated my hands without looking and gripped my shaft, a pulse of pleasure shooting up my cock as I stroked myself, watching her. Her lips parted, the color in her cheeks high and hot as she stroked herself, watching me. My fist swallowed my tip, slick and smooth, my eyes locked on her hand. The throb of my orgasm was hot, hard, urgent.

I let myself go to climb her body, to kiss her, to spread her thighs with slick hands and settle my hips between them.

Her hands rasped the stubble of my jaw, her thighs drawing up, her heat cradling my cock. Every flex of her hips slicked my length, and with a trembling hand, I hooked the back of her knee and pulled it into my ribs.

My name rode her breath, filled her eyes, whispered on her fingertips.

I retracted my hips, knees digging into the bed, hand on her pale thigh. And with that simple shift, the very tip of me settled against the very edge of her.

She stilled—ribs, hands, eyes. But her heart fluttered against my chest, afraid and alert.

I smoothed her hair, arrested by the feel of her hot center against my crown.

"Breathe, Melia," I whispered.

She drew a shallow breath in compliance, her eyes darting between mine.

"I love you," I breathed, my throat tight.

And she sighed, throat bobbing as she swallowed. Touched my lips in wonder. Whispered words I'd dream of forever.

"I love you."

I kissed her once more, kissed her with all my hopes and fears, swallowed all of hers as she kissed me back.

And I flexed my hips, breaching her gently.

She gasped into my mouth, her body locking from the shock. The resistance was immediate and complete, the heat of her gripping me with a strength that drew a pleasurable pulse from my cock.

I stayed seated where I was, lips lowering to press a kiss to her sweet mouth, to remind her. To give her a moment to warm to the sensation, to acquaint herself with the feeling, not needing more from her but her kiss. My fingers traced her breast, thumbed the tight tip. Trailed lower, found the mound of her, brushed her still-swollen clit until she was soft under me, the velvet vise of her body opening, her hips rocking, settling her body onto mine in invitation.

Another gentle flex, pressing into her by increment, heart thudding from barely maintained control. Her face tightened, ashen, lips flat. She was caged in my arms, my fingers in her hair and my eyes searching her face for distress, but she smoothed her expression. Rolled her hips. Urged me on.

Another thrust, and she had taken my crown and then some, gripping it tight, so tight. My breath trembled from restraint, my thighs shaking, torn between my desire to drive into her and my desire to not hurt her. But her hands slipped around my ribs to my back and applied pressure, telling me to do it. To go. To fill her.

But first, I kissed her again. I kissed her and told her I loved her, kissed her and told her I needed her. And with all the tenderness I could offer, I thrust my hips, hanging on to hers, holding her still as I breached her completely.

Our eyes were locked, her body trembling, lips parted and brows drawn. For a moment, all I could do was breathe, the feeling of my body in hers, her core so tight, sending a deep throb through my cock in the sheath of her body.

The sweetest moan passed her lips, the deep sound of pleasure-pain.

She breathed a string of words I couldn't understand and didn't need to. They were the mutterings of a plea, a desire, a need I felt in every nerve of my body.

I pulled out slow, gently rolling my hips to fill her again. The opposition eased, her core opening up, her body sighing. She buried her face in the crook of my neck, hanging on to me, rocking her hips. And I closed my eyes, held her to me, and gave myself to her.

Every pump of my hips brought an easing of hers, the rhythm of our bodies merging, matching. Her lips on my throat, a kiss, the brush of her tongue. Her fingers holding me to her, holding her to me. Her body, soft under mine, hot around mine. My heart aching and pumping and calling to her.

Because I needed her more than I'd ever needed anyone. I loved her as I'd never loved anyone.

I came with a thundering rush, a seize of my heart. I buried my face in her hair, buried myself in her body, rode my orgasm with a burst of lightning behind closed lids until the wave receded. And I marked every detail—her quivering breath against my skin, her small hands clinging to me, her thighs trembling. The scent of her hair, the softness of her, the warmth of her still holding me tight.

I kissed her hair, kissed her forehead, her cheeks, her lips—those faithful, honest lips. When I finally broke away, it was to gaze into her shining eyes. My throat clamped tight. She smiled up at me, lips together, her breath hitching as a heavy tear slipped down her temple and into her hair.

A small, gentle laugh brushed past her lips, and she sniffled once. "I... I'm sorry."

I thumbed the track left by her tear. "Don't ever apologize to me for how you feel, Melia." I said inspected her face with adoration. "Are you all right?"

And when she smiled, it was powered by all the things I felt, mirrored there on the curve of her lips. "Perfect," she whispered.

I couldn't speak, so I kissed her again, a searing kiss, a declarative kiss, a kiss of promise and veneration.

I rolled, bringing her onto her side with me and pulling out of her in the same motion. My arm was under her, wrapped around her back, and before she could assess anything, I hooked my other arm in her knees and sat, holding her to my chest.

She tucked her head under my chin as I stood, carrying her to the bathroom. I set her down next to the tub and turned it on, testing the water.

"A bath?" she asked sleepily.

I smiled down at her. "Thought it might be nice. Want a fizzy thing?"

She nodded, her cheeks high, the color bright and alive. Her arms had moved to her chest in unintentional modesty, though not quite covering her. She looked so small, so vulnerable, though her smiling lips told me of one of the many ways she trusted me.

I pressed a brief kiss to her temple before grabbing the basket and picking a pink one with a soap flower in the top that smelled like lavender. "How's this one?"

Her smile tilted. "That one's called a sex bomb."

I glanced at it, turning it over in my hands. "It's not going to give you an orgasm, is it? Because I've decided that's my job."

She stepped into me, still smiling as she laid her hands on my chest. "Well, we wouldn't want to put you out of work, would we?"

I grabbed her hip, lowering my lips on a track for hers. "No, especially considering how good I am at it."

She laughed just before I kissed her, reveling in the feeling of her hands on my skin and her body against mine. A moment later, I had her by the hand as I stepped into the gigantic tub, helping her in after me. And as the water climbed higher, I sat at the back of the tub with Amelia nestled between my legs, her head resting in the dip of my chest.

I gathered her hair, combing my hands through it as she sighed. Her arms rested on my knees, fingertips skating the rising waterline.

"How do you feel?" I asked, twisting her hair up into a bun with the help of a hair tie on my wrist.

I waited while she considered my question, seeming to put her thoughts in order.

"My body feels okay. No," she amended, "better than okay. It wasn't as bad as I imagined it would be."

I chuckled, lips together. "Maybe I should take back my claims of skill."

She sat, turning around between my legs. Amelia was beaming, the light within her radiating, shining its warmth and love on me like sunshine after a long, cold winter. "Oh, don't take it back," she said, wrapping her arms around my waist, bringing her breasts to my torso. "You are everything." The words were reverent, her eyes open and bright. "You're everything I could ever want, all I could hope for. Thank you for loving me, Tommy."

"How could I not, Melia? Loving you is the easiest thing I've ever done," I said simply, brushing my knuckles across her cheek before opening my hand, cupping the curve with my palm.

And when I kissed her, it was with hope I'd never known for the girl who owned me completely.

counted them in ... ruined me. Those
have haunted me, ruined me through fire in search
my kingdom. I have walked through fire in search
lic that would save us, that would give me
kept them in coffers, counted them
for my pain. Those sins have haunted
claimed my kingdom. I have wal
lic that would sa

For the Record

AMELIA

My chin rested on my hand, which rested on Tommy's cavernous chest. Slowly, I rose and fell with his breath, the long, deep inhale and exhale of perfect sleep.

His big hand cupped my shoulder, his arm holding me to him like a vise, even in the dead of sleep. The room was painted in violety-reds and crimson-oranges, the sun only just setting the city on fire with its light as we spun around it, just like we always had.

But my world spun around the man under my palm, powered by the heart drumming against my hand.

The quiet ache between my thighs was nothing like I'd thought it'd be. I'd thought the entire ordeal would be horribly painful, impossibly awful, that I'd be split in half by the imposing member residing in his pants. But I was right to trust Tommy. He showed all the tenderness and care he had in him, which was a lot. So much that it only hurt for the few seconds it took him to fit himself inside me.

As shocking as the pain was, it had faded, replaced by pleasure. But all feeling came in a chain of bursts, flashes of sensation each equal in their intensity. It had been so much to experience that all I could do was hold on to him, urge him on, ease the fear behind his eyes.

I was changed, rearranged, and every piece of me had Tommy's name on it.

The last thing I wanted to do that morning was answer the summons to Janessa's office. Tommy and I were leaving that afternoon for a quick trip to Chicago for a book signing, and as badly as he needed to be here, writing, I was looking forward to a weekend away. I imagined us walking down Navy Pier and taking a selfie in front of The Bean like cheesy tourists. I pictured sitting next to him at his book signing, like he'd asked me to, surprised that the thought of being there with his readers didn't make me feel anxious at all. And I fantasized about a couple of long, sleepless nights in a penthouse suite with my husband.

I smiled at him like a loon.

I wasn't afraid of anything. Not with Tommy by my side. I was untouchable. I could do anything.

For weeks, I'd been looking for a way out, but the answer had been right there. I only had to find my voice. And Tommy had taught me how to sing.

I had story angles to pitch. I had outlines and options. And I found myself certain I could convince her.

Because I wouldn't betray Tommy. Not for anything in the world. And when I left Janessa's office today, she'd know that to be an indisputable fact.

Tommy drew a noisy breath through his nose, curling his arm and squeezing me to him as he roused. His long, dark lashes fluttered, blinking open lazily, his black eyes stirring along with his cock.

"Morning," I said, smiling.

He twisted, tangling our limbs as he pressed me into the bed with his chest, his thigh between my legs. "Morning," he echoed the split second before his lips claimed mine.

The kiss was long enough to leave me limp and buzzing in his arms, but nowhere near long enough for me to be satisfied. When he broke away, my eyes stayed closed, and I sighed into the ether and melted into the bed.

A soft chuckle compelled me to look up at him.

I shifted my hips, stroking myself on his thigh, eliciting a moan from the base of his throat.

"Careful. Move like that, and I'll be tempted," he said with a voice gruff and rumbling.

I shifted again, ignoring the tenderness of the flesh between my legs. "Maybe I want to tempt you."

He nipped at my lips but didn't make a move to settle between my thighs like I wanted him to. "Tonight. I want to give you more time."

The wry smile I wore slid into a frown. "What if I don't want to wait?"

"Too bad," he teased, smirking.

My frown jutted into a pout. "How come?"

He leaned closer, that sideways smile a dangerous warning. "Because tonight, I don't want to be careful."

"Oh," I breathed, tingling heat brushing my cheeks.

His hand found my breast, tested its weight, squeezed gently. His attention turned to his fingertips, his body shifting to slide down mine. "Don't sound so disappointed," he said, surveying my breast with his full attention. "I didn't say you wouldn't get an orgasm." His lips closed over my tight nipple, teeth skimming the aching peak.

And Tommy made good on his promise, just as he always did.

A COUPLE OF HOURS AND several orgasms later, I stood in front of my vanity, back straight and face set in determination as I recited the pitches in my mind. I smoothed my shirt. Turned to check the back of my skirt. Leaned into the mirror to get a good look at my lipstick, wearing Loud and Clear like a talisman.

"You're gorgeous," Tommy said from behind me.

When I turned, it was with a smile and a flitting of my heart. "Thank you." I strode toward him, not stopping until our bodies were flush.

He brushed my hair over my shoulder. "Tell me you'll hurry back."

I smiled. "I'll hurry back."

"Tell me you're packed."

"All packed."

His hand slid down my back to cup my ass. "Tell me you're not wearing panties."

A laugh shot out of me. "Sorry, but I can't walk into Janessa Hughes's office without the comfort of underwear."

Tommy leaned in. "Then tell me you'll let me take them off the second you walk through the door."

"Deal," I said just before he kissed me too gently, seeming to take care for my lipstick.

Damn his good manners.

I sighed. "Let me get out of here so I can get back."

"All right. Tell Janessa I said to go to hell."

"I'll be sure to relay the message," I said on a laugh, turning for the living room.

A longer, less careful kiss at the door left me wishing I could fast-forward until we were on our way to Chicago.

Down the stairs I trotted, slipping into the backseat of the Mercedes. Tommy waited at the top of the steps, leaning against the doorjamb in a henley and jeans, hands in his pockets and a devastating smile on his face. When I waved, he lifted a hand.

He didn't go inside until after I was long gone.

The drive was long enough to brew swampy heat in my palms, but not long enough to prepare me, not with my nerves climbing. I couldn't go over my notes anymore, couldn't know them any better. There was nothing to plan, nothing to rehearse.

I just had to get in there and do the damn thing and hope to God I could sway her.

The office was frenetic as usual, a bustling beehive buzzing with energy that ratcheted my anxiety with every step. I was waved in by her secretary, and when the door opened, there Janessa sat on her throne, ready to pass judgment with nothing more than the flick of her wrist.

"Hello, Amelia," she said warmly. "I'm glad you found time in your busy schedule to check in." The hint of sarcasm was almost undetectable, leaving me wondering if I'd imagined it.

"I'm sorry. We've just been tied up," I started as I sat, setting my bag down.

"Oh, I'm sure you have."

Okay, no, that sarcasm was there, alive and sneering. My heart lurched once, slamming against my breastbone.

"Look at you," she said with a touch of condescension. "Don't you look lovely? I barely recognize you these days."

The jab glanced off me, and I smiled like I did in front of the cameras when I was afraid. "Hair and makeup—that's all." I reached into my bag for the stack of proposals, eager to do what needed to be done so I could get the hell out of there. "I've done a lot of work to get you some options on the article, and I think I've got a couple of really strong angles."

"I'm interested to see what you've come up with."

She didn't seem interested. She seemed predatory.

I ignored the thought and passed the stack across her desk. She flipped through them, her face closed off and locked up tight. And I waited, my confidence slipping. A clock ticked from somewhere in the room. I resisted the urge to locate it so I could stare it into shutting up.

"I'm impressed by your effort," she said with a pause, which I filled with a smile and a flash of relief.

"Thank you. I really thought maybe the rundown of Tommy's famous girlfriends would be a good one, coupled with the girls he's stood up for. He's just so protective over the people he loves—"

"Yes, I'm sure." She flipped through them again, shaking her head. "They're still editorials, Amelia. This isn't what I asked for."

Janessa set the papers down, folding her hands on top of them. Her eyes were steely, her back painfully straight and shoulders square.

"These aren't good enough," she said flatly. "We've already got the material for your fake relationship. I want to know about all the rest."

A fire ignited in my chest that climbed across my skin, up my neck, bursting on my cheeks. "I can't disclose that, and he can't either. Do you realize what kind of legal trouble he'd be in?"

Her lips, which had been flat and determined, curled in a wicked smile. "I knew it was true, but to hear it from the source is more satisfying than I thought it would be."

Fear, cold and sharp, dragged a painful line down my middle. "You can't do this, Janessa. I *won't* do this."

One of her brows rose in amused challenge. "Won't you?" Her eyes hardened to flint. "I knew you weren't cut out for this job the second you walked through the door. But *you* were somehow the woman he chose to play the lead in his big charade. This story landed in my lap, and I'm not about to lose it. So I'd like to remind you of a few things you seem to have forgotten. Not only do I have the power to get you the job you want, but I have the power to ensure you *never* get that job. I have another reporter—one with more ambition and fewer scruples than you—who's got a piece ready and waiting for me to publish. I assure you, it isn't flattering. Not for Tommy *or* for you."

The band on my lungs tightened. There wasn't enough air. "Vivienne."

She smiled, a smug twist of her lips. "So, what will it be, Amelia? Do you still think you can have your cake and eat it?"

I looked down at my hands, my eyes hanging on the wedding band on my finger, the diamond winking at me to the rhythm of my trembling hand. "No," I said quietly.

"Good," she said with an edge of triumph. "I'm glad you see it my way."

"No." The word was stronger than before, my chin lifting to level her. "I can't have it both ways. So, you win." I stood, reaching for my bag with my heart thundering. "I quit."

The only surprise was in her eyes as they widened and the slightest smudge of color on her cheeks. "If you quit, I'll tell Tommy everything you've told me."

My jaw clenched. "Go ahead. I haven't told you anything."

She rose like an angel of death, hands braced on the surface of her desk. "Do you really think that matters, Amelia? Do you still believe that the truth matters? You of all people should know better. No one cares about the truth. It's about what they *want* to believe."

My nostrils flared as I dragged a stinging breath through my nose. "Tell him what you want, Janessa. He won't believe you, not over me."

Her smile was cold and serpentine. "I suppose we'll see."

"Yes, I suppose we will," I shot, leaving her with a final hateful stare before turning on my heel and storming out of that building to the cycling tune of a single question.

How will I tell him the truth?

I only hoped I was right. He had to believe me.

If not, we were both lost.

TOMMY

My brow quirked when the doorbell rang. The first thought in my mind was of Amelia.

I hurried to the door behind Gus, whose barking echoed off every smooth surface. She was due home any second. I wondered if maybe she'd forgotten her keys, but as I passed the dish where we dropped them, it only held mine.

I opened the door with a smile that slid off my face and onto the floor the second I saw Vivienne Thorne standing on my stoop with a smug smile on her face.

Gus sniffed her, and she jerked away, brushing him back with enough force to convince him to obey, although he did so with a low growl.

I knew exactly how he felt.

"What the fuck are you doing here?"

That superior smile curled tighter. "Oh, just wanted to swing by. Where's your *wife*?" she asked, brushing past me before I could stop her.

"Oh, she's just down at the *none of your fucking business*, Vivienne."

She turned in the entryway. "She's run off to Janessa again, hasn't she? Telling her boss all your secrets." A laugh, a horrible laugh that made me want to grab her around the neck and throttle her quiet. "That's all anyone wants from you, Tommy. You know that as well as I do. You should just come clean, clear the record. Admit it's all fake. Admit they were *all* fake. Admit your whole life is a lie so we can sigh our collective *I knew it*s and get on with our lives."

I shook my head, my hands flexing and relaxing at my sides as I tried to grip the reins of self-control. "You're dumber than I thought if you ever believed you could goad me into telling you a single fucking thing. I'll tell you what. Grab your pen and paper and write this down—I love my wife, and you're not original. You're the same as every other bitch with an agenda that I've been ignoring for years."

Unfazed, she smiled. "And your sweet little Amelia could *never* be a bitch with an agenda, could she?"

The rage in my chest flared. I stepped into her, hooked a hand on her upper arm, and forced her toward the door. "You don't know one fucking thing about her."

"I know plenty. Like the fact that she's writing for Janessa, not for you."

The certainty in her voice struck me. I stopped dead with Vivienne half on the stoop. "I don't believe you."

"You always were a sucker. Did you really think she'd tell Janessa no? She wants your story, and Amelia will give it to her. In fact, I have it on good authority that she just handed over a stack of notes all about you."

"Liar," I spat. "You'd say anything to hurt us, to break us. No one's buying your line, Vivienne. So do us all a favor and give it up, for Christ's sake."

Her eyes were cool, too calm to be bravado. "How about you ask her when she gets home, Tommy? Since you're so sure of yourself and all."

For one full second, I stared at her before shoving her the rest of the way out the door. "Don't tell me what to do, you fucking snake."

She turned, opening her mouth to speak just as the door slammed in her face.

My hands shook as I walked through the house and straight for the bar, pouring myself a scotch, too many fingers to be considered any measurement.

I downed it in three painful swallows.

She couldn't be right. It couldn't be true. There was no way Amelia—*my* Amelia—would betray me.

There was no fucking way in hell.

And yet, Vivienne seemed to know something I didn't. Her

certainty had unnerved me, taken a sledgehammer to the foundation of my trust. That tingling in my gut was unreadable, nebulous and uncertain for the very first time.

I splayed my hands on the cool countertop, my palms so hot that a damp fog collected on the surface.

I'd ask Amelia to tell me the truth.

And I hoped to God it wasn't the truth I feared.

AMELIA

By the time I was climbing the steps to the house, my thoughts were practically spilling out of me, too many to contain, and all of them waited on the tip of my tongue to confess.

I walked through the door, scanning for him as Gus greeted me.

"Tommy?" I called, absently scruffing Gus's ears before stepping to the sideboard to deposit my keys.

No answer.

I stripped off my coat, the dread sinking, twisting my innards. "Tommy, I'm home," I said as I walked into the living room, stopping dead when I saw him.

He sat on the couch, legs parted, empty glass of what I guessed had been scotch hanging from his hand between his knees. Everything about him was dark—the draw of his black brows, the line of his lips, the hard cut of his jaw. But his eyes were black as midnight, churning with emotion.

I stood perfectly still. The silence screamed between us.

"What happened with Janessa?" The words were low. Calm. A velvet noose.

My mouth dried, my tongue sticky and thick. "Tommy, I need to talk to you," I said softly, stepping further into the room.

He watched me approach. Nothing moved but his eyes and the steady rise and fall of his chest.

I sat across from him on the surface of the coffee table, wanting to get eye-level with him to say what I needed to say.

Just tell him the truth.

His face gave away nothing.

I tried to swallow. My throat clicked. My hands found each other in my lap and clasped so hard, it hurt.

There was nothing to do but say it. And there was no way to say it but plainly.

"Janessa has been pushing me to write an exposé. She wants to know your secrets, and she wanted me to tell her."

A pause, pregnant and thick. "How long? How long has she been angling?"

"Since the first time I saw her alone after…after we got m-married." I took a breath to steady myself. It did no good. "But Tommy, I'd never—"

"Weeks. You've kept this from me for weeks."

"I…yes," I admitted.

"Did you write about me? Did you hand your notes to Janessa today?"

Sharp was my breath. Shocked was my realization.

I'd left everything with Janessa.

"I…I did."

The mask fell, his anger rising like a storm. "Help me understand, Amelia. Help me understand why you would do this."

I launched into the admission, a rambling, desperate attempt to come clean. "From the very beginning, she's wanted to know about you, and from the first moment I met you, I knew I could never give her what she wanted. I…I thought she would be appeased when we came to her with the concept for the article. But she only saw it as an opportunity for more. I thought I could fix it, that I could find a way to help you with the article and somehow give her what she wanted, but ... but I couldn't. I can't. When I took my proposals to her today, she rejected my ideas. She told me I had to choose. So, I did. I chose you, Tommy. I quit."

A flash of warmth shifted in his eyes for a moment before it was gone, replaced by cool distance. "What did you tell her? What does she know?"

A hot flush of shame climbed my neck, my cheeks, as I confessed. "O-one proposal angled your mom, her illness, what you've done for her, your childhood. Another angled y-your exes, your private and public life."

The ache in my chest roared, tearing open. I couldn't speak. I couldn't breathe.

For a long moment, he said nothing. I watched as his hand passed over his face, fingers pressing into his eyes. Cupping his mouth. Testing the bridge of his nose.

The breath he took shuddered with barely restrained fury. "You lied to me."

"Tommy, I never lied to you," I breathed.

"But you did." The words were so still, so hard. "The second you wrote about me, put my secrets, my life on paper, and handed it to Janessa, you betrayed me. Keeping it from me was its own lie."

"I didn't mean to leave them with her, but I was s-so upset and ... Tommy, I swear, I was going to tell you as soon as you were finished with the book." A rush of tears, my nose stinging, throat tight. "I-I didn't want you to worry, and I thought ... I thought I could find a way to fix it. I was trying to *protect* you, not hurt you. Because if I didn't write this story, someone like Vivienne would. Someone who would hurt you. I would *never* hurt you. Never."

"Never *intentionally*," he amended. "I know you didn't intend to hurt me. You didn't intend to break my trust. But you did."

My breath hitched, a tear slipping from my lashes to fall to my skirt, too heavy to roll.

He was a hundred miles away, the road between us crumbling with every breath. "Never once did I ever question you. Never once did it even cross my *mind* that you would lie to me. You married me under the promise of a job, and still, I trusted you completely."

My brows were knit together so tight, my whole face bent. "Tommy, I don't care about the job. I did it for *you*. The article was meant to help you, and—"

"That article was never for me. It was for *you*. But what's worse than knowing you were plotting with Janessa? I had to learn the truth from fucking *Vivienne Thorne*."

"Vivienne?" I whispered, trying to piece it together.

"She came here when you were gone to let me know exactly what you were doing. And I was naive enough to think she was lying. That all she wanted was to get between us."

My hands were stiff and foreign in my lap. I looked down at them, not recognizing them. "She's writing an article about you for Janessa," I said, staring through my fingers. "They're in it together."

A sharp inhale through his nose as he scrubbed a hand over his mouth. "*Goddammit*, Amelia. If you had trusted me, we could have headed this off. If you'd been honest with me, I wouldn't have gotten blindsided. Coming from you, I could have handled the truth. But coming from *her*?" He flung a hand at the door. "You should have fucking told me, Amelia."

"I'm sorry," I said through my tears, flowing freely. "I'm so sorry." I reached for his hand.

But he jerked it away, standing with enough speed and force to nearly knock me back. The pain in his voice was acute, a barb aimed at my heart. "I believe you. I know that you're sorry, and I know you wouldn't deliberately betray me. But you gave the enemy the blueprints of my life. You kept it all from me—the blackmail, her deceit. You went around me when it's *my* life on the line. Now she has it all, and we both know she'll use it. I've been betrayed like this before, but I never thought it would be you. This is my bruise, Amelia. This is my deep, dark bruise, and you just pressed it."

"Tommy, please," I cried gently. "I love you."

"I know that. I do," he said, emotion shaking his voice. "But I'm too fucking hurt to be reasonable." He turned his back on me, striding across the room, chewing through the space like a prowling animal.

For a moment, I sat stupidly on the coffee table, unable to parse what was happening. "W-where are you going?"

He paused, glancing over his shoulder with betrayal touching every beautiful line of his face. "To Chicago. Without you."

My breath skipped, my heart aching so deeply, I pressed my palm to it. "Is this the end?"

The vision of him blurred beyond the curtain of tears, but when I blinked, they cleared. And in that briefest of moments, I saw his regret, his love, his longing. But he shook his head, looking away.

"No. But I need time, space. We'll talk when I get back."

He disappeared into his room, slamming the door behind him. And I was left alone with my tears to consider my mistakes as I held the shards of my heart in my hands, counting them one by one.

offers, counted them in ... ruined me. Those ...
... have haunted me, walked through fire in search
... my kingdom. I have walked through fire in search
relic that would save us, that would give me ...
... kept them in coffers, counted them
... for my pain. Those sins have haunted
... claimed my kingdom. I have walk
... that would sav

Tsunami

TOMMY

The last thing **I wanted** to do was leave.

The only thing I could do was get the hell out of there.

Beyond the window of the Mercedes, the city rolled by. I didn't see it. Imaginings of a dozen scenarios drifted in and out of my mind. Amelia and Janessa, head-to-head, plotting a takedown. Janessa asking her to betray me and Amelia agreeing with a hungry smile. The two of them laughing, raising a glass to their cleverness. Me holding Amelia, telling her I loved her, but her fingers crossed behind her back when she repeated the words. In every vision, she was a villain with a wicked smile and an expression on her face I'd never, ever seen—conniving.

But my imagination was active enough to be able to picture it without effort, my suspicion speculating the worst of all scenarios strictly to hurt me. To remind me that I'd brought this on myself.

My heart howled that I was wrong, that she'd never plot against me. My brain said otherwise with stern, direct force. It had been silent for too long. My heart had steered us into an iceberg, and my brain was having no more of it.

Confusion was the closest I could get to a feeling. My emotions were a mosaic, and I was too close to see the whole. Manipulation in shades of orange. Betrayal in shades of red. Love in washes of blue like the ocean, brushing the edges of hurt in deep violet. Trust in fiery yellows, licking the oranges and reds like flames.

I loved her, and she'd hurt me.

She hadn't meant to break me, but she'd been careless all the same.

She'd given Janessa my life, the truths I'd kept concealed for so long.

But the loop always came back to the heart of the matter—I'd let my guard down, and this was my penance.

I tore myself down with frantic hands, the reprimand fierce and violent. I'd trusted her implicitly—stupidly—from the first. She'd had to do so little to gain so much of my trust.

The day's discoveries had shaken me to the foundation. It wasn't even that she had betrayed me. I knew deep down, under layers and layers of anger and fear, that she hadn't done it on purpose.

But I had betrayed myself. That, I found, was as difficult to reconcile as the knowledge that Amelia had been working with Janessa behind my back, had loaded the cannon for my enemy. Amelia touched my greatest fear. She was everything I'd been running from, and I'd welcomed her into my heart without hesitation.

I was living the blessing and curse of that choice.

The worst part of it all, the regret and guilt of my heart, was that I'd created her. I had corrupted her in ways beyond comprehension by putting her in this place, by tenderly setting her in the lion's den and assuming she would do exactly as I wished. But she hadn't.

Amelia. My Amelia. I knew her so well, knew every curve of her face, every fleck of gray and silver in the ocean of her irises. But being confronted and hearing her confession had taken everything I'd believed and scrawled an asterisk in blood red next to her name. The seed of doubt was barbed, a thorny, poisonous kernel of truth, hooking in my mind and in my heart, spreading with astounding speed.

My fist closed, elbow resting on the door. The vision of her as I walked away filled my mind. Her shining hurt, her searing pain had stripped me bare, left me raw, more raw than the betrayal. Because she loved me, and she was sorry. And I loved her, but I was hurt, too hurt to do anything but run.

Time would do me—*us*—good. Time would quiet my fears. Time would see the tsunami of distrust receding to leave the truth. But for the moment, I was caught under the wave, tossed and spinning in the undercurrent, trying to figure out which way was up and which way was death.

I only had to find the sun.

Honeybear

AMELIA

The morning sunlight cut through the room in a wedge of light, its cheer and promise lost on me.

Claudius lay curled on my chest in a swirl of vibrating fur as I stared at my ceiling just like I had all night, watching the surface shift in color from midnight to violet, the shadows receding as the sun rose.

I wished it were raining. Thundering rain, plinking the windows, some soundtrack of melancholy to match my mood.

I'd stopped crying at some point when the shadows were still deep and full of sullen sadness. But I couldn't say I was empty. I wished I were. I wished I'd felt nothing.

Apathy would be a release.

It was the first night I'd spent alone in weeks. I'd never noticed how cold my bed was, how empty it could be with nothing but my insubstantial body to fill the space.

Tommy was gone. And I couldn't help wondering if I'd lost him forever.

The long hours of the night had been haunted by his words, his voice, the hard look of pain, the instant distance between us. Haunted by my agreement with everything he'd said.

He was right. Every word, every accusation. I should have told him the second Janessa threatened me. I shouldn't have tried to handle it without him, not as disadvantaged as I was by inexperience. And I never, ever should have written about him for Janessa.

I'd thought I was helping, but I'd only hurt him. It didn't matter that I hadn't intended to.

As he'd pointed out, I had whether I'd meant to or not.

The road to hell was paved with good intentions, and I'd paved mine with brimstone, thinking it was gold.

But I was blind. I always had been.

I shifted, suddenly unable to stand being in this bed for another minute. Stubborn Claudius made no move to relocate, just cracked one green eye and seemed to tell me to relax.

"Easy for you to say," I muttered, gently shoving him off me.

I threw off the covers, swinging my legs over the edge where they dangled, toes pointed at the ground. I'd start the day without sleep, and as such, it seemed that the day before had never ended. I didn't know what in the world I'd do with myself.

I should have been sitting next to him at the signing, managing his line, taking pictures, sneaking kisses. I should have been in his arms. But his arms were folded, closed, unwilling.

With a shuddering sigh and a blink to clear my vision, I slid off the bed, my feet landing on the rug with almost no sound. Gus hopped to his feet from his station at the foot of my bed, but even he was subdued, his tail wagging lazily as he ambled over to me, ears flat.

I ran a hand over the curve of his skull. "Good morning, Gus."

He opened his mouth in a panting smile, leaning into my hand.

I nodded, busying myself.

Sarah paused, watching me as I filled up the teakettle. "I know you're not all right, so I won't ask you the obvious. But do you want to talk about it?"

For a moment, I didn't respond, just watched the bubbling water fill the copper kettle. It wasn't until the teapot was on that I faced her.

"I … I hurt him, Sarah," I said with my voice shaking, my eyes on my fingers where they rested on the countertop. "He's right. I should never have kept this from him. If I'd told him, we could have handled it together. I … I thought I could save him, spare him, but I only hurt him worse, and now … now he's gone." My voice broke. I swallowed my emotion, but it bobbed back up like a life vest.

"He'll be back," she said gently, speaking to fill the space while I collected myself again. "He's hurt and angry, but here's something you should know about Tommy. He is scared to death of pain. So when he does get hurt, it makes him furious. It's his defense, a shield he holds up, like a bear on his hind legs, roaring his hurt to anybody in his path."

I nodded down at my hands.

"But you know something else?"

My gaze lifted to meet hers, her eyes a velvety brown, her face soft. "When the pain ebbs, when his hurt eases, he'll curl up at your feet and ask your forgiveness. He just needs time."

"There's nothing to forgive. It was me who ruined everything."

"No, honey," she said with a shake of her head. "You gave him something to believe in. You gave him hope. And that will overshadow anything that comes between you. He loves you, Amelia. And he knows the truth."

"That I didn't intend for all this?"

"No. That you love him, too. And the way you love, the way you *both* love, dictates loyalty, inherently and without question." She reached for my hand, covering it with hers. "Honey, he will come back, and everything will be all right. I promise. Just have a little faith."

"I hope you're right."

"I know I am. Just give him time to lick his wounds. Trust him just like you want him to trust you, and I promise, everything will work out just fine."

My throat tightened, my hope rising for the first time since I'd walked through the door yesterday.

Everything would be all right. I just had to trust him and hope he trusted me in equal measure.

And like a fool, I put my heart behind my hope completely.

The Who and the Why

AMELIA

Expectations and reality so rarely aligned.

I'd expected Tommy to come home the next day. For us to come together, to apologize and beg forgiveness, to forgive and move on.

I did not expect to find a picture of Tommy's naked ass on Vivienne's Instagram.

She'd thoughtfully tagged me in the image—Vivienne looking freshly tossed and utterly gorgeous in the early morning light, and in the background was my husband, naked and asleep in a hotel bed on his stomach, the sheets tangled around his legs. His face was buried in the pillow in his arms, his dark hair curling and cascading over his shoulder.

I would know his body anywhere. But the damning, irrefutable evidence was the perfect globe of his ass, marked with the words *Made in the Bronx.*

The location tagged in the photo was the hotel in Chicago where

I knew Tommy was staying.

I knew because I should have been there with him.

My phone rested facedown on the bed for a long, long time before I found the composure and courage to pick it up again.

The article she'd linked the image to set another wave of helpless tears on me, the power and depth of which I hadn't experienced before.

The *USA Times* had published a spread written by Vivienne Thorne, titled "The Truth About Tommy." In great and explicit detail, Vivienne proceeded to tear down the construct of Tommy's image, built with years of care by a man who'd only wanted to be left alone. Every relationship, every public appearance, everything was a lie.

Including me.

She knew things she shouldn't, details she couldn't. She spoke words that were familiar, ringing of a voice not her own.

Because they were mine.

So many of her points were retellings of my notes, embellished and added to, inflated to the point of pomp and bombast. Janessa. It was the only explanation. Vivienne had gotten her job back, and Janessa had enough in my notes to damn him. She had taken the lead and ran with it, painting him as a charlatan, a fraud.

In his way, he was. But she'd left out all the important details.

She'd left out the why simply to destroy the who.

The end of the article had left me gutted, read between long stretches of holding my phone to my chest, unable to breathe, unable to see past my tears. Vivienne had made it her spectacular finale to recount her sexual encounter with Tommy, just last night in his hotel in Chicago after a fight with his fake wife.

It was a cool account of their interaction in the hotel bar, one that had inevitably led them back to his room, where they hooked up, where Tommy admitted all the things in the article were true. Confirmed from the source.

I wished then that he'd just broken up with me. Maybe then wouldn't have hurt so badly to know that he'd slept with Vivienne to spite me.

His characters had always been an archetype of him, and with that knowledge, I shouldn't have been surprised. He was so angry, so hurt. And as I looked at the proof of his betrayal, I found I couldn't reconcile the man I thought I knew with the man who would do this to me. To us.

But I reminded myself of an important fact.

It was all a dream. A fantasy. None of it was real.

It never had been.

My phone buzzed and dinged and lit up over and over again while I packed my things until I couldn't take any more. I shut it off, unsure that I'd ever turn it back on. I wrote a letter as tears rolled down my face, collecting at my chin. I stowed Claudius in his crate. I knelt at Gus's feet and held him around the neck and cried, telling him what a good boy he was, telling him how much I'd miss him.

And I left my keys in the dish when I walked out the door.

True Sins

TOMMY

Nothing about me was calm.

Not the thundering of rushing blood in my ears, not my pulse fluttering in the thick vein on my hand. Not my racing thoughts or the tight muscles of my body, legs bent, too long for even the first-class seat.

I waved the flight attendant off when he tried to offer me another scotch.

One more, and I might hulk the fucking hatch off the plane and take a dive.

My phone pinged and vibrated with messages, one after another after another. Messages from everyone—my agent, my editor, my brother and mom, a dozen reporters, all of my exes, and my lawyers.

Everyone but the one fucking person I needed to speak to.

My wife.

My texts had gone unanswered, my calls sent straight to voice mail. Theo had gone to check on her but she was gone. There was a note. He hadn't read it, but noted that she'd taken her cat with her.

Which meant she wasn't coming back.

My hand found my lips, cupped the bottom half of my face, scrubbed it like it would help me find words. Find a solution. Find answers.

The article had broken, and it had broken everything I'd built along with it. It had stolen everything I'd tried so hard to protect. It had robbed me of my cover, and now their sights were trained on me.

Vivienne's exposé was scathing, a dressing down that had stripped me naked. Legally, we were taking every measure we could. My lawyers were already fielding accusations from the lawyers of my ex-girlfriends, the contracts between us in question. The contract between Janessa and myself had been laid out and combed over. The *USA Times* legal team was, at that moment, on their way into meetings to sort out what the fuck had happened and who was liable.

My lawyers had asked if I wanted to shake down my contract with Amelia. But I'd told them to leave her alone.

I should have known when Vivienne showed up at the convention that something was so fucking wrong. But she was just being Vivienne, posturing and throwing her weight around, slinging barbs in an attempt to crack me open. And as always, I had blown her off without telling her anything but to fuck off.

I had decided this morning that Vivienne was perhaps the biggest mistake I'd ever made. And I'd made a lot of fucking mistakes.

She was the first person I'd pointed to when I sicced my lawyers on every one of the fucks who'd had a hand in this.

That deep ache in my chest throbbed when I thought about Amelia seeing that photograph. I'd had no idea Vivienne had taken it a year ago when we hooked up at this very same convention, in the very same hotel.

I knew the second I learned Amelia was gone that she had not only seen that photo, but she believed it.

That knowledge hurt worse than anything, beyond any betrayal, beyond all offenses. After everything, after all she knew, after all we'd been through, she believed Vivienne. She believed the lie that the newspaper told her, the fake pictures, the line. Everything I hated, everything I despised, she believed without question.

The knowledge, the realization, had gutted me.

She didn't trust me after all.

She thought so little of me, she believed that I had committed the unforgivable sin of my heroes. That I'd slept with Vivienne out of spite.

She hadn't even asked me for the truth.

And above all, that was the sin I found I couldn't forgive.

AMELIA

I knew he was coming back. I knew he would find me. I knew I would see him, face him, see the truth for myself.

But the man I found on my stoop was almost unrecognizable.

Tommy was thunder and lightning, a black cloud sparking with electricity. Black eyes. Black hair. Black shadow on his sharp jaw. Black, broken mood.

He said nothing. He didn't have to.

Silently, I stepped back, a wordless concession to his entry.

My heart, I found, was as black and bottomless as his anger. The chasm between us yawned.

My eyes lit on details of his body. His hands, where had they touched her? His lips, where had they kissed her? His eyes, had they been hot and smoldering for her? His hair, had she run her fingers through it? Had he whispered his pleas, told her of my transgressions? Had he wanted her all along?

I crossed my arms over my stomach, squeezed, tried to hold myself together as hot, angry tears stung my eyes.

Neither of us sat. We stood squarely before each other, unmoving.

"You left," he finally said.

The sound of his voice was a salty sting on the deep wound of my heart.

"You left first. Except I came home, alone. Where were you last night?"

The flash of pain behind his eyes struck me like lightning.

"It seems you already think you know. Does it matter what I say?"

Emotion seized my throat, rising up from my heart, uncontained. "Vivienne. Of all the women you could have fucked, you had to choose *her*. I can't believe you," I cried. "I can't believe you would do this to me."

He didn't move, but everything about him changed. Hardened. Darkened when I thought he couldn't be any darker, an eclipse of the moon on a starless night.

"If you think I fucked Vivienne Thorne last night, you don't know me at all."

The fiery rage in my heart went out with a hiss.

"You—" I whispered, but he cut me off.

"That picture was from the conference *last year*."

My mind tripped and stumbled down a hillside, unable to catch itself. "But…"

"Have I ever indicated I feel anything for Vivienne but the desire to make her disappear?"

I couldn't breathe. "N-no."

"Have I ever so much as even *looked* at another woman since I've been with you?"

Tears stung, no longer angry. They were sharp with shame. "No," I whispered.

"Then why, Amelia…why for the love of God would you think I would sleep with someone else? Especially someone who has been actively trying to ruin both of us?"

"I…" Too fast, the thoughts were too fast, the realization clicking like pins in a lock. "Y-you slept with her before. You…you were so angry, and I thought…I thought you…if you wanted to hurt me, you knew this would."

His Adam's apple bobbed. Nothing else moved. "You thought," he started, his voice controlled, the timbre ominous, "after all I've done to protect you, that I would fuck Vivienne to hurt you?"

"I…" I couldn't finish. My tears fell, guilt washing over me. "I…I did."

He drew a breath that sucked all the air from the room. "You don't trust me. But I trusted you completely. I always thought you were the naive one, Amelia. Turns out it was me."

Pain, sharp and cutting. "I…I'm sorry," I whispered, but the words weren't enough.

"You believed their lie—*the* lie, the press, everything I hate—instead of trusting *me*. You have betrayed me more deeply than I thought you capable of. And it's my own fault. For putting you here. For turning you into this." His fisted hands trembled violently enough to see the movement from feet away. Locks of hair shook infinitesimally. His voice shuddered when he spoke. "I think you should stay here until we figure out what to do."

"What to do?"

"About this. About everything. About us."

I shook my head. I couldn't see him anymore—he was a shining blur, a mirage. A dream. Tears spilled down my cheeks, soaking them.

"I'm sorry I dragged you into this. I'm sorry I put all of this on you.

And I'm sorry you couldn't trust me. Without trust, we have nothing."

It was too much, too much pain, too much to process, to understand, to grasp what he was saying. I needed time. I needed air. I needed him.

"Tommy, please," I choked, reaching for him as he stepped for the door.

But he backed away from me with his lips hard and eyes shining, his drawn brows betraying the emotion of his broken heart. "Don't," he warned. "*Please*." The word broke.

I retracted my hand, clutching it to my chest.

"Goodbye, Amelia," he said like it was the last time.

And then he was gone.

The Story They Want

AMELIA

The next twenty-four hours were a blur.

Katherine found me on the couch some time after Tommy left. I didn't know how long it had been. I wasn't sure how I'd gotten there.

Everything hurt. My thudding skull. My swollen eyes, the well of tears infinite. My lungs burning. My ribs hitching. The hollow space inside where my heart used to be nothing but a gaping hole with seared edges.

I was wrong, so wrong. And he was right. About everything.

I'd had everything I could have wanted and lost it all.

Somehow, I ended up in bed. I took something, put into my palm by Katherine, her face tight with worry as I told her everything.

And I cried. I cried with her holding me, her arms wrapped around me and whispers on her lips until I eventually fell asleep.

It was a dreamless, heavy sleep, the kind that left you hungover and worthless, a blank loss of time that would have worried me, if it hadn't been welcomed.

When I woke, the sun was high, my room bright, my heart missing. Gone.

I was empty.

My mind was slow, thick and hazy from whatever Katherine had given me. Judging by the time, I guessed a sleeping pill. I'd never been so grateful to lose a day. I wondered how many more of those pills she had. Maybe I could take another. Skip another day. Fast-forward in the hopes that, when I finally woke for good, I would be beyond everything.

Or better yet, that I'd wake to find it had all been a dream. A beautiful dream turned nightmare. But that wasn't how hearts worked. I wouldn't find peace in a coma—my pain would be patiently waiting when I woke. So I lay there in my bed, testing the edges of the wound in my chest with tentative fingers.

I embraced every moment of pain, relished in the sick sensation. The pain was my penance.

I retraced my steps, marked every decision made, looking for the point where it had all gone wrong. Trying to map out how I'd gotten here. Somehow, my love for him hadn't been enough. It hadn't been enough to absolve me. It hadn't been enough to guide me. My intentions, my designs, hadn't mattered.

All that mattered were the consequences. There was nothing to regret except choosing a different path. It had seemed so innocuous, the path I'd been on. It had seemed right.

That was one thing Tommy had been wrong about.

It *was* me who was naive. My inexperience had led me down a road that ended in a trap door, the floor speared with spikes. And here I was at the bottom, looking up at the square of light I'd fallen from, wishing I'd done everything different.

My door cracked open, and I caught a sliver of Rin. When she saw

I was awake, she opened it the rest of the way, her face bent in concern.

"Hey," she said so quietly.

I didn't speak.

She strode over, sat on the edge of my bed, searched my face. "Did you sleep?"

I nodded once.

For a moment, she just watched me, her face impossibly sad. "I am so sorry."

And just like that, I was no longer empty. The hole in my chest filled with grief, spilling over the top. Tears, never-ending tears, fell without obstruction.

She didn't speak, just laid a hand on my leg and held on to me.

At some point, the well of emotion emptied again. Rin handed me a tissue.

I gathered my strength enough to sit up, my hands slow and clumsy.

"What are you going to do?" she asked gently, handing me another when I'd spent the first.

I dabbed at my nose. "There's nothing to do, Rin." My voice was scratchy and rough from disuse.

"There is *always* something to do," she assured me.

I shook my head. "Y-you didn't s-see him. There's no coming back from this. I've hurt him too badly."

"But you love each other. There has to be a way, Amelia."

Val's voice came from the doorway. "She's right. There's always a way."

She walked in with Katherine in her wake and took a seat opposite Rin. Katherine sat on the foot of the bed. The three of them watched me with too many emotions on their faces to count.

"There's nothing I can say. He knows I love him. He knows I'd never hurt him. But in the end, that doesn't matter, does it? It isn't enough to rewrite the facts. I should have believed him. I shouldn't have written about him. I shouldn't have …" I dissolved again, wishing I could disappear, evaporate, vanish.

"Anyone would have believed the picture. That post was damning, Amelia," Katherine said with matter-of-fact pragmatism. "It looked real, and coupled with the article and the fact that you'd fought … the conclusion wasn't that much of a jump."

"I didn't even ask him. I didn't trust him. I betrayed him in the most brutal of ways. I-I just didn't know. He's the only man I've ever been with, the only man I've ever loved. And I thought I understood trust. I thought I trusted him. But he's right. When it mattered, when it came down to it, I didn't. It's just—" A sob racked through me, and I took a long breath, trying to calm myself. I couldn't stop crying. "It's just that I never really believed he could love me. I never believed I was enough for him. As much as I trusted him, there was always a part of me that didn't think myself worthy. The thought of him sleeping with V-Vivienne didn't take much imagination. And beyond that, I gave away his secrets. I sold him out."

"But you didn't mean to," Val insisted.

"But that doesn't matter." I stated the fact with quiet certainty. "I did."

"You can't give up." Rin shook her head at me, her brows drawn. "There has to be *something* you can do."

"You have to fight for him." Val's lips were flat.

"How?" I cried. "What could I possibly do? How could I possibly make up for this? For all of this?"

"Tell him," Katherine said. "Tell him the truth. Tell *everyone* the truth. The whole thing, the whole story."

My face bent in a frown. "What do you mean?"

"You had a story to write," she answered. "So write it."

I shook my head against the thought, but my mind hooked the thread and pulled it, the idea lengthening and unraveling in my hands.

Write the story.

Tell him how I felt.

Tell *everyone* how I felt.

That, I could do.

"I don't know if it will change his mind," I said softly, wishing with all I had in me that it could.

Katherine reached for my hand. "But it might. If you're honest and if he loves you, it might."

The words were already stringing themselves together in my mind, my hope nothing but flickering embers.

But embers were better than nothing. And with gentle care, with love and tending, I could try to coax them into a flame.

And so I squeezed her hand and said, "It just might."

The Truth About Tommy

TOMMY

Three days.
Two broken hearts.
One shitstorm.
Zero words on my manuscript.

I stared at the blank page with blank eyes and a blank mind. I hadn't written a word since before Chicago. The ending of the story had eluded me, my muse gone. I didn't know how the story ended.

I didn't know how *our* story ended.

In all the phone calls and meetings I'd had, not one of them had been with the one I needed, the one I wanted. There was only one person who could comfort me—the one who had broken my heart. We hadn't spoken, though not for lack of things to say.

There were *too many* things to say. And I didn't know how to say any of them.

I didn't even know where to start.

I'd had my hands full anyway attempting to straighten out the mess in an effort to ignore the gaping wound in my chest. The biggest win my lawyers had notched on their belt was Janessa's head on a platter. When faced with the lawsuit, the *Times* had smiled, said they would take care of it, and she had been dismissed immediately. The next in line had swiftly stepped in, and I'd found her to be much more compliant. A retraction was in the works, I'd been told. Beyond firing Janessa, it was the best any of us could hope for.

Vivienne had not gotten her job back after all, and the slander suit we'd slapped her with—along with an ominous revenge porn charge—sent her packing. Literally. I'd heard she was on her way to Los Angeles. If I had my way, she wouldn't be able to get a job at a newspaper more reputable than the *Enquirer*. And I often got my way.

My editor had been a much more difficult problem to solve. Thank God Steven loved the book enough to put up with my shit. I was just a few chapters from the end, and once that was turned in, he'd assured me things would be okay. Assuming the newspaper's retraction went out soon.

And assuming I could write the end.

Amelia's letter sat on the corner of my desk, folded and unfolded and folded again. A reminder.

I'd woken up in Chicago ready to come home and make it right. To work through it all, forgive and apologize, to hold her and move on.

But she'd been gone. And the letter that awaited me did nothing to mend my broken heart.

I'm sorry I hurt you so deeply that you'd seek comfort with her.
I'm sorry for all I've done.
And I'm sorry I wasn't enough.
I'll always love you.
—Amelia

I closed my laptop with a forceful snick and pushed back from my desk. The room had become foreign, my life foreign. Amelia had changed everything, all the way down to where and how I wrote. And sitting in this room again was only a reminder that I couldn't go backward.

I couldn't erase the last month with her. I couldn't pretend like things would be the same.

I didn't want them to be. But I didn't want to go back that far.

A week would have done just fine.

I missed her desperately. Every cold, quiet night without her. Hours spent wondering what she was doing, if she was all right, knowing she wasn't. Days spent trying to reconcile what had happened and how I could both not want to see her at all with the need to find her, to hear her voice, to know she was alive and loved me and was hurting just as hopelessly as I was.

I exited the room, though its morose energy clung to me like the cold, following me down the stairs. Gus's head rose, his eyes big and sad. He didn't get up, didn't bound over to me. He just lay there in his post in front of her door, watching me with accusation as I walked through the room.

"Come on, buddy. Wanna go for a walk?"

The trigger phrase always turned him into a hysterical bundle of fur. But today, he just lowered his head to his paws in refusal.

I strode to him and got down on my haunches. Stroked his head. Sighed.

"I miss her, too," I said.

He let out a sigh of his own.

Hand on my thigh, I pushed myself to stand, turning for the door. I needed to get out of the house. It wasn't even eight in the morning, and I'd spent the last two hours staring at an empty page, fruitlessly willing words to come. I refused to sit there all day again with nothing to show for.

I trotted down the steps and to Ma's place, looking for a distraction.

She sat on the couch, drinking coffee with a book. "Morning, honey," she said, smiling.

"Hey, Ma."

She slipped her bookmark in, and when she closed the book and I saw the cover, something in my chest twisted painfully. I sat next to her, thumbing the edge of the pages.

"*Lord of Scoundrels*. That's a good one. What part are you at?"

"Dain just kissed her in the rain and ran off, left her there in the street, all alone." Her eyes were soft with understanding. "You can't deny Amelia has good taste."

"No, I suppose I can't," I said softly.

"You holding up?"

"Not really."

"Still no words?"

I shook my head. "I don't know how the story ends, Ma."

"Well," she started gently, "a grand gesture wouldn't hurt. Forgiveness. Apology. Acceptance."

"I don't know how to do that. I don't know how to forget."

"Nobody says you should try to forget."

I didn't respond.

"I know you're hurt. I do, and you're not wrong to be. But you betrayed her trust, too."

I frowned, glancing at her.

"You didn't believe she was trying to protect you by not telling you."

I shook my head. "It's not that, Ma. I do believe her. I was—*am*—mad she didn't tell me, but I believe her. I hate that it went down like it did, that she gave Janessa ammunition, even though it wasn't intentional. But she didn't trust *me* when it came down to it. She believed *them*. She believed some bullshit article and Vivienne's lie."

"But how long will you hold on to that? You love her, Tommy."

"What is love without trust?" I thumbed my lip. "I was mad about her lying about Janessa. But I was broken by her lack of faith in me."

"I don't know if I'd say she lied."

"Omission is just another brand of lie. You know it as well as I do."

She drew a long breath and let it out slow. "She's just so inexperienced. I understand how she could have jumped to the conclusion."

"I can't. Not for the life of me."

Ma's face bent in determination. "Amelia has known you for years as a womanizer, thanks to you and your Teddy's scheming. You've slept with Vivienne before. You got in a fight with Amelia, left her here while you stormed off, pouting. Should I remind you that this is exactly what a character in one of your novels would do? Is it really so hard to see how she could have misunderstood?"

"She shoulda called me," I insisted, ignoring the truth of the rest. "She shoulda waited. Asked. Something. Anything but this."

Ma nodded. "She should have. But honey, all of this is a misunderstanding. A mistake. Do you really think you can walk away from her without a single regret?"

The question shot a bolt down my spine. It hadn't occurred to me to ask it so plainly of myself. I hadn't been ready to face that truth. But when I looked into my future, Amelia was there. She was right there. And I couldn't see myself without her.

I swallowed hard.

"Your weakness is this idea that you're invulnerable. But you can't go through life without being hurt. You can't love without risk to your heart. Amelia is the only thing that could truly hurt you, and you ran away from that pain because you're afraid of it. But honey, listen to me," she said, taking my hand, searching my eyes. "You love her. So get her back."

"I don't even know what to say to her," I said softly.

"Think about all the mistakes you've made, all the forgiveness you've been given. There's a place in your heart to give that back, offer an apology of your own. Do you think you could do that?"

"I…I don't think I have a choice," I said, the stony weight on my chest lifting, powered by glimmering hope. "I don't know if I can go on without her."

"If anybody can mend this, it's Amelia," she said with all the faith in the world.

And I believed her without question.

Theo flew into the room, gaze on the phone in his hand. "You haven't been online," he said, his brows drawn.

My chest seized. "What fucking now?"

His jaw was set. "The *Times* printed the retraction. You need to read it."

I took his phone, my mouth bone dry, heart stopping completely when I read the headline.

"*My Month with Thomas Bane: The Real Truth About Tommy*" by Amelia Bane.

My gaze shifted to Theo's, a torrent of thoughts exchanged in that single glance. And then I dropped my eyes to his phone again and read.

Everyone thinks they know the truth about Tommy.

He's a player and a rake. A rogue and a menace. He's irreverent and charming, a scoundrel worthy of headlines in all of your favorite gossip columns. He's trouble with a capital T to start and an oh, my at the end.

Some of that is true.

Most of it isn't.

A month ago, none of you knew my name. I was just a painfully shy book blogger with a new job at the Times.

A month ago, I wasn't married.

A month ago, I'd never been kissed.

And then I met Thomas Bane.

If any of you have had the pleasure of meeting Tommy, you know that he is one of the most magnetic, charismatic, and convincing men on the face of the earth. And when he asked for my help, there was only one answer I could give.

Never once, not for a single minute, have I regretted saying yes.

There is so much that I could say about Tommy. I could speak gospel about his dedication and work ethic, his rise from obscurity to build an empire. I could speak volumes about the fierceness of his love, the depth of his loyalty to those he cares for—his family.

But the testament I want to give is my own.

Our marriage was fake. That's true.

Until it wasn't. Because I fell in love with Thomas Bane.

I know why you believe the lies about him. We believe what we want, what we're fed. Thomas Bane, Nazi. Bad Boy Bane, the public menace. Thomas Bane, the liar. The heartbreaker. The charlatan who's been fooling us all, if you believe Vivienne Thorne.

I can't blame you for that. I believed the lies, too.

It's how I lost the only man I've ever loved.

But here is the truth about Tommy. He taught a girl who was afraid how to be brave. He showed her how to love without condition, to trust without question. He gave her hope. Showed her the depth of his heart, unlocked the gate to his life, himself, without hesitation.

He gave me his trust, something he's not granted to any woman before.

And I betrayed that trust when I believed the lie that Vivienne Thorne published.

Tommy has let you all believe the lies before because he fabricated them himself. He wanted you to believe what he gave you because it misdirected you from the things he truly loves. But this lie was different. Because with Vivienne's lie, he was hurt, though not because of the lie itself.

But because I believed it.

No, I've never regretted marrying the most loyal, honorable, and loving man I have ever known.

But I have so many other regrets.

I'm sorry I didn't trust him. I'm sorry I didn't come to him when Janessa Hughes asked me to expose his secrets. I'm sorry I was so naive to think I could bear the burden on my own. That in trying to spare him pain, I only caused him more.

But my greatest regret is betraying my love by believing Vivienne's lie without a single question.

Vivienne conveniently failed to mention in her salacious recount of their tryst that it happened a year ago. She left out the facts—that his past fake relationships were meant to protect him, protect his heart and family from this exactly.

The best thing I ever did was agree to become Amelia Bane. Because knowing Tommy has forever changed me. The depth of his love, the breadth of his devotion, the hard line that exists between right and wrong. The man beyond the wall is so much more than I could put into words. More than I could explain to you. He showed me what it meant to love and be loved. And I learned the hard lesson of how not to love and the truth of faith.

Faith is complete and absolute. Faith cannot be shaken. Faith believes, even when what you can see betrays what you know.

I only hope that you all get the chance to know him now that the wall is gone. Now that there's nothing between you, I hope you can see him. I hope you can somehow know the man I love, and I hope that you will trust him in the ways I didn't but should have.

I hope you fall in love with him as I did.

And I hope you learn faith of your own.

I swallowed the dry lump in my tight, stinging throat, reading the article again. Soaking up every word, hearing the truth of her apology over the aching depth of my love for her.

I met Theo's eyes, my heart thudding. "Did you know?"

"That she wrote the retraction? No. That she's right? Yes." He watched me for a second as I sat stunned on the couch. "What are you gonna do?"

I held his black eyes with mine, knowing there was only one thing to do.

"I'm gonna figure out how to tell her I'm sorry."

Shake the Heavens

AMELIA

The social media frenzy when I'd married Tommy was nothing compared to what happened when the *Times* published the article.

Calls, emails, requests for my presence on a multitude of media outlets flooded the *Times'* office. Everyone had questions, and everyone wanted to know what was next. When was the next installment coming? Had I heard from Tommy? Were we okay? Would we be?

His silence was all the answer I possessed.

The article was a love letter, that was true. But I was no longer naive enough to have hope for forgiveness. My crimes were too grave, the lesson learned hard. My only true hope was that he had read it and knew I loved him, that I was sorry, that I should have had faith. Even if he didn't love me anymore, even if he didn't want me. I wanted to set the record straight, and I had.

No, I didn't expect him to forgive me.

But I'd be a liar if I said that under all of that, in the depths of my heart, I could put out the quiet fire that hoped for a second chance.

I'd been sitting on the couch for a few hours, listening to music, watching the fire crackling with Claudius in my lap. A book sat forgotten on the couch next to me. My phone sat silently on the coffee table. I'd set it to Do Not Disturb, and the only exceptions on calls it would allow through were from my friends and Tommy.

It had been lifeless all day.

Claudius rode my torso as I drew a heavy sigh and let it go.

I wondered what Tommy was doing. Was he missing me like I was sick over him? Had his anger ebbed at all, or was it still the inferno I'd seen when last we spoke? Had he finished the book? How had it ended?

How would *our* story end?

I didn't know. And I didn't know if I'd ever know.

The doorbell rang, sending me off the couch cushion by at least three inches. Claudius bolted off my lap and up the stairs for my bedroom.

I pressed a hand to my skittish heart, too many hours of quiet broken by the startling, innocuous doorbell.

"Coming," I called as I wound around the couch, reached for the doorknob. Turned. Pulled.

Died.

Tommy's visage was there on my porch, tall and dark and beautiful. His hair was loose, the scent of soap and leather swirling into me in eddies.

His face betrayed nothing. The set of his lips. The depths of his eyes.

"Tommy," I breathed.

He nodded once in lieu of a greeting. "Can I come in?" he asked cautiously.

"Of course." I stepped out of the way, the flush hot on my face.

I didn't see the manila envelope in his big hand until he passed me.

My guts twisted, my eyes locked on the envelope, my chest prickling with needle-sharp pain.

Divorce papers. Those were divorce papers.

This was it.

This was how it would end.

Tommy stopped just inside, turning to face me as I closed the door.

I held my chin up, kept it still, breathed in. Breathed out.

He looked down at the envelope. "I...I'm sorry to come by unannounced."

"It's okay," I said quietly, fighting back a hundred other things I wanted to say.

"I needed you to look over something for approval. I was going to email it to you, but I really thought it needed to be in person. After everything we've been through, I owe you that much."

He extended the envelope. I took it.

"You don't owe me anything," I muttered, opening the envelope, doing my level best not to cry.

"Yes, I do."

But I didn't speak, didn't look up. My eyes were locked on the packet in my hand, my heart climbing my throat.

The chapter title was "Forgiveness."

I read so fast, I had to force myself to slow down, to read every word.

Wynn had come to the fae palace, seeking Aislinn out after she disappeared. He'd rejected her, thinking she'd betrayed him. But her machinations had been to save him. He just hadn't realized it until it was almost too late. He knelt at her feet, her hands in his.

"I have collected sins, kept them in coffers, counted them in silence as markers for my pain. Those sins have haunted me, ruined me. Those sins have claimed my kingdom. I have walked through fire in search of the relic

that would save us, that would give me absolution. But there is no relic."

Fear and shock gripped Aislinn. All they had worked for, all they had endured, for nothing. "It is gone?"

"No," he said softly. "It is you."

"Me?" she breathed, grasping for understanding.

"My absolution is found in you. The key, the truth, was found in abandoning what I'd thought I knew. Only one power exists that could harm me—my love for you. And my love is what will save us all. Forsaking you is the sin I will not survive, cannot forgive. Tell me I am not too late. Tell me there is still a chance, and I will rewrite the stars. I will shake the heavens and mark them with your name." He reached for her face and brushed a sparkling tear from her cheek. "Forgive me, Aislinn, though I do not deserve it. Because without you, I am lost."

I tore my eyes away and met Tommy's. His mask had cracked, and I saw his fears, his sorrow, his love.

"You finished it," I whispered, swallowing my tears, unable to let myself believe that art still imitated life, that Wynn's feelings were Tommy's.

"Just now. I've been up all night. As soon as it was finished, all I could do was shower and come here. To you."

I smiled up at him. "I'm just so happy for you, Tommy. You did it. In one month, you did it."

"Only because of you." He took a step toward me, his eyes smoldering. "I didn't know how to end it. Didn't know what to write. For days, I sat staring at a blank page, waiting. But I couldn't write the end. Not until I knew what to do about us."

My smile faded as he edged the truth. "Oh. Yes, of course." The disappointment in my voice was impossible to contain. I tried. "What did you decide?"

Another step. The tilt of his lips. He reached for my hand. "That

I love you."

My heart stopped painfully, a dead thunk in my chest. "After everything I've done?"

He took the envelope, tossing it on the couch without looking away from me. "You weren't the only one who was wrong. I know you. I know every corner of your heart. I was just too upset to see beyond myself to the truth. You, Amelia Bane, are the purest thing I have ever known. And if I lost you, I would never forgive myself. I would never escape it. Because I love you, Amelia. Forgive me for not trusting you with Janessa. Forgive me my anger, my pain, the time I needed to see reason. *I will rewrite the stars. I will shake the heavens and mark them with your name. Because without you, I am lost.*"

Tears spilled down my cheeks. "Forgive you? It was me who was wrong. I never should have doubted you."

He thumbed the cool track of my tears. "Swear to me you'll always come to me. Promise me you'll always hear my side."

"Always."

"Forever?"

My brows knit together. "Forever?" I echoed.

He took me in his arms, cupped my cheek, gazed into my face. "Marry me again. Marry me forever. Let me love you until the end of days. Save my kingdom. Save me, my angel. Marry me and be mine. I'm already yours."

With the sweetness of deliverance, I smiled up at my husband and whispered the word I would always say when it came to him.

"Yes."

And with the sweetness of relief and joy, he sealed the promise with a kiss.

Starting Now

AMELIA

"**C**ome home," **he whispered when** he broke away, his lips grazing my cheek, my jaw, my neck.

I sighed at the ceiling. "Anything you want."

"You. All I want is you."

He captured my mouth, the kiss deep with possession and desire, with the freedom found in forgiveness. And for a moment, that was all we needed. Just each other.

We hurried upstairs. I hastily repacked my things while Tommy picked up Claudius, holding my cat to his broad chest and petting him, cooing his hellos and sentiments. I chuckled, setting the crate on my bed and opening it up.

"Claudius has turned you into a cat person."

"Well, he's such a good kitty, aren't you, Claude? You're a good boy. Gus is gonna be so happy to see you."

I beamed. "Oh, I've missed Gus so much."

"He's missed you, too," Tommy said, his blunt fingers tenderly twiddling the top of Claudius's head. "He's been camped out in front of your room since you left. And he's been giving me the silent treatment."

"Claudius has been glued to me. I can't get anything done because he's been in my lap for days. But honestly, I don't think it was for my comfort. I think it was for his. He missed you, but not as much as I did."

Tommy deposited Claudius in his crate. "I'm sorry. For all of this."

"Please, don't," I said softly, closing the metal door. "Tommy, I am such a fool. I don't know why you would forgive me for this."

"Because I love you. Because you would forgive me. Because you did the best you could. Because if your greatest sin was that you didn't ask me about Vivienne, then we're doing all right. I just needed time. Thank you for giving that to me."

I laughed. "I published a love letter to you in the *USA Times*."

He shrugged, stepping into me. "I'd already forgiven you, Melia. That article gave me hope that maybe you'd forgive me, too."

His arms wound around my waist, and as he pulled me into him, my hands came to rest on his torso, the heat of his body welcomed and sorely missed.

"There was never anything to forgive, not from me. I...I can hardly believe you're standing here after everything. Because you were right."

One of his shoulders rose and fell. "Just because it was justified doesn't mean it was right." He reached for my face, inspected it, thumbed my cheek. "But I would have always come around, Melia. I could never have let you go."

Tears welled in a rush of gratitude and relief. "I would have been here, waiting."

He tilted my face to his. "And I would have always come for you."

His lips brushed mine, delicate and sweet.

Claudius meowed impatiently from the confines of his crate, and Tommy broke away with a chuckle. "All right, let's get you home," he said to the crate as he picked it up. "And you, too, Mrs. Bane."

And he took me under his arm, and we did just that.

We walked the blocks home, the winter sun high and distant, the sky big and dusty blue. I clicked neatly into his side as we strode down the sidewalk, talking about what had happened since we parted. I'd known about Janessa—when I'd approached her office about the article, I'd found it occupied by someone new, a woman far more amenable than Janessa had been. Vivienne was gone, too, and I felt immeasurable relief that we were separated by an entire continent.

But best of all, Tommy had finished his book. Blackbird hadn't dropped him because of Vivienne's article, and they were especially pleased after my response was published. But more than anything, they loved the book so much that the acquisition was enough for them to overlook the media fire. And in fact, his editor was going to fast-track the book to use the media draft to promote it as our story. Tommy showed me the cover—Wynn and Aislinn standing on a clifftop, overlooking a mountain range, the wind whipping their cloaks, the light brilliant and hopeful. The book was already up for preorder, and Blackbird had already busted out the big guns, pushing promotions everywhere.

The first thing we did when we reached the house was go straight downstairs. Sarah was waiting anxiously with Theo, their faces lighting up with joy and thanks I felt in my marrow. There were hugs and tears, laughter and thanks.

Relief. We were all relieved, and that feeling carried with it gratitude and a simple rightness that none of us could deny.

And then we went home.

The second the door opened, Gus pounced, knocking me back into Tommy. With a slobbery, humid mouth, he licked at my face, barking intermittently at earsplitting levels. Tommy wrangled us all the way into the entryway, hooking Gus by the collar to cease the assault.

"Look, boy, look," he said, hanging on to Gus with one hand while he unlatched the crate. "Look who I brought with me."

Claudius strutted out, and Gus froze all but for his cautiously wagging tail. With a mewl, Claudius pranced over and ran the length of his body against Gus's front leg.

With a bark, he bounced, sprinting off in the direction of his basket of tennis balls.

I watched him, laughing, my face opening with a whoop when Tommy picked me up. I was cradled in his arms, my hand on the scruffy line of his jaw, his face turned down to me, brimming with adoration.

"Where are we going?" I asked on a laugh.

"To bed."

"But it's two in the afternoon," I teased.

"I've spent nearly a hundred and fifty hours without you. Almost a week of sleepless nights, awake in the dark, thinking of you. I intend to make up for every one of those hours, starting right now."

"I missed you, too," I said just before he kissed me.

Blindly, he carried me into my room, laid me down in the bed that felt more like ours than mine. Pressed me into the bed with his heavy body. Kissed me with the lips I loved so well.

Emotion welled within me, filling my chest with a deep ache, stinging my eyes with its truth. I could have lost him. I thought I had. Surely, this was a dream, and any moment, I would wake up back at my place with nothing but Claudius to comfort me from my loss.

But when I opened my eyes, there he was. The scent of him was real, clinging to me as if it wanted to consume me. The feel of his hand on my jaw, on my neck, was true, solid and possessive, stroking my skin with devotion, as if he couldn't believe it was real either.

Somehow, it was. Somehow, he'd come back to me. Somehow,

I'd been given another chance. And this time, I wouldn't risk losing it, not for anything.

"I love you," I whispered, a tear spilling, rolling away.

"I know, Melia," he breathed, surveying my face. "It's in everything you do, impossible to miss. And I would forgive you anything because of it."

"I'll never give you a reason to forgive again."

His smile, small and sideways, tugged at his lips. "Everyone needs forgiveness. I'll beg yours again someday, and you'll beg mine. Because love isn't perfect, but forgiveness is absolute. I will always forgive you if you'll promise to do the same."

"I will. I do."

"Then nothing will come between us again."

His kiss told me of his conviction, and mine spoke of the promises I'd made to him, the promise to trust, to believe. Because losing him had taught me the lesson of a lifetime.

I would always side with him. Because without trust, there could be no love. And my faith in him was as absolute as his forgiveness of me.

The kiss deepened, our breath noisy, my heart aching. Our bodies wound together, my hands skimming over the curves of his body, tasting his hot skin. A shuffling shift, and his shirt was gone. A twist and a breaking kiss, and mine was on the floor next to his. He was fire, simmering and sweltering, the heat of his lips, his skin, his tongue tangling with mine and his hands on my waist, on my breast, on my cheek, in my hair.

My hands were just as starved for him—they traced the smooth ridges of his stomach and down, opening his zipper, slipping inside to feel the silken weight of his length in my palm, stroking him with reverence and need.

The moan on his lips tightened my thighs, contracted my core. His cock pulsed in echo, his hips circling to drive himself into my hands. But when my hips rose to meet him, his hand clamped the curve, pressing me into the bed as he kissed me, thrusting slow, steady strokes.

With a pop of our lips, he broke away, feathering kisses along the delicate skin of my jaw, over the fluttering pulse at my neck. The heat of his tongue drew a lazy circle on my skin. Licked the column of my throat. He held the weight of my breast in his big palm. Unfastened my bra with a snick, drew it down my arms, and flung it away.

I watched, heart thundering against his lips as he licked a lazy trail between my breasts. His broad shoulders bulged and flexed as he shifted down my body, his hands deft as he worked my pants down my legs until they were gone and my panties along with them. I was arrested by the sight of his big fingers hooked in the delicate lace, the tan of his skin against the pale of mine.

One of those hands splayed across the inside of my thigh to open me up. Then the other—anticipation locked my lungs. His eyes were down, regarding my body with delicate heat, every place his gaze brushed licking fire on my skin.

I couldn't seem to breathe. The fire had consumed all the air.

His hair hung around his face, shrouding him in the slightest of shadows, darkening his already dark features.

Exposed and unafraid, I lay before him, sacred and invulnerable. He settled between my legs, spread wide to accommodate the breadth of his chest. His arms hooked outside my thighs, the motion squeezing my thighs in the vise of his arms, my body locked down by nothing more than his biceps and forearms. I shifted impatiently against his hold, knowing it would do no good, begging him to do what he intended all the same.

He obliged. His lips descended, his breath hot against the edge of me, my own breath still with anticipation. And he closed his eyes just as his tongue brushed its silken tip to my center.

A gasp of pleasure shot my lungs open, a sigh eased them again, the relief of contact mingling with the possession of his mouth. My hands slipped into his glossy black hair, fingers raking through the thick locks as I watched him, felt his tongue trace the ridges and valleys of my flesh, taking his time with the swollen tip of me that craved his attention so desperately.

My awareness slipped, my body no longer under my control. But my hips shifted and bucked, seeking pressure, needing his weight on me. I wanted him in a way that his lips and tongue, though expert, could not provide.

I whispered his name, twisted my fingers in his hair, but he didn't stop. Laid a hand on his shoulder, lifting my torso to reach him, to pull him, to beg him without words to come to me.

For a moment, he didn't heed, though I knew he'd heard. So with a restive shift of my hips, I unlatched him.

His eyes were molten, ebony shot with crimson, his lips glistening with my sex. I wanted to taste them.

So I did.

Swollen and lush were his sensual lips, slick with the salty taste of my body. My arms locked around his neck, and when I shifted my weight to lie back, he let me take him with me, one hand planted in the bed, the other removing his pants.

He laid his glorious weight on me, the crush of his body stealing my senses. His hips rested between my legs, his torso so much longer than mine that, even with that misalignment of our hips, my face was tilted up to carry on kissing him. I was surrounded by him, held captive by his body. His arms caged me. His broad chest was my shelter. His lips occupied my heart.

My hips shifted, cradling his hard length in the cleft of my body, and his hips answered every flex with one of their own in opposite direction and equal force.

With a hard stroke, his body lifted from mine, the cold air cutting between us.

I mewled at the loss, admiring the long stretch of his body as he reached for the nightstand, the rippling muscles over his ribs, the heavy curves of his chest. He knelt between my legs, the thick cords of his thighs like pillars, his lids heavy, eyes hooded. The rasp of his hands rubbing together, the shine of the lube on his skin. The sight of his cock filling his big hand, the pink tip appearing and disappearing in his fist.

I rose again, unable to keep watching without touching him. His lips met mine, my hands covered his, then replaced them as he braced himself, lowered us. But I didn't let him go—instead, I brought the tip of his crown to the threshold of my body, shifted my pelvis to settle his hot flesh between my rippling, aching lips.

His hand slipped between us, tracing the topography of my clit, setting a swallowing pulse through my core that brought him a millimeter deeper. He felt the desire, the permission, the plea of my body and gave it what it wanted, gave me everything I wanted, pressing into me with stinging heat.

And I settled onto him with a gentle shimmy, allowing him as deep as he could go.

The pain fell away, and the pleasure rose to take its place until it was forgotten.

His breath rattled from restraint, his length thumping a single pulse. And when I was relaxed and open to him, he moved.

My hands hung on his waist as he pulled out of me in a slow, aching stroke. And when he filled me again, there was no resistance, just a slide of his body into mine and a deep sigh of pleasure from our lips. My thighs were slung over his, his thumb shifting languidly around my clit as he rocked into me and out of me, unhurried and deliberate. The sensation overwhelmed me, the fullness, the glorious strangeness of his body inside mine, the lightning shocks from the point where his thumb worked my body, the hot, slow burn simmering in my womb, radiating across my skin, arresting my mind. There were only the points where we touched, nothing else.

I lost my sense of self, caught in a fever pitch. He teased the heat in me, fanned the flame, set me on fire with the wildness of my need for him. And he knew what I needed when I didn't, knew how to move when I couldn't, knew where to touch, where to press, where to love me inside and out. My eyes closed, chin tilted, lungs straining, rhythm racing until it broke with a cry from my lips and a lock of my body, ribs to hips to core, a frozen moment of limbo that kicked into motion again with galloping thunder.

He lowered to meet me, his lips grazing my chin, my cheek, my forehead. My body clamped around him, impossibly tight, impossibly full, his hips slowing—not for lack of want, but for lack of space. But my body didn't care, just pulled and flexed and drew him deeper.

The second the pressure eased, my body languished, he thrust again, filling me with a slam that jostled my body from the force. A low moan of pleasure slipped past my lips, my heavy arms curling around his neck. An echoing moan from the base of his throat. A jolt as he hit the end of me and retreated. His breath labored. His hips circled. A pause of his body buried deep within mine, as if to wait, to hold off, to prolong his pleasure. But it was no use. With a hard, long thrust, he filled me up and sighed my name, the sound choking in a grunt as he came.

The last time, I'd been too preoccupied to recognize anything beyond myself. But as he spent himself, I cataloged everything. The pinch of his brow, the tightness of his eyes, slammed shut against the feeling. His full lips, parted and gasping. The cords of his neck, tight and straining. The lock of his muscular thighs. The thick length of him pulsing inside me. The feel of his hand on my face, the way his lips tasted of salt and sex when he kissed me. The sated, heavy feeling in my womb, the lazy weight of my arms and legs wrapped around him.

He broke the kiss, his hands on my face, thumbing my lip as he looked down at me.

"Are you all right?" he asked gently.

"Perfect," I whispered.

And for the first time in my life, it was the absolute truth.

THE SUN HAD GONE DOWN some time ago, though I couldn't have told you what time it was. That particular unit of measure had ceased to exist in the long hours we spent in bed, talking and kissing and touching and loving.

I didn't know if there would ever be enough time to love or if my heart would ever get its fill of him.

I suspected that well was infinite.

I lay half across his chest, my arm draped lazily over him, his arm hooked lazily around me while he toyed with my hair, wrapping long strands around square fingertips.

"Can we stay like this forever?" I asked on a long, heady sigh.

"Without a doubt."

I smiled, shifting to rest my chin on the back of my hand. He tucked his hand behind his head, fanning out the thick muscles of his arm. Those ridiculous lips of his tilted sideways.

"What are you smiling about?" he asked.

"Your ridiculous lips."

"Hmm. I thought it might be my ridiculous elbow." He wiggled the joint that mechanized the hand behind his head.

"That too. And your ridiculous arms. Who has arms that big?"

"Giants. And wrestlers."

I chuckled. "And your ridiculous eyes. The first time I ever met you, I was sure you were the devil."

"What changed your mind?"

"Who said I've changed my mind?"

He tipped his head in a laugh.

I watched him with delight. "But you know what's the most ridiculous of all?"

"What?" he asked, those devil eyes sparking with mischief and adoration.

"Your ridiculous heart. Because somehow, that muscle in your chest chose me."

He unfolded his arm, slipped his hand into my hair, twisted to put me under him. And he whispered words that etched themselves on my heart, "I'll always choose you, Amelia."

Tommy kissed me—a soft, long, deep press of his lips—his fingers tasting the skin of my neck, the strands of my hair.

With a ridiculous sigh, I looked into my husband's face and knew he'd be mine forever.

Epilogue

AMELIA

I do.

Two little words.

One promise of forever.

The lights were low in the reception tent, the garden beyond our little glowing haven illuminated by the full moon on a cloudless night.

On the most magical night of my life.

And this time, my dress was white.

Tommy and I swayed on the dancefloor, surrounded by all the people we knew and loved. The ceremony had been a blur, though less than the first time. This time, I wasn't nervous about the kiss. I wasn't nervous about the man at the end of the aisle.

In fact, I wasn't nervous at all.

Marrying Tommy was the easiest thing I'd ever done.

My father spun my mother around the dance floor, winking at me as they passed. Sam and Val were lost in their own little world, their smiles soft, her hand enclosed in his, clutched to his chest.

Gus sat uncharacteristically obedient next to Tommy's mom in her wheelchair, the furry beast wearing a bow tie and white collar, mouth open in a panting smile. Rin and Court swayed nearby, and when she laughed at something he'd said, his smile broke like sunshine through a cloud. And then there was Katherine, smiling so widely, so blissfully as her baby daddy held her close, I almost didn't recognize her. Not only for the open expression on her normally inanimate face, but for the swell of her belly that kept them from canoodling right there on the dance floor.

I'd tell you all about him, but you'll have to hear that one from her. How Katherine ended up accidentally pregnant is too good not to hear direct from the source.

The dreamiest sigh slipped out of me.

Tommy chuckled, speeding up to whisk me in a circle and turn my thoughts back to him, which didn't take much. He was the sum of my universe, heart and soul. Even his body was a grand, stately fixture, commanding all of my attention from his hand nestled in the small of my back to his black, bottomless eyes, infinite and filled with adoration. Adoration for me.

Love, I'd decided, was magic.

"You're beautiful, Melia," he said with that sideways smile of his.

A little laugh escaped me, though my cheeks flushed. "I think you've said that about a hundred times tonight."

"And I'll say it a hundred more."

I shook my head at him with an unbridled smile on my face. "I love you."

"I love you, too. I still can't believe I convinced you to marry me. Twice."

"Well, to be fair, you're very convincing."

"I am, aren't I?"

"And modest."

He shrugged a shoulder. "Such is my curse. I knew I had to have you from the start. No one else could put up with me."

"Oh, it's not so hard."

His smile tugged a little higher. "Ma would disagree."

"Theo, too," I added playfully. "But it's never been hard for me. I think I loved you somehow before I even knew you. Before you were even real and fully formed in my life, even when you were nothing more than a headline in a magazine. I think somehow, I knew. And now you're the headline of my life, past, present, and future."

"*Thomas Bane, Tamed.*"

I giggled. "*Amelia Bane, Beast Tamer.*"

That earned me a full laugh. "No one else. No one loves me like you."

"And I'll love you until the day I die," I promised.

For a moment, he watched me, cataloging the details of my face. "You saved me."

"No, you saved yourself. I only told you you could."

But he shook his head. "Not only that. I didn't believe, before you. Love was as real to me as Bigfoot or Santa or Hogwarts."

I chuckled.

"But then you came along. And now I believe in magic. My heart is full of you, Melia. And I didn't know I could carry so much in me. I love you with a fierceness I don't understand and don't care to. I only want to keep you forever."

My heart skipped a beat, thumping when it started again. "Well, I hope there's room in your heart for one more."

His brows drew together, his feet slowing. "One more?"

I nodded, my cheeks high and smiling and warm from the secret I'd kept for a solid three days. It had to be a record, and it damn near killed me.

"Melia," he said cautiously as we came to a full stop in the crowd, music and motion flowing around us. "Are you … are we…"

I couldn't say it out loud. So I nodded again like a fool.

His hand slipped around to my belly where he pressed his palm. "A baby. We're having a baby."

"And on the first try," I joked.

But Tommy wasn't laughing. He was smiling the most brilliant smile I had ever seen grace his face, the gesture bright enough to light us both up like a brazier.

And before I could say another word, he swept me into his arms and kissed me like a man who had everything he wanted in the world.

And I kissed him back, knowing I did too.

ALSO BY STACI HART

BAD HABITS
With a Twist
Chaser
Last Call

THE AUSTENS
Wasted Words
A Thousand Letters
A Little Too Late
Living Out Loud

THE TONIC SERIES
Tonic
Bad Penny

THE RED LIPSTICK COALITION
Piece of Work
Player

THE HARDCORE SERIALS
Hardcore: Complete Collection

HEARTS AND ARROWS
Paper Fools
Shift
What the Heart Wants: Novella 2.5
From Darkness
Fool's Gold: Novella 3.5

SHORT STORIES
Once
Desperate Measures
Nailed

WELL SUITED

KATHERINE

"**O**h, fuck."

I wish I could have said that disbelief was the emotion I felt as I held the small plastic stick in fingers I knew to be mine, but were for some unknown reason utterly unrecognizable. My gaze fixed on the tiny window where a blue plus sign stared back at me with unflinching clarity.

There was no disbelief, seeing as how I knew exactly when and how, and with whom it happened.

When: approximately five weeks ago.

Who: one night stand.

How: broken condom.

If birth control hadn't made me an irrational, blubbering mess, my uterus would not be occupied by a zygote.

No, I corrected myself—not a zygote. At this stage, it was an embryo, and would have a heartbeat, tail, and tiny nubs that would become arms and legs. My photographic memory recalled an image

I'd seen in sex-ed during junior high of something that looked closer to an extra-terrestrial than a baby.

My stomach rolled at the thought. Or at the realization. Or because the surge of hormones was giving me morning sickness. Or in this instance, afternoon sickness.

I swallowed back my lunch, forcing it down my esophagus where it belonged before shifting my train of thought before I really did vomit.

I cataloged my feelings with the clinical detachment I approached everything with. Shock was at the top of the list, based on my rapid breath, clammy hands, racing pulse, and the dizziness that rose and fell in waves. The reason, I deduced, was that an occupied uterus had no place in my current plan, life or otherwise. My dinner plans for sushi were out the window for sure.

I lowered myself to sit on the closed toilet, holding the pregnancy test in dead, foreign hands. My back was ramrod straight, my shoulder blades pulled back, nose in the air sucking oxygen like it would stop me from vomiting. Resisting was beginning to seem futile. I wondered absently how long I could iron stomach it before I'd lose my lunch.

The thought made me gag again.

I gripped the reins on my galloping thoughts, pulling them to a halt so I could find the road again.

I needed to decide what I was going to do.

I had always wanted to procreate, assumed that I would. I'd allotted myself a single child to appease the instinct to continue my genetics, one I knew was sentimental and driven by a desire for immortality more than a desire for love. And the upside to this unforeseen path was that I didn't have to wait to find a suitable mate.

I'd already found one.

Genetically, he was the cream of the crop. As a physical specimen, he was ideal—his musculature a study in symmetry and strength, his height imposing, dominant. He was perfectly masculine, a man who thrived on control and command, and beyond that, he was highly intelligent and resourceful.

Really, I couldn't have hand picked a better genetic pool.

My mind briefly ran over my financials, deducing quickly that my job at the New York Public Library would suffice to support myself and the embryo. A nanny would be necessary, of course, but who didn't have a nanny in Manhattan?

With a deep breath and a curt nod at my reflection in the bathroom mirror, I decided.

This was the perfect opportunity to achieve a goal, and it seemed silly not to take it simply because it wasn't in my plan. It had landed in my lap. Or, more accurately, my uterus.

With that resolved, I stood, set the pregnancy test on the counter, and got down on my knees to empty my stomach.

A rush of irrational sadness arrested me as I swiped involuntary tears from my cheeks and turned to the sink to brush my teeth. Because all I truly wanted was to tell my friends. Not for validation, but because they were the people who I shared everything with. And the comfort of sharing this with them was something I thought I might need, judging by the unfamiliar twist in my chest. But they were all gone, living their own lives with their boyfriends and husbands and fiancés.

And I was here alone. I didn't even have Claudius the cat anymore—Amelia took him with her when she got married.

I'd text them later and ask them to come over, which I knew they would honor without question. And maybe I'd swing by the shelter and get a cat of my own.

But first, I needed to go find Theodore Bane and tell him I was having his baby.

WELL SUITED

COMING APRIL, 2019

Get a release email alert: http://bit.ly/1E3iJeO
Add to Goodreads: http://bit.ly/2VTfuI6
Follow Staci Hart on Amazon: https://amzn.to/2DJIihi

THANK YOU

Some books are easier than others to write.

This one fell into the "others" category.

From page one, I have been in love with this story, and after the long, hard hours of planning, plotting, editing, rewriting, and fine-tuning, that love has grown to depths I couldn't have imagined. So first, I would like to thank you, reader. Thank you for reading, for letting me into your life. I hope you fell in love, too.

My husband, Jeff, is a flesh-and-bone hero. Every day leaves me wondering how I got so lucky to have landed a man so devoted, so supportive, so willing to put up with the unpredictability of my career and, I'm not ashamed to add, my mood. I could not do this without him standing behind me, reminding me in those moments where it all feels too hard, like too much, that I could do it. That he believed in me. Thank you for always being strong enough to keep me standing.

Kandi Steiner is this beautiful anomaly in a big, dark world. Even when she's down, even when she's sad, she shines with a light that is impossible to put out. We don't go a single day without talking, and that companionship is vital to me, necessary, cherished. Of everyone I know, she understands me on levels I don't understand myself. Kandi, I love you so much. Thank you for always showing up, for always sharing your love, and for always loving me back.

A year ago, I reached out to Kerrigan Byrne through her author page in order to tell her not only how brilliant she is, but to thank her for her stories. Because they changed me, changed the way I write, the way I look at stories. And when she messaged me back, we found a quick, deep friendship that has become an indispensable part of my life. Plotting with her is one of the great privileges of my career. Sharing our lives, our joys and pains and everything in between has become a treasured part of every single day. Kerrigan, I adore you so deeply, so madly. Thank you for all you have done for me, for all the ways you've changed my life.

When I proposed to Abbey Byers that we work together for developmental editing, I never imagined how close we would become. Even though she is very busy with an incredible and demanding career, she always finds time to call, to read, to message me. Our brains are twins, our thought process so similar, that our conversations sometimes feel like I'm talking to another version of myself. As someone who processes everything verbally, I'm sure you can imagine that this is a particularly useful trait Abbey and I possess. And when we come together, it's fireworks. Abbey, thank you for your humor, your devotion to these novels, and for just being who you are.

Karla Sorenson has been privy to the inner workings of my cuckoo brain for years now, and one of these days, I'm certain she'll finally be done with me. I will subsequently shrivel up and die, because I love her so deeply. And thank God she loves me too—she lets me achieve a level of codependence that is unheard of in Karlaland. She always delivers the truth, patiently discusses story issues with me ad infinitum (and much to her discomfort). Sometimes I push too far. And she always finds a way to forgive me, to love me beyond my faults. Karla, you are a saint, and I am so thankful for you every single day.

Honestly, I feel like I've won some sort of award in receiving help from Kyla Linde. Her critical mind has become another essential part of my process. And her friendship has become an essential part of my life. It is so rare to have people in your life who understand you so deeply, and Kyla is one of those people for me. She is always there for me, always willing to help, always there with a steady hand and stellar advice. Kyla, thank you for everything. Just everything.

Carrie Ann Ryan is an absolute joy. It doesn't matter what life throws at her—she holds her head up and never stops looking forward. She inspires me so deeply, in all ways. She is kindness embodied and strength in flesh. Carrie Ann, thank you for your help, your advice, your friendship.

Sasha Erramouspe deserves an award—she reads every book I write half a dozen times before it's finished in an attempt to help me sort through the mire of my thoughts. She never fails to make me laugh, and is always ready and willing to help. I am blessed with her kindness and generosity every day. Sasha, I am so thankful you are a part of my life and a part of these books.

Tina Lynne—you, my darling, are a treasure. Thank you for your hard work and dedication. Thank you for always taking care of me. Thank you for handling such a huge part of my business so I have more time to write. You are everything to me.

Ace Grey—your love and support are such a joy in my life. Thank you for your unending encouragement, your willingness to sit down with me and hash out the minutia of feedback, even when it's tedious and exhausting. You are brilliant, my friend. Thank you.

To my beta readers—Sarah Green, Kris Duplantier, Kathryn Andrews, Mary Catherine Gebhard, Danielle Legasse—thank you so much for reading this under such inconvenient circumstances. Getting the manuscript in parts over the holidays was a huge pain in the ass for you, I know, but each and every one of you helped form this story, helped make it the best it could possibly be. You are crucial to my process, and every one of your voices are heard in this final version. Thank you for your time, your energy, your advice.

Jana Aston—thanks for pointing out that men who smirk are experts at cunnilingus. It's legiterally true.

Marjorie Whitehorn and Alleskelle Fraser—thank you for being master hair petters. I love to send you both snippets, especially on hard days when I'd rather curl up and *just not*.

Jenn Watson of Social Butterfly PR—thank you for the entirely other form of hair pets…the kind that motivate and drive positivity. Thank you for always taking such good care of me.

Sarah Ferguson—thank you for running my releases like a boss and never getting bent when I'm late and forget things. You da real MVP.

To Jovana Shirley and Ellie McLove—thank you for always making my manuscripts so shiny and clean.

To Lauren Perry of Perrywinkle Photography—once again, you have pulled out a win! You're magic.

Nadege Richards—thank you for my BEAUTIFUL interiors. You are so unbelievable talented.

To every blogger, bookstagrammer, and reader who has been a part of this book in any way, thank you. Without your love, without your support, these books wouldn't be possible. It's all for you.

ABOUT STACI

Staci has been a lot of things up to this point in her life: a graphic designer, an entrepreneur, a seamstress, a clothing and handbag designer, a waitress. Can't forget that. She's also been a mom to three little girls who are sure to grow up to break a number of hearts. She's been a wife, even though she's certainly not the cleanest, or the best cook. She's also super, duper fun at a party, especially if she's been drinking whiskey, and her favorite word starts with f, ends with k.

From roots in Houston, to a seven year stint in Southern California, Staci and her family ended up settling somewhere in between and equally north, in Denver. They are new enough that snow is still magical. When she's not writing, she's gaming, cleaning, or designing graphics.

FOLLOW STACI HART:

Website: Stacihartnovels.com
Facebook: Facebook.com/stacihartnovels
Twitter: Twitter.com/imaquirkybird
Pinterest: pinterest.com/imaquirkybird